D1603907

'Set against the glittering background of 1940s Harbin and Seoul, colonial Korea takes centre stage in this page-turning melodrama. Endless Blue Sky comes with a new vibrancy and presents a new world; utterly pro-European in its ideology and peppered with avant-garde ideas on love and marriage, on success, fulfilment, and happiness.'

—KEVIN O'ROURKE

Translator of *Our Twisted Hero* by Yi Mun-yol

'Endless Blue Sky depicts the complex identity and dreams of a colonial Korean traveling to Manchuria to find the West. There, he attempts to overcome his identity as a colonial subject, the influence of the Japanese empire, and the culture of the East. The novel vividly depicts various aspects of East Asia circa 1940; opium addiction, kidnapping, Russian refugees, Harbin dance cabarets, and symphony orchestras. This novel deepened the spatial and cultural imagination of Korean novels in the colonial period, raising issues of globality and locality.'

—LEE KYOUNGHOON

Associate Professor, Dept. of Korean Language and Literature, Yonsei University

'Devotees of Korean literature in English translation tired of reading the same handful of canonical short stories by colonial period writers will welcome Steven Capener's new annotated translation of Endless Blue Sky. Finally we have another full-length novel available to us in English from this period, and by one of modern Korea's greatest lyricists and stylists.'

—ROSS KING

Professor and Head of the Dept. of Asian Studies, The University of British Columbia

ENDLESS BLUE SKY

A NOVEL BY LEE HYOSEOK

Translated and Introduced by STEVEN D. CAPENER

HONFORD STAR

This translation first published by Honford Star 2018
honfordstar.com
Translation and Introduction copyright © Steven D. Capener 2018
All rights reserved
The moral right of the translator and editors has been asserted.

ISBN (paperback): 978-1-9997912-4-7
ISBN (ebook): 978-1-9997912-5-4
A catalogue record for this book is available from the British Library.
Cover illustration by Lee Kyutae
Book cover and interior design by Jon Gomez

Printed and bound by TJ International

This book is published with the support of the
Literature Translation Institute of Korea (LTI Korea).

CONTENTS

INTRODUCTION

Lee Hyoseok was born in 1907 in Pyeongchang, Gangwon province, Korea. He graduated from the prestigious Gyeongseong 1st High School (Now Kyunggi High School) and then entered the English Literature Department of Gyeongseong Imperial University where he distinguished himself, writing his graduation thesis on the Irish poet John Millington Synge. He debuted as a writer while still a college student, publishing 'The City and the Ghost' (1927) about the increasing number of homeless people (ghosts) in the city of Seoul. After graduating in 1928, he continued to publish short stories that often depicted characters with socialist leanings, earning him the reputation of a 'fellow traveller' writer sympathetic to the socialist cause.

In 1931, he married Lee Gyeongwon, the daughter of a middle-class family. In 1933, he joined the modernist coterie the Group of Nine along with fellow writers Yi Taejun, Park Taewon, and Yi Sang. In 1934, Lee was hired to teach literature at Sungshil Technical College in Pyongyang. He lost both his wife and his youngest son in 1940 and met an untimely death in 1942 at the age of thirty-six.

In the mid-1930s, Lee's writing moved away from proletarian themes to embrace a distinctly modernist style. His short stories after 1935 were characterized by a lyrical tone and an emphasis on the primacy of nature over human artifice. Works such as 'Mountains' and 'Fields' are representative of this shift; however, there were two other palpable thematic shifts that accompanied this new natural lyricism: bold depictions of sexuality that were ahead of the times (and which included extra-marital sex and homosexuality) and a privileging of Western (European) high culture.

One of the aspects of Lee's depictions of sexuality that was extraordinary for the times was that he gave female characters a high degree of sexual agency, depicting them choosing sexual partners for pleasure ('Bunnyeo') and fantasizing about homosexual encounters with other female characters

(*Hwabun*). Lee seemed to enjoy turning the tables on the patriarchal mores of Korean society in the 1930s by creating sexually liberated femme fatales such as the one in 'The Sick Rose' that gives both of her partners syphilis. Such sexual freedom seemed to be part of a larger desire on Lee's part to be free from the conformity that he felt was strangling Korean society. In *Endless Blue Sky*, a novel serialized in the *Maeil Daily* newspaper in 148 installments from 25 January 1940 to 8 July 1941, Lee expresses his frustration with Korean orthodoxy when his protagonist laments that Koreans adopting the traditional white clothing signalled the death of colour in the country.

Lee stated in an essay that he felt no particular emotional attachment to any one place in Korea, that he had no 'hometown'. Furthermore, several of his protagonists, in what are clearly authorial interventions, state that they feel their spiritual home to be the cultured West. He was personally fascinated with the music, art, dress, and food of the West and, according to one of his students, kept a bar of butter in the desk drawer of his office. He was a coffee lover and stated in an essay that he would gladly travel miles on a rocking bus for a cup of mocha coffee. His literature was also shaped by foreign literary influences from Chekhov, Blake, and Mansfield to Walt Whitman. All of these characteristics helped to form his literary style and themes, and *Endless Blue Sky* is, undoubtedly, the culmination of all of these influences.

In this novel, Cheon Ilma, in many ways a personification of Lee, travels to Harbin in Manchuria (a surrogate Europe for Lee) where he very literally marries himself to the West in the form of the beautiful Russian woman, Nadia, who speaks English, plays classical music on the piano, and clearly represents the means to fulfil Lee's longing to transcend the limitations of the time and place of his birth, whether it be the fascism of the imperial colonizer Japan or the stultifying conformity of the Korean Confucian tradition. It is significant that the novel does not end with Ilma leaving Korea to live with his Western bride in a European country but with him bringing Nadia, this symbol of Western beauty and culture, to live with him in Korea. She wears *hanbok*, studies the language, and loves the food. This can be seen as Lee's belief that Western culture, if combined with that of Korea, could serve to help the country overcome the difficulties it was experiencing due to colonization and backwardness.

Lee was a cosmopolitan who was overtly antagonistic to expressions of ethnic nationalism. In the story, while in Harbin, Ilma's friend Byeoksu reacts with disgust at hearing another Korean say how nice it is to meet a 'compatriot'. Byeoksu responds with the word 'idiot' and refuses the proffered handshake. In *Endless Blue Sky*, Lee also makes clear his belief that love transcends blood. He emphasized that love and mutual understanding can overcome minor differences, such as food and language.

> '... whether one's hair is black or red, whether
> one speaks the same language or not, all sit
> at the banquet of life as equals, and there
> is nothing remotely unnatural about this.
> Differences in lifestyle are not fundamen-
> tal obstacles to harmony. Whether one eats
> bread or rice is an inconsequential difference.
> When love is strong enough, the assimilation
> of the human race is as simple as can be.'

At the same time, Lee was not immune to the effects of assimilation himself. While he was obliquely critical of Japanese imperialism, he had clearly internalized some of its logic. In an essay titled 'The Shell of the Continent', he talks about the backwardness of the residents of the colonized Manchuria (which we are supposed to understand represent the Chinese). Lee, while being extremely critical of how Koreans lived in Manchuria (implying most of them were involved in drug dealing and prostitution), makes his views clear when describing virtually the only Manchurian to appear in the text. While marvelling at the 'grand readjustment' that was sweeping across Manchuria (colonial modernity), Ilma spies a Manchurian relieving himself in full view of the train:

> 'Of course, this grand readjustment was still in its infancy; it would be some time yet before its completion. For example, when the train departed and passed by a long stretch of slums bordering the station, something suddenly brought a smile to Ilma's face. At the base of an embankment, squarely facing the train, a Manchurian had removed his pants and was leisurely relieving himself. One might call it a humorous scene in the fresh morning air. In any case, it was a far cry from the rather solemn scene at the station. It was difficult to say just how many generations would have to pass before such behaviour also might be readjusted.'

That these somewhat disparate characteristics co-exist within the same novel (and writer) speak somewhat to the complex nature of world in which Lee Hyoseok lived. What can be said about him was that his belief in the healing power of art and love, his universalism, his empathy for the empty husks of the world, and his vision of the possibility of happiness were all sorely needed as the clouds of war were gathering over the Pacific.

In the end, Lee was a dreamer. His alter ego Cheon Ilma uses the word 'dream' some seventy-seven times in the novel. Lee dreamt of beauty, art, love and freedom – all obvious themes in *Endless Blue Sky*. Lee died before seeing whether his dreams would ever be realized. He succumbed to meningitis in 1942 at the age of thirty-six. He was at the height of his literary powers, and one is left to imagine what his contributions to Korean (and world) literature would have been had he enjoyed a longer life and been able to write in a better world.

Steven D. Capener
Seoul Women's University

ENDLESS BLUE SKY

1. A BOUQUET

It seemed as if the late summer sun had stopped moving in the sky, making the heat of the afternoon even more oppressive.

The torpor that lay over the grounds of Seoul Station was in sharp contrast to the ringing clamour inside, indicating the imminent arrival of the 3.30 express train bound for Xinjiang. A single hired sedan made its way to the fore of the countless black automobiles arrayed in front of the station, and from it emerged a man holding a bouquet of flowers. It was the novelist Mun Hun, rather plainly attired. After checking the time on the station tower clock, he entered the building. He smiled somewhat self-consciously at the awkward appearance he knew he was presenting by holding such a large bundle of flowers that was attracting so many stares.

'Bloody flowers, it's not as if I'm seeing off a woman or anything...'

While walking through the lobby, Hun ran into the young medical doctor Pak Neungbo, who was also roaming the premises as if in search of something. He was one of the all too many freshly-minted doctors, little black tuft of a moustache and all, that one could see on the streets these days.

'You bought flowers. Good thinking.'

'A bit embarrassing, but I figured it was okay between close friends.'

'What should I get?'

They exited the lobby and paced about in front of the station store.

'I know. Whiskey. You've got to be drunk to venture out on to those Manchurian plains. No one goes to Manchuria sober.'

'Splendid.'

The two of them – one holding a bottle, the other a bouquet – continued to look for Cheon Ilma, the mutual friend they had come to see off, but he was nowhere to be found.

They went through the lobby once more, looked inside the tearoom, and then ran up to the eatery on the second floor, all without success.

'I guess spending too much time in Manchuria begins to affect one's sense of time.'

'This trip's different though; I'm sure a lot's going into his preparations.'

'If he keeps this up, Ilma may just settle down in Manchuria.'

Ilma had a reason for being late. The regular coach ticket to Harbin he had purchased a few days ago had unexpectedly been upgraded to a deluxe first-class ticket today. Thanks to the patronage of the president of the *Hyundai Daily* newspaper, with whom coincidence had recently brought him into dealings, the present trip was dubbed a commission. Such work carried with it preferable treatment with regard to travel expenses, as well as considerations relating to the company's image, and, as such, the order was put in for a deluxe first-class ticket.

By the time he had gone down to the agency, turned in his original ticket, and gotten the new one, the train was getting ready to depart.

There were only thirty minutes left before departure when

Ilma and Kim Jongse, a fellow newspaperman who the president had ordered to see him off, finally got in the car for the station. A certain satisfaction welled up in Ilma as he ordered the driver to step on it while sinking back into the plush seat.

'It's my first time in deluxe first-class. With a press pass you probably ride in the deluxe cars all the time, but it's a first for me.'

'You happy? Don't waste this chance to turn your life around.'

'Having my regular coach-class life bumped up to deluxe-class status is almost too much to take in.'

'I wish you'd quit constantly crying about how poor you are. If they put you in the ultra-deluxe first-class you'd probably faint. You've been given the job of a distinguished cultural envoy by the paper – why are you so worried about something so small as a rail ticket?'

'Cultural envoy – at least the title sounds nice.'

'Just get up there and successfully close this deal. If things go well, the company, for its part, will certainly reward you, and you'll be on your way up in the world.'

'For some reason, I have the feeling things are going to go well.'

Ilma's duties as a cultural envoy were actually quite simple. He was to go to Harbin and negotiate the invitation of a symphony orchestra. Although there was no mention of an occupation on Ilma's business card, while writing commentaries on current cultural topics and critical essays on music, he had naturally come to be considered, by himself and others, as a culture mediator. Recent displays of his talents in the field, including successfully arranging for the performances of renowned theatrical and dance troupes from Tokyo, had brought Ilma to the attention of certain people. One of them was the president of the *Hyundai Daily*, who now had his sights set on the Harbin Symphony Orchestra and had hired

Ilma as his representative in the negotiations for a performance. It was something Ilma could have arranged on his own, but, knowing the newspaper's backing would prove advantageous, he immediately accepted the president's terms and began preparing for the trip.

'Anyway, now that I'm a cultural broker, I can rub shoulders with you newspapermen.'

The truth be told, today Ilma felt a sort of pride regarding the work he was now doing for society.

'In any case, there is no one who would consider you a mere cultural broker.'

Jongse's reply was, of course, not meant derisively.

'There may be some who privately don't like the fact that I received a liberal arts degree and yet am engaged in this sort of work, but I'm not the least bit ashamed. In fact, I'm quite proud of it. I guess everyone's different, but even when I hear that most of my classmates have risen to become department directors and doctors, I still feel that what I'm doing is right for me.'

'It would be impossible to enjoy your work without that pride. Honestly speaking, I found the performance you arranged by that theatrical troupe from Tokyo a lot more culturally significant for the common people than all the doctoral dissertations being published these days.'

'I'm not exactly sure why, but I feel really proud to be going on this particular trip. I've been all over Manchuria. I'm so familiar with it that it feels like an outing in my neighbourhood, but I've never felt both so anxious and happy about going.'

'You're already thirty-five, right? You've lived more than half your life; isn't it about time you started to really make something of yourself?'

'When I think of my age, I do feel a bit embarrassed, but I'm pretty sure there will be some good things ahead. I can't keep going on like this ...'

As the car stopped in front of the station, so did their conversation.

When Ilma got out he was holding a trunk. The thought of the long trip before him suddenly caused his baggage to feel like it weighed a ton. On this day, he entered the deluxe first-class waiting room imposingly – shoulders, back, and chest out. Compared to the times he had slunk in with an economy ticket, the atmosphere could not have been more agreeable. Hun and Neungbo, who had been running around with their flowers and whiskey, ran up to him and blocked his way.

'How do you feel about going to Manchuria?'

'Why are you two making such a fuss? Is it right that I should see two such close friends together at the station when I haven't heard from either of them in months?'

Ilma, who had spent such a long time in solitude, was in fact gladdened by this small expression of friendship.

'Isn't this trip particularly important? I'm your friend, but I'm also a citizen. I can hardly wait for you to return with good news and plenty of quality performances, as well.'

'What do you think of my present?'

As he took the bouquet Hun thrust toward him, Ilma, despite his indifferent countenance, was rather thrilled. A bunch of flowers so pure could mean nothing but sincere concern for his happiness. He was touched by the humanity of the gesture.

'Must novelists always give such novelistic presents?'

'It might have looked better coming from a woman's hand. At any rate, there's something awkward about a man holding a bouquet.'

'Do you know how many years it's been since I've thought of a woman?'

'I'm no novelist, so here's a doctor's present.'

As Ilma finished tucking the bottle of whiskey from Neungbo into his trunk, the following message rang over the loudspeaker:

'*The train for Xinjiang is now boarding!*'

Standing up to join the crowd heading for the gate, he could not help comparing the serenity there to the utter congestion of the economy class waiting room. Though Ilma had certainly never longed for class advancement or the complacency that comes with extravagance, this simple realization of the differences between the two waiting rooms made a deep impression on him.

'You look about ten times better today.' Jongse, in either complete awareness or complete ignorance of Ilma's feelings, laughed heartily.

When Ilma, having grabbed a window seat in the deluxe first-class car, came back out on the platform, he looked upon the three friends before him with a feeling of promise and satisfaction. The robust figures cut by Neungbo, Jongse, and Hun – or, put another way, a medical doctor, a newspaper reporter, and a novelist – stood in bold relief against the crowd. When he considered the importance to society of each of their stations, he found them even more impressive and was suddenly overcome with a sense of pride at being their friend. And immediately following his happiness at having such companions, the realization arose in him that he must somehow distinguish himself in order to feel equal to them.

'You'll pay for that nose someday.'

Jongse had said this in jest, but Ilma took it to heart. There was Chunhyang's nose and Lee Doryeong's from the classic Joseon-era love ballad. It was not insignificant that to these he had decided to add his own and measure himself against his friends for one more push forward.

'Three people, and one person, and ...'

The three people seeing him off and him, the one person leaving. Though he was leaving to bridge (to the degree it was possible) the gap separating them, he also felt it appropriate that he do his all not to fall short of their expectations and solicitations.

Are all these merely the useless musings leading up to a journey?

This was the state of Ilma's mind today: much too nervous to erase such thoughts.

'The one regrettable thing, as I mentioned earlier, is that we have no women with us. This is a meaningful send-off. It certainly wouldn't do any harm to have a bit of colour.'

Hun, as if trying to follow up on what he had said in the waiting room, brought the topic of conversation back to women. It appeared as if he were disappointed that, among the colourful groups of women about the platform, theirs was the only group that stood alone, isolated like a band of Puritans.

'At this point, what use do I have for women?'

'That stubbornness will get you nowhere. No matter what the occasion, women always brighten up a scene.'

'Spoken like a true novelist.'

Neungbo took it upon himself to answer. 'Ilma said he's going to find the best woman in the world and have the finest love affair with her. Until then he's going to cover his eyes and ears; he's determined not to play around. It will take a very special woman to get his attention. A merely average woman showing up for this send-off would have done nothing for him.'

'Do you think it's right to be so stubborn just because you failed in your first attempt at love? I don't know how you can live so rigidly.'

'Don't you worry. Someday I'll have a woman who'll surprise you. You can say whatever you want till then.'

'A world-class love, do you mean like the Duke of Windsor?'

'Who knows what will happen?'

'As long as you're going on this trip, you might as well bring back love along with art.'

'I hope all goes according to my wishes, but who knows what the future holds?'

While all of them were laughing heartily, an announcement for departure came over the loudspeaker, followed by the ring of a bell.

'It's only a brief parting. I may look different upon my return.'

'We'll be counting the days till you get back.'

Ilma got back on the train and looked out on his friends through the window. Now, as he was departing, he felt the distance between them widen and the feeling that he was the one leaving deepen.

Be brave. A real man can redraw the map of the world. One, two, three!

As soon as the train began moving, Ilma steeled his nerves and waved out of the window. The figures of his three friends waving their hats faded into the distance.

The blue silk seats were immaculate, and their backrests were draped in white cotton, but these were not the only things different about this car; the appearance and bearing of its passengers also set it apart from standard class. Whether soldiers, government officials, businessmen or ladies, their attractive and smart appearances silently boasted of their places at the top of society.

Ilma could not help but wonder where he ranked among them. And though he had purchased his place among them merely by adding a bit of money to his standard-class fare, he could not help but feel it was all sort of magical. He had made this trip so many times, only a month ago in fact, and on the very same train, but that day was his first with a business ticket.

Having no vase, he put Hun's bouquet, still wrapped in waxed paper, on the windowsill. When he looked about the car, the pleasant movement of the train brought with it a stream of thoughts about his voyage. With those flowers and in that car, he felt he was happy; he certainly wasn't unhappy.

He thought of the title 'On a Journey with a Bouquet of

Flowers'. Even though he had taken the path of the wanderer frequently over the past few years in search of he knew not what, never had a trip felt this right; this time felt like nothing less than the road to happiness.

Happiness – for the first half of his life, just how well had the goddess of fortune looked after him? The sixteen years he'd spent in school had been by no means favourable. Rather, they were a time of uncertainty and anguish. Even once he had finished school, it was not a path to easy advancement and success that awaited him. Following his own path in search of work to his liking had brought him to try his hand at today's unconventional and somewhat absurd business. But it was a wholly original and arduous path with neither predecessor nor guide. Far from smooth, the first half of his life had been crooked and thorny. Even failing at his first love paled in comparison to the tragedy he had suffered just a few months ago – the loss of his mother, the last living member of his immediate family, had dealt his spirit a crushing blow. He felt it was his final misfortune.

He'd gone to her as soon as he received the telegram, but she was already in critical condition. Being alone, she'd gone to live with a close relative, and it was there that she'd fallen ill. The fact that Ilma had put off living with his mother until his own life became more stable, at which time he had planned to bring her to Seoul to finish her life in peace, made his grief all the greater. He was beside himself and merely cried inconsolably at her sickbed for several days. His crying turned to wailing when, in her final hours, he realized the depth and consistency of his aged mother's love. In her will she had left him a small plot of land; though too insignificant to be called a fortune, she had held onto it for all those years. Trifling as it was, it pained Ilma to his bones. But as death is a natural part of life, he simply had to deal with his feelings and wipe away his tears. Putting the past behind him, Ilma summoned all his courage. He sold off his inheritance, said farewell to his relatives, and returned to Seoul as if being chased by something. He was now truly alone, with no one to care for and no one to care for him. But even amidst suffering and death, life goes on. He gritted his teeth and was swept back out into life.

That's all in the past. I hope this is the end of my misfortunes as well.

In fact, Ilma began to feel a keen premonition that this would spell the end of his ill fate. When he stepped out into the streets with the money from his inheritance, the desire to embark on some new enterprise welled up within him. This was partially what brought him to agree to his present duties as a cultural envoy with an unprecedented combination of anxiousness and expectation.

In the deluxe first-class car today, his expectations once again soared, and he thought this trip, begun holding a bouquet, was headed straight for happiness.

A new heart, a new beginning…

This thought kept coming to him, making the scenes passing his windows all the more to his liking.

*

It was seven in the morning when he awoke after a night in the sleeper car. The train was stopped at Bongcheon station.

We're all the way into Manchuria now.

Rubbing his eyes, Ilma looked out the window onto the dim platform. He had passed this way many times before, so nothing struck him as particularly curious, which is why he had slept so soundly. But when he saw the gang of coolies working lazily in the station yard and the attitudes of the station attendants supervising them, he could not help but feel the change in the times and the movement of history. Something about it was imposing and serious so that it gave a distinctly different impression from that of six or seven years ago. This was because the old had been replaced by the new, and a grand readjustment had begun. Ilma could not look upon the tremendous changes over the past several years without a combination of wonder and lamentation. He experienced these emotions whenever he travelled this road.

Of course, this grand readjustment was still in its infancy; it would be some time yet before its completion. For example, when the train departed and passed by a long stretch of slums bordering the station, something suddenly brought a smile to Ilma's face. At the base of an embankment, squarely facing the train, a Manchurian had removed his pants and was leisurely relieving himself. One might call it a humorous scene in the fresh morning air. In any case, it was a far cry from the rather solemn scene at the station. It was difficult to say just how many generations would have to pass before such behaviour also might be readjusted.

Unable to rid himself of the smile from the morning's scene, Ilma washed, tidied up a bit, and then had breakfast in the dining car, after which he returned to his white-backed seat. His mind clear, today felt like yet another enjoyable day on his journey. He looked out upon the broad Manchurian plains. The boundless plains had neither mountains nor streams but were covered in green vegetation and abundant grain. Here and there, clusters of sunflowers ripened yellow, strong and splendid as if having drunk in the very essence of the sun. If any man looked after these plains he was now hiding, for not even his shadow was visible upon the great expanse. Ilma could not contain his sense of wonder at the thought that on these fertile plains, though infinite time had passed, history was now, unbeknownst to any man, being rewritten.

It is not the innocent plains that change but the men who rule them, the masters. Truly, only men can change.

Other thoughts followed this one like a runaway horse and galloped along the plains.

The train had passed Chollyong, and Sipyongga was almost in sight. It appeared that a railroad police officer had begun making his rounds. Ilma immediately recognized him, though he was dressed in plain clothes, as he began checking seats from the far end of the car. Once he had received a business card, the officer usually moved on without saying much. He remained a bit longer in front of Ilma's seat, however, because there was no mention of an occupation on his name card.

'Where are you going?'

'To Harbin.'

He had gone through the same routine twice already, once with a police officer and once with a customs agent when crossing the border the night before. And he had also been through it innumerable times on his previous trips, all of which allowed him to maintain an attitude of composure.

'What for?'

'I'm on my way to Harbin to invite a symphony orchestra, but I'm not sure what to call my job. Though it's a type of cultural work ...'

As he made his way through this awkward explanation, the thought occurred to him that he should have had some business cards printed for this work with the newspaper, even if it was only temporary. In order to produce the card he had received from the president of *Hyundai Daily* to show that he was, in fact, affiliated with a newspaper, he reached into his pocket and pulled out his organizer.

'How much money are you carrying?'

'I only brought a few hundred won.'

He pulled out his notebook as he gave his reply. The many cards he had placed between its pages fell and scattered, but a single piece of paper, folded many times over, stood out among them.

There was no need to pick it up and unfold it, for it was a lottery ticket, nothing special to Ilma, the officer, or anyone, for that matter, who had spent considerable time in Manchuria. It was a single National Prosperity Lottery ticket, issued by the government of Manchuria.

'What's with the lottery ticket?'

Ilma smiled as he replied to this question from the plain-clothes officer, 'I bought it on one of my many trips to Manchuria.'

'But only residents of Manchuria are allowed to purchase these.'

'Well, I'm not a resident, but I may as well be. I am here so often that I buy a few each year.'

'Have you ever won?'

'Ha, I wish. No, I lose every time.'

It appeared a single lottery ticket had been enough to put the policeman's mind at ease.

'Why don't you pick some numbers for the 10,000 won prize?'

'Having your numbers drawn from among the hundreds of thousands out there doesn't happen to just anyone. It's the kind of luck you might happen to see once in a lifetime. You make it sound so easy.'

'There's not a single Manchurian who doesn't buy one each month. Some even say they live in Manchuria for the pleasure of buying lottery tickets. In fact, I have one too.'

'We're just the same, you and I.'

'If I had 10,000 won, you think I'd be a goddamned cop?'

Considering the policeman's own confession, it seemed that all those living on the plains were exceedingly familiar with the dream of the lottery. All men carried the desire for good fortune in their hearts; it could hardly be considered a crime.

Truth be told, no Manchurian could resist the temptation of the lottery. The government, using the great fortune associated with winning as bait, divided its financial burden among hundreds of thousands of citizens. With the money thus gathered, it awarded a few tens of thousands of won to winners, while using the remaining several hundreds of thousands of won for national relief projects. But, much more than from a clear conception of such important relief works, the average citizen's impression of the lottery came from the allure of, and excitement at, the possibility of winning. They had no need to consider the precise relief project from which the benefits of this huge sum, to which they had each contributed, would trickle down to them. Rather, people in the city bought tickets there, while farmers in the countryside quietly asked those venturing to the city to buy them tickets with a few won of their hard-earned money, and travellers like Ilma bought a couple for amusement on their journeys and kept them crumpled in their pockets. It was enough for all of them to await the announcement on the fifteenth of the following month and, discovering whether they had won or lost, to laugh or cry accordingly. Whether they tasted the great fortune of winning or the pain of losing, what was truly important were the dreams and worries brought by the thirty days of excitement and stimulation leading up to the fifteenth of the coming month. The rich dreamt the leisurely dreams of the rich, while the poor felt the desperate desire of the poor, but the inspiration and stimulation of the experience was the same for all. When they were fortunate enough to win, they could dance with joy, and when they lost they could just choke back their tears, quietly buy another ticket, and keep it with redoubled excitement while awaiting the results of the coming month. They might spend an entire lifetime being deceived, but, if they could live in constant anticipation, was it not a bargain?

'It's a sort of national gambling.'

Ilma had no reason to be overly critical of this national event for he, like a Manchurian, purchased that month's happiness for a few won each time he passed by Shingyeong.

Now that he thought of it, even the officer who had come to question him admitted to participating in this gambling. It appeared that all people took pleasure in the same sorts of things.

The officer had begun quite sternly, but, thanks to the

ticket, his face had softened, and, without asking any further questions, he disappeared toward the rear of the car with a smile. Ilma was so pleased that he even purposefully unfolded his ticket for another look. It was composed of five sheets, each of which had the following numbers clearly printed on it: 3 7 5 2 5. He smiled again and mumbled to himself.

'3 7 5 2 5, thirty-seven thousand five hundred and twenty-five – is this a lucky number, or an unlucky one?'

*

Having passed Sipyongga and arrived at Gongjuryeong – or Princess Pass – Shingyeong was now no more than an hour away. The feeling of excitement at the unexpected good fortune brought by the lottery ticket still fresh, Ilma basked in a proud feeling of pleasure at the trip.

Gongjuryeong – the name was beautiful no matter how many times he heard it. In front of its rustic station lay flower beds with crimson salvias in full bloom and a sparse elm grove, beyond which he remembered its quaint streets. As he imagined the residential area, with its roads lined with old Russian-era buildings, on the far side of this small city, it brought him pleasure to consider just what sorts of lives were being lived there.

Was it named Princess Pass after the legend of a princess?

Lost in such thoughts, Ilma was still looking out his window in wonder when the train began to move.

'What are you staring at?'

Someone had suddenly appeared at Ilma's side and covered his eyes with her hands, depriving him of Gongjuryeong's scenery.

Even though she did not give off the warm air and fragrance of spring, her soft hands and voice were enough to tell him she was a woman, but, beyond that, Ilma was powerless to guess who she was. That said, he also felt no need to push her hands away and so, softly questioned her.

'Who are you?'

'Why don't you guess?' the woman replied in a clearer, higher voice, after which she affected a laugh.

'Are you a nymph fallen from the heavens?'

'Why not say I'm a princess come down off the pass?'

'But I don't know a single person in Manchuria.'

He did not know any women in Manchuria, and it would have been impossible to get to know one on such a short train ride.

'I followed you all the way from Seoul. I'm sure you never dreamt that I slipped onto the same car as you yesterday afternoon. Although now you should know who I am.'

She removed her hands, but, of course, Ilma was able to speak her name before turning to face her.

'Is it you, Danyeong?'

Upon actually seeing her, his eyes opened wide in surprise.

'What are you doing here?'

'I was certain when I boarded the train, but I worried the whole night through about whether what I was doing was right or wrong. I didn't sleep a wink.'

As she plopped down listlessly in her seat, Danyeong's face, which should have been happy, was filled with gloom.

'Just where do you think you are going, following me like this? I think you're lying.'

Ilma stared straight at Danyeong, who was dressed rather extravagantly, his shock not abated in the least. With her hair permed and cut in a bob, her make-up heavy, and her impeccable Western-style outfit, she brought a singular splash of colour to the otherwise dreary car. People took notice, though no one needed to say a thing; her appearance made it obvious she was an actress. Perhaps due to her having agonized through the night, to Ilma, who saw her quite regularly, she appeared a bit haggard.

'I have no idea what I'm doing. Even though I'm afraid of what might happen, I just can't seem to control myself. I knew you were travelling deluxe first-class, of course, and even saw you from a distance at the station with Hun and the others but actually coming to see you proved to be difficult. I tossed and turned all night, then, as we got close to Shingyeong, I forgot my pride and just came running to you. You must be surprised, but please forgive me. Now that I see you, I feel ashamed again, but last night I could think of nothing else.'

'Following me here is no good. As I've told you so many times before, my mind is set. I couldn't change it even if I wanted to. What use do I have for women? I am determined to stay absolutely focused until I achieve my goals.' There was an unmistakable tone of reproach in Ilma's voice.

It seemed proper to call Danyeong an actress. After all, she was under exclusive contract with Bando Studios and appeared on the silver screen in a couple of new films each year. Most knew her as a femme fatale, and she was quite famous in the struggling movie industry. On screen she received applause, while on the street she was recognized by fans, often becoming the topic of conversation. But Ilma paid much more attention to her sordid private life than to her social position as an actress and, as a result, was left with the impression that she was unwholesome. When he became aware of her chaotic personal life and frequent liaisons, he began to consider her not as someone beneficial to society, but rather as a noxious insect poisoning it. Of course, he knew that this unsound society was capable of producing at least one such pathological individual, but the more he thought about it, the greater his disgust grew, albeit not without a touch of pity.

Although he had long been aware of Danyeong's adoration for him, Ilma had remained aloof. For one, beyond his criticisms of her character, she simply was not his type. And, secondly, he really had no use for women at the time. Having rebuffed her on numerous occasions in Seoul, he'd had no idea she would follow him, let alone appear so far along on the journey. Ilma could not help but be taken aback.

'When we are apart, I become brave. When we meet, my courage fades, only to return when we are apart again. At this rate, I may follow you my entire life.'

Such sultry displays of passion only made Ilma more uncomfortable.

'Think of Hun. Aren't you ashamed?'

The novelist longed for her, but Danyeong hardly acknowledged his existence.

'I can't help it if I don't like him. For some reason I could never love Hun. Though I do appreciate that he's interested in me.'

'I feel the same way about you. Hun is my friend. Just thinking of what it would do to him is more than enough reason why I could never be with you. Look, he's the one who gave me this bouquet.'

Danyeong just hung her head, not saying a word.

In the midst of the silence, the train pulled into its final destination of Shingyeong. Ilma felt relieved at the release this provided from the awkwardness of sitting there with Danyeong.

'What are you planning to do? I'm going to take the afternoon train to Harbin, so why don't we say goodbye here?'

Danyeong went back to the third-class car, retrieved her things and walked with Ilma out of the station. The sight of her walking along like a kicked dog bothered Ilma.

'We will say goodbye, but why don't you stay in Shingyeong for one night? You still have a long way to go.'

'I'm too busy to dawdle. I'll stop by on my way back.' Closing his ears to Danyeong's suggestive offer, he steeled himself against the temptation.

'Then can we at least go somewhere and have a meal together?'

'Let's eat here.'

By the time he had wrangled her into the crowded station restaurant and found a seat, Danyeong was crying. She wiped her eyes with a handkerchief and then blew her nose into it. Even this seemed seductive and so Ilma said, in as cold a voice as he could muster, 'If you don't have any special plans, why don't you go back to Seoul on the next train? I don't think it's a good idea for you to be all the way out here by yourself.'

This was too much for Danyeong and her face blazed red in anger.

'Are you trying to insult me? And why do you care anyway? Isn't that a completely different problem?'

'It's just that I'm worried about you, and ...'

'Just please stop ... I get it. After you've been hurt by your first love you can't let another woman in. Miryeo? Is Miryeo the only woman in the world? Is she better than all other women? If you happen to see her, please let her know how I feel.'

By bringing up the name Miryeo, Danyeong was intentionally rubbing salt in a deep wound, and this instantly set Ilma off.

'How dare you!' he shouted, but Danyeong didn't even flinch.

'I know all about it,' she said with a great show of irritation.

Deciding that further argument would be pointless, Ilma clenched his teeth and began to write a telegram on the restaurant table.

Arriving Harbin at 6 p.m.

The telegram was going to his good friend Han Byeoksu, a reporter for the *Harbin Daily* newspaper. He would separate from Danyeong here and leave by himself for Harbin on the one o'clock train.

2. A CERTAIN FAMILY

The editorial offices of the Hyundai Daily *newspaper.*

*

True to its status as a major newspaper in a capital city, the external appearance of the building was impressive, and the scale of the spacious, bustling interior of the editorial offices was no less imposing. It was late in the morning, and dozens of employees were toiling at their assigned desks to prepare the evening edition of the paper. Pens were racing across manuscripts, desktop phones rang incessantly, and there was a continuous drone of voices.

A young woman came out of the president's office, wound her way through the maze of desks and stopped in front of the entertainment desk where Kim Jongse was absorbed in his manuscript. At one time, Jongse had made a name for himself at the social affairs desk, but he had since moved to the entertainment desk.

A man that possessed both of these talents was very useful to the newspaper. It was the day after Ilma had been sent off to Manchuria; Jongse's excitement had cooled, and he was now able to concentrate.

'The president would like to see you.'

In response to the office girl's words, he looked up and, brushing a wisp of hair out of his eyes, said, 'I'm quite busy, what's this about?'

'He says it'll just take a minute.'

Throwing down his pen, Jongse followed her to the president's office. His first thought was one of annoyance.

The president, who had been talking with the editor-in-chief, quickly offered Jongse a seat.

'Sorry to bother you when you're busy. Sit down for a moment.'

Whether the reason for this summons was something irritating or pleasant, when Jongse was busy he didn't like to be disturbed.

'Give the article you're working on to someone else; I need you to go somewhere.'

Seeing the smile on the normally illiberal president's face put Jongse at ease.

'It seems like this project is going to be a success.'

Jongse immediately intuited what this was about. 'Are you talking about the plan to invite the symphony orchestra?' he asked, guessing what was coming.

'Not only was this the right time for this plan but your recommendation to send Ilma was good work as well.'

'Well, there's no doubt Ilma will do a good job.'

'We'll have to wait to see how it all turns out, but the praise and positive responses have been rolling in. By phone and letter.' The editor-in-chief appeared pleased as he looked through the postcards and letters on the desk, 'We just got a phone call from someone who is in discussions with the editor to unconditionally sponsor the event, but we wanted to hear what you think since you're involved in this project.'

'If they want to sponsor it we should accept. The project will thrive, and we'll get good PR from it.'

As if Jongse's amiable response was just the answer he wanted, the editor-in-chief said, 'We agree on this, then. In fact, this is not a small undertaking for the paper, and the early positive responses are very reassuring.'

The president added, 'You know who it is. His name's Yu Manhae of the East Asia Trading Company. He just called from his home offering to sponsor us and said if we send someone over he's ready to come to an agreement.'

'Yu Manhae? Even though he's a businessman, he's quite familiar with cultural entrepreneurship. His proposal is a decent one.'

'Yu Manhae is a clever person who intends to make a profit in this project, that's why he accepted the offer.'

'Foreign trade may not be doing well, but I'm sure he has made several hundred thousand won in metal goods and gold mining. He's said that he'll invest a thousand, or even ten thousand in a cultural enterprise, but that won't even put a dent in his pocket. There's no reason to turn down such a rare offer.'

'I want you to go and meet him.'

'Of course, I'll go. Since I'm already involved in this project, I'll wrap this up no problem.'

Jongse's answer pleased both the president and the editor-in-chief.

*

Yu Manhae. I suddenly get to go see Yu Manhae. This should be good.

Muttering to himself after returning to his seat, Jongse hastily wrapped up the article he had been writing, handed it over for editing to a colleague sitting next to him, and left the office.

Even if this is fate, it's somewhat incredible. It seems I run into him every time I turn around.

In addition to the excitement of being assigned to go see the young businessman Yu Manhae, the unexpected events of the morning held another hidden significance for Jongse. Yu Manhae was of interest to Jongse not only because he was a well-known businessman but, truth be told, also because he shared a strange bond with Jongse's friend Ilma. When seeing Ilma off at Seoul Station, Ilma had been going on about the failure of his first love; and the name Miryeo, which Danyeong had vexed him with in the Shingyeong station restaurant, was not only the name of that first love but was also the current wife of Manhae. For people who knew about this strange connection between Ilma and Manhae, it was a topic of clandestine conversation, and the memory of that time was still enough to upset Ilma. Of course, as Ilma's friend, the situation was of great interest to Jongse. The concern of Ilma's friends over this situation was widely talked about, and, of course, the way things had turned out between Ilma, Manhae, and Miryeo had been affecting Ilma ever since.

Ilma and Manhae were a year apart in school and Miryeo had been the object of both of their desires. In the mundane world, they say the best weapon with which to win in love is wealth. Victory between Ilma and Manhae was decided by this commonplace criterion. Ilma's defeat was attributable to the fact that he was a lowly scholar who had graduated from a college of liberal arts, while Manhae's victory was due to the fact that he was a law graduate who had inherited a large fortune. Only time would tell whether Miryeo had made the right choice or not, but while things had turned out the way Manhae had wanted and he was happy, Ilma's disappointment had been immense. Ilma was invited to the wedding, where he hid himself in the crowd and cried softly like a movie actor. Seven or eight years had passed since that dramatic scene.

While Ilma had, up until this very day, been making his way along a rocky path, Manhae had been utilizing his substantial capital to get into the trading business, which had flourished to the point that he could enter the steel and gold mining industries, thereby increasing his fortune and making a name for himself as a young entrepreneur. The obvious distinction between the two of them was a continuing source of public attention and had captured Jongse's interest as well. It was as if there were two lives being played out in the same city, one happy and one sad, and the vicissitudes of these two lives were secretly a topic of interest to their friends. This was the cause of the excitement that Jongse felt upon being given this unexpected responsibility.

This is no ordinary stroke of fate.

This was just too delicious to keep to himself, and so Jongse looked for Hun in their favourite teahouse, but it had not opened yet. Feeling vexed at not being able to sit and indulge in some juicy gossip with anyone, Jongse, partly to look more dignified, changed his mind about taking the trolley to Seodaemun and caught a taxi instead.

'To Yeonhuijang, and step on it.'

Feeling the same sense of adventure as when going out to cover an accident while working in the social affairs division, he sat back in the seat.

The comfortable, shiny car ran along the trolley line, went up the street to Geumhwajang and then entered the street to Yeonhuijang. Pointing out the fancy red roof of the Western-style house that stood out even in this neighbourhood, Jongse once again gave Yu Manhae's name to the driver.

*

In the parlour of Manhae's red-roofed Western-style house earlier that morning, there was a discussion under way between him and his wife. After finishing a late breakfast and retiring to the parlour to leaf through the morning edition of the paper, Miryeo brought her husband's attention to one of its pages.

It was the *Hyundai Daily*. He took in the article with one glance.

'That's quite a project,' Manhae exclaimed. It was an article about the symphony orchestra invitation. The project was reported in block letters in a five-column article.

'Joseon's* music society is quite something if they can bring in a foreign symphony orchestra.'

Miryeo could not suppress her delight at the news.

'How many people do they think can appreciate such music?' asked Manhae.

'What are you talking about? Don't you know that in the last few years the average person's level of musical sophistication has vastly improved?'

'How much could it have improved? Do they really know anything about it? They're just acting as if they do.'

'If you're not careful, you'll be the only one who doesn't know anything about it. Soon you'll be the only one who could be called modern that doesn't know who Beethoven or Chopin is. Do you actually think there are people who wouldn't like to hear such music?'

When it came to things like music or art, the couple never agreed. Miryeo was a thoroughly modern woman who, having received a specialized college education, was extremely cultured with an especially good knowledge of art and culture. On the other hand, Manhae, in spite of the excellent education he had received, had a lower than average, superficial understanding of such things and was unyieldingly conservative in his views.

'The project is proceeding after taking account of the general populace's level of cultivation. Would they attempt such a large project recklessly? It's an extremely valuable undertaking.

* Joseon was the name used for Korea during the colonial period.

We aren't the only ones who're happy to see this kind of project get off the ground.'

However, Manhae, not fully comprehending, had a different opinion. 'Simply put, it's nothing but vanity. The project is vain and to approve of it is vain. They are trying to drive simple citizens into the same pit of vanity.'

'What do you mean, vanity? Why is it vain? Is it fair to label as vanity the citizen's attempts to understand art?'

For some reason on this particular morning, Miryeo just couldn't abide her husband's opinions and ended up losing her temper. As her tanned face took on a look of aggravation, she stared into her husband's equally tanned face. It had only been a couple of days since they had returned from a two-week vacation at the beach.

As they went to the same place every year, their vacations did not provide any novel sense of happiness to the couple. That said, the trips were not unpleasant either. After returning from the annual event that played out as if scripted, the couple was lazily spending a few torpid days at home experiencing a completely new sense of fatigue. As it was the height of summer, there was no particularly pressing business, and Manhae had not gone to his office but was resting up at home. As far as a family goes, it was just the two of them and the hired help; the small household meant that Miryeo spent every day with her husband, which she found tiresome. When people feel stifled, they are apt to give vent to their feelings for no apparent reason. On this particular morning, that unexpected newspaper article was the thing that ignited the explosion.

Miryeo's face turned red and blood rushed to her temples. Compared to her husband, whose straight nose and shining eyes gave off a softness that concealed a lively nature and, therefore, gave off no particular impression other than amiability, Miryeo's face possessed a strong tenacity. She had been the talk of the town before she was even thirty, and her exceptional countenance was without a blemish, like a genial flower. Was it that a beauty who can control her aggravation seems even more attractive? The knitted brow on her tanned face made her seem exceptionally beautiful on this morning.

'Vanity, you say. You are only insulting yourself with such talk by displaying how little you know.'

'If it's not vanity, then what is it? One's belly has to be full before worrying about culture. If pursuing music or art without being able to feed yourself is not vanity, tell me what is.'

Manhae too was not going to give in easily, and an unexpected confrontation developed between the couple.

'It seems you think that food is the only thing people need to feel satisfied. Music is a kind of nutrition as well. You talk only about the stomach but forget the soul.'

'So music alone can fill an empty stomach. Why don't you try living on nothing but music then?'

'Ha! You go on like that, all the while pretending that you're engaged in some big enterprise when you're just a merchant. You use the word "businessman" and think the world is yours, but do you know that behind your back people call you a miser? Why is it that cultural projects can only happen after one is living well? Can't you see that even the poor desire such things?'

'Ah ha, since there are so many people like you, the culture business must be thriving in this poor land.'

'That's enough! Just know that they're all better than you.'

Giving rein to her anger, Miryeo threw the newspaper down on the table and got up. The paper hit her cup, spilling tea all over the tray. Seeing that she ignored the spill and disappeared into the hallway, Manhae decided to hold his tongue and not exasperate her any further.

There are few households where the wife's voice does not grow louder with time. The husband's world is outside the house, where he can enjoy all manner of power and authority, but once he sets one foot inside, all things are in the hands of his wife. Oddly enough, it was not thought shameful that the same beard that was haughtily stroked outside the house was yanked on by the wife inside. This was especially true in the case of Manhae's household, and when Miryeo raised her voice, there was nowhere to hide. As this had been Manhae's fate since the first days of his marriage, and as it was only after much supplication that he had won Miryeo's hand from among those many competitors, he had from the beginning been a devoted husband who, for the most part, endured his wife's obstinacy. Even when taking great pains to please his wife, there were many times when he could not read her mind. He had been making such efforts for the eight years they had been married. For Miryeo's part, she hadn't been happy with the marriage from the start, and, what's more, the monotonous home life gave rise to a powerful sense of ennui. On top of that, the only thing her leisured life left her with was a feeling of weariness. She was sick of her husband's business, which lacked any sense of taste, and the fact that her desire to add some culture to her life had not been taken seriously caused her dissatisfaction to grow.

'Wait and see. The day will come when I get involved in the culture business,' Manhae said in a soft tone while looking down at his wife.

'When will that be, in the next life? Seeing as how the only thing that concerns you twenty-four hours a day is your gold mine, what else could possibly interest you?'

'I have no choice but to be concerned with money if my business is going to thrive. But that doesn't mean that money is my ultimate objective.'

'Oh please. I've asked you to make a children's music institute, but did you listen? You also ignored me when I asked you to make a music academy. And now you're saying that you're going to do something? If you don't want to be involved, I'll do it by myself.'

'Let's take our time and think of something.'

'Getting involved in bringing this symphony orchestra here would be a worthwhile thing to do. It's not just something for the newspaper, anyone could do it.'

'We're already too late.'

'What do you mean, too late? Is there any reason we couldn't support it? If you did, you would gradually become better known, which would help your business.'

'Support, well ...'

'Look, how about this?' Her anger having cooled, Miryeo took her husband's arm and pointed to the telephone on the desk. 'Make a phone call right now.'

Pulling her husband to the phone, she said, 'Call the president of the *Hyundai Daily*.'

And so, the president of the paper was contacted and support for the symphony orchestra project was offered. Miryeo's fury abated, and Manhae was finally free from that tense atmosphere and could relax. For the first time in a long while, the thorny mood within the house had completely dissipated.

*

The president had summoned Jongse and discussed the matter of sponsorship with him. Jongse then headed for Manhae's home for a more detailed discussion. When he found himself ringing the doorbell to the foyer of the Western-style house in Yeonhuijang with the brightest roof in the neighbourhood, the couple had already come down to the yard and were finding respite from the sun on a bench in the shade of a tree.

Upon hearing the bell, Miryeo said, 'That must be the person from the paper.'

Moving up to the hallway with quick steps, she stuck her feet in a pair of slippers and headed for the foyer.

'The president sent me. I'm from the entertainment division.'

Receiving Jongse's card with a smile, Miryeo welcomed the

morning guest. Jongse well remembered Miryeo, but her rec-ollection of him was not so vivid and was limited to a vague memory of who he was. However, as that morning's business had come about at the couple's instigation, the reception she extended was especially hospitable.

The parlour was hot and humid, and so Miryeo ushered Jongse into the garden. It was a bright late summer day and the garden, with the cool shade from its cherry tree and the flickering shadows of fish in the small pond, was much more comfortable than inside the house. The wooden chair in the shade looked cool, and the wooden table painted white also had a refreshing appearance. Jongse and Manhae knew each other by sight but their familiarity ended there. Feeling somewhat embarrassed by the fact that he had rushed to get involved in the project as talk of it grew in the city, Manhae got up slowly to greet Jongse as if reluctant to leave the garden.

'Your paper is undertaking another great project. I'm sorry I didn't go to express my thanks personally and have caused you the trouble of visiting me.'

'It's quite alright. I consider it an honour to have the chance to come see you like this.'

Jongse's response reflected his genuine feelings on several levels. Of course, discussions on the project were one thing, but Jongse was also thinking about what big news today's visit would be when he conveyed it to his friend Ilma.

'Actually, this is more my wife's project, and it was her mak-ing a fuss about it that brought you here. As far as support goes, I don't know what would be appropriate, so I have been waiting for some advice.'

'What do you mean, a fuss? It's just that I don't think it's good for a woman to do nothing at home all day and wanted to get involved in something,' while giving her a husband a subtle rebuke, Miryeo joined the conversation with a smile.

'Anyway, if one has the energy, one should get involved with some kind of project. There's been a lot of talk that sooner or later, as a well-known businessman, you would be starting some project or another.'

At Jongse's instigation, Manhae became magnanimous, and Miryeo became more talkative.

'There were a lot of plans. We talked about starting a nursery and thought about opening a music academy and forming an orchestra.'

'That's good news,' Jongse chimed in as if he had been waiting for his chance. He continued, 'Well, why don't you take this opportunity to create and support a music academy that we can put a name on? Anyway, in this kind of thing using the name of an organization is more appropriate than the name of an individual.'

'How much are you putting into this project?'

'We are thinking of ten thousand won.'

'Well, I'll contribute half of that. Shall we think of a name for the music academy?'

Thanks to Miryeo's handling of the negotiations, things had been decided in an unexpectedly easy manner.

The three of them quickly came up with the name Nokseong Music Academy and discussed having the newspaper promote the new enterprise.

'Nokseong Music Academy. That sounds magnificent,' Jongse casually commented, and the couple readily agreed with him. With that, the day's business was concluded.

'It's a name full of hope.'*

Hearing her husband's approval, Miryeo's mood turned to delight.

'It has a gentle sound, but that makes sense seeing as it's an

---

* Why the name 'Nokseong', which means 'green star', is hopeful is unclear. Nokseong was also the name of the first art and film magazine published in colonial Korea (first edition, November 1919). This magazine included articles on art and 'moving pictures' that included profiles of famous actors and actresses. Charlie Chaplin was featured in one issue.

academy for women only. We'll hire only those who have a genuine interest and basic grounding in music. We will form and give training to a choir section, an instrumental section, and one or two symphonies. Of course, we want to produce talented individuals, but by training a choir, orchestra, and a symphony we can create enthusiasm for a music culture in this country. Education, finances, and all other aspects of the academy will be managed by women, so it will have its own unique character that can't be found anywhere else.'

'That's an excellent plan. And you already have the look of the young future dean of the academy.'

Manhae was caught up in Jongse's enthusiasm and became bolder.

'In that case, I'll invest two hundred thousand won. With that much capital we could put together a decent academy right away.'

Miryeo had never seen her husband change his mind so rapidly. It seemed that Jongse's encouragement had helped bring an unexpectedly quick result.

'Two hundred thousand won! I've never heard such a thing come from your mouth. It seems you finally understand the culture business. If you had figured this out earlier, the Nokseong Music Academy would already have been established, and we wouldn't have lost the Harbin Symphony Orchestra negotiations to the newspaper company.'

Jongse smiled at Miryeo's lament. 'That wouldn't have been possible this time. Give support to this project, and next time you can have exclusive control.'

'What a waste.'

'We've sent Ilma. He's the best man for the job. He's been gone a day, so the negotiations should start soon.'

'Wh–who did you send?'

'The cultural critic Cheon Ilma.'

The information, so casually tossed out by Jongse, was news to the couple and caused a great deal of surprise.

'Ilma?' While Miryeo repeated her question with wide eyes, the name could only form soundlessly on Manhae's lips.

'Are you saying you didn't know? It hasn't come out in the paper, but everybody knows about it.'

While being surprised at the fact that the couple had not already heard about Ilma, Jongse could not help but marvel at the fact that he was the one breaking this news to them.

'They sent Ilma.' Miryeo, deep in thought, uttered the intriguing name.

'Ilma is a fellow alumnus.'

Manhae spoke the name as well, and while it was pronounced the same by the couple, the whirlwind of emotions it caused in each of their hearts was quite different. Quickly perceiving what was in each of their minds, Jongse, feeling his breast flutter, did his best to break the frightening silence that had settled over them.

'Ilma is a talented guy. His analyses as a music critic are always very incisive. His ability makes him the best man for the job.'

'Even when he was in school, he was known for his ability.'

As Manhae regained some composure and was able to sound natural, Jongse, again carefully trying to gauge his emotions, replied, 'It's true that he hasn't achieved the recognition he deserves and has had trouble finding his niche, but someone of his calibre is sure to succeed.'

Choosing his words for their impact on the couple and raising his voice for effect, he praised his friend, but Miryeo, as if to conceal her innermost thoughts, maintained a stubborn silence throughout.

*

That evening, Jongse appeared at his favourite tea house with a proud look as if the whole world had been blessed with happiness and began to wax eloquent to Neungbo and Hun.

'Guess where I went today?'

Putting on airs, Jongse tossed out another question.

'Whom did I meet and what did we talk about?'

Hun jeeringly replied, 'Did you go to hell?'

'I went to see Manhae.'

'Was Miryeo there as well?' Neungbo, finding his voice, sat up straight in surprise.

'Not only did I meet Miryeo but I heard about an incredible project.'

'What project? How the hell did you wind up meeting them?'

'Well actually, it was because of Ilma, so I can't really take any credit, but meeting them after so long was really something.'

'I wonder if they look the same as they used to. Everything changes so fast these days.'

'Maturity seems to have made her twice as beautiful. If she was a red rose in her twenties, I could compare her to a carnation now, a slightly worn red carnation. That is the best comparison to the beauty of a woman in her thirties. Perhaps it was the fact that her skin was a bit tanned from their trip to Gajae beach, but she looked more attractive than ever. I felt again today how happy Manhae's married life must be.'

'And so, how unhappy Ilma must be,' Neungbo added with a tone of admiration.

'It's not entering her thirties that accounts for her beauty. Miryeo is a natural beauty. She has a face one would walk a thousand *li** just to look at. Just the fact that you got to see her today should make you happy.'

'This is going to make Ilma even happier than it did me. The proposal that beauty suddenly made …'

Jongse conveyed the gist of the plan he had heard that afternoon to establish a music academy with two hundred thousand won worth of capital and to use the academy to

*   *Li* is a measurement of distance equalling about one third of a mile.

support the invitation of the Harbin Symphony Orchestra. Further, he told them that the couple had not agreed to all this knowing of Ilma's involvement but had found out about it only after everything had been agreed, causing them great surprise at the unexpected twist of fate.

'Hum ...'

'That's an incredible project.' Hun as well expressed his surprise at the turn of events.

'Anybody that wealthy would want to get involved in some kind of project. That would certainly help the culture business in this country thrive.'

'So what do you make of all that ambition? Is it the result of ennui that has crept into their married life? At any rate, they are about at the point in their marriage when boredom sets in, but the basic problem is that Miryeo has a stronger personality than Manhae. He had to practically beg her to marry him, and now that he's older, he's at his wife's beck and call.'

Jongse added his own comment to Neungbo's analysis. 'The fact that they don't have a child after eight years of marriage is probably a source of dissatisfaction to Miryeo. Manhae is not exactly a monk once he's outside the house. Whether that's the reason they don't have a child, I can't say, but that attitude must cause some problems.'

'That's why the Nokseong Music Academy will be established, support will be given to the Harbin Symphony Orchestra, and she will have contact again with Ilma. This is some very strange karma indeed.'

'When Ilma gets back, he's not going to be happy. Once a fire is lit, it's not put out so easily.'

'Can those passions be rekindled in Ilma? Well, we can never really know what's in another person's heart.'

'Enough talk, send a letter to Manchuria right away. I wouldn't be surprised if he comes running back here,' Hun said in all seriousness to Jongse.

As the topic shifted from Miryeo to Ilma, the three

continued their idle chatter on the topic of their missing comrade.

'The bachelor will be excited to get that letter.'

'He's become an old bachelor waiting for this opportunity.'

'Doesn't he always fulfil his responsibilities?'

After congratulating Jongse for bringing them the good tidings regarding their friend, they then wheedled him into buying the drinks for the evening.

Neungbo suggested going to see Eunpa, so they headed towards Namcheon and the Sillagwon* bar.

They ordered drinks and, after Eunpa served them, the talk, which had started with Ilma, turned to the topic of happiness.

'People are always saying happiness this and happiness that, what the hell is happiness anyway?'

The response was thus: 'Happiness is happiness, what else would it be? Happiness is nothing more than that which tells you what's not unhappiness.'

'Then what's unhappiness?'

'The ancient philosopher Plato said that human happiness was comprised of four things: health, beauty, strength and money. Isn't the difference between happiness and unhappiness whether one has these things or not?'

'If one had all four of those things one would certainly be happy.'

'Are you saying that unhappiness can become happiness? Does that mean that happiness and unhappiness depend on a person's state of mind?'

'I heard a story about a person named Piccadilly who was condemned to death. When he stood in front of the guillotine, a woman was brought forth and he was told that if he married this woman his life would be spared. After looking at the woman he found that she was lame. He said that if he

* Sillagwon (실낙원) is the Korean translation of the title of Milton's poem *Paradise Lost*.

were to be killed so be it, he would not marry the woman and so gave up his life. So, to Piccadilly, death was the preferable choice of the two. Marriage is not always better than death.'

'He's a crazy fool. Whether she's crippled or not, he should have married her, it's preferable to dying.'

'I have another one! The philosopher Posidonius was extremely ill and had taken to his sickbed when a friend came to ask a question about philosophy. As he felt sorry for his friend he said, "Pain is nothing to me. Even when I'm suffering, I can think and speak of philosophy. Suffering, no matter how severe, holds no power over me. Even if I suffer the pain of death, I will never say suffering is unhappiness." Can we say, then, that to Posidonius pain is unhappiness?'

'They're all crazy. What use is the silly talk of a petty philosopher? In discussing happiness, the most important thing is common sense. Happiness is happiness, unhappiness the same, it's simple. All this other talk is meaningless nonsense.'

It was Neungbo who was insisting on the common-sense theory, while Jongse was attempting to give the issue deeper consideration by using the example of the philosopher. After Neungbo's retort, Jongse changed the direction of the conversation. 'Well, would you say that you're happy?'

'There are all kinds of happiness. Whether I could say that I am happy right at this moment or not, I'm not sure, but I don't think I'm unhappy. I'm at my favourite bar the Sillagwon with Eunpa at my side, drinking with my friends, how could I not be happy?'

'I could understand if it was the *nagwon*, but what's so happy about the Sillagwon?'*

Everyone laughed at Jongse's witticism and Neungbo, changing his tone, said, 'Of course, it's possible to imagine being happier than I am right now. When I open my clinic and set up house with Eunpa, I will be happier than I am now.'

* *Nagwon* means 'the Garden of Eden'.

'And when I become president of a newspaper and Hun writes a Nobel Prize-winning novel ...'

'That's right!'

'Those are impressive dreams you have, Mr Medical Doctor, but where's the money for your new clinic?'

Eunpa, laughing along, raises her glass to Neungbo's lips.*

Hun as well was enjoying the drunken joviality and the discussion of happiness. Alcohol makes the heart magnanimous, and when one's heart is open, one's imagination is free to soar.

Neungbo opens a hospital, Jongse becomes president of a newspaper, and I win the Nobel Prize ...

'If I win the Nobel Prize, what happens to Ilma?'

'Just imagine that he becomes the wealthiest man in town.'

'That means he'll be a multi-millionaire. Richer than Yu Manhae.'

'If that happens it would mean the end of Manhae.'

'And things will work out between Ilma and Miryeo. Ah, fantasizing is fun.'

'It's not just fun, perhaps such fancies are the only real happiness.'

'Can that be? Would anything be sadder than if everything we've been saying were nothing more than fancy? Every once in a while, such fancies have to become reality to be fancies. If not, they're not worth being called fancies.'

Hun, taking over the discussion of happiness, raised his voice in a chivalrous manner: 'Then you'd better get to work winning that Nobel Prize.'

'Anyway, Ilma has to become the richest man in town.'

'You have drank too much.'

'He has to. We're not that happy right now. I can't help but think that better times are coming. Is life worth living without such hopes? You can't blame a person for having hopes.'

---

* Here, the author inexplicably changes to the present tense.

'It's too much to think that this is all there is and then we die.'

'Human history is always changing. Would the Creator begrudge us if our lot were to improve? Among the kings of Macedonia that followed Alexander, there were those who committed all manner of crudities in the streets of Rome. And they say the kings of Sicily served as teachers in the schools of Corinth – human history is always changing. Beggars become kings and kings, beggars ...'

'Does anybody have any use for a king who becomes a beggar? Think only about the beggar who becomes a king.'

'Okay. A beggar becoming a king – I win the Nobel Prize and Ilma ...'

'Drinking is a good thing. It has made such nice, pleasant gentlemen of you all.' Eunpa made her contribution to the reverie, and the drinks she served had already made the men drunk by early evening.

Among them all, Hun was the worst drinker, and his discussion of fancy soon turned to prattle and then, inexplicably, to tears, managing to create a scene in the midst of the boisterous drinking festivities. They hadn't been this pleasantly drunk for a long time.

After parting with his friends and plopping into the seat of the car he had summoned, Jongse headed for his home in Seongbuk-dong. Recalling this later, collapsing into bed after the long night of drinking all seemed to have happened in a dream.

Jongse wasn't able to open his eyes until well after noon the next day, and even though his eyes were open, his brain was not really working. He was still drunk: his face was red, and his body hot.

He gulped down a bowl of cold water and lay back down. He was neither awake nor asleep but in a state somewhere in between.

This state of grogginess continued till evening. It was in this condition that he received a single telegram from Ilma.

Negotiations going well. Don't be surprised
at news of ten thousand won winnings.

He dubiously read the telegram over twice, but the message didn't change. *Don't be surprised at news of ten thousand won winnings.*

What does that mean? Ten thousand won winnings? How did he win ten thousand won? What luck could have brought him that kind of money?

Putting the telegram down he mused, *It's a strange dream, Ilma – ten thousand won – what does it all mean?*

Hun being still groggy, this all seemed like nothing more than a dream. It was huge news and an enormous surprise. However, far from dreaming, Hun was, in fact, up and sitting in front of his desk, and in front of his eyes was a real telegram and not something from his imagination.

Trying to clear his head, Hun took another few gulps of cold water.

3. TEN THOUSAND WON

The sequence of events that had lead up to Ilma sending Hun the telegram reporting his ten thousand won winnings was as follows. After barely managing to extricate himself from Danyeong's grasp at Shingyeong station, Ilma had boarded the afternoon train and arrived at Harbin around five o'clock that evening. Byeoksu had received the telegram and was on the busy platform to meet him.

'I thought you'd be in a standard-class car, but ...'

Expressing his surprise at Ilma's emerging from a deluxe first-class car, he came running to take the trunk from him.

'The sun rose in the west today.'

'And things are looking up for you.'

'Who has any use for a shabby cultural envoy?'

'I read your letter and also saw it in the newspaper.' In addition to being quite perceptive, working for the newspaper kept Byeoksu abreast of everything that was going on. 'I'm honoured to be able to walk together with a cultural envoy or whatever it is they call you.'

'You should enjoy the privilege while you can, before long

I'm likely to become so popular that you won't even be able to stand next to me.'

'Since you've been coming to Manchuria, you've turned into quite the braggart. Don't make boasts you can't keep.'

With his stout frame and a clay pipe clenched in his teeth, Byeoksu cut a solid figure. In the ten-some years since he had come to Manchuria, his face had become tanned dark, and his appearance had definitely changed. His uncle Han Unsan had, early on, opened a pharmacy called the Daeryukdang* with a large amount of capital and this had brought Byeoksu to Harbin where he had spent his youth doing various jobs. He had wasted much of his time unsure whether it was money or something else that had brought him all the way to Manchuria.

'Let's go straight to the Daeryukdang.'

Byeoksu, as usual, insisted that Ilma stay with him, but today Ilma's response was different.

'I need to stop imposing on you. If I don't, it'll be impossible to return all the favours I owe.'

'Are you saying you're going to stay in a hotel?'

'Not just any hotel. I've reserved a room at the Modern Hotel.'**

'The Modern Hotel ... that's great!'

'It's frequented by people involved with music, so it should be a good place to make some contacts.'

As Ilma paced back and forth, a porter came running and asked if he was the guest who had sent the telegram. The porter had come from the hotel to meet him. He hoisted Ilma's trunk and followed him outside to where a car was waiting. After Ilma and Byeoksu were seated in the car, it exited the

---

* Daeryukdang (대륙당) translates as 'Continental House'. The word 'continent' was understood to mean mainland China or Manchuria.
** The Modern Hotel actually existed in Harbin at the time of the story.

drive and headed down the street. As the car crossed the streetcar tracks and passed over the Jaehong Bridge, the broad city could be seen, brilliantly bathed in the light of the setting sun, and the Songhwa river could be dimly perceived in the distance. The car shot down the hill and raced toward the Puristan district.

The foliage of the roadside trees was changing colour, and here and there the ground was covered in fallen elm leaves. Perhaps it was that the change of seasons came a couple of months early here, but the stifling late summer heat that was felt in Seoul was, in this northern city, replaced by a refreshing coolness. The impression he had of the city now was quite different than the one he had received when he had visited in mid-summer.

This impression became even stronger when they entered Katiskaya Boulevard. Both sides of the street were lined with old buildings, and people were strolling about – it was like a corner of Europe. It was as if he had come to a foreign country,* and Ilma's heart raced every time he experienced this feeling. The change in colour of the dress of the men and women was even more interesting than the change of seasons.

'For some reason, whenever I come here, I feel like I've arrived at the place I've been searching for.'

'You've been infatuated with Europe for a long time now.'

After arriving at the hotel and its familiar counter, he signed his name and went up to his room. He unpacked, bathed and groomed himself, and, as if issuing orders, said to Byeoksu, 'From today I'm the boss. You've got to stick with me and do what I say. Okay, let's get dinner together.'

With that he gave Byeoksu's shoulder a push toward the restaurant.

---

* Of course, Ilma is in a foreign country in that it is not Korea; however, Manchuria has been annexed by Japan and so is part of the same empire as Korea. What Lee really means here by 'foreign' is Western.

They enjoyed dinner in the hotel restaurant, Ilma speaking of Joseon and Byeoksu of Manchuria. By the time they had talked of the Harbin music scene and finished dinner, night had fallen. Ilma wanted to get to work as quickly as possible, but it was impossible to visit anyone at this hour, and his desire to enjoy his first night on the continent was greater than his desire to go right to work.

Byeoksu was already aware of this desire. He knew exactly what his friend wanted to do. 'It's not really that early, shall we head out?'

'Where to?'

'There's nothing you haven't seen here. You know where we're going.'

'Why are you trying to tempt me so early?'

'When you travel, are there such things as travel morals?'

'Actually, I was just thinking about that place myself.'

Looking at Ilma as if to say, 'See?', Byeoksu prepared to get up from his seat. 'It seems the person who is always asking about you has some special interest in you.'

'Who are you talking about?'

'Whaddya mean who? Nadia, of course.'

'Nadia asks about me?' Ilma stood with his mouth open, his heart suddenly aflutter. 'Truth be told, the first thing I think of when I come to Harbin is Nadia. Did she really ask about me?'

'You're really something. Other people could be here ten years and nothing interesting happens to them. You must have some special gift with women.'

'Nadia's different from other women. She may dance in a cabaret, but I don't think she's like anyone one else I know.'

'That's a strange thing to say.'

'She deserves better.'

'Foreign women put feelings before anything else, so they don't fall for some half-hearted approach. The fact that you won her heart so easily means that you're quite the ladies' man.'

The two had come out of the hotel and were walking down the street. The streets, lit up at night, looked more radiant than during the daytime. This street was not paved but laid with cobblestones, and its uneven texture under their feet added to the foreign feel of the place at night. While feeling the breeze coming off the Songhwa river, they headed north down a main boulevard to where the Moscow Cabaret was located on the right side of a crook in the road. The dance hall was down the stairs in the basement.

It was a long, dark room with only a few guests, who, it seemed, felt it was still a bit early to start dancing. As the two sat down, Nadia came running from a table where she had just finished eating. Her sudden appearance didn't seem real to Ilma, who was so happy to see her that he felt like he was dreaming.

'What brings you here? When did you arrive?' For a foreign woman there was something vaguely Asian about her calm demeanour. 'I hear about you often from Kasper Han.'

'After arriving, I went to the hotel and then came straight here.'

'Will you stay for a few days?'

'I have some business to see to, so I'll be here until it's concluded. It could be quick, or it could take a while.'

'Stay for a while if you can.'

'*Spasibo.*'*

Her words were music to Ilma's ears.

When speaking with Nadia, Ilma used English or broken Russian and while the language and emotions were different, his international outlook and the fact that it was Nadia, made it possible for him to harmonize with her without the slightest awkwardness. Even though they had only met a few times, he felt like they had known each other a long while.

While dancing to the music, they grew more comfortable

* 'Thank you' in Russian.

with each other. That night, he danced to the very last song with only Nadia.

*

Just after midnight, Ilma took Nadia out of the cabaret to get something to eat and to chat. By the time he sent her home in a car, the night had grown late. After saying goodnight to Byeoksu, he returned to the hotel. The two a.m. bell could be heard as he was crawling into bed. This was how he spent his first night on the continent.

The next day, due to the festivities of the night before, Ilma slept in and left the hotel unusually late, but when he thought of the time he had spent with Nadia the night before, he had no regrets.

Ilma's first order of business was to go the head offices of the railway. This was the sponsor of the Harbin Symphony Orchestra. The newspaper company had already approached the director of public services, whom Ilma met to ask for assistance, and so his response was very positive.

'I received a letter from the president and expressions of support from several other places. It's a fine project. We're fully behind it. Not only is it important for the culture of Seoul, but it also brings honour to the symphony orchestra and aids its development. Even if we hadn't been approached from outside, this department has wanted to engage in a similar project of its own. Anyway, I hope the project is successful and will do what I can to help things proceed smoothly.'

Ilma was very happy with the cooperative attitude of the director, and the two shared their frank opinions about cultural exchange – things had gone unexpectedly well, and it turned out to be a very enjoyable meeting.

Being pleased at how smoothly things were going so far, Ilma made an appointment to meet the director again at a later date and left the railway offices. It was almost noon.

Calling Byeoksu, he arranged to meet outside the hotel for

lunch and had the horse-drawn carriage head for the Pang-wans restaurant. He must have been late in arriving because when he got there, Byeoksu was already waiting out front. The upper floor of the large building housed a hotel and restaurant, while the lower floor was a department store. Byeoksu, who had been pacing in front of the door, came running when he saw Ilma. Grabbing the carriage, he said in an excited voice, 'Don't be shocked.'

'About what?'

'Does it sound like I'm going to give you bad news?'

'I don't know. Why do I feel nervous?'

'What was the number of your lottery ticket?'

'What about my lottery ticket?'

The two entered the department store and as Ilma fumbled in his pocket planner for the ticket, Byeoksu pulled him towards the counter.

'Wasn't it 37525? Look at that.'

'37525 – what are you talking about?'

'It's you. You're the winner. You've won first prize.'

Ilma stood with his mouth open, lost as to what was going on. 'Am I dreaming?'

'This is no dream, you're wide awake. Today's the fifteenth of the month, the day they announce the lottery winners, and you won – ten thousand won.'

'Ten thousand won!'

It so happened that the second, third, and fourth place winners were also announced on that day and people were crowding around the counter. Ilma dazedly approached the counter with his ticket in his hand where the employee con-gratulated him with a smile.

'This turned out well. For some reason, our store has picked the winner several times over the last couple of months. Thanks to that, the store is always crowded, and we couldn't be happier.'

The people milling about to catch a glimpse of what the lottery winner looked like stared Ilma up and down.

'On the coming twenty-third of the month, go to the Central Bank and pick up your entire ten thousand won winnings in cash. There will be a handling fee of three per cent.'

The world around Ilma was spinning, and the words of the employee were barely audible.

Eschewing lunch, Ilma and Byeoksu left the department store and headed for a post office. The first person who came to his mind was the novelist Hun. He felt that his luck on this trip had come from the bouquet of flowers Hun had given him.

Don't be surprised at news of ten thousand won winnings, Harbin.

Even after sending this telegram and leaving the post office, his body still felt flushed, and the world still spun.

*

In order to cool his excitement, Ilma decided to walk along the street for a bit with Byeoksu.

How is it that I was the one picked among all those thousands of people? How is it that ten thousand won came into my hands?

The more he thought about it, the more it all seemed like a dream. He was still in a daze. The crowds meandering about the streets seemed like schools of fish moving around in another world. Why was he the one picked from among all these people? What kind of fate was this? Had Lady Luck picked him out of the blue like a blind man drawing straws? Are there such things as fortune and misfortune?

When contemplating the matter of good and bad luck, which is normally taken for granted, one might come to doubt that there is any design to the universe, and the result is greater confusion.

'It seems like this is the reason for all these trips to Manchuria.'

'It hasn't hit me yet. I can't think straight.'

'Luck, seen from the outside, seems like something bright

and shiny, but once one is inside it, it's nothing special.' Byeoksu understood Ilma's confusion.

'When something is completely full, it might seem empty. It's sometimes hard to tell the difference.' Byeoksu, it seems, had perceived what was in Ilma's mind.

'Are you saying that you can tell emptiness but not fullness?'

'Fullness and emptiness can look the same.'

The people passing by were all living at the whim of varying states of good and bad luck, but they all appeared essentially the same. Ilma's great fortune had not changed the houses lining both sides of the street, the many carriages coming and going between them, or the leaves trembling on the trees along the boulevard in the least – they all looked the same as they had yesterday.

'For example, is there any difference between me and this beggar? There's nothing special about me and nothing vulgar about him. Is there anything about our faces that could tell you what's in our hearts?'

After giving the beggar a few coins and sending him on his way, nothing had changed. It sometimes seemed there was a strange and mysterious harmonizing force in the affairs of the world, and then sometimes it seemed there wasn't. And Ilma had no idea how to comprehend it.

'There's nothing to think about. Luck is luck. Ten thousand won is ten thousand won. That's all there is to it. What else can there be?'

Once again becoming the realist, Byeoksu raised his voice as if trying to bring Ilma out of his reverie. 'Thinking too much will only spoil things. When something good happens, it's best to take it in your stride. Worrying too much can ruin everything. In reality, winning the lottery can lead to either comedy or tragedy.'

Byeoksu gave several examples of what he meant. 'There was the person that got so excited at the news of winning the lottery that they fell out a second storey window. And there was the person who worked as a domestic servant and, upon hearing the news of winning the lottery, lost their mind and took the first train for their hometown without even stopping by their place of work or their boarding house. And there were the cases of husbands who won the lottery while away from home, but their wives took the ten thousand won and ran away, and upon their return they filed missing person reports and lawsuits which were either won or lost ...'

'That's enough. Why are you telling me all these unlucky stories?'

Ilma's reaction encouraged Byeoksu.

'Now I'm getting through to you. There's no reason for you to split hairs like this; no matter how you look at it, luck is luck, and ten thousand won is ten thousand won.'

'Splitting hairs? How am I splitting hairs? It's just too much to take in all at once.'

'Pick up the money using my name. There could be complications because you're not from here. My name is safe.'

After all the excitement had subsided enough for them to relax, the two suddenly realized that they were hungry.

After lunch, when Ilma had gathered his wits, the significance of the ten thousand won began to sink in.

The pleasantly full feeling of his stomach and the contentment in his heart were not due to the food but to the ten thousand won. They were the results of the satisfaction that the thought of the money gave him.

Even an ordinary sight like that of the dishes scattered seemed to take on special significance, and the sumptuous meal had filled him with contentment.

Just now I am more content than anyone can be, and there is nothing further I could wish for.

Ilma, like a king who commanded the entire world, could not have been more satisfied. There was no one before whom he would kneel. *I'm the master of my world*, he went so far as to think to himself. It was as if all had been prepared just for him.

The table, the food, the streets, and the people – even the heavens and the earth – as if all had been placed here for him. He wasn't thinking straight. He still had not come back to reality.

'What in the world are you going to do with ten thousand won?'

That was the next problem. Byeoksu had abruptly brought him out of his reverie. Between the two, Byeoksu kept his feet more firmly rooted in reality.

'I don't know. What should I do with it? For the time being, I don't want to worry about what to do with the money. I just want to enjoy the idea of it.'

'You're satisfied with just the idea of it? You're a romanticist. A miser is happy just to have gold, but gold exists to be used. There is no significance in having ten thousand won if you're not going to use it.'

'Well, let's think of a use for it. Is there a business I could start with it that would be right for me? What should I do? Let's think of the best way to use the money.'

'Are you worried there won't be anything to do with the money? Everyone will have their own idea about that.'

'"Ten thousand won for a modern man",* that's a delightful-sounding title, isn't it?' Byeoksu said while luxuriating in his own fantasies, watching blue cigarette smoke curl up from his fingertips.

'One could do a lot for the poor with ten thousand won.'

'What's the first thing you want to do?'

'Um ... build a small cultural residence.'

'What will building a house do for you? After you build it will it feed you?'

'Well, if you don't like that idea, how about I buy a car?'

'A car? That's like horseshoes on a dog.'

---

* Lee seems to use the term 'modern man' (현대인) to refer to a level of Western-style education and culture that would set one apart from the pre-modern Korean.

'I could take a luxury trip.'

'You've always wanted to do that.'

'I suppose you think you can't buy love with ten thousand won?'

'Love? Buy love with money? That's the kind of thing I'd expect you to say.'

'Do you think you get love with your heart? You're a very naïve modern man.'

'There are other things besides money that you can give to someone you love, and to a poor and lonely pers...'

In the midst of this utterance, Ilma thought of Nadia. Her image, destitute and lonely, suddenly materialized in his mind.

'For example, if Nadia wanted me to, I could give her all of the ten thousand won.'

'Hmm, Nadia. Does she have that big a hold over you?'

Lonely Nadia, who had lost her father in Manjuri* and buried her mother in Harbin a few years ago; she lived with her aunt and worked in a cabaret, not even earning one won a day. When it came to being poor and lonely, Ilma knew of no woman more deserving of pity than Nadia. In fact, it was her pathetic situation that drew him to her.

'You'd give everything to Nadia? Well, I wouldn't put it past you.'

'That's right.' Ilma stared at the far-off mountains, his face brightening at this new thought.

*

The next day – the day after Ilma won the lottery – the talk of his winning had filled the streets of Shingyeong.

After the humiliating parting with Ilma at the station, from which she had walked away in resentment, Danyeong was out today for a leisurely stroll. Her splendid attire made

* A Chinese city in Inner Mongolia that sits on the border with Russia.

her stand out in the crowds, and her appearance, reflected in the store windows, brought her a feeling of satisfaction.

She wasn't alone; a driver accompanied her. Even though Ilma had rejected her, Danyeong was not worried about not having admirers.

'Why do you look so shabby today? After ten years in Seoul, can't you learn some refinement? Your appearance, the way you walk, you look like a hillbilly.'

However, the object of this rebuke was anything but a hillbilly. A driver in name only, he was none other than the prominent president of Bando Studios, Kim Myeongdo. Even though he was a mover and a shaker in the film production world, he was completely under Danyeong's thumb. After receiving Danyeong's telegram, he had come from Seoul by car as fast as he could. She had called him to assuage her anger at the way Ilma had treated her. Being completely captivated by Danyeong, this didn't bother Myeongdo, and he was only too happy to come running.

While he had given Danyeong roles in several of his movies, he had yet to make any headway regarding his furtive desires and was just one of the several men at her beck and call who hovered around her. Whenever they met, he squandered large sums of money, but his obsession with her meant he could be shooed away at her command without one word of protest.

The fact that they looked like a peacock and a shaggy dog when they were together was more a result of Danyeong's excessive extravagance than Myeongdo's unremarkable appearance. No matter how one looked at it, Myeongdo did not give the impression of a movie executive out with a female movie star but seemed more akin to a servant trailing after a socialite.

'I don't care if you call me a hillbilly. As long as you give me what I want, you can call me your slave.'

'Whether you care or not, I'm embarrassed. Just look at you. I shouldn't have called you.'

'What are you saying? That I should just inconspicuously shuffle along behind you?'

'Whether you shuffle or not, straighten up and walk more briskly. Does walking in Manchuria for the first time wear you out like this?'

'Okay, straighten up and walk more briskly – how's this?'

'No matter how you walk, it's annoying.'

Myeongdo's appearance, trudging along like a student in front of his teacher, was a pathetic sight.

In trying to keep up with the rapidly moving Danyeong, Myeongdo's stumbling attempts at walking like a scholar looked like the workings of a bellows, and this brought him to the side of the street where a sign in front of a store caught his gaze and brought him to a halt. In the meantime, Danyeong continued on her way.

The sign was an announcement of the lottery results. Lotteries were a thing of interest to Myeongdo. The piece of paper he found after looking through his notebook was a lottery ticket. He had asked a friend who had travelled to Manchuria last month to buy it for him. Danyeong had stopped and was looking back at Myeongdo staring intently at his ticket number and comparing it to the lottery results. She thought he looked like a stout fireplug.

What's he staring at?

Having no choice but to go back, she stared over his shoulder at the lottery ticket.

'Wait, do you have a winning ticket?'

Myeongdo smiled at her question. 'Ha! Fat chance. How could I have a winning ticket among all these tens of thousands of people?'

'That's right. Did you think just anyone could be a winner? Luck is called luck because it's rare; if it's common it can't be called luck.'

'Well, it's supposed to come around once in a while, but it never does.'

'Stop complaining. Let's go.'

Danyeong started herding Myeongdo ahead of her like a barnyard duck.

'If the last numbers had been right ... I only needed three more matches to win.'

After entering a teahouse and ordering, the griping continued to emanate from the fireplug.

'If you're not blind, you know how rare such things are – why do you go on like that?'

'It's a pity, the more I think of it.'

'Just think that it wasn't your turn. You're acting greedy. Luck can go to other people too.'

'The thought that it wasn't my turn is depressing.'

At the same time that Myeongdo went through money like it was water when he was with Danyeong, he could be stingy and vulgar in his desire for material gain, not wanting to lose anything to anyone. This was his disposition, and it had probably gotten him where he was today. As it was, he was on his best behaviour in front of Danyeong – if he had been alone and had learned who had won the lottery, he would have been a sorrowful sight, consumed with disappointment.

'Who was the rascal that got my luck? Why is he luckier than me? I'd like to see what this guy looks like.'

'Is there any reason to know who won? Why do you speak ill of another's luck?'

'Whoever it is has two eyes, one nose, and one mouth.'

There was, of course, no way to know that Ilma was the lucky one they were talking about. How surprised they would have been had they known. Yet not knowing was, no doubt, preferable for Myeongdo. Not knowing it was Ilma allowed him to imagine the situation as he pleased. He, of course, had no way of knowing that a few hours later he would come to know the result. Whether the future is near or far, not knowing what it holds can be both a necessary and a fortuitous thing.

'Forget about the lottery and get ready to leave for Harbin.'

This order from Danyeong was the result of the shadow of Ilma lurking in her heart, but she had no idea that he was also connected to the lottery business. Her thoughts of him had nothing to do with the lottery and she could not in her wildest dreams have known of his involvement. She had suddenly thought of Ilma out of the blue, and that thought had caused her to want to leave for Harbin as soon as possible.

'You want to leave for Harbin? I only arrived yesterday and you won't even let me have a day of rest but want to leave already?'

'What is there to keep us here in Shingyeong any longer? Nowhere is more fun than Harbin.'

'That's your opinion. Do you think I feel the same?'

'Well, the truth be told ...' Here Danyeong felt it was necessary to put news of Ilma into Myeongdo's ear. She thought it would be less awkward if he knew of Ilma's presence in advance than if they suddenly met. 'Ilma is now in Harbin.'

Myeongdo gave a start.

'He didn't get off at Shingyeong but went straight on to Harbin. As you know, he's there on that symphony orchestra business.'

'So you were rejected by Ilma and you called me, is that it? What does that make me?'

Myeongdo had been aware for some time that Danyeong was infatuated with Ilma, and his own relationship with him was an awkward one. Hearing this sudden news, his face took on a look of displeasure, but no matter what his relationship with Ilma might be, his feelings for Danyeong trumped everything.

'What do you mean, what does that make you? Are you two enemies or something? A couple of gentlemen like you two will have no problem getting along.'

'You really know how to use people. While you drag one around like a scarecrow, your heart is with the other one.'

It wasn't necessarily a protestation. It was more like the pitiful appeal of a hen-pecked husband.

4. A NIGHT ON THE CONTINENT

In the meantime, it was decided that they would go to Harbin. Danyeong would not have stood for any other outcome. And no matter what his real intentions were, Myeongdo would not have been able to carry on without humouring Danyeong's whims. Having said that, it wasn't that Danyeong had won, nor had Myeongdo lost. It was merely the natural outcome of the type of relationship they had.

'You know how much I respect you.' Feeling satisfied, Danyeong was attempting to beguile Myeongdo. In fact, she secretly felt some gratitude toward him.

'You call this respect? Now I've seen it all.' Myeongdo pouted like a slighted child.

'Since there are so many things I want to do it might seem like I'm using you, but if you really didn't want any part of it would it be possible? Why would I single you out among all those men? Think about it and tell me if I'm not right.'

'Don't play innocent. You're just seeing which way the wind is blowing and then telling me what you think I want to hear.'

'Wait a minute, why wouldn't I respect you? And what do you have to be so upset about?'

'That's enough about respect. Quit toying with me. I'm a man, too. I can't pretend to be a stone Buddha for the rest of my life.'

This wasn't the first time that Myeongdo had revealed his heart's real desire. That feeling which had sprung up from the first time he had met Danyeong and that had captured his feelings ever since was the reason he could control his desires, but it was also the reason that he became enthralled any time he was near her.

However, every time Danyeong heard such talk, she felt nauseated and her skin crawled. She habitually got angry and expressed her irritation.

'What do you mean, saying I'm toying with you? When have I toyed with you? If you don't want to go to Harbin, don't go. Why do you keep griping?'

'Who ... who's griping?' This time Myeongdo wavered, feeling chagrined. 'Who said anything about not wanting to go to Harbin? Of course, we're going. Let's take the night train.'

Almost pleading, he desperately tried to calm Danyeong's irritation.

While walking down the street after leaving the teahouse, Myeongdo tried everything he could think of to smooth the pretty little complainer's ruffled feathers.

'Before autumn, I'm planning to start production of a new film. This time too, of course, you have to play the lead. There are a lot of women who call themselves actresses, but none are worth a damn. You're the brightest star among them all.'

'I don't buy that. Even if I agree to appear in your movie, you don't have to butter me up like that.'

'So, you'll appear in the film? Oh, thank you. I'll develop a good part for you, so you must agree to do it.'

'Well, if I like the part I'll take it, if not I won't. I don't want to keep appearing in second-rate movies. There's nothing in that for me.'

'Don't be so dismissive of the movie industry. Before long, we're going to make a big splash.'

Every day, toward evening, Myeongdo had a ritual he performed. This entailed going to a dance studio where he would practice his social dance skills. Due to his bulk, he was an awkward dancer. Every time he came to Manchuria, he would quietly search out a backstreet studio, but he still hadn't gotten the hang of it. He felt so strongly about learning to dance that whether he was there for one day or two, he would never miss the chance to practice.

On this day as well, this was the most important order of business. Leading the way, he went to his favourite dance studio where he spent half the day monopolizing the young instructor and whirling around the floor as if he were doing gymnastics.

As dusk began to fall, he remembered the train to Harbin and left for the station with Danyeong.

*

The Daeryukdang Pharmacy on Jidan Street was the best in the vicinity. It occupied a space in a large building facing the street, and in addition to the pharmacy, a large family occupied the living quarters. Byeoksu, as if he were in his own home, resided comfortably in the small room next to his uncle Han Unsan's room. He spent most of the time he was not at the newspaper in this room.

Owing to his frequent visits, Ilma was acquainted with Unsan. Feeling bad that he hadn't stopped in to say hello even after having been in Harbin for several days, he dropped by the pharmacy. Byeoksu had been anticipating this. His work that day had taken him outside his office, and this meant that he was not following any particular schedule and seemed to have a lot of leisure time.

Actually, it was Ilma who was really at leisure. He had quickly finished his duties in the span of a couple of days.

He had met the director of the railroad office one more time, had visited the director of the music academy, and had consulted with the manager of the Modern Hotel. In this way, he had concluded the negotiations for the symphony orchestra. At this point, it was just a matter of waiting for the day the orchestra would depart. They would leave for the performance tour that coming October. Until the day that he met them in Seoul, Ilma was a completely free man. His options were to return right away to Seoul, or stay awhile in Harbin. Having such leisure was a very pleasant experience. Needless to say, he spent his days feeling very much at ease. It was the first time he had ever enjoyed such a relaxing trip.

*

Unsan and Byeoksu shared the same stout appearance, only Unsan more so. Put another way, Unsan was a larger version of Byeoksu. Whether it was the gleam in his eyes, the fat yet firm body, or his tendency to go against the grain, he was the type that could get by even in this inhospitable environment. Perhaps it was the decades of hardship that had turned his hair half white, and even though his face was deeply lined with the years of struggle, he was known with envy as the successful proprietor of the Daeryukdang Pharmacy and was satisfied with his life. He had made his way following the fortunes of the continent and now was seen as a sturdy fellow who could not be ruffled or taken advantage of easily.

'Do you know how my uncle succeeded here?'

Byeoksu had once told Ilma about his uncle's past.

'Well, success usually means accumulating wealth. How has your uncle accumulated his wealth? Surely it's not ill-gotten?'

'Well, there's not much difference. He didn't actually take other people's property, but his methods weren't honest either.'

'Well, good or not, he must have made his money selling drugs, what else would he have done?'

'You're right, that's how he did it. But not the kind of drugs you see here on display. The kind you sell in secret. The kind that melts the spines of the Chinese and the Manchurians. He did a huge business in it.'

'Hmm.' Ilma understood what Byeoksu was saying. 'Isn't that dangerous?'

'Why wouldn't it be? It's a desperate business. Because of that, it's profitable. Just about every Korean in Manchuria who could be said to be successful has walked the same dangerous path. It's the only path that's really open them.'

'Are you saying it's honourable or dishonourable?'

'Honourable? Every Korean I see in Manchuria reminds me of the drug trade. Koreans and drugs – could there be anything more dishonourable? No matter what else they might do, this is what they're known for. He may be on the straight and narrow now, but Uncle's past is dark indeed.'

Byeoksu's tone was one of discontent toward his uncle. Even if Byeoksu were to starve to death and die with a heart full of resentment, he would never compromise his principle of always doing the right thing.

Knowing what he did about Han Unsan, Ilma could see that he was anything but an ordinary person.

'I was happy to hear about your great luck.' Han Unsan gave Ilma a careful once over. Apparently, he considered Ilma's luck to be extraordinary. 'Manchuria has always been a tough place; it doesn't seem possible that someone that's not from here could come into that kind of luck. It seems like Lady Luck has really taken a shine to you.'

'Lady Luck is blind, that's why she came to me. If she actually knew what she was doing would she give me money?'

'These days ten thousand won might not be that much money to some people, but to me that's a huge number. It's been over twenty years since I came to Manchuria – do you think I had even ten won in my pocket when I first arrived? Luckily, I was able to get to where I am today, but I built it all with my bare hands. There were times when I practically starved. I faced death several times. I think now it was all providence.'

'I can only imagine what that must have been like.'

'These days things have gotten so much better that luck walks in on its own hind legs, but when I think about the last half of my life I get goosebumps and break out in a sweat.'

'If someone is going to do the kind of business you did, Uncle, they would have to be prepared for that kind of life,' Byeoksu chimed in.

'Do you think there's an easy way to make a living in Manchuria? It's all a difficult risk.' This was part excuse and part protest.

'It's true that this is a fairly simple place. If one is willing to work hard one can make a living. People these days have it easy. No matter how hard they think they have it, it's nothing compared to what people used to endure.'

Turning again to Ilma, Uncle Unsan said, 'If I had ten thousand won, I would try some kind of business, but people these days don't think like that.'

'More than business, people need to be able to live first.' Byeoksu again answered for Ilma.

'Because of that kind of thinking, you're still living like you are at your age. These modern youths have no spine,' Unsan said, but this was met with a retort from Byeoksu.

'It's not that we don't have will, it's that we've chosen a different way. We don't have to do things the same way you did in the past.'

'Whether that's true or not, will is will. One always has to have an ideal; if the ideal is lofty, then the will is strong, even though you might ask if I had such a thing. Such ideas don't occur to youth these days.'

Listening to Unsan, who had made his living selling drugs, talk about ideals was somewhat awkward for Ilma; however, unexpectedly hearing this word gave him a feeling he hadn't had in a long time.

Modern man has vague ideals – such a statement didn't seem to be merely dogmatism or nonsense. If, for instance, Ilma were to ask himself what his ideals were and how firm his conviction in them was, he didn't think he could give a ready answer. Staring out of the window, he thought of how the sudden windfall of ten thousand won had caused him to reflect bitterly on his lack of ideals in the past. His gaze losing its focus, Ilma asked himself what sort of ideals the people busily coming and going on that street might have.

'What sort of ideals should a modern person have?'

'How should I know? These modern youths should know that better than anyone.'

While only half listening to their conversation, Ilma continued to gaze out of the window. A shadow that had been wavering about the front door appeared once again and scrutinized the inside of the store.

Perhaps because Ilma's and the shadow's gazes inadvertently met, the guest entered the pharmacy. Only after pushing the glass door inward and entering did the attention of those inside turn to the visitor.

That morning's customer was a young, foreign girl. She looked to be around seventeen or eighteen. She was relatively small with a white complexion.

As all eyes suddenly turned to her, she seemed quite self-conscious.

After bashfully examining the faces in the store, she went to the counter staffed by an employee. Carefully watching her from behind, Ilma had the feeling that he had seen her before.

The girl spoke in a low voice at the counter, after which the employee approached Unsan as if reluctant to deal with the situation alone and whispered something in his ear. Unsan gave his consent with an expressionless face. After bidding the girl to wait, the employee went into the interior of the store.

'I think I've seen her somewhere before,' Byeoksu quipped

to Ilma in a low voice. 'Now I remember. She's a dancer. She dances in the Sunggari Cabaret. She looks completely different in the daylight.'

'She's awfully young to be a dancer.'

'It's too bad. You can't tell at night, but she really doesn't look well. She's obviously addicted. It's a shame for someone so young.' While muttering this lament, Byeoksu put his mouth to Ilma's ear. 'Do you know what she's here to buy?'

'She's here for medicine, what else would it be?'

'That's right, medicine. She's here for her medicine.'

Ilma realized he hadn't gotten the drift of what Byeoksu was saying. 'Are you talking about "that"?' He finally understood.

'Look at her. She's really addicted.'

'Such a young girl. Now I've seen everything.'

'Haven't I been telling you? When people see Koreans in Manchuria this is the first thing they think of. They think that all Koreans are doing this on the sly. It's an obvious assumption here because this is a pharmacy, but in other places as well – that's probably what people think when they see us in the streets. If a Korean owns a pharmacy, people are always slipping in to buy drugs.'

'What happens if ...?'

'Of course, it's illegal. Even after putting up a sign that says "pharmacy" and filling the store with all kinds of ordinary merchandise ... truth be told, people still do a lot of this kind of business. It's a dangerous thing to do.

'Such a young girl mixed up with that stuff. She must be slowly killing herself.'

'Manchuria is a big complicated abyss. It's a vast place, and there's no way to know exactly what lurks beneath the surface here.'

'A complicated abyss. Doesn't that make it more interesting?'

It wasn't the time or place to discuss such a heavy topic, so with this flippant comment, Ilma once again turned his inquisitive gaze to the young girl.

The employee, who had disappeared into the back of the store, reappeared with something wrapped in blue paper and put it down in front of the girl.

The girl paid, and while the bill was being settled, Unsan looked at Ilma as if searching for something to say that would justify the unsavoury transaction that had just been witnessed. Perceiving Unsan's intention, Ilma turned away and, with Byeoksu, rose as if to leave.

As Ilma hesitantly stood, the young girl crossed in front of him. He got a good look at her as she brushed quickly past him, head bowed, holding the packet of drugs. Her face, which at first had appeared white, had, upon closer inspection, a yellowish tinge. Her skin was lax and lacklustre, like a lump of wax. Her earlobes, the nape of her neck, and her hands were all yellow. Her thin body, which trembled slightly, gave no more of an impression than a fragile leaf as it brushed past – it was obvious that she didn't have much time left.

Ilma followed Byeoksu out of the store where he saw the young girl, staggering slightly, meet a friend waiting on the other side of the street. As she turned to greet the girl they could see it was none other than Nadia.

'What's going on? Nadia, is that you?'

Ilma had approached Nadia, and his unexpected exclamation caused her eyes to open in surprise and her face to take on a flustered look.

'I'm surprised to see you here. I'm out today with Emilia.'

Upon hearing the name Emilia, Ilma looked again at the girl, who, at that point took first notice of him.

'I just saw Emilia a moment ago.' In response to Emilia's look of suspicion, Ilma said, 'In the pharmacy.'

'Oh, is that so?' At this, Nadia looked even more flustered. 'Emilia's a close friend, but she's not well and I'm worried about her health.' She spoke in high-pitched voice while starting to walk.

'Actually, I have some worries as well.'

Byeoksu, who had been walking with them, begged off due to work at the newspaper, and Ilma continued on with Nadia.

Feeling more comfortable with just Ilma, Nadia briefly introduced Emilia, who seemed more relaxed than she had before. She seemed happy to have a new acquaintance. Seeing Ilma and Nadia walking comfortably together, Emilia moved off to one side.

'We're on our way to Emilia's apartment, would you come with us?'

'If it's alright with you I'd be happy to accompany you. I've nothing else to do with myself.'

'Good. I hate the stares we get when just the two of us are out walking.'

Of course, she was referring to Emilia's unwell appearance. Her sickly countenance wasn't so obvious at night under the street lamps, but walking down the street in broad daylight and full view of the passing crowds was a miserable experience indeed, especially because of the contrast with Nadia's healthy complexion.

'Both Emilia and I are orphans. But at least I have my aunt's house; Emilia lives alone in an apartment. She doesn't know what happened to her parents. She came here when she was small and practically raised herself.'

In such sad circumstances, there was no reason not to be honest. Ilma was a great comfort to Nadia, who was like someone adrift in the middle of the sea waiting to be thrown a lifeline.

'She begged the cabaret owner to let her work for a few hours at night to earn money and the rest of the time she spends lying in her apartment. She doesn't have any friends. I do what I can, but there are many times when I can't take care of her. With so many other troubles already, why she had to get into that stuff I don't know. She is so addicted that she can't go an hour without it. It's a cursed life. It's so pitiful I can hardly bear it sometimes.'

'That is a shame. This is the first time I've ever seen this kind of thing. Suddenly Manchuria frightens me. It has so many different faces.'

'It is a frightening place. It's a pit of unhappiness and evil. And here in Harbin, there are too many unsavoury places to count.'

'I don't know whether it's a good thing or not, but my impression of Manchuria is the opposite of what it was yesterday. I guess I'm saying that it's not all fun, and that's depressing.'

In the middle of this utterance, Ilma suddenly stopped in his tracks. Nadia had turned to the side and caught the suddenly collapsing Emilia. While Ilma and Nadia had been chattering away, Emilia had been trembling, and she had finally collapsed.

Ilma hurriedly caught a passing cab and helped Emilia into the seat. Nadia gave the name of the apartment to the driver, and the car sped off.

*

Emilia's room was in a corner of the second floor of a small, back-alley apartment building. Ilma and Nadia practically had to lift her onto the bed, after which they hurriedly opened the packet of drugs she had bought. This was the only form of treatment they could give her: getting the drugs into her system as quickly as possible to see if they had any effect. Her need for the drugs was what had caused her collapse. That thirst could not be slaked with a sip of water but only with the injection of a few grams of the drug.

The response was rapid. A few minutes after finding her syringe in a drawer and injecting the right amount of the drug into her, the colour returned to her face and her eyes opened. Her recovery was so complete that it was hard to believe she had collapsed earlier. She gazed for a moment at Ilma, then closed her eyes and buried herself under her blanket as if in embarrassment. Perhaps it was because Nadia had gone through this several times before, but her skill in attending to all aspects of the process was obvious. Whether it was measuring the drug, using the syringe, or cleaning everything up afterward, it was clear that she wasn't figuring it out as she went, but that she was long since accustomed to the routine. And it wasn't just her skill; her concern was like that of a mother or an older sister. Her kind-hearted care for the girl exceeded that of simple friendship. Without Nadia, there was no telling how much lonelier and more forlorn Emilia would have been.

Ilma found himself moved by Nadia's tenderness, and once things settled down he had the chance to inspect the room. In the single room there was a wardrobe and household utensils piled up here and there. There were several trunks under and beside the bed, which seemed to speak of an unstable, wandering life. A tea set was spread out on the table, and there were numerous cigarette butts scattered everywhere. All of these things and the squalor bespoke the lonely life the young girl had been enduring.

The building outside the window blocked out the sky save for one small precious slice – like a wedge of rainbow – which barely managed to fall into the otherwise dark room. On the wall opposite the window, there hung a solitary picture. It was the picture of a still young woman. The gentle smile coming from that one picture seemed to soften and brighten the gloomy atmosphere of the room.

'That's Emilia's mother,' Nadia explained, staring absent-mindedly at the picture. 'It's the only picture she has managed to keep, and it is her constant companion. Because her mother is always there looking down at her, when she is exhausted she comes back to this poor excuse for an apartment as if it were her real home.'

When it came to mothers, Ilma knew that Nadia also was without her mother. Having turned away when speaking in a low voice of Emilia's mother as if she were speaking of her own, Nadia suddenly realized that Ilma had not responded and turned back to him, trying to affect a smile.

'Well now, if you haven't seen and heard everything.' And with that, she stopped arranging things in the apartment.

'What do you mean, seen and heard everything? I don't think it's bad that I unexpectedly came to this room and have seen all this. In a way, it worked out well in that through you I got to meet Emilia. People feel and become aware of more in times of misfortune than in times of happiness.'

'Let's go. She looks to be asleep. We'll back come again when she's awake.'

Seeming to be reassured by the sleeping form of Emilia, Nadia tucked the bedclothes around her. Ilma rose and, giving Emilia's sleeping face a parting look, opened the door.

'Let's go to the hotel.'

While walking side by side down the stairs, a new, meaningful glance passed between the two.

The unexpected incident with Emilia had brought them closer. After witnessing Emilia's misfortune, their hearts had reached a new level of communication. The result of this misfortune was the creation of love.

Their actions were agreed upon without the need of words, and so their movements were in harmony without any verbal communication. Walking down the street, eating, breathing – all these things were completely coordinated.

The two spent the entire day together until Nadia had to go to work. After lunch in the hotel, they went into the hotel theatre to catch a matinee. The title, *The Back Streets of Paris*, had attracted Ilma's attention, and Nadia had agreed.

The small theatre was full, and the movie had been playing for some time. Feeling their way through the dark, they found seats in the very back. After their eyes became accustomed to the dark, they could make out the other people. They were mostly foreigners and seemed to be composed of couples. In the midst of all those couples, Ilma and Nadia had now also become a couple. There was no way to know whether the foreigners were married couples or dating, and in the same way, there was no way for the other couples to know the nature of Ilma's and Nadia's relationship. Married or dating – actually, Ilma wondered as well what kind of relationship they had and what kind Nadia wanted.

The chaotic backstreets of Paris on the screen gave Ilma another taste of foreign sentiment. The light-coloured roofs, the apartments, the bars, the thoroughfares, the music, and dancing that were seen in the movie – the scale of that life, clean and appropriately gay, could also been seen in Harbin. For that reason, Ilma felt even closer to it and was drawn even deeper into the film.

A poor young French girl developed feelings for a young foreigner. The girl worked in a laundry and, while delivering clothes to a boarding house, the two began to care deeply for each other. The young man was Arabian, and he had come to Paris to learn to paint; he was an awkward *e'tranger** who was still struggling with the language.

In the beginning, due to the language barrier, they mostly communicated with facial expressions. If the girl would smile, the boy would smile too. In addition to studying painting, the youth was also working very hard on his French. When he was able to express himself to a certain degree, he said to the girl, 'Are you really interested in me?'

The girl smiled at his stammered query and nodded her head. 'Of course.'

'But we can't communicate very well.'

'It's enough to see with my eyes and feel with my heart. Is language so necessary?'

'What do you think about the fact that our countries and our races are different?'

* The original expression used was *aetrangje* (에트랑제).

'Our countries may be different, but we see with the same eyes. Does it matter that they are of different colours?'

'Even so, I care for you more than you care for me.'

'Wait and see who loves whom more.'

The girl fell into the boy's arms and openly confessed her love. The young man went to the girl's house, and they strolled together through the streets. They went for tea and to dances together, and the boy painted her portrait on his canvas. Knowing the girl's home was a poor one, he tried to give her money, but she firmly refused it.

Unfortunately, around the time that the two agreed to be engaged, the young man got news that his father was not well, and he had to rush back to his country. He promised to return after settling the inheritance of his father's estate and putting the affairs of his household in order, but a year passed and he had not returned. Did he have a fiancée in his home country, or had something happened to him? Even his letters had stopped coming. But the girl continued to wait for him. She watched the eastern sky, waiting for the one she loved to return.

In one way, it was like a beautiful fairy tale. While appearing unrealistic, each scene was coloured with just enough reality to make it seem natural. What appealed even more to Ilma was the smooth, spontaneous way in which the love between the two developed. The fact that the object of the Parisian girl's love was not a Parisian, but an Arabian youth also heightened Ilma's interest.

'Isn't it enough to see with these eyes and feel with this heart?'

The way the girl spoke of her unconditional love sounded wonderful. A love that transcends language and blood – he thought it a rare thing.

The film ended without the return of the Arabian youth. The lights came up as the forlorn face of the girl was etched into all the hearts in the audience.

Nadia seemed to have been affected in the same way as Ilma by the movie. As the tension subsided, Nadia said in a melancholy voice, 'Isn't she pitiable?'

'The story ended too soon. If it would have gone on a little longer ...'

'I wish the young man would have come back.'

'Well, they fell in love with each other, so the writer seems to have gotten his message across.'

As if not satisfied with this Nadia said, 'The young man seems heartless. No matter what happened in his country, he should've come back. How can he just forget the girl who is waiting for him?'

Ilma, looking back, said, 'Asians are generally cold-hearted like that. They don't have a strong sense of responsibility.'

'Well, not everyone's the same. You can't say that all Asians are like that. The youth should have brought his wealth back to Paris or sent for the girl. The story doesn't make sense if they are not happy together. To not do so seems pointless.'

Thinking that Nadia's opinion was typical of a foreigner, Ilma said, 'After all, it's only a movie. And movies are not reality.'

'Well, reality should be different from what we see in the movies. It's a good thing this movie's not reality.'

Ilma was happy to hear this from Nadia. Her negative reaction to the movie was an expression of her hope for reality.

As the next movie started, the two left the theatre and continued their conversation. The movie had unexpectedly provided them with a topic related to affairs of the heart. And the incident with Emilia had, in a short span of time, created a feeling of solidarity between them; their conversation returned to the topic presented by the movie.

'How beautiful it is to think of a world without borders. Especially in this cold-hearted world.'

'Yes, I agree.'

'Is there anything other than love that can erase borders?

The Arabian youth is in no way inferior to the Parisian girl and she is in no way better than him. They each see in each other only a human being. Can there be a more beautiful world than that?'

'That's the way I see it too; all people are the same. Europeans, Asians – there are only individual differences. On the whole, none are better or worse than another.'

'If people could only get rid of their prejudices and be more open-minded, how beautiful the world could be.'

Ilma burbled on about this fantastic idea, the simplicity of his feelings almost childlike.

Nadia was experiencing the same feelings as Ilma and even their steps were in synch as they walked. Ilma was feeling a sense of closeness to Nadia similar to that which the Arabian youth felt for the Parisian girl.

*

As night came to the street, Ilma was at the Moscow Cabaret. He was not only the first customer that night but also the best. From the hotel to the theatre, and then until Nadia had to go home to prepare for work that evening, the two were together, and even after that, Ilma headed for the cabaret early.

Byeoksu stuck to him like a shadow. After coming in from the office, he quickly hurried out of the house on Ilma's heels.

'Where in the world have you been all day?'

Byeoksu pestered Ilma about what he had done for the half day they had been apart.

'We went to the hotel, then to the theatre, and to a tea house – a typical course, nothing unusual about it.'

'Well, the course of your day may have been typical, but that of your heart certainly isn't. It must have had a few twists and turns.'

'Well, I must admit that there was something different about my feelings today.'

'You're smitten with her.'

Ilma spoke as if to himself, his tone changing and his heart fluttering: 'It seems that motives in love are connected with fate. In some cases, no matter how long you work at it, some loves are not meant to be while in other cases love happens quickly. There seems to something that decides it in an instant for both sides. That's what I think happened with us. It's not common that people's hearts are changed so quickly.'

'Do you think this is already love or something like it? Love isn't decided so easily.'

'That's the thinking of someone who doesn't understand European customs – the idea of love at first sight. Without that instantaneous feeling of certainty, you can't call it true love. I saw a movie called *The Back Streets of Paris* about an Arabian youth that falls in love with a Parisian girl. I haven't been moved like that in a long time.'

'Are you saying what you felt in the movie is related to what you are going through now?'

'There's probably a subtle connection. Perhaps I or Nadia are seeing it as we want to see it – maybe that's why I haven't felt this good about anything in a long time.'

'Then be sure you catch her, and don't let her slip away. And you have to be serious; a woman like her is rare. I'm sure about this. Having Nadia will add happiness to the luck that you got with the lottery ticket. Time will show you I'm right.'

Warming to his task, Byeoksu began to wax eloquent. 'There are two types of women in Manchuria. Even if both can be called flowers of the continent, they are very different in quality. You saw the sunflowers covering the plain on the train ride here, didn't you? There is the sunflower, and then there is the poppy that grows in the shadows. These are the two types of women. The sunflower stretches itself towards the sun, while the poppy plant flounders in the shadows, and instead of stretching up, it rots. Take Emilia, who we saw this morning at the drug store; she's the poppy plant. It's a shame, but there's nothing to be done. And Nadia – she's a sunflower.

She is a hundred and eighty degrees the opposite of Emilia. As long as she faces the sun, there's no limit to how far she can stretch. You must become her sun.'

'I went to Emilia's apartment today. It was a depressing experience.'

'Just depressing? Do you know how many women like Emilia there are here? It's all the fault of the continent. The reason I sometimes get sick of this place is because I see so many poppies. I hope you only see the sunflowers. Become Nadia's sun.'

In the midst of this banter, Nadia suddenly appeared.

She looked to have just come from her home where she had changed clothes. Her face shone differently than it had in the daytime. Byeoksu's sunflower analogy kept coming to Ilma's mind, and he had already started to think of Nadia as a sunflower.

In no time the hall had filled up with guests, and the music had started to play. It wasn't such a large hall, but still, when it was filled with several dozen people, the atmosphere was lively. It was difficult to tell where Ilma's party had wedged itself into that tumult. Half the patrons were foreigners, and the other half were locals. While the foreigners all had different backgrounds and their appearances ranged from dark red faces to pale white, the locals were a diverse bunch as well. Being smack in the middle of the crowd, Ilma could tell that they weren't all Manchurian. Being caught up in the midst of a crowd of people of different nationalities did not necessarily result in a feeling of closeness among the different groups; there was a vague sense of awkwardness and, here and there, an uncomfortable look.

Following the music, one by one the different groups began to rise from their seats. However, while they were all sucked into the same swirling dance, they did not form one mass but circled in their own orbits, like oil and water, unable to mix.

The music and dancing were mixed with drinking. People

generally began to dance after reaching a certain stage of inebriation, but even in the midst of the evening's excitement brought on by the combination of music, dancing, and booze, Ilma could feel a sense of disharmony created by the disparate elements that had gathered there.

And the first thought that arose out of that feeling of disharmony was:

Nadia and me. Are Nadia and I really a match?

The concern that they would look awkward together welled up in his mind. While watching the other people undulating on the dance floor, this worry quietly filled his heart.

'Since you've spent half the day with her, why don't you let me at least have one dance?'

Byeoksu quickly grabbed Nadia's hand and rose from his seat. Nadia, unable to refuse, gave Ilma a smile and started to dance. All Ilma could do was remain in his seat until a dancer he was not familiar with passed by, at which he rose and followed her. She gladly assented and as they held each other and gave themselves over to the dance, she was furtively appraising Ilma.

'What's your name?' he asked.

'Anna.' After promptly answering him she smiled and said, 'You and Nadia, right?'

The question was unexpected.

'How did you know?'

'Because you never dance with anyone else.'

'And?'

'I saw you walking together in the street today. You looked happy.'

Feeling a sense of pleasure at hearing such unexpected things from this unexpected woman, Ilma said, 'So do you think we look good together? We don't look awkward?'

'You look very good together. The ideal couple.'

At that moment Byeoksu and Nadia danced past them,

prompting Anna to say, 'You look much better together than they do.'

'Really?' While there was a touch of doubt in his voice, he was also quite pleased.

'It's not enough to just look good together; your feelings must be in harmony as well.'

'Perhaps.'

While not being totally convinced by what Anna had said, Ilma started looking around for Nadia.

Seeing Ilma searching for Nadia, Anna whispered, 'You made a good choice.'

'...'

'I mean Nadia.'

'What do you mean, choice?' The insinuation in Anna's words caused Ilma to prick up his ears.

'You chose well picking Nadia.'

'What do you mean?'

'I mean you selected well.'

'What if I hadn't?'

'I say that because there are so many people who don't.'

'Is she a fish that I selected?'

Anna smiled at Ilma's joke. 'First, your choice is a good one because she's pretty.'

'And?'

'Second, she's kind.'

'Third ...'

'You two are a good match.'

'Anything else?'

'In Nadia's situation, she needs someone like you.'

'Her situation?'

'She's living with her aunt, but it seems that she's not comfortable there because she's said she wants to move out.'

'I've also heard something about the aunt, but I didn't realize it was that urgent.'

'She comes from a very good family, and it seems now they're extremely picky. Her uncle was a Major General under the Czarist government. He was her mother's older brother. Since it's her mother's house that has survived, it's much more difficult for her than if it would have been her father's. She's been talking a lot about how it's even more uncomfortable being around her uncle than her aunt – then you came along.'

'Like the ferry that appears just when it's needed.'

'It's a very special ferry. Who wouldn't want to take the ferry if the ferry boat was you?'

'Me ...?'

'Nadia looks happy. It's good this has happened to her.'

'Nobody likes to have their leg pulled.'

'Who's pulling any legs? I'm just telling the truth.'

Ilma didn't know if it was pleasure or embarrassment he felt at Anna's words, but his heart was filled with something.

'Don't dance only with Nadia; give me a dance too every once in a while.'

When the music ended, Anna removed her hand from Ilma's and went back to her seat.

As Ilma searched for Nadia with his eyes, the music started up again before she could return to her seat. It was the tango. Just when the soft music had brought the enjoyment to a peak, Nadia appeared in front of him. Without a word, they came together on the dance floor. The rhythm between them was immensely pleasurable, and it seemed like the music caressed every inch of their bodies.

'I heard some interesting things just now from Anna.'

Nadia responded right away to Ilma's remark. 'She talks a lot.'

'She spoke very highly of you.'

'We're very close. More so than the other girls.'

'She says we are a good match. And that she saw us in the street today. She went on about how pretty you are, and how kind, and about what a good choice we both made.'

While passing on exactly what Anna had said, Ilma was not his usual self. He was a bit tipsy on the music and all the praise.

'She really does talk a lot. What business is it of hers who chooses what? Seems like she's jealous.'

'There's nothing to get upset about. A good choice is a good choice; nobody can come between us now.'

Ilma suddenly went silent and gave a shudder. He had just then seen something over Nadia's shoulder that made him do so. Next to them a couple was spinning around, dancing awkwardly – and the woman was Danyeong. Ilma stared, trying to figure out who it was she was with.

The person spinning around in front of Danyeong was none other than Myeongdo. The sight of the pair gyrating like a couple of monkeys was laughable.

What are they doing here?

Meeting them in this place and time was a total surprise. Of course, far from being pleased at seeing them, Ilma was taken by a feeling of annoyance.

What a pain in the neck.

He danced off in another direction with Nadia, but the pair stubbornly continued to appear before them. This seemed to be the work of Danyeong. Lurching back and forth, smiling all the time, Danyeong continued to gaze at Ilma over Myeongdo's shoulder.

'Surprised?' her stare seemed to say.

'Not a bit,' Ilma's expression replied.

'If that's not a look of surprise, what is it?' was the response from Danyeong's eyes.

'Why are you jumping around like a shaman sorceress?'

'What business is it of yours?'

'Because you're irritating me.'

'What concern is that of mine?'

'You're an embarrassing sight. You and this chump are a good match.'

'Whether we are or not, what's it to you?'

'Then why do you keep following me? See? You're back again.'

'Do you think you can be rid of me that easily? I'm always going to be around to bother you.'

'Go ahead, do your worst.'

'You say that while trying to get away.'

While this conversation was conveyed through their glances, Danyeong continued to pursue Ilma around the dance floor. If Ilma turned right, she would turn left; if he went left, she would go right, continuously wavering in front of him, obsessed with remaining in his sight. Ilma tried not to let her enter his peripheral vision, but he was unable to keep the whole affair from getting on his nerves.

What can I do with her? I can't stomp on her.

As it happened, the music at that moment was quite monotonous. He wished the song would end, but it kept going. Ilma merely spun his body absent-mindedly in a way that resembled dancing.

The best way to ignore Danyeong was to look at Nadia, so he fixed his gaze on the back of her shoulder and hugged her even more affectionately.

He put his face in the nape of her neck and could smell the fragrance of her hair. While losing himself in that fragrance, he thought about nothing but seeing Nadia in front of him, feeling nothing but Nadia. Holding Nadia carefully like she was a bouquet of flowers, he moved away from the centre of the crowd and danced around its fringes.

This further incited Danyeong. Assuming a prim air, she pulled Myeongdo around like a cow.

It happened when Ilma had reached the band, eyes half closed, still lost in Nadia's perfume. A sudden collision almost sent them sprawling.

'What do you think you're doing?' Nadia demanded in an angry voice.

Danyeong had swung her and her partner's bodies into them. In the face of Nadia's anger, Danyeong assumed a sulky air and once again grabbed Myeongdo's hand.

'Why do you have to always be gadding about?'

But by the time Ilma shouted this, the other pair had started dancing again.

'So what's it to you if I do?'

Nadia responded to Danyeong's muttered remark with a disgusted look. 'Who are they?'

'She's an actress or something. And the guy is president of a film company. Even though they don't look like much, when they're in Joseon, they put on airs as if they're famous.'

'She's a poor excuse for an actress. The same goes for the president.'

It was a long, tedious dance.

When the music stopped, Ilma quickly returned to his seat as if the thought of more dancing was too much for him.

Danyeong and Myeongdo quickly sat in Byeoksu's seat.

When Ilma did not even look at them, Myeongdo, feet numb from dancing, said, 'My apologies.'

He was referring to the bumping incident.

'He's not a very good dancer and doesn't see the people in front of him,' Danyeong added flippantly.

'Is it such a big deal if people bump into each other when they're dancing? Isn't smiling when someone bumps into you the proper etiquette?'

'Where did you learn that?'

In response to Ilma's rebuke, Danyeong said, 'Oh, are you still angry?' Face flushing, she took the conversation in a completely different direction. 'Introduce us.'

She meant, of course, that he should introduce Nadia.

'You two seem to be very affectionate.' Her sarcastic tone was annoying.

'Why are you sticking your nose in my business again?' Ilma yelled.

'Just like the saying "a woman in every port", you seem to have one everywhere you go. I didn't know that was why you came to Manchuria so often. It looks like you two already have a special relationship. You're acting like quite the gentleman, but it's clear to see that you're quite the ladies' man. Of course, I don't count, but surely you haven't forgotten the name Nam Miryeo.'

'Seems you make it your job to worry about other people's business.'

'Of course, I worry. Why wouldn't I?'

Nadia's curiosity growing at Ilma's rising voice and the conversation she couldn't follow, she spoke in a tone of annoyance to Ilma in a language only he could understand. 'After her rudeness, why is she being so long-winded?'

'This two-bit actress is just acting like a fool.'

'What's she going on about?'

'They've come from Joseon for kicks and are making a fuss for no reason.'

At this point Byeoksu returned to find his seat taken. 'Who are our guests?'

Standing with a confused look on his face, Myeongdo introduced himself. 'I'm Kim Myeongdo of Bando Studios. This is Choi Danyeong, one of our actresses. We were somewhat bored in Seoul, so we made the long trip here for some fun. It's nice to meet some compatriots here in this foreign place. Are you enjoying yourself?'

So saying, he extended his hand. Seeming to find the word 'compatriot' disagreeable, not only did Byeoksu not take the proffered hand, but he retreated from the table as well. 'Idiot.'

The word 'compatriot' made him feel ill at ease; it carried no authenticity or even meaning and sounded like nothing more than slick nonsense. Byeoksu's displeasure at that word was not really the result of his irritation – it was just that it was a meaningless and unnecessary thing to say in that situation.

As the music started again and Byeoksu was moving away

from the table, Nadia stood up as if stifled by the atmosphere and led him to the dance floor, where they started to dance.

Ilma, left alone, could not suppress his anger. 'What do you mean by annoying people like this?'

'What are you talking about? Why are you worried about what I'm doing? I came here on my own two feet. Are you trying to tell me what I can and can't do?'

Myeongdo, seeming to feel embarrassed, offered an explanation. 'I didn't anticipate all this excitement. I was just sitting around in Seoul when I got a telegram to come to Shingyeong with no explanation, and then I was dragged here.'

'What's your intention in always following me around?'

'I told you I came here on my own two feet, and I go where I like. Intention? What intention would there be?'

There was no limit to Danyeong's coyness.

5. THE FLIGHT OF ACHILLES

Mid-morning at the Bukman*Hotel

*

It was a beehive-like four-story building facing the street. Myeongdo and Danyeong had the front and back rooms of the second floor.

As Danyeong was busy washing her face, Myeongdo came into her room without knocking.

'Who is it?'

'Me.'

Knowing full well who it was when she had asked, this was a game that Danyeong and Myeongdo played with each other.

'You just come in without permission?'

'Do I really need permission?'

'Of course, you do. This is a lady's room.'

'Someone pretending to be a lady, maybe.'

'What? This won't do. Out you go.' Rising from her vanity table, Danyeong turned on Myeongdo.

---

*   Here, Bukman has the meaning 'northern Manchuria'.

Myeongdo saw that she was in the same state as when she had risen, wearing her nightgown, her thin underwear discernible underneath. Her neck and bosom rose out of her bedclothes, and beneath, her white legs and feet were visible. Danyeong well knew that this vulnerable look was a dangerous poison to Myeongdo. No matter how familiarly she may act in front of him, she was not without a woman's sense of shame.

'I said leave.'

Coming near her, he could smell her perfume and temptation began to stir. Her calves, which appeared through the folds of her gown like flower vases, caught his eye and cast a spell over his senses.

'You remind me of an elementary school teacher when you're cross like this, treating people like little students.'

'You are a naughty student that never changes his ways. If you really were a student, you'd be at the bottom of the class.'

'Don't be so mean. Let's compromise. Look, I'll sit with my back turned.'

Myeongdo looked ridiculous as he turned a chair to face away from Danyeong's vanity table and sat down in it.

'Why are men so shameless?'

Having no other recourse, Danyeong went over to the bed as if struck with a sudden thought, pulled off the blanket and draped it over Myeongdo's head.

'Are you trying to suffocate me?'

'Just stay like that. If you don't like it, you can leave.'

'This is like being in hell.' Myeongdo's voice coming out of the blanket sounded like a mosquito.

Choosing to stay under the blanket rather than leave the room implied that Myeongdo would rather remain in darkness as long as he was next to Danyeong. Seeing a middle-aged man sitting calmly under a blanket was a pitiful sight.

This is disgusting. He's acting like an animal, she thought. 'You're contemptuous because you act so disgustingly.'

'What would I have to do to not be disgusting?'

'Act a little more dignified.'

'You mean act cold like Ilma?'

'Shall I let you in on a secret?' Becoming merry at the mention of Ilma's name, Danyeong's voice softened. 'Speaking honestly about women ...'

'Yes?'

'They don't like really persistent men.'

'...'

'A slightly cold, arrogant man is more appealing.'

'You're talking about Ilma, aren't you?'

'This isn't just about Ilma. This is how most women feel. Don't gripe, just listen. I'm going to give you the secret of how to win in love.'

'Hurry up, I'm suffocating in here. I can't breathe.'

'Wait! Stay like that for a minute.'

Myeongdo's apparent intention to throw off the blanket startled Danyeong into yelling in surprise. She was in the process of changing her underthings. She put a gown on over her chemise and quickly pulled on her stockings.

*

To outside observers, the couple using those rooms looked to be a very loving one, and in spite of the reality of the awkwardness between them, when they came out all dressed up, they seemed an affectionate pair, at least to the hotel staff. In fact, when they descended the stairs together, in spite of the fact that they used separate rooms and that inside their rooms their relationship was like that of a cat and a dog, they looked like a married couple. As they went up and down the staircase, they were the object of people's scrutiny, and no one who saw them suspected that they weren't husband and wife. This was actually what Myeongdo wanted, and even if he was the recipient of ill treatment at Danyeong's hands, as long as it was in private, he could descend the stairs with his chin up.

'At any rate, it was fun.'

As there was no one to see her do it, Danyeong glanced at Myeongdo, who was tittering giddily.

'Tormenting Ilma yesterday.'

'Yesterday you were meek as a lamb, and now you laugh about it? That's rather small of you.'

'I didn't know you were so brave. I thought you would be on your hands and knees in front of Ilma, but you were quite bold. That's the way to deal with a man, you can't be namby-pamby about it.'

As he was speaking, Myeongdo suddenly realized that he was not only talking about Ilma but about himself as well, and this brought a bitter smile to his lips. If Danyeong's attitude toward Ilma was bold, then how much more fearless was she when it came to him? This realization made the insult all the greater.

'Stop worrying about what other people do and try not to act so weak in front of Ilma. It makes me sick to see you being so worthless.'

'Between men such a thing isn't important. But I like your attitude. Of course, I like Ilma's attitude too.'

'That's enough.' Becoming irate, Danyeong went downstairs first.

The two were always the last to breakfast. There were few customers in the restaurant. The waiter began to set out breakfast dishes in front of them. They had no choice but to pretend to be a couple in front of him.

'When we bumped into them and they almost fell over, that woman Nadia yelled something, what was it again? Oh yes, she said "What do you think you're doing?" with a very annoyed look on her face. That was very satisfying.'

Myeongdo was muttering about the events of the past night as they ate; at his mention of Nadia, Danyeong's ears perked up, and she was compelled to add her own comment.

'How far do you think things have gone with Ilma and that Nadia? Are they really together?'

'Judging from what I saw last night, they are more than just together, they're a couple.'

At Myeongdo's instigation, Danyeong became even more agitated and heartsick. 'Damn it!'

'You can't judge that book by its cover. Ilma appears gentlemanly, but he's actually quite the rake.'

'What can I do? I can't scratch his eyes out.'

'If you did, it would just drive him to Nadia.'

'What does Nadia have that I don't? I'm better than her in every way ...'

'To me, you're ten times more beautiful than Nadia, but you have to seem that way to Ilma.'

Danyeong's anxiety was a welcome sight to Myeongdo. 'Damn it all.' But it was not Danyeong's game to fold after one hand. The deep sigh she let out was a sign of the firm resolve coiling inside of her. 'This is far from over. It's time to play for keeps.'

Losing her appetite to the wrath she felt in her heart, Danyeong left the table and in a fit of frustration said, 'Let's go to the Songhwa river.'

'Whaddya mean, go to the river? Do you think it's the middle of summer?'

'It will be refreshing, we can get some air.'

As she said this, she spied the poster on the wall promoting the horse races.

'Look at this, they're having races.'

'Very good.'

'Let's go and watch the horses.'

The two left the hotel for the races.

The autumn season's races had begun. In Seoul as well, Danyeong had gone to the races and bet on the horses several times and so was no stranger to the track.

They took Shinshi Street and stopped by a department store on the way.

The Chulim* Department Store, under foreign management, was the best in all of Harbin. All the employees were foreigners, but what really drew the interest of the customers were the blonde-haired, blue-eyed female staff waiting on people. There was more than just one language being used. One could hear Russian and English, and the mix of languages emanating from all about the place gave it the feel of an international department store. The goods on display on all floors gave of the subtle glimmer and pleasing vibe of Europe. This was not the result of anything that could happen in a day. This glow that suffused the place was the product of strong traditions, accumulated and passed down over a thousand years. It was like a small display case of Europe itself. Inside the throng of people, Danyeong could sense the European atmosphere and the special feel in the air. Here she was able to experience the real smell of civilization.

Her objective was to buy a pair of binoculars. She went to an upper floor to the luxury goods department, and as she was selecting a pair to her liking an attractive blonde employee approached.

'Are you going to the races?' she asked in a girlish voice.

'Listen, we are really going to need these at the track,' Danyeong explained to Myeongdo.

'To see the horses' legs with. That way you can see which horse is ahead and by how much,' Myeongdo added.

'Yes, to look at the horses, and the scenery, and the people ...' Danyeong said as she put the binoculars to her eyes and adjusted the focus. 'Look at that.'

Through the window, the far-off image of people coming and going filled the lens.

'That one there.'

* The name means 'autumn forest'.

As the focus was fixed on the distance, Myeongdo had to fiddle back forth with the adjustment.

'You're going to miss a world-class beauty.'

Finally, as he found the right focus, 'That's it. There, do you see her?'

'If I can find beautiful women with these things, I guess I really do need them.'

The female employee who had been watching them smiled and asked, 'Do you like them?'

After buying the binoculars and leaving the department store, Danyeong was as happy as a child, as if she had just discovered something wondrous.

'Aren't your eyes enough? Do you need these things to spy on life?'

'One can see it twice as well.'

'It feels like cheating on nature.'

'This way I can invent life all over again.'

They got into a car and asked to go to the racetrack.

They raced along Magagu Street. This was a residential district lined with old, stately elm trees that gave it the feel of another world as they cast their shadows on the road. As they left this area, they came onto a broad expanse of plain. Coming around the airfield, Danyeong put the binoculars to her eyes. She could see the distant racetrack approaching, and the figures of people shimmered in the lenses.

The racetrack was just a spot on the wide plain. But, on closer inspection, it was itself a wide plain.

Inside it was bustling with people, and the only place not crowded was the grounds of the track. What was it that these thousands of people – men and women, young and old – had gathered here for? There's no place people won't go if there is money to be made.

Was it that there wasn't enough drama in ordinary city life? Did people come all the way out to this plain to experience blood-boiling, heart-stopping drama? Their fates were left to the legs of the horses, which would decide whether it would be boom or bust that day. Fortune brought laughter and misfortune tears. The excitement and discouragement, the joy and disappointment, these emotional ups and downs that constituted a day at the track are what brought people out to stand around that oval and watch the horses run.

Three or four of the day's races had already taken place.

As Danyeong and Myeongdo entered the track, the fourth race was just finishing. People were scattered here and there among the seats in various states of joy or disappointment, and many were going down to the windows to place a wager on the next race. Myeongdo and Danyeong were in the midst of that pulsing wave of people. Like the streets of Harbin, the racetrack was also a display case of various nationalities and races. In the middle of all those unfamiliar faces and all that strangeness, they were both taken with an excitement that sucked them into the clamorous mix.

The seven or eight horses that were to run in the next race had been brought out into the yard. The jockeys, holding their whips, had led them lovingly out to where they were displayed in order to help the spectators make a decision on how to bet. The contest of these horses' abilities would decide the fate of the spectators who bet on them. The spectators inspected the horses carefully in order to appraise their chances.

A jockey in a red outfit with a red cap led out a horse named Sun. His lanky and high-spirited form first caught Danyeong's eye and then her full attention.

'I want to bet on that horse.'

Her sudden decision caused Myeongdo to look carefully at the horse.

'It might look good, but it won't run. Horses are like people, strength is more important than size; just being big isn't enough.'

His opposition only strengthened her resolve.

'What are you talking about? Appearance is the first

consideration. Without that, how are you going to judge what it has inside? The outside must be good for the inside to be worth anything. Can the horse be strong if it looks worthless? That's the one. Just wait and see if Sun doesn't win.'

Surprisingly, Myeongdo stuck to his guns. Believing himself to be right, he decided that he liked either Achilles or Mentalcha for the next race.

'I've had several years of aggravation because I was taken in by the appearance of horses at the track. There are other things to look at besides physical appearance. Let's see, there's a look of shrewdness and reliability. These are the most important things with both people and horses. An imposing look is no use at all. For instance, I think Achilles or Mentalcha are both superior to Sun, but let's wait and see. It won't take long to find out.'

'It's like you to say something like that. In what way is Achilles better than Sun? Is that what you call your horse sense?'

'We'll know in a bit. Why are you being so ornery?'

'It's obvious Sun is the horse. Hurry up and place my bet on him.'

Being right was of no use. Not being able to stand up to Danyeong's obstinacy, Myeongdo had no choice but to follow her down and place a bet on Sun. Buying two five-won race tickets, they returned to their seats and, facing the oval track, waited for the bell to start the race.

The fifth race started. The signal sounded, and the horses were off. Thousands of eyes strained to follow the flight of the horses like drawn bowstrings. All eyes followed the steeds as they made several laps around the oval track. As the laps mounted, the wave of tension uniting the spectators was released, and each person was propelled toward a climax of either elation or disappointment. Sun was a game horse and, while at first it looked like he was falling behind Achilles, with a couple of laps left he pulled into the lead.

A surge of effort by the horses was met with a clamour from the stands and the roar of voices. Many people, it seemed, had bet on Sun. Danyeong, being one of them, came half out of her seat, waving her arms and screaming as he passed.

'Look at that. you said Sun wouldn't win. I know what I'm talking about.'

In her delight, she could not help but rib Myeongdo. As he had bet on the same horse, he was not outwardly displeased, but secretly he was disappointed.

'There's still one lap left.'

So saying, he looked to Achilles, who seemed to be struggling three or four horses back. Having declared his preference for Achilles, a part of him wanted that horse to win. He was in a silent competition with Danyeong. Of course, Achilles was doing his best, and the green-clad jockey with his whip was lying flat along his neck, urging him on, yet a large gap had opened between him and Sun.

'Even if it were two laps left, how could anyone catch him? There's no way he can lose.'

'It will be decided in the last minute.'

'The race is already decided, what last minute? Are you thinking that Achilles can still win? Look how far behind he is.'

'Let's start celebrating.'

'Look at him run!'

'Half a lap.'

'He's soaring.'

'A quarter lap.'

'He's flying.'

'A little more.'

'He's flying ... fly, fly ... that's it!'

'Hurray for Sun!'

People came out of their seats and the sound of their cheering rolled across the racetrack. Sun had come in first.

'Hurray for Sun!'

'Hurrah!'

Hats flew into the air, handkerchiefs were waved, and the seats shook with the excitement of the crowd. The spectators all rushed to come down from their seats.

Caught in the rush, Danyeong's beret was twisted on her head, and her handbag was pulled by the crush of bodies. Myeongdo was just able to catch her arm and lead her toward the infield.

'What do you think? That was great.'

'Thanks to you I bought a winning ticket.'

'I told you I know what I'm talking about. From now on, just buy the tickets I tell you to. We can't lose.'

'Just because you were right once, do you think you're going to win every time? I have my own way to judge. Sun won't always win, and Achilles won't always lose.'

'You insist on that even after he lost?'

People were crowding in front of the window to collect their winnings.

The payout for Sun was a little over twenty won, and since Danyeong and Myeongdo had bought a ticket each, they pocketed around forty won. As Sun had been a popular bet, the payout wasn't so high. However, as this was Danyeong's first time to bet on a horse and her first winnings, she was overjoyed.

'If I had known, I would have bought a dozen tickets.'

Her greed had been unleashed.

'That would be two hundred won.'

'And I knew he would win ...'

'You're getting greedy.'

'I'm going to bet on Sun again. I like him.'

'It's not a good idea to go with the same horse every time.'

'Just look at the results.'

Sun would rest one race and appear again in the seventh race.

Danyeong wheedled Myeongdo into betting all their winnings on Sun. What's more, they each bought a lottery ticket. Since it was Sun running in the race, Myeongdo could not disagree with Danyeong and, after meekly following her instructions, he returned to his seat.

The seventh race started amid the heightening anticipation. The excitement intensified as the course conditions were broadcast over the loudspeaker.

This time as well, attention was focused on Sun. The horse's every action caused the spectators' nerves to tingle. The circular seats were a confusion of screams and sighs. Would the outcome be fortune? Wealth? Black or white? Fate was left to the horses that had been wagered on, and everyone stared at the bustling oval track.

As with the earlier race, after a few laps Sun started to pull ahead of the pack. Every time he passed another horse, Danyeong would let out a scream and jump up and down in her seat. With two laps left, Sun was leading the other horses. Inside the roar of the crowd that sounded like a cyclone, Danyeong felt heat run through her body as if she were in a dream.

'This race is turning out just like the last one.' Half out of her seat, the binoculars never left her eyes.

'So it seems. It's as if today's races are being run just for you.' In fact, Myeongdo was quite pleased.

'What do you think of my technique? I'm in complete control here.'

'I didn't know things would go this well. We did the right thing coming to the races today.'

'Figure out how much we will get if we win this race. At twenty won each, that's one hundred and sixty won, at thirty won each, that's two hundred and forty won ...'

'At fifty won apiece, that's four hundred won – at one hundred won each, that's eight hundred won.'

'That's eight hundred won that I earned.'

'In any case, I'll buy you whatever you want. A muffler or jewellery ...'

'A muffler or jewellery ...' Repeating Myeongdo's words like a parrot, Danyeong suddenly put the binoculars to her eyes. 'Wait, over there.'

'Why? What's wrong? Sun is winning.'

'Isn't that Ilma?'

The binoculars clearly showed Ilma and his companions in their seats some distance off.

'He's with Nadia and – who's that other woman?'

The other woman with Ilma and Nadia was Emilia. Ilma was also holding a pair of binoculars and enthusiastically watching the race.

'Ilma is here,' Myeongdo said in a voice of surprise, while Danyeong had already forgotten the race and would not move the binoculars from the group. 'He's first again. Sun is first again ...'

Danyeong paid no attention to Myeongdo's cries, seeing nothing but Ilma. It appeared that they hadn't bet on Sun; their faces clearly showed their disappointment.

*

Emilia had finally felt well enough to get up, and her condition had improved to the extent that Ilma and Nadia had brought her along for a combined picnic and a trip to the racetrack. Ilma was new to the races, but both Nadia and Emilia were familiar with betting on the horses. However, Ilma had his own ideas, and when it came time to bet he stuck stubbornly to his opinion. After inspecting the horses, he would bet on the horse he liked no matter what advice Nadia might give to the contrary. He had continued to lose, and by the seventh race he had nothing to show for his efforts but a string of failures.

When Danyeong had discovered them in her binoculars after the seventh race, they were in a disappointed funk. The three of them, Ilma in the middle of the two women, all had the same expression on their faces.

'Look at that. Sun is going to win again.'

A flustered Nadia said to Ilma, 'I told you to bet on Sun.'

An irritated Emilia responded, 'So what if he wins? The races are only half over.'

Ilma outwardly was maintaining a calm composure, but on the inside, he was feeling impatient. His pockets were growing empty, and more than anything else, he was becoming dispirited.

'I'm betting on Sun in the next race; I don't care what anyone says,' Emilia declared in the annoyed voice of a child.

'Look. Look at that.'

'Sun came in first again.'

'Damn it.'

The screams of delight coming from the seats around them demoralized the three to the point that they didn't have the will to get up out of their seats.

Danyeong was able to see all this from a distance.

'That's just what you deserve.'

Due to her contrary nature, the sight of their disappointment brought her pleasure.

'That's what you get for trifling with me.'

Danyeong's and Myeongdo's winnings for that race were over two hundred won. Practically jumping with joy, Danyeong had the desire to wave her earnings in front of Ilma's face. She even wanted to smack him across the face with the money.

Myeongdo was barely able to restrain her from rushing over to Ilma and his party, and it was decided they would keep an eye on their movements from where they sat.

Danyeong, for fear of missing something, never took the binoculars from her eyes.

Ilma and his party sat out several races in the lounge and by the time the tenth race came around, the day had lengthened, and there were only three or four races left.

As the slanting sun shone down on the racetrack, the noise

had become even more cacophonous. Fate had been decided for most of the people in the seats. The winners had won, and the losers had lost, and for most, the day's fortunes had already been decided. Only those with some energy and courage left could still do battle with Lady Luck. Ilma was one of them.

When the tenth race was about to begin, Ilma summoned his remaining pluck and bought the last ticket at the betting window.

He bet on Achilles. As it turned out, Sun was also running in this race. It was the exact same field as in the fifth race. Sun had won the fifth race by a large margin. It was a simple matter for most people to choose between the two horses. As with the fifth race, the choice was Sun, and compared to the crowd gathering in front of that window, the only people standing before Achilles' window were Ilma and his party.

In addition to Ilma, Myeongdo too, it seems, had discovered Achilles and was impressed by his appearance. Even though he had lost money on that horse in several races, he didn't hesitate to bet on him one last time.

Myeongdo's decision to bet on Achilles this time was the result of Danyeong's insistence in placing her money on Sun again. Danyeong was completely taken with Sun, and Myeongdo couldn't deny that their wins and their two hundred won earnings had all been due to that horse.

After several failures, Ilma's decision to bet again on Achilles was not taken lying down by Nadia.

'You're betting on Achilles again?' Her tone was not one of disappointment but of opposition.

'This is the last time.' Ilma's tone this time was one of entreaty.

'You keep saying "this time, this time," and you keep losing.'

'This time will be different.'

'How do you know?'

'If fate always turned out the same, there would be no

problems in the world. But the fact that it doesn't is what makes life interesting.'

'Are you saying that fate is going to change this time?'

'He obviously thinks so. That's why he insists on betting again.' It was fairly easy to placate Nadia, but Emilia was being obstinate. 'Anyway, I won't be fooled this time.' Thus grumbling, she added, 'I'm betting on Sun. I don't like Achilles.'

'Don't complain later.'

'I don't care. I'm betting on Sun.'

There being no help for it, he placed a bet on Sun for Emilia and put everything he had left in his pockets on Achilles – he was able to buy five tickets. With his final one won, he bought a lottery ticket as well. He put everything he had, do or die, on that race. This was an exciting adventure, going head to head with fate. (Reporting the results of that adventure, the way the dominoes eventually fell, to the reader, is a source of no small delight to the author. What follows is a faithful rendering of the facts, but the author cannot but feel a sense of marvel at the unbelievable happiness that was to come. It is reassuring to know that such fortune actually exists in this world.)

For the first few laps, Sun led the pack. As many people had bet on Sun, a large number of them were on their feet facing the running horses, cheering him on. It was like a crowd cheering a sports competition. They were cheering for Sun, their champion.

Danyeong, having bet on Sun, was among those screaming their support for him; but, at the same time, she kept her binoculars trained on Ilma and his party. Seeing that he was sitting quietly, not cheering, she surmised that he hadn't bet on Sun, and a part of her took secret pleasure in this. However, this time, her pleasure was to be short-lived. Sun's supremacy was about to end.

With two laps left, Sun started to lag, and Achilles, who had been at the rear of the pack, started to surge. In a half lap, he passed horse after horse until he was in the lead.

'Yeah!' Ilma let out a yell in spite of himself and jumped to his feet. 'Go Achilles!'

The fact that no one else was cheering for Achilles meant that Ilma was the only one who had bet on him. The people in the racetrack suddenly became quiet as if they had been doused with cold water. No one had predicted this run by Achilles.

'Sun has fallen behind, and Achilles is going all out.' The voice reporting the progress of the race through the loud-speaker was more excited than usual.

The invigorated Achilles looked as if he would soar right into the heavens, and the green-clad jockey on his back looked as light as a bird's wings. The finish was now right before the leading horse's eyes.

'Yes! That's it! Just a little more. Ah! Hurrah! Achilles, you did it!'

Achilles had come in first. It seemed like a miracle. Ilma screamed till his voice went hoarse, and Nadia clung to his neck with tears in her eyes. They were the only peo-ple overcome with joy among the thousands venting their disappointment.

This was what they call a windfall. Ilma took all the win-nings for Achilles. It was the kind of luck that came from tak-ing a chance.

Each ticket paid seven hundred won, and, at five tickets, that made their winnings three thousand five hundred won. What's more, as unbelievable as it was, the lottery ticket had hit as well, paying twelve hundred won. The total was the whopping sum of almost five thousand won. It was all so sur-real that Ilma found it all almost too much to believe.

'I can't believe this is happening to me.'

Nadia was holding Ilma's arm and trembling. 'What are you going to do?'

'I feel more afraid than happy.'

'Why do you feel afraid? You didn't steal the money.'

This was somewhat reassuring; however, when he took the five thousand won worth of notes in his hand, his heart was racing.

Why is this luck coming to me? he thought while his heart experienced a strange anxiety. 'I feel like I'm in another world.'

Emilia felt no confusion about her delight. 'The hero of the day. Our hero.'

She suddenly had a newfound respect for Ilma.

While it was Achilles that won the race, it was Ilma who had bet on him. Achilles was Ilma and Ilma, Achilles. The hero of the day was simultaneously Achilles and Ilma. It suddenly seemed to Emilia that Ilma was soaring in the clouds.

'I'm sorry I was so stubborn. I had no idea things would turn out like this.'

She was embarrassed at having opposed Ilma and alone betting on Sun.

In contrast to Ilma's fortune, there was a large group of unfortunates, amongst whom Danyeong was the most unfortunate. She had lost the hundreds of won she had won earlier, and her good fortune had been totally reversed. Just thinking of it made her grind her teeth.

It was one thing when Myeongdo had won, but there was no way he was going to take losing because of Danyeong quietly. He gave voice to his displeasure.

'What did I say? This is what happens when you take those kinds of chances.'

'Who knew this would happen?' Danyeong replied sourly.

'All you could think of was Sun. You didn't listen to what I was trying to tell you.'

'You say that now that you've lost. You weren't complaining when you won. What about the two times you won?'

'Where are those winnings now? It's all your fault.'

'Okay, so it's my fault. That's the end of it. Why are you getting so mad?'

She was already disgusted enough at seeing Ilma celebrating

through the binoculars, and this abuse at Myeongdo's hands was too much to take, fuelling her anger.

'Those wretches have stolen our luck. They've even taken our winnings.'

The more she thought about it, the more aggravated she became.

'I'm not going to take this lying down. Let's go over there.'

Dropping the binoculars, Danyeong pulled Myeongdo into the crowd.

When they appeared in front of Ilma's group, her tone was sarcastic.

'Very impressive. You have a flower on each arm. Let's have a look at the hero's face.'

As if remembering the events of the evening past, Nadia turned away with a look of disgust.

'Did you follow me to the races?'

'I want you to know that some of your winnings should rightfully be ours.'

Thinking that any further conversation would only cause useless aggravation, Ilma grabbed Nadia's hand and headed in the direction of the car.

Dusk was coming down, and the racetrack was almost empty.

6. THE BANQUET

After returning to the hotel in the car, Ilma called Byeoksu at the newspaper.

The four of them had decided to go to a banquet.

When Byeoksu heard about events at the track he turned white with astonishment. The colour of his face actually changed.

'First the lottery ticket and now the track. It's all too easy, I can't help but be afraid.'

'Just think that you were fortunate. Is there any reason to be worried?'

'It's not luck. Who gets this lucky?'

'Accept misfortune as misfortune and fortune as fortune. There's nothing to worry about. If you worry when you are lucky, what in the world do you expect from life?'

'To just be ordinary.'

'If that's what you want, why have you come all the way to Manchuria? Are you saying you came all this way to be ordinary? Anyway, you've now taken all the good fortune there is in Manchuria for yourself and left none for us.'

'That's a cheery thought. That this too is life. I guess I should take life as it comes. Is there any other way?'

The specially prepared banquet table in one corner of the restaurant was particularly splendid this evening.

Taking special pains to make Nadia happy, Ilma ordered some dishes that were not on the evening's menu he thought she would like. The small celebration of the day's success was also a gesture to Nadia of Ilma's feelings for her.

There was a basket of flowers on the white table, and a bottle of champagne rested in a bucket of ice. The delicately flavoured dishes brought out in turn by the waiter were not enough to satisfy Ilma.

'Is this what they call luxury? Is this the best we can do for a banquet?'

'When you're full of energy, nothing satisfies. Once you have luxury, it stops being special, and you want something more valuable. But in fact, there's no such thing. The food a king eats and that which we eat is not so different. The substance is the same.'

In spite of Byeoksu's words, everything still looked insufficient to Ilma. This was due to his new affluence.

However, to Nadia, that evening's banquet was exquisite, and she felt very thankful to Ilma. She was thankful for the meal but also for the kindness Ilma showed her.

'This is the finest meal I have ever had.'

It was a frank confession, and her honesty was enough to bring tears to the eyes of those present.

'Not even on my birthday or at Christmas have I had a meal like this. Of course, I'll never forget my birthdays when my mother was alive and she invited the neighbours over, and we had stacks of sliced bread and whole roasted duck. That was the best time of my life. But, apart from that, I've never had such an enjoyable time as this.'

'Then let's enjoy ourselves.'

Nadia's story clearly evoked similar memories in Emilia

and she said, 'Just think of this as your birthday, and I'll think of it as Christmas.'

'In that case, let's lift our glasses to the two of you.'

Ilma motioned the waiter over to fill their glasses. After the pleasant sound of the cork popping, the four of them proceeded to get tipsy on the bubbly champagne.

Nadia did not object to her glass being refilled, and soon her face was a rose pink.

Emilia left directly from there for work at the dance hall, but Nadia decided to take the night off.

Having grown even tipsier, they realized that they couldn't go out in their condition. After dinner, while sitting in the lobby with its red carpet, listening to music, Ilma felt that he couldn't be happier, and, in fact, he couldn't have been. He felt as if he were a balloon floating gently in the air.

If there was one thing lacking it was the fact that he still wasn't completely certain of Nadia's feelings. In the days that they had been seeing each other, he had developed a good idea as to what her feelings were; however, as a woman's heart is not an easy thing to know, he couldn't relax until he was sure of her affections. It had gotten to the point where Ilma could not be without her. Somehow, she had become the most important thing in his life, and he couldn't imagine a day without her company. In spite of the fact that he suddenly had fifteen thousand won in his trunk, this alone was of no special value. His own existence by itself was also nothing special. It was by living for someone precious that one found meaning and light. To Ilma, that precious other was Nadia. For her, he could give up everything he had. The problem was Nadia's heart. That would decide everything.

Mixed in with his contentment was one small thread of concern, no larger really than a thin tendril of cloud drifting across a full, round moon. Nadia's feelings were not so complicated, and she was relatively forthright in expressing them. The extent of the affection that Nadia had come to feel for Ilma over the last few days was the clearest and most honest measure of her feelings. What's more, he wondered if her satisfied countenance was not a sign that her feelings had deepened. Actually, Ilma's concern was a sweet little grumble arising from a contentment that he would himself realize a few short hours later.

'I'm trying to think of how to show you the best time possible.'

As Ilma spoke, Nadia looked as if she couldn't be happier.

'If you do any more for me, I'll never be able to repay you. I'm as content as can be.'

Luxury was drinking all the champagne you wanted, and pleasure was enjoying music and dancing. There's nothing more enjoyable in life than that. Even if Ilma had tried to discover something more pleasurable, it would have been a waste of time and so, he figured, why fight a good thing.

They went to the Waltz House on a relatively quiet street that Nadia knew of. In the clean dance hall, they became drunk on several bottles of champagne and were so swept up in the fun that they danced the waltz over and over.

This was a waltz dance hall, wherein were played both the Vienna waltz and the Paris waltz, the melodies of which are slightly different – one is refined and one modern. The waltz is meant to be danced by people in love. To dance the waltz is to whirl where one will until one can whirl no more.

Nadia and Ilma danced several waltzes in a row. They whirled wildly until they were dizzy and out of breath. Ilma, ready to collapse, plopped down on a sofa. Nadia followed him and after sitting, rested her head on his shoulder. She was tired; alcohol and dancing had taken their toll on her. With her head on Ilma's shoulder, she spoke as if talking in her sleep.

'I'd like to go somewhere, anywhere, far away … shall I go to Joseon with you?'

The last part caused Ilma to sober up.

'I think I know Joseon well now.'

She continued to surprise him.

He wasn't even able to ask how she had come by her knowledge of Joseon but could only stare at her.

'I know Joseon through you. I think Joseon must be like you.'

It didn't seem to be the alcohol talking. There was a light in her eyes and her voice trembled slightly.

'...'

'And I think I could love Joseon.'

It was a good thing he was drunk. He felt a new courage at her words and pulled her into the crook of his arm.

'What could you love about Joseon?'

'Anything, everything – the people, their nature.'

'I have been imagining you wearing Joseon clothes for quite a while now. I've thought how beautiful you would look in a Joseon skirt and short coat.'

'They say Joseon people wear white. It's as if they are always in evening wear, it seems so fresh and nice.'

'And they always wear traditional shoes. Blue material with red laces, several yellow strings attached. These shoes worn with white socks, a white skirt, with a black jacket is a sight that can only be seen in Joseon and is one of its beautiful faces.'

'And the pottery flower vases that have been made since the old days are also wonderful.'

'In the past, our ancestors were among the most cultured in the world. They made wonderful pottery and were good painters and musicians.'

'I want to live in the midst of such accomplishments. I want to wear white clothes, look at pottery and paintings, and listen to old music.'

'I can't believe what I'm hearing. But I could hear it ten or even a hundred times, and I wouldn't tire of it.'

'Then I'll say it ten, a hundred times. I can't wait to live in that kind of Joseon.'

Before she was even finished speaking, Ilma pulled her

back onto the dance floor where they once again melded into the crowd. At that moment, this was the only way he knew to express what he was feeling.

'Sometimes, the hardest thing in the world becomes the easiest. Those words were exactly what I wanted to hear from you. And they came so readily.'

As the dancers stepped noisily to the waltz, the two circled about, being sucked into the centre of the dance. Among all those couples, there were none happier than Ilma and Nadia. They floated above the crowd like a bird over water.

Byeoksu seemed to have intuited what was happening between them, because at some point in the evening he disappeared from the hall. Ilma searched for him from the dance floor but was unable to see him. While Byeoksu had disappeared, the crowd had increased, indicating that the night had grown late. Nadia's fatigue was obvious, and she hung on Ilma's arm.

'My body feels unusually tired tonight. But my mind is wide awake. Let's go somewhere comfortable.'

The two called a car, climbed in, and sank tiredly into the seats. They headed for Ilma's hotel as if it was the most natural thing in the world.

When they arrived at the hotel and Ilma asked for the key at the front desk, he got a surprising answer.

'I gave it out earlier.'

'You gave it out? To whom?'

At Ilma's surprised query, it was the employee's turn to be confused.

'A woman came earlier and asked for the key. I thought she was travelling with you, so I gave it to her.'

'A woman? I haven't been travelling with any woman.'

Of course, of the two, Ilma was the more surprised.

'She insisted that she was traveling with you.'

'What are you talking about? I'm not travelling with a woman.'

Hearing Ilma's agitated voice, the concierge realized his error and became even more embarrassed. 'Then I've made a mistake.'

'Yes, you have. Please get the key back.'

Ilma and Nadia followed the employee up the stairs to the second floor.

When they reached the room and knocked, someone inside replied, 'Who is it?'

Together with the coquettishly lilting voice could be heard the sound of shuffling slippers. Even without hearing the voice, Ilma knew that the intruder was Danyeong. The sound of her lilting voice filled Ilma with rage.

'Who's banging on the door waking people up this late at night?'

'Open up.'

Hearing Ilma's voice, Danyeong's became even more languid. 'Ah, it's the occupant. Do you think that scares me? If you're alone, I'll let you in, if you're with her, I won't.'

'Do you know what's going to happen if you don't open this door right now?'

Opening the door at the sound of his yell, Danyeong's relaxed form appeared in the doorway.

'Look at you, going around like you're a couple. You win at the track and pick up a girl; you're certainly in high spirits, aren't you?'

'I want you to hear from her whether she is travelling with me or not.'

This was an order from Ilma.

'I want you to acknowledge your mistake here and now.'

Bowing deeply, the concierge was gripped with fear.

'Get her out of here immediately. This is your responsibility.'

'My, aren't you making a fuss.'

As Ilma turned to go without giving any indication that he had heard Danyeong, Nadia was already descending the stairs.

Ilma hurried after her. Much more than Danyeong's

behaviour, more than anything else, the most important thing to Ilma at that moment was what Nadia was thinking.

'Nadia, I know that you won't misunderstand what has happened.'

As an expression of the displeasure she felt, Nadia remained silent for some time.

'She's the last person on earth I could ever fall in love with.'

When they were halfway down the stairs, they heard the sound of Danyeong throwing a tantrum, crying, and flailing about. The cry was that of a child that hasn't gotten its way. The sound got gradually louder.

'She's unbelievable. To follow me all the way here and make this kind of a scene. This kind of obsession is exhausting to both parties. And what's it good for? I tell you, it's useless.'

Even if Nadia had not heard these words, she harboured no misunderstandings regarding Ilma. She had met Danyeong several times and had realized that this was a case of one-sided love, and this was borne out by the cold demeanour Ilma maintained throughout the whole situation.

The more aware she became of Danyeong's efforts, the more her antipathy toward her grew. She was immeasurably pleased by Ilma's cool response.

When they reached the lobby, Nadia plopped down in a seat. 'I'm exhausted. And we have nowhere to go.'

'Of course, we have somewhere to go. Soon we'll be able to use the room. As soon as they get rid of the trespasser.'

Ilma dropped into the seat next to Nadia.

*

It wasn't until two days later that Nadia emerged from Ilma's room.

This was, of course, the result of her love for Ilma, but it was also a form of rebellion against her home, specifically her aunt, the wife of her father's older brother. The couple had not been so kind to Nadia. This caused her great sadness. She was unable to appeal to her aunt's affections or share her troubles with her. Their relationship was strained, and there was a coldness between them. Nadia was afflicted with the constant sorrow of the orphan, and she felt as if she were only a temporary boarder in their home. She had been waiting for a long time for the day when she could leave. Nadia's actions that evening were, in fact, evidence that she had decided to leave her family. From the moment she had made up her mind about her feelings toward Ilma, she had been waiting for this day. She was leaving her old home and taking the first steps in a new life.

'Before I leave this place, I have one request. I want to visit my mother's grave to say goodbye.'

That afternoon, Ilma granted her request and decided to visit the gravesite with her.

Nadia bought a bouquet of flowers and a thin candle. She intended to place them at her mother's grave.

They rode a horse-drawn carriage out of town for twenty minutes on the broad roadway for a distance similar to that of the racetrack. Carrying her bouquet, Nadia rode in silence. The whip of the driver flapped in the air, and the red petals of the bouquet fluttered. Becoming aware that the air had suddenly turned chilly, Ilma felt a new, cool sense of exquisite affection creeping into his heart. How had it come about that he had met her, fallen in love with her, and was now riding in this carriage with her? There was no denying that she was riding beside him now with a bouquet of flowers. It didn't seem real, rather like a dream. Like the change in seasons, it was a strange and wonderful thing. While it was a happy occasion, there was also something sad about it. The more he thought about this, the more he felt human life was a mystery. Was the reason that Nadia was staring silently ahead with a shadow dangling from her long eyelashes due to the fact that she was feeling something similar? The two sat silently in the chilly wind, lost in their own thoughts.

As they passed a brightly coloured Buddhist temple, the entrance of the cemetery appeared, giving an indication of how large it was inside. There were flower vendors on both sides of the entrance, waiting for visitors with their multicoloured wares.

Inside the entrance was the Uspenskia Monastery, and behind that, the broad, tree-covered cemetery opened up. Both the monastery and the cemetery were empty, and this gave the feeling of a deserted house and its garden. The dozens of graves were now the occupants of that garden. They were lying silently in the shadow of the trees, watching over their garden. Even though it was a cemetery, it seemed more like a secluded, peaceful grove. In the shade of the thin poplars and delicate zelkova trees rested long, square stone tombs with headstones, lamps burning on either side, and bouquets of flowers. The graves looked like small, elegant arbours. There were so many such graves that the place felt like a park. There was nothing frightful or revolting about the scene; it was as if nature were putting on a performance in the quiet and solitude. Paths lead off into all corners of the cemetery through the gaps in the trees, white poplars lined the lanes, and there were benches placed here and there for people to sit, rest, and reminisce or meditate.

It was early autumn and the leaves, tinged with autumn colour, hung beautifully from the branches of the trees or had fallen and covered the paths. Even the songs of the birds had ceased, and the rays of sunlight filtering through the trees of that lovely, silent autumn grove created an enchanting world. As if out for a stroll, Nadia and Ilma ambled along the pathways.

After taking several paths, Nadia came to stop in the shade of a tree.

'This is where my mother lies.'

Her voice was soft as she approached the grave; there was a small gate in the white stake fence that surrounded it. Nadia opened the gate and went in. Ilma surveyed the grave from outside the fence.

There were an almost infinite variety of sizes and types of graves in the cemetery, but this one was not particularly large or well adorned. The tombstone was small and the grass around it was tall. The flame had gone out in the glass lantern, and both the flowers that had been placed there and the ones in a bottle had withered up. On the tombstone were her mother's name, date of death, and a few words about her life written in Russian. Below this was a picture of her embedded in the stone. Nadia looked just like her.

Ilma removed his hat and bowed his head in front of the picture.

He felt a bit awkward in front of the grave of a stranger, but when he thought that this was Nadia's mother, the feeling disappeared, and more than anything, he was moved by Nadia's devotion.

Watching Nadia place the flowers before the grave, light the candle in the lantern, and stand for a long time in an attitude of prayer, her clear and boundless devotion to her mother was plain. Ilma thought the scene, one of solitude, was like something from an old painting.

As Nadia turned to face Ilma after finishing her prayer, her eyes seemed misty with tears.

'I haven't been to see her for so long. It looks like an untended grave. When I think how forlorn and hurt she must feel in that grave ...'

In fact, she was crying. Using the handkerchief she had dried her tears with, she began to clean the tombstone. She wiped away the dust and polished the letters. Her motions were earnest, as if handling a precious object, as if wiping a face clean.

According to the date on the tombstone, she had passed away several years before. Ilma was touched by the fact that Nadia's love for her mother had not lessened in that time.

Feeling his eyes start to fill with tears at the emotions he was feeling, Ilma retreated to a nearby bench. Before long, Nadia also came out and stood next to him. He could see the traces on her face where she had wiped away her tears so as not to be seen crying.

'I'll take nothing of this place with me when I leave. Nothing about life here or my family appeals to me. The only thing that bothers me about leaving is my mother's grave, even though she will always be with me in my memories.'

'You're not leaving forever. While you keep your mother's memories alive, you can come back sometimes to visit.'

'While I'm gone, it won't take long for her grave to become a shambles. The lantern will go out, the flowers will wither, and the grass will grow ...'

Arising from the bench, the two made their way back down the path.

The way to deal with sadness is to leave it behind. She could not stay there forever. Nadia put her memories of her mother behind her and looked resolutely ahead.

The cemetery was a park. The late sun was warm on their backs. New leaves had fallen under their feet.

There was no way to tell what might be hidden in the vastness of that interior. As they rounded the bend of a path, Ilma could make out the outline of a person in the shade of a tree. It was a tall, slender young man standing there silently. It was unclear whether he was out for a stroll or had come to visit one of the deceased.

As it turned out, it was someone Nadia knew. As they approached, the youth raised his hand. Nadia spoke as if slightly surprised.

'Ivanov. What are you doing here?'

'I came to lay some flowers at my father's grave. What a surprise to meet you here.'

Seeing Ivanov staring at Ilma, Nadia quickly introduced them.

Maybe it was because of the fallen leaves, but Ivanov's clothes made him look forlorn. Summer having passed, his light purple suit did not match the season and gave him a shabby appearance. There was no lustre in his wide, round eyes as they stared vacantly at the world. His eyes had not always been so cold. A cold world had given him such an indifferent look.

He and Nadia seemed extremely close. They spoke to each other very comfortably and in an intimate tone. Ilma could follow the gist of their rapid speech, but there were parts that he missed.

Being their first encounter, he didn't want to intrude on their conversation and intended to stand quietly, but, feeling uncomfortable, he ended up walking a few steps away. Nadia, as if trying to reassure him, quickly followed. With a wave, Ivanov set off down a path.

'He comes to my uncle's home often. When my uncle was a general, Ivanov was an officer. He and my uncle seem very close,' Nadia explained, walking next to Ilma.

'Everyone at this cemetery looks forlorn. I guess anyone who comes here would look that way.'

'These graves left a multitude of orphans on the streets. Poor, helpless orphans with nowhere to turn. It's hard to say whose fault it is.' There was a tone of resentment in Nadia's voice.

'Is Ivanov one of them?'

'He may not look it, but he's a musician. One with nowhere to play. The cabarets have all the musicians they need, and he was turned down at the hotels. If he had a car he could make a living, but where's he going to get a car? It's a waste of good talent.'

She meant he had no choice but to become one of the many taxi drivers in the city. Being touched by his sad plight, Ilma said, 'Why is it that life never turns out right for the really talented?' His voice sounded like a sigh.

'He said in all seriousness that he might be better off begging.'

'…'

'When I said I was going to Joseon, he said with a sad smile that things had turned out well for me.'

The smile on Nadia's face was also an extremely sad one.

There was a futility to having met Ivanov and hearing his story. Hearing the sad tale of a total stranger was depressing and even irritating. Unlike hearing a happy story, hearing of someone's misfortunes was a wearisome thing. Added to this was a futile feeling of depression in Ilma's heart. He felt an oppressive sense of anxiety.

Ilma had already been openly coming and going at the hotel with Nadia and walking in the streets with her, but after they left the cemetery, the impressions he had gotten there did not fade, but rather caused him to view what he saw in the streets completely differently.

Of course, this didn't mean that his happiness had evaporated. But the impressions he had received here among the fallen leaves had tempered the unfettered joy of yesterday with a reflective coolness. It was comparable to a child who suddenly goes from laughing to crying. Just as the tears that follow laughter can be another way to express happiness, what Ilma was feeling was not unhappiness, but the pangs of self-reflection.

How many more unhappy people than happy ones are there in the world? Ten times? A hundred times more?

This wasn't the first time he had entertained such thoughts, but unlike before, this time they weren't abstract musings.

When he walked the streets, the majority of people he saw were poor, pitiable folks. Every time he travelled, he felt that there were too many people, and that most of them were unfortunate. If he had to make a comparison it would be to a red ant pile swarming with ants, all fighting amid misery just to survive. Humans, far from being noble, were a lowly species. No different from animals, they were ignoble and sordid.

People were empty husks floating on the water. Something with weight and substance would sink, but crushed, empty husks float aimlessly on the surface of the water, spinning helplessly. Humans were mostly such empty husks. Most cities were the same, but Harbin, in particular, was a city of empty husks. The streets were international display cases of empty husks, harried by life, wandering in bewilderment. Such thoughts were not new for Ilma, but today they came to him with redoubled intensity.

Beggars came and went, grabbing his sleeve. If he gave a few coins, another beggar would see and attach himself to Ilma. The beggars were not just the old and women. There were young people and even children. If he gave some money, they were happy, but even if he didn't, they did not mind. They would not pester him further, but immediately go on their way. Even the lowliest husk did not seem sad, but rather somehow optimistic. That optimism was even more painful to see.

The shabby clothes of a girl selling flowers were indistinguishable from those of the beggars. With her head wrapped in a towel, she stood on a street corner, and instead of hawking her wares, she stared vacantly at a far-off field. Her filthy feet were clad in tattered shoes. They weren't shoes, actually. They were rotted pieces of cloth. How many bundles of flowers she managed to sell in a day, and how an empty husk like her managed to survive, was truly a mystery.

On a bench across the street sat a blind musician playing an accordion. He was a former Russian officer who had lost his eyes in battle. He was an intriguing sight. His dark glasses caught the light; he was fully absorbed in, and swaying to, the melodies that flowed ceaselessly from his instrument. Was it a song of longing for his lost home, the far-off Danube river? Was it a song of nostalgia for all the things he'd lost – the river, nature, his village, his neighbours? The plaintive strains of the melody flowed, filling the street. However, passers-by were oblivious to that beautiful and precious song. People rushed here and there on their own business, paying no heed to the song, as if such sentimentality was forbidden in the competition for survival that defined this place. The beautiful strains of the accordion merely grazed people's ears, then flowed over the pavement and disappeared. Even if, occasionally, someone threw him a coin, he had no way of knowing who it was, and his fingers continued to move on the accordion. He was completely absorbed in his song. It was his song, played for himself, a pathetic, empty husk who longed for his home. The song touched Ilma, heightening his melancholy.

Was this one the only empty husk? The shabbily dressed throngs who were busily going about the streets were also empty husks. Ivanov, who he had met at the cemetery, was an empty husk. The sick Emilia was an empty husk. And was not Nadia an empty husk? There was no doubt.

Then what am I?

Ilma knew that he, too, was an empty husk. Even if he had won fifteen thousand won, and even if he was engaged in the culture business, he was nothing more than an empty husk. He and Nadia had come together precisely because they were empty husks. Empty husk was itself a class. If one of them hadn't been an empty husk, they could not have come together.

Thinking about it this way, Ilma decided that being an empty husk was not such a bad thing. Was this the happiness that comes from unhappiness? Being seized with such emotions, and with his departure from Harbin fast approaching, his appreciation of Nadia grew.

7. THE TORTOISE AND THE HARE

Even though it was early autumn in Seoul, the sun was still hot, and it shone brightly on the streets. Seoul was two months behind Manchuria when it came to the seasons.

On that particular day, nowhere on the street was hotter than the conference room of the East Asia Trading Company.

The young president, Yu Manhae, had called in his general director, Lee Dongyeol, and his managing director, Choi Seongsu, and the three of them were so engaged in intense discussion that he didn't even have a chance to wipe off the sweat that had appeared on his brow. The sweat was not the problem. They were at an important crossroads, a point when fate was to be decided.

'What are you talking about, Director Lee? What are you trying to do to me? Do you think what you're saying makes sense?'

Manhae was so agitated that his voice trembled, but Lee Dongyeol was as cool and sharp as a knife blade.

'Well, you can be surprised, but that won't change the truth. I don't like having to tell you this, but it's my job to inform you of the real situation. It is a very difficult thing to give you such unsettling news, but as the company is facing a crisis, there is no way around it.'

It was not easy to surprise the young president, but there was no getting around the fact that the company was facing difficulties.

'Your problems are all of our problems. In fact, on my way to Seoul in the car I cried inside. I wanted to scream.'

'Is it true? Is there nothing we can do?'

'We have no choice but to believe the technicians. Already a couple of different technicians have reported back. This is the third time. Since all the reports are the same, there's nothing we can do but believe them.'

'Are you sure? All three reports were the same?'

'The initial appraisement was false. In fact, it was a trick. We were deceived. How could a vein play out like that after only three months?'

The Hungcheon gold mine, which had cost a million won, had started to show signs of failure after only three months. General director Lee Dongyeol, who had gone out on a site inspection with the technicians, had returned to Seoul after several days. He had just given his report to Manhae, who had been waiting impatiently to receive it. Manhae had gone pale, and his blood had run so cold that he didn't even notice the sweat on his brow. The beads of sweat ran down his neck and into his shirt.

When someone is confronted with a situation that makes their face turn blue, they tend not to notice that they are sweating. What's more, when they are carrying others' fortunes on their shoulders, they may assume a stolid, serious, cool expression on their pale face. But the serious expressions on both Lee Dongyeol's and Choi Seongsu's faces were attempts to bite back a surging anger.

'The vein of gold is running very thin, and the gold content in the broken rock is extremely low. It's mostly veins of granite; it seems unlikely that there is any gold in the white rock.

Things have been looking bad for a long time. The engineers are discouraged and the miners exhausted and lethargic.'

Not a muscle moved in Lee Dongyeol's tanned face with its firm eyes.

'It's a remote place, so the roads are rough. I've been rattling in a truck for a couple of days and I'm beat. On my way back, all I could think of was what a wretched place it is. The technicians voiced the same disappointments and complaints ...'

With each word, Manhae's colour worsened, and the sweat poured off him. And for good reason, Manhae had invested almost all he had in the mine, and it was his livelihood.

It was not just the one million won he had spent to buy the mine; he had spent another million in buying the equipment and making improvements to the facilities. In order to come up with the two million won, he had not only mobilized all his holdings but had also borrowed from several places. Compared to his investment in the mine, his holdings in the trading company and the Daechang Metal Works were no larger than a flea's liver. The mine's failure meant the destruction of his career. Turning white like that was the only way Manhae could maintain some semblance of composure.

'Call the manager of the mine to come down. Send a telegram now.'

After the incredible discouragement he had just experienced, this was all he could come up with as a solution. It was the desperate gesture of someone who doesn't know what else to do.

'Even if you call the manager, nothing about what I've told you will change. What I've told you I heard directly from him, it's the same as if you were speaking to him.'

Lee Dongyeol felt sorry for the young president. This problem required wisdom and the right response, but what he saw now amounted to no more than children's games.

'I'll send a telegram now requesting that the manager come. But that's not the problem.'

Calling a courier and informing him of the message, Lee Dongyeol looked in turn at Yu Manhae and Choi Seongsu.

'There's no way around the fact that the mine is exhausted; don't you think we should look into how such a mine was purchased in the first place?'

'Speaking plainly, seeing that this was clearly fraud, there's no way that this was a legitimate purchase transaction.'

To this response by financial director Choi Seongsu, Lee Dongyeol replied, 'Exactly, it was obviously fraudulent. Even though we can't turn back the clock, isn't there something we can do? The broker who negotiated the deal, Bak Namgu, is here; maybe we can get him to negotiate on our behalf.'

'What good will negotiating do now? Taking legal action will have no effect, and weeping and wailing won't accomplish a thing...'

Before Choi Seongsu was even done speaking, Manhae's voice erupted, causing the other two to go silent. 'Fraud? Illegitimate transaction? A one million won illegitimate transaction? Oh my god!'

Unable to contain his rage, he brought his fist down on the table, his entire body shaking. 'Was it Bak Namgu that brought this destruction on us? Has he destroyed my life?'

Sweat flowed from him like tears, soaking his collar. 'There's nothing we can do now. The damage is done. It's infuriating to think we were taken in so easily. These days, the idea of gold mining is all the rage. I was infatuated with the idea and rushed too quickly into the deal. We should have done a more thorough scientific investigation into the quality of the ore veins before we made the purchase.'

'This is all useless talk now. Even if we can't take legal action against Bak Namgu, we can confront him and see if we can get anything out of him.'

Lee Dongyeol agreed with Choi Seongsu's comments.

'That's what I'm talking about. Let's meet him and sound him out. Perhaps there's a way to get some concessions...'

'How can we get any concessions at this stage from such evil people? Everything gone in one morning. I don't know if this is real or a dream.'

Manhae was gradually getting a grip on himself. The eyes in his pale face regained their clearness. This presented a chance for the other two to honestly air their feelings.

'If I can be frank, you took on too many things. Our trading company is a big enough enterprise by itself, as is the iron-works. On top of that, investing in a gold mine didn't make sense. Wasn't I against it from the start? I've been worrying about how we're going to deal with this situation.'

'The zeal for gold has always ruined people. Whether now or in the past, it has always been a kind of disease.'

The young president rose from his chair as if not liking what he was hearing. 'Are you two going to torment me as well? Call Bak Namgu, or whatever his name is, right away.'

*

That evening, Manhae made an appointment to meet Bak Namgu. He arranged a party in a comfortable room that had been prepared in the Sangnokwon. It was the kind of party that Manhae had thrown on innumerable occasions in the course of doing business. That evening, however, he was agitated by an odd feeling, different from any he'd had before. This was not due to anything as concrete as concern over whether the evening would end in success or failure but to the possibility that it might be neither. It was the feeling of vexation and frustration when one is unable to find their way out of a thick fog.

The negotiations were left to Lee Dongyeol and Choi Seongsu, and they had asked for Cheongmae, but, while it was only early evening, she was already taking care of guests at another banquet in a nearby room. They dined there almost every other day and always had Cheongmae entertain them, so it was regretful that they had lost her to another engagement on that particular day. Manhae and Cheongmae were quite close. Manhae was very fond of Cheongmae, and she was grateful for Manhae's help. A relationship that had started with material support had grown from affection to love, and now Manhae occupied an important place in Cheongmae's heart. The long-time, close nature of the relationship made the fact that Cheongmae was unable to attend the party even more regrettable. What made it a difficult situation was that Manhae had not summoned Cheongmae to better help him host Bak Namgu, but because he himself wanted her there.

'A banquet? What kind of banquet starts so early?'

Trying to appease Manhae, who, out of depression, was unreasonably moved to anger, the waiter, rubbing his hands in supplication, replied, 'They are from a newspaper.'

'Why would a newspaper company banquet start so early?'

'It's a meeting of the *Hyundai Daily*. The president is hosting some people tonight.'

'When they finish, send her over here.'

'Of course, sir.'

'And pull her out and send her over from time to time.'

'Yes, sir.'

Being faced with such an urgent situation and feeling uncharacteristically anxious, the slightest thing caused him to lose his composure. The gentle Manhae, who never raised his voice like he had to the waiter, was angry that evening. Actually, the cause of his anger was not Cheongmae, but the enormous personal shock he had received that day. The bolt of lightning from the blue that was the news of the mine had melted his spirit, agitating his soul to breaking point.

Instead of Cheongmae, two unfamiliar *kisaeng** were brought into the room, and while they were waiting, Bak Namgu appeared, somewhat late. It is typical for the one being hosted, much more than the host, to be at ease and

---

* *Kisaeng* were female entertainers.

somewhat arrogant. Manhae's side was worried that something else would go wrong, and Bak Namgu for his part, far from being sorry for his tardiness, was imperturbable, not showing any reaction.

'Mr Bak, you look so relaxed, life must be good these days.'

Bak Namgu smiled at the flattery, finally showing a hint of regret. 'How could I be relaxed? I'm too busy.'

'It's good to be busy. Nothing gets accomplished if one isn't busy.'

'The problem is, I'm only busy without accomplishing anything. And I worry that I'll spend the rest of my life like this.'

'Don't be modest.'

Whether he saw Choi Seongsu's smile or not, Bak Namgu once again assumed a serious expression.

He looked like a cold-blooded creature with his dark, calculating appearance. His unyielding, tough character was a stark contrast to Manhae's soft, accommodating personality, and Manhae seemed no match for him.

Even after they all had a few drinks, Manhae had yet to break his silence, and so Lee Dongyeol began exchanging words with Bak Namgu.

'According to the talk going around, you've been involved in several big projects lately. Are you still mainly involved in mining? How are things going?'

Bak Namgu was very careful about his speech and behaviour, not letting anything slip.

'Well, the mining business is difficult and doesn't return much profit, and after trying my hand at it, sure enough, nothing seems to go right. There's nothing easy under the sun.'

'No profit? If there's no profit in it, why is every Tom, Dick, and Harry chomping at the bit to get into it? The value of gold these days has people running around like crazy. If there's no profit in it, would people be foolish enough to go to all that trouble for nothing? What are you saying? No offense, but you are not a foolish person.'

As Choi Seongsu let out a belly laugh, Namgu started to open up.

'Mr Choi, you're not familiar with the situation. When it comes to business, I don't like to lose money. This isn't something I like to broadcast, but, speaking frankly, not only is the mining business experiencing difficulties, but the economy, which was thriving, is also in the doldrums. No matter what the conditions, there is no business as unpredictable as mining. Suddenly people are getting out. Only people with large holdings are staying in. The smaller investors have, for the most part, gotten out, so this is advantageous for those who stayed in. I'm one of those that got out early. And since I had nothing else to do, I invested in real estate. Even if the mines aren't doing well, the land always keeps its value so big mistakes are rare. Even though there isn't a large return on land investments, they're steady so I find myself coming back to real estate after trying my hand at other investments.'

Once he started talking, he had quite a bit to say. Even though he was speaking a bit confusedly, there was a slight undertone of satisfaction and gratification in his voice at having said what he wanted to say.

'You can be so nonchalant because you got what you wanted out of it before getting out,' Lee Dongyeol said with a forced smile. 'I'll bet you made a bundle just this year,' he added, giving Bak Namgu a thumbs up.

'Absolutely not,' Bak Namgu said, shaking his head from side to side. 'Mr Lee, don't jump to conclusions. If I had made any money do you think I would still be in this business going around like a pariah? If I had made even a tenth of what you think, I would have changed my life and be relaxing right now. What an absurd thing to say.'

Pretending to be deeply afflicted, his disingenuously smiling face betrayed his satisfied attitude.

The single thumb in the air was meant to signify one million won. The meaning of that gesture was well understood in their world. It was the symbol for that daunting amount. The one tenth that Namgu referred to was one hundred thousand won. His attitude suggested that even if he hadn't earned the entire amount signified by the thumb, he was probably close. He was the hottest broker in the city.

'It's a perilous business. If you do okay you're lucky; nine out of ten times things don't go well. It's such stressful work that I really do need to get out of it as soon as I can.'

'Why are you only talking about yourself!?'

This sudden clap of thunder rendered all present mute. Manhae, who until then had not said a word, could no longer contain his anger, and he let out a whale-like bellow. The other three could not even look at his red, angry face.

'What are you going to do about my problem?'

While Manhae's scream had silenced those in attendance, it quickly brought them back to the reason for that evening's meeting.

In particular, Bak Namgu's body became hot, his nerves were set on edge, and his concentration narrowed.

Of course, Namgu had not neglected to gauge the atmosphere; however, the sudden shout had heightened the tension and focused his attention. Feeling somewhat embarrassed that he had been absorbed in his own private affairs, Manhae's unexpected voice had brought him back to the issue and put him on his guard.

'What are you going to do about my problem?'

Seeing Manhae unable to constrain his agitation, Lee Dongyeol said, 'President Yu, try not to get so excited, let's discuss this coolly. Nothing will be solved by raising your voice, try to be calm ...'

'Is being calm going to fix things? What in the world are you going to do about my problem?'

'Why don't you tell me what you are so upset about?' Namgu feigned total ignorance, his face taut.

'What? Tell you what I'm upset about? You've ruined me,

and you're pretending not to know anything about it, God damn it ...'

Dongyeol, concerned about what sort of imprecation might fly out of Manhae's mouth, quickly cut him off. 'Business these days isn't going well at all. The mining business is particularly a problem and is a source of concern for us.'

Taking on a concerned look, Namgu said, 'Say, how is that business doing?'

Namgu looked as if he had just recalled that particular enterprise.

'It's a failure.'

'A failure? Why, that can't be ...'

'The vein has run out, and the mine is on the verge of closing.'

'That can't be ...'

'Stop pretending you don't know anything about it.' Not being able to restrain himself, Manhae again raised his voice. 'Because of your worthless mine, I'm ruined. This is no time to feign ignorance. Take it back. You have to do something.'

'What are you talking about?' At that point Namgu stared directly at Manhae with a serious look and said in a strained voice, 'This is the first I heard of any of this. You're talking about mine closings and being ruined, but what do you expect me to do about it? Do you want me to scream and shout all to no avail? What do you expect from me?'

'I want my money back. If selling me a mine that was about to close for one million won isn't fraud, what is it? I want my one million won back. And you can take back that worthless mine.'

'Fraud? Why are you using such harsh language? What has happened that the goodwill we shared a few months ago when we concluded this transaction has turned to such anger? Who can see into the core of a mountain? Was it my mountain that you bought? I'm a middleman. I merely bought it from someone else and sold it to you. How could I know what the mountain would yield?'

While what he said made a certain sense, Manhae was in no mood to listen. 'In any event, the mine I bought from you has ruined me. I can't believe the unfairness of it.'

'I don't know about you being ruined, but what if the mine had yielded ten million won? Then what would you have said to me? Success or failure in this is a matter of luck; why are you abusing me like this? How could I know how much gold the mountain contained? If you're going to rage at someone, rage at the person who sold me the mine. Don't you understand what I'm telling you? You can talk about bankruptcy or ruin all you want, it won't do any good. Trying to blame your bad luck on me won't do any good. Now, what do you have to say?'

Manhae looked as if he were about to jump out of his seat. 'You two leave us alone for a minute.'

Hearing the radical change in Manhae's voice, Lee Dongyeol and Choi Seongsu became suddenly uneasy.

'What are you planning to do?'

'I want to talk to him alone – you two leave the room for a minute.'

'Alright, but try to stay calm.'

The two experienced a vague worry, but after voicing their concern, they left the room.

In fact, they were really no longer needed there. Manhae and Bak Namgu were locked in their own confrontation to which no additional advice or support would be heeded. The two had private matters to discuss. And while Lee and Choi thought it the right thing to leave them alone, they could not entirely free themselves of worry. Manhae was already agitated, and Bak Namgu was becoming that way. There was no way to predict what could go wrong.

'The night is not going to end well; something's going to happen.'

Lee Dongyeol and Choi Seongsu whispered to each other in the hallway. Keeping an eye on events in the room from the hallway and speaking to each other in low tones, the two decided there was nothing else to do but retire to a nearby room and drink, whereupon they asked a passing waiter to prepare a room.

When they heard from the waiter that the room was ready, they headed in that direction, but, just as they arrived in front of the door, they unexpectedly met Cheongmae coming down the hallway. Being happy see them, she swished her skirt. This was a winsome form of greeting.

'I'm sorry I couldn't be with you tonight, there was a previous reservation.'

Her smile revealed teeth as white as pearls. Her eyes caught the lamplight and shone like drops of water.

'If you had been there tonight, the president would have been in a more relaxed mood. Tonight's meeting is really important, and the mood in the room right now isn't too good.'

After hearing this from Choi Seongsu, Cheongmae said, 'So Bak Namgu is here.' Repeating what she had heard from the waiter, she asked, 'Are they talking about the Hungcheon mine business?'

'The mining business isn't for ordinary people. One minute you're on top of the world, the next you're beside yourself with rage; it's best left to madmen.'

Cheongmae already had an idea about the state of the mine, and so it wasn't inappropriate of Lee Dongyeol to state his feelings like this in front of her.

'So, tonight's meeting needs to go well.'

'He's not one to easily give up. It seems ominous that he asked us to leave the room. Go in for a minute and see what they're doing.'

'Okay. I'll be right back.'

Cheongmae walked softly toward their room.

Choi Seongsu and Lee Dongyeol sat across from each other in their room and began to pour beer each for the other. It was a simple table with no dishes of food, adorned by only beer bottles and glasses. Not being able to think of anything but the problem in front of them, they'd shared several glasses of beer in silence when the door suddenly opened and Cheongmae burst in. It was only briefly after she had gone into Manhae's room that she came running out in a great fright. Her eyes were open wide in shock.

'It's an emergency. Quick, you must get in there.'

'What's wrong? You look like you've seen a murder.'

'A murder may be about to happen.'

At that point Lee Dongyeol became alarmed. 'Murder?'

They got up from their seats.

'When I went into to the room, it was like two wild animals facing each other. Something was glittering in front of the president, and when I looked more closely, I saw it was a knife. A dagger. I was so surprised I ran out without saying a word.'

'A dagger, you say?'

Choi Seongsu and Lee Dongyeol dashed from the room.

*

After the two had left the room, Cheongmae didn't have the nerve to return to Manhae's room so she went back to her seat at the *Hyundai Daily* newspaper banquet.

The festivities had reached their peak. The room was noisy and the table was strewn with food and drink.

Dozens of people were milling around, some sitting and some standing in a scene that resembled a busy marketplace. People were busy pouring each other drinks.

'Cheongmae.'

'Why are you getting so many calls?'

'Are you sure you aren't cheating on us?'

Deftly dodging the proffered hands that came stretching towards her from those who had spoken, she made her way to the side of Kim Jongse.

When she sat next to Jongse, who was drinking by himself at one corner of the table, he said, 'Do you think I don't know where you've been?'

Cheongmae replied naturally, 'Manhae is here.'

In fact, she had been about to appraise Jongse of the situation in the other room.

'The broker Bak Namgu must have come also.'

'Something bad has happened.'

'Are you talking about all the money he spent on that gold mine? What has happened?'

'I saw something terrible.'

'Did you see a lump of gold?'

'This is no joking matter.' Cheongmae started to leave the noisy room. 'Let's go somewhere quite.'

She plucked at Jongse's sleeve. Jongse, perceiving that something was wrong, followed Cheongmae out into the hallway.

After opening a window, which looked out onto the garden, and then sitting on the sill, he asked, 'What happened?'

'I saw Manhae and Namgu fighting.'

'What do you care if those two pigs fight each other?'

'There was a dagger on the table.'

'What? A dagger?' At that point Jongse gave her his full attention and asked, 'Is the mine he bought from Namgu in big trouble?'

This information had whetted his appetite as a newspaper reporter. He knew of the situation with Namgu, but the news that Manhae and Namgu were in a life-and-death confrontation was a new and interesting turn of events.

'Manhae is demanding that Namgu take the mine back, and he is refusing. This argument is not going to be resolved easily.'

'This is good. There's no way Namgu's going to take back the mine, but Manhae is no pushover either.'

'Something's going to happen tonight.'

'The end is near for Manhae. He had a meteoric rise that

had everybody talking, but the career of our young entrepreneur is going to be a short one.'

'What should we do?'

Jongse responded to Cheongmae's anxiety in a low voice. 'You'll lose a sponsor, but what is that to me?'

'Don't talk like that.'

'You got too close, and now you're the one that's getting hurt. To you, Manhae was the main dish while I was just dessert. It's better this way, we won't have to see him around any more.'

'I asked you not to talk like that.'

'Have you agreed with me even once? All you cared about was money. It's as if you have no heart.'

'Why are you being so contrary? Don't you care how I feel?'

'Why don't you ask yourself who's more important to you, Manhae or me. Or is money the most important thing?'

'I said stop.'

Just then, a loud scream came from Manhae's room, cutting off their conversation and causing them to stare in that direction.

After staring speechlessly for a moment, the two finally rushed down the hall towards Manhae's room.

It was not just one person's shouts that could be heard behind the closed door but a swarm of voices all mixed noisily together. In all the shouting, Manhae's and Namgu's agitated voices were clearly the loudest.

Jongse and Cheongmae did not immediately open the door but stood in the hall trying to figure out what was happening, but they could not make head nor tail of the jumble of excited voices.

'Are you trying to kill me?'

This voice was obviously Namgu's.

'Take back the mine and return my million won!'

And, of course, the adamant voice repeating this demand was that of Manhae.

Dongyeol and Seongsu were between them, trying to keep

them apart, and mixed with their voices were those of several waiters as well.

Suddenly, from inside that unseen wave of noise came the sound of something smashing and the renewed sound of struggle.

'I said that's enough!'

'Argh!'

No longer able to just stand by, Jongse opened the sliding door. Cheongmae as well rushed in behind him.

The fight was already well along and the small room was a shambles. The table was a mess, there were shattered dishes everywhere, and Manhae and Namgu, while being restrained by Dongyeol and Seongsu, were growling at each other like animals.

Unfortunately, blood had already been drawn. The knife fight had gone back and forth. It wasn't clear if Dongyeol and Seongsu had been unable to keep them apart, or if the damage had been done before they had arrived, but both Manhae and Namgu had sustained wounds. It was hard to tell where they had been cut, but they looked like a couple of demons who had been splashing about in a pool of blood, their faces and hands red with it. The screams had been the result of the mutually inflicted wounds. A blood-covered dagger glinted gruesomely on a seat.

'What are you just standing there for? Call a car immediately,' screamed Jongse at a waiter, not knowing what else to do. 'How could you let things get out of hand like this?' This time he aimed his recrimination at Dongyeol.

'They're both stronger than us, what could we have done?'

Dongyeol's response struck home, and Jongse continued weakly, 'What the hell is all this? This happened because you tried to keep this quiet, and no one called for help.'

The extent to which the commotion in the room had disturbed the entire place became clear when the waiter came back to announce that the car was ready. The guests from all the other rooms had come out and were crowded into the hallway. They had even crowded into the room so that the sliding door could not be closed, adding to the chaos.

Jongse and Cheongmae were swallowed up in all those people and ended up in a corner of the room. The site of the fight became like a crowded market place, and people's attention shifted from the two combatants to the noisy atmosphere of the room.

'Even if they say people are born into this world to fight, this is a huge disgrace.'

While so muttering to Cheongmae, Jongse, with the help of a waiter, managed to extract Manhae. Before the crowd could surge out of the room, Jongse was able to get him out and pull him to the car.

'Let me go with him,' said Cheongmae, to which Jongse replied, 'I guess I can forgive you that on a night like tonight.'

And then he added, 'This would make a great story for the social page.'

As he sent the car off, he was already thinking of a good title for the article.

After getting first aid at a nearby hospital, Cheongmae took Manhae to her house. She led Manhae, whose head and hands were wrapped in white bandages, into her room where she took off his clothes, put him in bed and covered him with a blanket. Lying in bed, covered with bandages, he looked like a seriously injured patient.

'What was it that Jongse said? This would make a good story for the social page?'

In the midst of all that had happened, Manhae's attention was on Jongse. His first words after lying down were about what Jongse had said.

'Why are you worried about that? Worry about getting better.'

'What else did he say? "I can forgive you on a night like tonight?"'

'Forget about it. What does it matter what he said?'

'Well, his newspaper article aside, he seems to have a keen interest in you.'

His response was evidence of the strong feelings Manhae had for Cheongmae. Hearing Jongse's remarks to Cheongmae had only intensified his feelings for her, and he felt that she was the most important thing to him at that moment. This was also the reason he had pretended not to know that the car was not going to his house and had let Cheongmae bring him here. Manhae's wife, Nam Miryeo, was not an easy woman to control. Except for when he travelled, he had never spent a night away from home. Tonight, he was going to break that custom. He was ready to spend the night with Cheongmae. He felt a stronger love for her now than ever before.

'Don't worry. Jongse is Jongse and you are you. Why are you worried about him?'

'Jongse! So, you do think about him! Arrggghhh!' Manhae, as if in anguish, grabbed his back, contorted his face, and let out a groan. 'I thought I got the better of that bastard, but he hurt me ten times worse than I hurt him.'

'What good does it do to fight like that? It only causes rumours and disgrace.'

'The guy wouldn't listen to me at all. He's a crafty bastard.'

'Did you expect him to listen? You know who he is. He's a skinflint who has been playing that game for over ten years. It was a mistake to confront him like that.'

'That son-of-a-bitch ruined me. I'm bankrupt, finished.'

His voice choked as if he were about burst into tears.

He seemed like a child under the blanket. A dark cloud seemed to hover over his brow.

'That's no way for a man to act. If your resolve is firm, your future won't change. Life can't be overturned like a toy boat.'

'My life's already been overturned.'

'Then turn it right again. That's the meaning of ability.'

'...'

Manhae was silent for some time.

'Cheongmae.' He called her name in an unusually low voice. 'Do you truly love me?'

'Where did that come from?'

'There's nothing as strange as the feeling of being in love. You might say you are in love, but when you think about it, you realize you're not. You might think you hate someone, but you really love them. Forget money, or fine words, or position; can you love a person just for himself?'

'Is there room for doubt? Do you need to ask?'

'I'm asking because I have a request.'

'…'

'Will you leave with me? Leave everything behind, just the two of us, maybe go to Shanghai.'

'To Shanghai?' Cheongmae, looking surprised and not surprised at the same time, was momentarily at a loss. 'Well …'

8. UNDER ONE ROOF

The next day dawned.

There was a great commotion in Manhae's normally quite house.

The commotion was being made in the spacious house by the clamorous voice of one woman. It was the kind of loud voice one might hear when the master of the house is away.

In fact, the master of the house was away. Manhae had spent that night somewhere else, and even by late morning there was no sign of him. It was the first such incident in almost eight years of marriage. It was no surprise that his wife Miryeo's voice was so loud.

There was no family, only a young maid. For that reason, she unjustly had to bear the brunt of Miryeo's tirade.

'So, you're saying that there was no hint of anything strange yesterday when he left the house?'

Miryeo and Manhae slept in different rooms and arose at different times, and their schedules at home did not always coincide. It was often the case that by the time Miryeo got up, Manhae had already had breakfast and left for work. The day before had been such a day. She had slept late, and her husband was already gone when she arose. Therefore, the night before last was the last time she had seen him.

'He didn't say anything, and there was nothing out of the ordinary.'

Miryeo was not satisfied with the maid's answer. 'And there was no word from him last night?'

As Miryeo had gone out in the afternoon and come back late, it was natural that she would ask the maid if there had been any news from her husband during her absence. It was actually the maid, not Miryeo, who took care of the house. Miryeo, like Manhae, was mostly concerned with her own personal affairs and left the running of the house to the maid. It was common that they would convey information to each other through the maid. However, on this occasion, the de facto manager of the house had no information to give.

'There was no word from him.'

'Is that possible? Is it possible that he spent the night away from home without sending word? Since you've been working here, has he ever done anything like this? Well, has he?'

Being pressed, the maid became nervous. 'He's never done anything like this. Not even once.'

'That's right, never even once. So, what on earth is going on?'

Seeing Miryeo stamping her foot impatiently, the maid was at a loss as to what to say. 'Well ...'

The maid was stunned by Miryeo's tantrum. The maid, who occupied an important place of responsibility in managing the household, had always looked strangely on the habits of this peculiar couple. They lived completely independent lives under the same roof. The idea of being an individual was more important to them than the idea of being a couple. Calling them a couple was a way to say they lived in the same house, but their behaviour was not that of a couple. They slept in different rooms and at different times, and they often ate separately. The times spent amicably together in the same room were exceedingly rare. She had no idea in what country such strange behaviour might be normal; the maid had always regarded it as odd. Furthermore, enjoying their separate lives as they did, the maid couldn't understand why the wife was so upset that her husband had spent a night away from home.

If the doorbell had not just then been rung, there was no telling how long the maid would have been tormented.

Running to the door, the maid found Hyeju, wife of commercial college professor An Sangdal, standing there.

'Welcome.'

The maid was unusually happy to see Hyeju. In contrast to the clamorous household, her light, casual attire was a comforting sight.

'Please come in. The lady is at home.'

Being relieved to see her, the maid, without waiting for instructions, ushered her quickly into the reception room and announced her arrival.

'Professor An's wife is here.'

The two women had been close since school, and Hyeju remained a good friend to Miryeo.

The maid, as well, was familiar with her through her frequent visits to the house. The maid was especially happy to see Hyeju as it was likely that her visit would help Miryeo to calm down. At the sound of the maid's voice, Miryeo's colour somewhat returned to normal, and she came into the reception room.

'What's a professor's wife coming around this early for? Why are you dressed up so nice this early in the morning?'

They shared a very comfortable relationship and often greeted each other with such banter.

'What do you mean early? It's almost noon. And look at you. Is this any way for the president of the Nokseong Music Academy to look?'

Only after hearing Hyeju's teasing did Miryeo realize how

she must look, and this caused her to glance at the clock on the wall. As her friend had said, it was nearing noon.

'I'm so mad I don't know what to do,' she said as she plopped down into a chair. 'Does Professor An ever do this kind of thing?'

Staring at her, Hyeju replied, 'What? Does Professor An ever do what kind of thing?'

'Go out and not come back. Stay out all night.'

'What do you mean – he didn't come home?' Hyeju could not contain her surprise. 'Such a thing is unheard of. How could a husband spend the night under another roof?'

As Hyeju added fuel to the fire, Miryeo became agitated all over again. 'It may not be something to get angry over, but I can't help it.'

'In a way, it's the natural result of your individualism* – what are you getting so angry for? No matter what he does, just think of it as him exercising his free will. You lose if you let it make you angry.'

'I guess I haven't perfected my individualism. What do you think I should do?'

'Is there a husband in the whole wide world that isn't an individualist? We can't say it's good or bad, that's just the way it is.'

'Is Professor An that way too?'

'Well, even if he doesn't stay out all night, that doesn't

---

* Here they are using the term 'individualism' (*gaeinjuui*) to indicate a modern Western mode of behaviour indicating independence from Confucian norms. For women of the time (especially women characters in Lee Hyoseok's works), it can be seen as a kind of proto-feminism. Conversely, as her husband Manhae will later allude, the notion of 'individualism' was also used to indicate Western self-interest as opposed to Asian group-orientedness. This was a concept that was promoted by public intellectuals from the late 1930s, both Japanese and Korean, in an attempt to demonstrate the spiritual weakness of America and Great Britain in the lead up to the Pacific War.

mean I know what he's really thinking. All men are probably the same when they're first married, but after seven or eight years, they lose their concern for the family. They're always sneaking around, and there's no way to know what they are thinking when they're not home. They don't allow their wives to intrude, even a little, into those thoughts. Is there any way to tell what's really in their minds? If you're lucky, the thing that he's passionate about and that occupies his mind is scholarship, but there's no way to actually open up his heart and see what's inside. Ultimately, we're all alone. Whether it's the husband or the wife, the only one we can really trust is our own self.'

'Wait a minute. Even you talk like that? The Hyeju with the sweet home that everybody envies ...?'

'I won't say that my home is not a sweet one, but I am an everlasting sceptic when it comes to the idea of married couples.'

'I don't buy the idea of married life. I'm mad now because of what has happened, but if I really make up my mind to take revenge, there's nothing stopping me. The idea of revenge is a satisfying one. There's nothing keeping me from leaving a marriage with no love in it.'

'That's enough talk of revenge. C'mon, let's go out.' Hyeju changed the topic to something she thought would interest Miryeo. 'Actually, I dressed up like this to go see a movie. *Southern Carrier** is showing. It's about time we saw a good film. Hurry and get ready. I'll wait.'

Acknowledging that this was just the thing to cheer her up, Miryeo changed clothes and put on her make-up.

---

* This is the 1937 movie adaptation of the 1929 debut novel by Antoine Marie Roger de Saint-Exupéry titled *Courrier sud* or *Southern Carrier*. De Saint-Exupéry wrote the screenplay and dialogue of the film.

*

It took more than an hour for Miryeo to get ready. In the meantime, Hyeju amused herself by listening to the phonograph and browsing through a picture book, while thinking to herself, *This is the ultimate in individualism. She doesn't care whether her husband comes home or not. The most important thing is putting on her make-up and taking an hour to do it.*

In any case, Hyeju's visit and the resulting conversation had calmed Miryeo down. As the two left the house side by side, there was no trace of worry on Miryeo's face; she looked like a relaxed, leisured housewife.

They had a late lunch at a grill,* and then went to the theatre where they watched the newly released *Southern Carrier*.

Miryeo was transfixed by the plot from beginning to end. She had never seen a movie that so captivated her. She was nearly beside herself with delight and emotion.

It was the story of the young wife of a government official who is posted to a remote region. She is not suited to the lifestyle or her surroundings, and her older husband is far from being the man she dreamt of in her youth. It turns out that a visiting pilot is a childhood friend of hers. Through him, she recovers her youthful dreams and is reinvigorated with hope. Their love is kindled on the burned-out coals of yesterday's affection, and there is nothing their passion can't overcome. She betrays her husband and her family and the two of them take flight. Even though their journey is short, it is an exceedingly happy one.

To Miryeo, the story up until that point was important and necessary. Everything after that part of the plot, however, seemed like tedious preaching.

So, there are forlorn woman over there, too.

* The original text uses the English word 'grill' transliterated into Korean (그릴), and in fact, the concept of the Western lunch grill was a familiar one in 1940s Seoul.

Thinking this to herself, she was completely taken with every scene that Jany Holt was in. Miryeo keenly felt the tragedy of a loveless family.

Watching that beautiful story for an hour and a half, Miryeo, as if she had discovered some important truth, felt a mixture of frustration and satisfaction – for some reason she felt simultaneously pleased and vexed. As she walked down the hallway with Hyeju, she asked, 'What do you think of their solution?'

'Well, I can't say that it's wrong. If you were to ask me what else they could have done, I wouldn't have an answer.'

'This is like a new discovery to me. Like the feeling of finding a new continent. I'll never forget this movie as long as I live. When I go home, I'm going to cry all by myself.'

'I wish they had ended it differently. It was like something out of a morality textbook. There's no reason to follow up that kind of ending with such misfortune.'

'Even that kind of misfortune would be worth it. During the time they were together, they experienced the strongest feelings of their lives; compared to that, such misfortune means nothing.' Miryeo had become excited, as if she were talking about her own situation.

Even after ordering tea in a teahouse, Miryeo's agitation had not subsided, and while she was lost in her own thoughts, Hyeju made a discovery that surprised them both.

On the social page of that day's newspaper was an article about the fight between Manhae and Namgu.

'What could have happened that he wouldn't come home?' Hyeju murmured, while pushing the paper toward Miryeo, whose eyes, wide with surprise, ran down the article.

'Due to his anger at the failure of the Hungcheon gold mine, Yu Manhae, president of the East Asia Trading Company, fought with the broker of the mine sale, Bak Namgu, resulting in injuries to much of his body. He left the scene with the assistance of the *kisaeng* Cheongmae. The failure of the mine, into which Yu Manhae had invested most of his holdings, is likely to result in bankruptcy ...'

Miryeo threw the paper down and immediately set out for Manhae's company.

'Where in the world is the president?'

In the face of her interrogation, neither Lee Dongyeol nor Choi Seongsu were inclined to say that he was with Cheongmae, and so both answered that they didn't know.

Fighting, Cheongmae, bankruptcy.

Miryeo had several reasons to be surprised.

It was not until late that night, after Miryeo had been anguishing over what to do for many hours, that Manhae appeared with his head wrapped in a bandage.

'You look like you've been to hell and back.'

The absurd sight that her husband presented rekindled Miryeo's anger.

His countenance, resembling a wounded soldier, head and hands covered in dirty bandages, looked more shabby than pitiful.

It was not the poor husband who'd fought with the evil broker and had lost his business that occupied her thoughts, but this base thing that had crawled in late after spending the previous night in a *kisaeng*'s house.

'How can you come home looking like that? It would be better if you hadn't come back at all.'

'You don't even know what happened.'

'What could've happened that you had to stay out all night?'

'Just slow down so I can explain.'

'Try explaining who Cheongmae is.'

Becoming flustered at being suddenly exposed, Manhae said, 'Cheongmae's not the problem. Suddenly I am faced with an extremely urgent situation.'

In spite of her husband's agitated fidgeting, Miryeo did not lose her composure.

'So, you fought with Bak Namgu over the Hungcheon

mine. What does that have to do with you not coming home?'

'That's right, it's all as the newspaper article said; the businessman Yu Manhae is ruined, he lost his fight with Bak Namgu, he's been overtaken by all his competitors, and become the laughing stock of the city. There's nothing left but a large, black pit that he's being sucked into little by little.'

'And in the midst of all that your family means nothing? Who's more important, Cheongmae or your wife?'

'She happened to be there and helped me get first aid is all. There's no Cheongmae or anyone else ...'

He sounded like a child making excuses.

'Don't try to worm you way out of this. You should be ashamed of yourself. Don't forget that trampling on the value of your family is a direct challenge to me.' Not being able to control her rage, Miryeo arose from her chair and stood trembling.

Manhae's philandering outside the home had not started with this incident. Miryeo knew only the Manhae that she saw at home. She had no way of knowing what he did when he was away from home. His world of freedom was much larger than hers, and it was no more than child's play for Manhae to deceive his naïve wife. It's not that Miryeo didn't have her suspicions, but without seeing it with her own eyes, there was nothing she could do.

The source of the rift in their relationship was this attitude of Manhae's, which, along with a loss of trust, had caused Miryeo's love to cool. Originally, it was Manhae's entreaties that had led to the marriage, and once Miryeo's feelings had started to cool, it didn't take long for them to turn to ice.

'It's your coldness that drives me outside.'

While Manhae was blaming things on his wife, she felt that the cause of all their problems lay with her husband. In fact, it was this practice of each blaming the other that had caused the current situation.

Miryeo's feelings were not necessarily the result of jealousy. Actually, her feelings for her husband were not strong enough to arouse jealousy. It wasn't jealousy and it wasn't love. It was indignity. She felt a powerful sense of affront at her husband's betrayal of his family. This was what had upset her so deeply.

'Do you think I'm satisfied with this relationship?'

In her anger, she grabbed anything that came to hand and threw it, one object hitting the mirror hanging on the wall, which shattered and crashed to the floor. This time it was her turn to challenge her husband.

'Are you going to make a big deal out of this small matter while we are facing a much bigger problem?' Manhae's voice had finally started to rise, but, as it rose, it made Miryeo angrier, not more reasonable.

'Which one is the big problem and which the trifling matter? The family is the small matter and what happens outside is the big problem. Why bother with a family that is nothing more than a small matter?'

'So what if the busy husband spent a night away from home?'

'Are you saying that that's a man's right? Who came up with that? You're supposed to be a modern man who has received a modern education. Do you have even a little of the pride of a modern man? You're just a barbarian that's been cleaned up a bit. Why don't we see if this is only a man's right? Let's see if it's a wife's lot to just sit at home waiting to die.'

As if to emphasize her point, Miryeo left the house without looking back.

The courage to do so did not come from her identity as a wife but from the belief in her equality with her husband. It was a daring, unwavering courage.

The anguish suffered by Manhae this night was far worse than that suffered by Miryeo at his hands the night before. As the night deepened, Manhae wasn't able to sleep a wink waiting for his wife to return. Just as Miryeo had spent a miserable night in her separate bedroom, so too did Manhae spend such a night in his.

'Humph. So, she's getting back at me.'

Even while giving a snort of anguish, like Miryeo the night before, he was becoming angry. When Miryeo sauntered in the next morning, his mounting anger combined with his mental exhaustion resulted in a yell escaping his lips.

'What do you think you're doing!?'

'Why? It stings, doesn't it? I slept in a hotel. Compared to me sleeping in a hotel, how do you think I felt knowing you slept at a *kisaeng*'s house? You need to learn first-hand how evil men's chauvinism is, how shameless and detestable are the husbands of this world.'

'Because I'm a cultured person you can get away with this; if I were really a barbarian, someone might get murdered.'

'What's that? Murdered, you say?' It was Miryeo's turn to get angry. 'That's precisely the kind of thing a barbarian would say. So, you still haven't gotten rid of your prejudice? Can't you get over the arrogant notion that only men are human?'

'It's too bad that you were born in Joseon. If you had been born in Europe with its advanced individualism and moral culture, you could have lived freely, but you had the misfortune to be born in this backward country where you have to endure men's abuse.'

Needling her this way was not an attempt at compromise. It came from the anger he felt boiling up.

'Is this ridicule? Why don't you try becoming like a cultured European man? Don't blame women for everything.'

'Goddamn education!' Manhae finally exploded. 'These people pretentiously learning European manners or individualism and then talking about male-female equality, or the wife's status, or such nonsense are really a sight to see. These country bumpkins running around talking about civilization or culture while reeking of soybean malt and paste ... and this nonsense about revenge. A woman taking revenge on her husband, ha! Do you think I care about this loveless marriage? Shall I put an end to it once and for all?'

'Who's the one that made this family in the first place?'

'Who made it? Why, it was you, the half-baked culture lover.'

Manhae shared one tendency with his wife. Something flew through the air and this time, instead of the mirror, it was the wall clock that was smashed. The glass broke and fell with a crash, and the pendulum stopped its swing. The two were silent.

'Right. You're exactly right. It's over. Actually, this is what I had been hoping for.' With that she went to her room and began packing her things.

A couple of hours later, with two trunks packed full, a savings account passbook, some cash, and a few other personal effects which were close to hand, she left the house. She got into a car and headed for the main street.

She had no thoughts such as, *Wow, I actually left.* In her agitated state, her whole body seething, she could only head for a familiar street.

She went back to the hotel she had stayed at the night before and got the same room. Dropping her luggage in the middle of the room and plopping down on the bed she felt as if she were in a dream.

Well, here I am.

At the same time as this reassuring thought went through her head, she felt as if something heavy were pressing down on her back.

It was a kind of anxiety, a fear one feels when one goes out on a limb.

She needed courage. She needed courage to drive away the fear and confusion. While reproving herself for her weak conviction, she concentrated entirely on the fervour of her actions.

I just did what I had to do.

There was no need for self-reflection or regret. Things had turned out the way they had for a reason. She must accept and affirm the reality in front of her. Other thoughts were useless and harmful; she put all her energy into steadying her wavering heart.

If the truth be told, there was a part of Miryeo that had been secretly hoping that this day would come. Even love spats were long a thing of the past, like a stream that had run dry. She felt that a large part of the reason for this was her husband's attitude. This was a convenient way to look at it, but, at the same time, if Miryeo looked deeper into her heart she would find that the problem was related to his basic humanity. This problem of fundamental humanity, which had not previously occurred to Miryeo, was most likely what had brought things to this conclusion. Miracles do not only occur in the home, and mystery always exists where it cannot be seen. The attempt to escape from the here and now is the expression of the mind's search for miracles and mystery. No one knew better than Miryeo that a life without mystery is not worth living; in the end, it was her husband that had brought her to this realization. It was his attitude that had pushed her into this course of action. In a sense, it was the result of a consensus, and for that reason, there was no hesitation in making the decision. If there had been mistakes and wrongs done, her husband was to blame – such thoughts helped Miryeo to strengthen her resolve.

Summoning her courage, she got up from the bed. In an attempt to become comfortable in her new temporary home, Miryeo changed her clothes and tidied herself up. After coming downstairs, she decided that she needed someone to talk to, and so found a message boy to send for Hyeju.

Hearing Miryeo's story over lunch in the restaurant, Hyeju's calm expression did not reveal any sign of surprise.

'Well, you certainly are braver and more determined than you look. So, you left home?'

In fact, her nonplussed expression was the result of her great surprise.

'Every generation has its Nora. The Nora buried in the ground would, no doubt, be happy to know that another Nora had been born.'*

'Well, I'm not the family Nora, I'm the Nora of humanity. I want to free myself from anything that restricts humanity.'

'Like the heroine in *Southern Carrier*. We saw the movie the day before yesterday, and you're imitating it today. That's incredible.'

'Things did turn out that way. But I'm a heroine without a hero.' With a bitter smile on her face, Miryeo toyed with her table knife.

'Just getting upset doesn't solve things. You have to take the proper legal steps.'

'Of course. I'm going to get a lawyer and finalize things. I'm not acting rashly, I've thought about it, and this is what I have determined is best.'

*

After Hyeju left, Miryeo, perhaps as a result of her worries, suddenly felt exhausted. Going up to her room and lying down, the accumulated fatigue of the last couple of days pulled Miryeo instantly into a several-hours-long deep sleep.

When she opened her eyes, the twilight had turned the room yellow. With the sun about to set over the western hills, the sky outside the window was a sea of gold. The uneven skyline of the city was slowly fading into the dusk, and the unmoving air gave the room a stuffy feel.

The queer yellow of that twilight was inexplicably unsettling, and so Miryeo moved to the window and lowered the shade. The room immediately descended into a deeper gloom. She found the light switch on the wall and flipped it

---

* This is a reference to the character in Ibsen's *A Doll's House*.

but turning on the artificial light before the sun had fully set gave the room an even more stifling feel. Turning the light off again, the room was darker than before.

'How annoying.'

Going to the window and raising the shade, the yellow twilight flooded into the room again. The heartbreak of that last moment when everything was sinking into darkness made it seem like the room was on fire.

Miryeo plopped down on the bed and buried her face in her blanket. Her bones ached, and her body trembled.

'Why am I so sad?'

Feeling as if she was losing control of herself, she suddenly began to cry. She kicked her feet and sobbed like a baby.

After the events that had changed her life in the house she had been living in up until this point, she was suddenly overcome in that room by a tempest-like loneliness. It wasn't the house that she had left after being betrayed that she missed. Miryeo, at that moment, had no idea what might be the cause of her desolation and emptiness.

In the end, it was nostalgia. After awaking from her sleep, she was seized with a frightening feeling of nostalgia. She longed for a something, and a someplace. Without knowing what or where, she was filled with a burning longing for something that was not the here and now.

What is it I want?

Ashamed of the way she was acting, Miryeo dried her tears and changed her clothes. Feeling restless in her room, she came down the stairs and entered the lobby. She could hear music. People were passing the time before dinner listening to music. Miryeo joined them. A duet was playing a light sonata by Mozart, but the clear, pleasant melody made her feel sad. Each strain of the music heightened her nostalgia and spoke to her dreams. To the dreamer, music is often a sad thing. But sad things are sometimes pleasurable. While listening absent-mindedly to the music and enjoying this kind of sadness, Miryeo became aware of a man who had come and sat next to her. Realizing that it was Kim Jongse, whom she had met at her home, she could not feign ignorance.

'I visited your home recently.' Jongse's earnest look of concern seemed to express what he wanted to say. 'I know why you are here at this hotel. Newspaper reporters are second only to God in knowing what's going on in the world.'

That means that people already know what has happened, Miryeo thought and, regarding Jongse with trepidation, she tried to change the subject.

'I'm afraid we've caused you needless trouble because of the Nokseong Music Academy. There has been a setback which will affect things, but, I assure you, we will provide the support that was promised.'

'I was with Manhae the night of the fight, so I think I know what the setback is. No matter how things work out between the two of you, I hope that the music academy is completed as planned as there are great expectations for its success.'

'Due to this sudden urgent matter, I haven't had time to think about the project.'

'Regarding that, there will be a chance later to talk about it. I am busy today as well. Ilma is coming back from Manchuria. I came to arrange a room ...'

'Ilma?'

'Yes. He's coming back ahead of the symphony orchestra. He's not coming alone, so I must make arrangements for the proper room.'

Jongse's words brought Miryeo to a state of tension and caused her body to flush.

9. A STAR IN THE SKY

Pak Neungbo was in a room on the second floor of the Cheongun Apartments, passing the early evening sitting absent-mindedly in a chair.

He had come home early from the hospital. The reason was that he had received a telegram saying that Ilma would arrive on the evening train. He was lost in meditation while awaiting the time to depart for the train station.

'How can someone's fate change so drastically in only a month?'

He was surprised at the change in his friend's fortunes. It was the kind of rapid, incredible change one witnesses when mixing things in a test tube.

Ilma had been the beneficiary of two amazing windfalls, had fallen in love on top of all that, and was now returning home. It was as if that luck had been waiting for him to come and get it. The Ilma that was coming back was in an entirely different situation than the Ilma that had left. The fact that this change in fortunes had happened to an especially close friend that Neungbo had spent so much time with, and that nothing noteworthy had happened to him, Jongse, or Hun in that time, made these events all the more fantastic to him.

And what has happened to me during that time?

His body had gone through its metabolic processes, and there had been the routine of daily life. That was it. Whether there had been any change in his cells during that month he didn't know, but not a thing in his life had changed. He hadn't added even one book to his bookcase, and a film of dust had accumulated on his microscope. His relationship with his love, Eunpa, continued on in a lukewarm fashion without anything that could be called progress. For some time now, Eunpa's entreaties that they set up a small home just for the two of them had changed from jest to earnestness, but as he still lacked the confidence to take such a step, there was no movement on that front. Things had come to a monotonous standstill.

And I'll be leaving this apartment.

His room was next to Ilma's. For some years now, they had come and gone between each other's rooms under the same roof like brothers, but now Ilma was bringing back someone to whom he was even closer. He would leave this apartment, and the two of them would make a happy nest of their own.

While he was lost in dreary contemplation of the sadness of such changes, Hun suddenly knocked on his door. He was going to the station with Neungbo to meet Ilma.

'You're going to lose a comrade.'

Neungbo had arisen, and he and Hun stood in front of Ilma's door. He was easily able to open it with the key to his own room.

The room looked desolate without his friend there. The dishes of a bachelor were to become the dishes of a newly married man. While running his finger over the dust on top of the desk, he thought how unbelievable the whole affair was.

'I'm losing my friend to a blonde beauty.'

'He always said he would experience a great love in his life. Is this it? Is this the result of his love of European culture?'

Hun, more than Neungbo, was able to understand and empathize with Ilma.

'If you have a ridiculous dream, you end up doing ridiculous things.'

In fact, Hun's dream was quite similar to Ilma's. He was caught in the grip of a futile nostalgia. The place he longed for was not here, but over there. It was the Western countries that had produced modern civilization. But it was Ilma, more than anyone else, who had boldly sought the object of that nostalgia and imported his dream. Hun felt that he understood Ilma's mind better than anyone.

'Ilma has actually realized his dream. He's one of a kind.'

'C'mon. Let's go see the blonde beauty.' Neungbo, looking at his wristwatch, urged Hun out the door.

After picking Ilma up at the station, taking him to the hotel, and dropping him off, Hun and Neungbo could not get the image of Nadia out of their heads. Upon seeing Nadia's beautiful face, they momentarily forgot their friend Ilma.

'Who does she look like? Which movie star?'

'Doesn't she remind you of Luchaire? Corinne Luchaire, the French actress?'

'That's it. That's who she looks like. That gentle, pure face.'

'What a catch. He really chose a good one. She doesn't have one flaw.'

'If I were Ilma, there'd be nothing further to desire. What more could he want? I don't see how he could do better. To want more is just being plain greedy.'

'In the end, it seems that Ilma's dream had something to do with Asia after all. The more I look at her face the more Asian it looks. Her eyes, her eyelashes, her nose are all Joseon. The only difference is that her skin is white, and her hair is blonde.'

'Ilma's dream is our dream. We are all dreaming of this one perfect type. Well, we've added some beauty to this city. The women that fancy themselves as beauties won't even be able to take a deep breath in front of Nadia. Those star-like eyes ...'

Those eyes that had looked directly at them without wavering at the station when Ilma had introduced them were still vivid in their minds. And in the car on the way to the hotel, even while looking with wonder at all the new sights, Nadia had not for a moment lost her dignity or grace. This was the cultivation that comes from long tradition showing through.

It was early evening, and with the idea of having dinner, they set out for the Sillagwon. Having just finished putting on her make-up, Eunpa came running out.

'Why didn't you take me to the station with you? What's the blonde beauty like?'

'After seeing Nadia, looking at you is like looking at a post. We can't see you as a woman any more.'

In spite of this taunt by Hun, Eunpa relied naturally, 'Okay, so you were that surprised by her. How did she catch that stuck-up Ilma's eye? Now I really want to see her.'

'My idea of what a woman is has changed. After seeing her, the women I see in the street all look two-dimensional.'

After hearing Neungbo's impressions, Eunpa finally became sulky.

'That's enough worship of the West. It doesn't suit the two of you. This obsequiousness to things Western is like a beggar drooling over something he can't have. It's the disgusting behaviour of a barbarian.'

Smiling affably at Eunpa's indignation, Hun replied, 'Who's worshipping the West? We're worshipping the beautiful. Beauty is an absolute thing like the sun. Whether it's Eastern or Western, there's nothing wrong with prostrating oneself before the beautiful. There's nothing shameful or disgusting about it. You give yourself away with that kind of indignation.'

'Is beauty everything?'

'I'd better think again about marrying you, Eunpa.'

'Okay, I'm sorry. We'll do it your way.' Eunpa laughed along with Neungbo, and the mood reverted back to one of jovial banter. 'If you were that surprised, does it mean that she is more beautiful than Miryeo?'

'Hmm. Miryeo and Nadia. It's just my opinion, but I think Nadia is more beautiful.'

In the midst of this, Jongse suddenly came running in. He had been making his rounds until late at the hospital.

'Who do you think was the most disappointed at the news of Nadia and Ilma?' Jongse asked this question before even catching his breath.

'Miryeo. I saw her in the hotel, but I could barely stand to see the grief on her face. She was standing off a way, watching them with a blank face.'

After seeing his friends off, Ilma went up to his room on the second floor with Nadia. Nadia seemed to have forgotten the fatigue of the trip and had a look of delight on her face. The streets were larger than she had imagined, and the fact that Ilma's friends had eagerly come to greet them had given her a very pleasant impression on this, her first trip out of Harbin.

'I had no idea the hotel would be this nice. There are very few hotels in Harbin that are decorated this splendidly.' Her satisfaction could be seen on her face and heard in her voice.

'Western civilization has made a lot of inroads here, at least outwardly.'

'I love your country. I think I can be happy here.'

'This hotel is not the only face of Joseon. There are many dirty sights outside. I just don't want you to be disappointed.'

'There are two sides to every place. If there is a bright side, there is always going to be a dark side. Why would I be disappointed?'

The bellboy opened the door and brought in several trunks. After Ilma asked about bathing and meals, the boy gave him the key and left. When they were finally alone in the large room, a powerful sense of relief flooded through him at finally having reached his destination after the long trip.

Nadia looked even lovelier in this room furnished with

items for the personal use of a couple, including a large bed, a wardrobe, and a vanity. Overcome with relief, she stood absent-mindedly for a moment.

Opening the northern-facing window, they looked down into the lowering dusk of evening at the octagonal pagoda in the courtyard below.* Nadia stood at the window, surveying the sights with a look of curiosity.

'Is that a Joseon house?'

'It's an old-fashioned one.'

'It looks spacious and refined. It seems similar to the houses in Manchuria.'

'It's the same style Asian house.'

'I think I've always understood Asia, but now I think I can appreciate its beauty.'

'Even if you can appreciate its beauty, there is no way to not be strongly disillusioned by the ugliness. And there is always more ugliness than beauty.'

'But that ugliness creates a feeling of sympathy.'

'Beyond that pagoda is a stream and beyond the stream, a slum. There are slums everywhere you go, but Joseon is one big slum.'

'Then let's live together in this slum. Beauty is not the only thing people want.' Turning and leaning her body into Ilma's, Nadia said, 'If you're going to understand me, you should know that I'm not such a shallow woman.'

She looked earnestly into Ilma's eyes. 'I didn't follow you here on a whim, and I didn't come because of your unexpected good fortune, nor because we are from the same social class. I left everything and came with you because I trust you and truly love you.'

This was the strongest expression of her feelings that Nadia

---

*   Here, Lee seems to be referring to the pagoda on the grounds of the Chosen Hotel, Seoul's most luxurious lodging establishment at the time that opened in 1914.

knew how to say, and that word 'love' was a frank confession of her innermost feelings. It was the best way she knew to say that she deeply cared for and highly respected him.

'Do you think I don't know that?'

'Then don't misunderstand me. Trust me like I trust you.'

Leaning deeper into his embrace, she waited for a demonstration of his affection. They held each other like it was the first time to do so. With the fresh feeling of being a newly-wed, Ilma thought his new wife was the most important thing in the world to him.

If the bellboy had not knocked and informed them that the bath was ready, there's no telling how long they would have remained like that.

*

Unlike a dormitory, there was no reason for the lifestyles of the guests in the hotel to follow any one pattern. Whether it was dining or resting in the lobby, the guests did these at their leisure and according to their own schedules. In this atmosphere, Miryeo's schedule was quite different from that of the other guests. She was especially careful to avoid times when other people congregated. She came to dinner earlier or later than the other guests. She came to the lobby when the likelihood of meeting other people was the slimmest. She was still concerned about rumours spreading.

After hearing about Ilma's return from Jongse the afternoon before, she had felt an inexplicable enervation, and the time she spent in her room had increased. She was in the grip of something that was the opposite of courage, call it resignation. For some reason, she felt afraid.

Meeting Ilma was a matter of no small import. When she thought of it, she felt a strange emotion, a mixture of hope and disappointment.

The noisy sound of footsteps in the hallway announced the arrival of Ilma's group. It was difficult in the spacious hotel to tell when people were arriving or leaving, but that evening Miryeo did not miss the noisy sound of voices in the hallway.

After the noise had died down, she asked the bellboy the particulars.

'There are new guests in the north corner room,' the boy explained. 'A man just came back from Manchuria with a blonde beauty. It's really incredible. I've seen international couples before, but these two are really something.'

Miryeo already had some notion about Ilma's relationship from Jongse, but hearing directly from the bellboy about the 'blonde beauty' and the 'international couple', she felt a hot, prickly sensation, and her heart began to pound.

'They sound like quite the guests.'

'We've seen a lot of foreign women here but never one like her.'

This was enough to drive Miryeo crazy. As she felt her spirit crumble, she wanted to hear no more of the bellboy's talk.

That night she stayed in her room. And she was the last one to breakfast the next morning.

She felt cowed, confining herself to her room. For two weeks, she had remained in her room like a prisoner. The emotions of the day before had taken another big bite out of her heart.

The warm afternoon sun filling the western window helped her to gather her wits. She changed her clothes and went down the stairs to get some fresh air. Passing the sunroom* and going out to the rear garden, the fresh-looking ivy climbing the rock wall caught her eye. The bright, red-coloured leaves brought the realization that autumn had quietly arrived.

Actually, on this day, Miryeo had chosen her red lined jacket over her light summer jacket. The colour of her jacket

---

* Here, Lee is no doubt referring to the famous sunroom of the Chosen Hotel; a large glass enclosed terrace where guests could sit in luxury enjoying drinks among tropical plants.

happened to match the colour of the ivy as if each was boasting of their autumn colours to the other. Both looked fresh and bright under the afternoon sun. Because Miryeo could not see herself, she could not make a judgement as to whether she or the ivy was the prettier. Looking at the colours of the ivy had awakened her to the sensation of autumn in the air.

However, there was something in the garden more beautiful than the ivy.

As she walked across the grass toward the rear entrance, a brilliant bundle of colour coming down the stone stairway caught her eye. It was also the colour of the ivy. This figure in a bright red dress was of much more interest to Miryeo than the ivy. Of course, she knew who this unusual couple was.

It was Ilma and Nadia. The two of them were enjoying an afternoon walk in the garden.

Miryeo hesitated, but, as the two had already seen her, she couldn't really beat a cowardly retreat, and while she stood staring blankly, they came toward her.

Nadia as well had seen Miryeo from a distance and was also aware of the fresh feeling of autumn. The beautiful colour of the summer jacket, which was the same as that of the ivy, had caught her attention, and she turned to Ilma. 'It's true what you said about Joseon women dressing beautifully.'

She had recalled that Ilma had once told her about the beauty of the white clothes and ornamented shoes worn in Joseon.

'White clothes have their own beauty, but the colourful clothing worn in spring and autumn are also beautiful. It would have looked even better if she had worn the ornamented shoes with that long skirt.'

'I want to dress like that once. The short skirt and shoes look like Western dress, like a two-piece.'

Forgetting how attractive her own appearance was, Nadia continued to admire Miryeo's stylishness while walking lightly across the dried grass.

At the same time, Miryeo was totally absorbed in her appraisal of Nadia. She was mesmerized by her red dress and golden hair.

The only person at that moment who could judge the beauty of both women was Ilma. Neither Miryeo nor Nadia could see themselves, but Ilma could view them both.

After leaving Harbin, Nadia looked lovelier today than Ilma had ever seen her, but the sudden appearance of Miryeo clad in Joseon dress surprised him. While staring at her, he and Nadia had, without thinking of their manners, come quite near to her.

Pretending not to look while doing so; pretending not to be surprised when one is; feigning ignorance; whether these are the acts of a cultured person or not, they are the cold-hearted habits of the modern man. However, when one is truly surprised, one loses the wherewithal to act aloof. This was the case with Ilma's and Nadia's eyes as they looked upon Miryeo. Wavering slightly, Miryeo affected a similar air of nonchalance, and as she pretended not to notice the two, they had the opportunity to observe her as they passed.

They were truly a happy couple. The two looked as proud as peacocks. While she was standing in uncertainty, not being able to turn and look at them and feeling dreary at the contrast they made with her own lonely countenance, Ilma turned back around and spoke to her.

'Excuse me, but aren't you Nam Miryeo?'

At the sound of his voice Miryeo turned and, for the first time, looked directly at him.

'Ah, it is you.' There seemed to be a deep, sentimental reverberation in his voice. Eight years had piled one on top of the other, and the sentiments, both cherished and forgotten in the layers of those years, seemed to be heard in that voice as if alive again.

For Miryeo as well, the feelings of eight years ago seemed to suddenly leap over that chasm of time to this moment, but her desolateness and sadness outweighed any renewed emotions or feelings of joy. The feelings of eight years ago were now meaningless in front of this happy couple. When she thought of how she had finally freed herself from the entanglements of those eight years, she realized the grave and heartless consequences that time had exacted. In a moment, hope and joy were extinguished by the sadness of disillusionment.

After introducing Nadia to Miryeo, the two spent some time speaking to each other in friendly tones.

Was she being introduced as the wife of a friend, or as a sponsor for the Joseon performance of the Harbin Symphony Orchestra? Ilma translated the smiling Nadia's words.

'Nadia is very happy to meet you and is thankful for your support for the invitation of the symphony orchestra.'

But Nadia's smile of gratitude, far from being welcome, tormented Miryeo. The joy of the world was not hers to have. Seeing happiness in the faces of other people only reminded her of her own loneliness.

*

After returning to her room from her walk in the garden, Miryeo was lost in deep thought until dinnertime.

She had never thought she would meet Ilma under such circumstances. He was an unchanging object of her dreams, and the home her heart longed for.

The night, a few days ago, that she'd cried in the twilight of that room in the grip of a heartbreaking nostalgia, the reason had been a longing for something she couldn't clearly identify. While Miryeo may not have been fully aware that Ilma was the object of her longing, she did feel the sadness of her dream and the loneliness of the path she had taken. After having met Ilma, she knew that the path was blocked, and the dream was over. Her heart was torn by an inconsolable despair and loneliness.

The time did not seem to pass so she arose, and in order to clear her mind, she washed and sat in front of her wardrobe. At that moment, the bellboy knocked and entered.

'I've been sent by the corner room,' he said, proffering an envelope containing a letter. 'I believe they have invited you to dinner.'

Hearing the boy's pronouncement, Miryeo opened the envelope, which contained a note from Ilma. She read a few lines.

Nadia would like to invite you to a banquet this evening. It would be our honour if you would join us.

'They asked me to bring back an answer. There is no need to write a note. I'll convey your message directly.'

The bellboy's urging allowed her no chance to read further or even think about whether she should accept or not; she had no choice but to give her assent then and there. In fact, there was no reason to refuse.

After the bellboy had left, she wondered if giving such a prompt reply might not be seen as unpolished. However, she quickly changed her mind and decided that, no matter what Ilma's circumstances might be, there was no reason to avoid him.

By special instruction, the banquet table set for the three of them was much larger than normal. Miryeo sat on one side of the table while Ilma and Nadia sat across from her, greeting the guest of honour with a bright smile.

'I just met you today and this is my first banquet after arriving in Joseon. Please don't think of this as boasting. After meeting you in the garden today, I hoped we could become friends.'

Miryeo was confused as to whether these were Nadia's words or Ilma's. In the same way, she had no way to know if tonight's banquet was Nadia's idea or Ilma's.

'I feel that I should learn about the country I now live in. I'll need a good friend to help me, so I was very happy to meet you today. Having seen how lovely and dignified you are, I hope we can enjoy a long friendship.'

After conveying Nadia's words, Ilma added, 'Become her friend and teach her.'

As she did not want to ask Ilma to interpret for her, she did her best in the English she could remember.

'I'm very fortunate to have met you this way. I'll do my best to become a good friend to you.'

Encouraged by Miryeo's short answer, Nadia also switched to English.

'I have a lot of plans. First, I must learn the Joseon language. It's the language of the place I love. Second, I want to know about Joseon clothes. I really want to wear them.'

'I'll show you everything I know.'

Ilma looked with wonder at the two of them conversing.

*

When Nadia had told Miryeo that there was a dance in the hall that very night and invited her to join them, Miryeo had readily accepted; however, when she got back to her room she began to regret her decision.

She had accepted the invitation after being moved by the totally unaffected kindness of the couple, but from the banquet on she hadn't been completely comfortable. What's more, she wondered how she could show up at a dance and mingle with those couples in her single, lonely state.

She felt embarrassed by the kindness showed her by Nadia. She could not say that she herself was as unselfish and innocent as Nadia. Having no knowledge of the subtle relationship between Miryeo and Ilma, Nadia's heart was like a pure, white sheet of paper. But Miryeo's heart, due to the feelings she held for Ilma, which could not be spoken, was complicated and tormented. While Ilma and Nadia had their own level of understanding, there was also an indistinct something that passed between her and Ilma. The couple had no idea that, next to Nadia, she felt ashamed and guilty. While harbouring these complicated feelings, she decided that, in her present situation, sitting naturally with this couple would not be proper manners.

But she had already agreed to go. There was a part of her that wanted to lean for support on the happy Nadia's subtle praises, and so she changed her clothes to go out. Fortunately, not all the people there would be couples. As there would be other singles there as well, Miryeo wouldn't be particularly uncomfortable sitting with Ilma and Nadia.

Was it an expression of goodwill? Friendship? As soon as the music started, Nadia asked Miryeo for the first dance. Not knowing what was going on, Miryeo was led to the floor wondering if women really danced with each other. The other people watched the two in fascination. Feeling self-conscious at being the centre of attention of the crowd, nevertheless she was grateful for Nadia's gesture and so was able to enjoy that strange dance.

When the dance ended, Ilma applauded. Next was the couples' dance. After a few dances, a single foreign man asked Nadia to dance and, when she accepted, Ilma took the opportunity to dance with Miryeo.

While turning around the dance floor holding on to Ilma, Miryeo was suddenly struck with a notion. It seemed as if dance had been invented so that two people could stand holding each other. If not for dance, how could two people so easily have this kind of contact?

'I don't know whose idea this evening was, the banquet and this dance, but I feel terribly sorry.'

'It was all Nadia's idea. She has no ulterior motives, it's all because she likes you.'

'That makes me feel even sorrier.' Seized with a frightening thought, Miryeo danced them into a quiet corner. 'This isn't the right place to tell you, we should talk somewhere quiet, but ... well, everything has changed.'

'You're talking about the reason that you're staying in this hotel.'

'How did you know?'

'I heard about it from Jongse. I heard about Manhae's failure and what happened between the two of you.'

'At this point it's hard to say whether it was my fault or Manhae's. I left because I couldn't stand to stay any longer, but now everything I see increases my agony.'

Realizing that this was a veiled reference to them, Ilma said, 'It's too late. Too much has changed now to fix all the things that have gone wrong.'

'People who have already found their places can't understand how desolate the latecomer feels. Their stares, which seem to mock you, make you feel strange, ashamed ...' She was unable to finish her words as her heart sank, and the strength left her body.

'Well, we can't blame the world for the way things are.'

The calm, somewhat indifferent tone of Ilma's words was frustrating. These were the satisfied thoughts of someone whose belly was full, not the agonized appeal of someone in torment. There was already a large gulf between their two hearts.

'Is the world so blameless while I'm suffering like this and you're so happy?'

'Of course I'm not talking about, or intending to talk about, my happiness.'

'You're a star. A star in the sky. The more I look the farther you recede until you are just a speck in the heavens. I can stretch out my arms, but you're already out of reach.'

Miryeo was suddenly taken with a distressing thought that caused her to fall silent.

What was her relationship with Ilma that she could torment him with such emotional appeals? The legal procedures had not even been finalized; she was still another man's wife. It was not right, while being legally married, to confess her heart to Ilma like this. It was shameless of her to subject him to such uncomfortable talk. Reconsidering her actions, she suddenly felt that even dancing with him like this was dangerous.

When the music ended, and she once again took her seat, she felt as if she had been placed inside a cloud of misery. She was more comfortable observing the other people dance. Watching the beautiful couple Ilma and Nadia; they looked like something from a dream, and at the same time, she felt that star receding farther into the sky. It was a shame to only be able to watch, and now her sense of fear was dissipating.

Pleading fatigue, Miryeo left the dance hall and went back to her room.

She tried to not to think of the couple, but their image stubbornly refused to leave her mind. It was like seeing a star fall right in front of her eyes only to suddenly disappear again into the heavens, like having something that was almost within her reach and yet so far away that it couldn't be grasped. When she thought that the best she could do would be to look up at that star for the rest of her life, a dark cloud seemed to drop over her vision.

Have I made the wrong decision?

When she thought of the actions she had taken, those actions and today's situation were completely different things. She had not acted based on any clear calculations, she had just acted, but the results were not what she had wanted or expected. It was not that hope and happiness would result from her actions. She had anticipated that her decision would bring loneliness and sadness; even so, she did not regret her actions. However, at the same time, she was enveloped by a vague anxiety.

The next afternoon, feeling distressed and deciding to go out for a walk, she met Jongse in the hallway, who had come to see Ilma, and heard some quite unexpected news from him.

He spoke in an earnest voice as if he had been waiting to convey this news to her.

'Have you heard about Manhae?' he asked in a low tone.

'Why? Has he been in another knife fight?'

'He's taken off. He's run off to Shanghai with his lover.'

'What? To Shanghai with his lover ...?' In spite of her attempt to act calm, she couldn't help but be surprised at this news. 'What do you mean he's run off with his lover?'

'He's run off with Cheongmae. You know, Cheongmae the *kisaeng*. I had an idea something like that might happen, but I didn't think he would pick up and completely disappear so quickly. Actually, since I was somewhat involved with Cheongmae, this is a very awkward situation. There's nothing more embarrassing that having my name mentioned in connection with this.'

Miryeo went back to the house she had so hurriedly departed. The dark house was just as she'd left it. When she arrived, the housekeeper rushed out, overcome with relief, and took Miryeo's hands in hers. The desolateness of the empty house had almost overcome her.

'Please don't leave again.'

In the dark hallway, the housekeeper's face was contorted as if she was about to cry.

10. THE WILL OF THE SEASON

Autumn had enveloped the streets and seeped into everyday life.

The colours were beautiful, the outfits of the women were eye-catching, and a fresh fragrance filled the air in front of the fruit stalls.

The colours and fragrances of the season brought people to a higher state of tension, and a new will could be felt in the luxuriance of life. It was as if autumn was the season of volition. The volition of exuberant life overflowed in every cell.

The leaves turning colour on the branches of a tree in the garden did not signify decay, rather it was as if they had been invigorated by life.

In that clear, bright autumn morning, Hun felt the resilience and soaring energy of the season.

He was in the office of the president of Bando Studios. He was sitting across from Kim Myeongdo, who had just made an ardent request of him. As he stared out the window at the branches of the trees in the garden, he felt that mysterious power surging up.

The request was for a movie script. In order to make the request, Myeongdo had sent someone to invite Hun to come.

'We would be greatly honoured if you would write a script for us.'

Hun was not uninterested in Myeongdo's earnest proposal.

'Of course, you'll be compensated to your satisfaction.'

Myeongdo, who had started the film company as something of a hobby, was president in name, but he practically ran the company single-handedly, taking care of everything from planning to finance. Negotiating the terms of a script and its compensation, needless to say, was entirely up to him.

'Compensation is not the problem ...'

'Then there's no reason to refuse.'

'I don't know if I can come up with anything in such a short period of time.'

'It's true we are pressed for time as we want to finish filming before autumn is over, but I'm hoping you can come up with something special.'

Myeongdo took Hun's hesitation to mean he was close to agreeing and hurried to conclude things. 'I have confidence that you can finish in two weeks.'

Standing up without waiting for an answer, he dragged Hun outside.

Even though the movie company was used only for administrative matters and not as a film set, the entire building was used as a boarding house, and the sight of actors, actresses, and staff bustling about through it gave it a gaudy atmosphere. Hun could not deny that the special atmosphere of the movie company was stimulating.

Coming out to the street, Myeongdo led Hun toward a grill.

As the luncheon started, Myeongdo said, 'There's a reason we're in a rush on this particular film.'

He spoke as if he were about to reveal a great secret. 'It was the request of the actress Danyeong, whom you know well, that you write the script. It was such an earnest request that I didn't know how to turn it down ...'

'It was Danyeong's request?'

This was surprising news that left a strong impression on Hun.

'Of course, since Danyeong is appearing in the movie, her part should be written to suit her.'

'It was Danyeong's request?' While repeating his question, the image of Danyeong flashed through Hun's mind.

'Truth be told, for the past few years, I have had to deal with all manner of frustrations due to Danyeong. I've never seen a woman so difficult to manage.'

It was odd that this appeal should come through Myeongdo, but then, Hun was not unaware of their relationship. It was just that, when it came to Danyeong, Hun had his own emotional entanglements.

Thorns on a sweetbrier, that's what Danyeong was like. She was like a passionate red flower surrounded by thorns so that people could only look at her with desire but dared not touch. However, there is one thing the sweetbrier blooming on the hill desires: the coral of the sea. Day and night, the sweetbrier, looking down on the blue sea, dreams of the red coral, but the distance from the hill to the sea is too far. Smelling the tide on the breezes blowing up from the beach, the sweetbrier is unbelievably sad. The flower can smell the coral on the breeze but cannot go down to the sea and meet it. Staring endlessly at the coral, the sweetbrier is constantly forlorn. There are always many welcome swallowtails flying about, but to the sweetbrier, locked in its dream of the coral, nothing else matters. Preparing its thorns, it has been busy keeping people at bay. No one can touch it. All they can do is stare longingly at that ripe flower.

Myeongdo was one of the many men around Danyeong who cursed those thorns, but only Danyeong and Hun knew that Hun was also one of those men. It was a decadent flower, but it was the appeal of that decadence that pulled Hun to it.

'That flower is evil.'

Even while hearing such criticism from his friends, it was precisely because this flower was evil that he could not stop his feelings from growing. The attraction to the beauty of evil is a surreptitious kind of affection that persists through the ages.

Hun also knew that Danyeong was infatuated with Ilma.

He had once said to Ilma, 'I don't know what kind of fantastic love it is that you want to experience once in your life, but what is it about Danyeong that doesn't qualify? It may be that she is too red a flower, but doesn't that also make her right for that kind of fantastic love?'

These weren't words of concern or advice.

'Love is matter of taste. Just because someone matches your taste doesn't mean they match mine. If she is that much to your liking, why don't you do something about it?'

Responding gloomily to Ilma's reply, Hun said, 'It's not just a matter of my taste, Danyeong has her own tastes as well.'

Ilma had brought back his fantastic love from Manchuria in the form of Nadia. Hun was well aware of how much this had agitated Danyeong's feelings. While he felt pity for what her heart was going through, this didn't reduce his affections for her one bit. Hearing of Danyeong's request through Myeongdo today, Hun could barely suppress his feelings.

Just as they were finishing lunch, Hun saw Danyeong appear at the entrance of the grill.

Danyeong had been at the movie company while Hun and Myeongdo were in there talking. Sometime after Hun and Myeongdo had left, Danyeong and some of the other actors had followed them. It was obvious that she had come to find out the results of the meeting.

Myeongdo called Danyeong over. They hadn't come for

lunch, and so, when Hun and Myeongdo left the grill, she followed Hun out.

'There's something I've been wanting to talk to you about.'

The three walked together.

'President Kim, would you leave us alone for a bit. I have a request to make.'

Myeongdo stood staring blankly as Hun and Danyeong walked off together.

Thinking that Danyeong's dispirited appearance must be due to the autumn season, at the same time he was also aware of the hint of a shadow hanging over his heart. Autumn is not only the season of will but also the season of sentiment. While feeling the strong will of life, Hun was also taken with a surge of sentiment.

Upon entering a quiet backstreet, Danyeong pulled a pack of cigarettes from her purse. Hun watched her in fascination as she lit her cigarette with a practiced hand.

'I'm smoking more than I used to these days,' Danyeong said, smiling as she exhaled a trail of smoke.

'It may be that women are more courageous than men; I've been trying to learn how to smoke for ten years, and I still can't do it right,' Hun confessed. 'I'm not able to learn to smoke because I'm afraid of it. I'm afraid of what would happen if I persisted in trying. In that sense, you're more tenacious than me.'

'At first it tasted poisonous and bitter, but gradually the taste became smoother until I came to like it. It seems people are even able to develop a taste for poison.'

'That's a poison I'll never develop a taste for.'

As if to say, 'watch this', Danyeong exhaled a long tendril of smoke as she spoke.

'When I'm angry, cigarettes are the only thing I want. It's not like I smoke them because I like the taste. I try to smoke away the time. I smoke to try to calm my feelings.'

'The reason you smoke isn't that simple. "The reason

Danyeong smokes." This could be the name of an essay on autumn.'

'Since I've been back from Manchuria, I smoke five packs a day. It's as if I'm trying to hide in the smoke.'

'Hide yourself in the smoke ... maybe I should try smoking again.'

Throwing away a half-smoked cigarette, Danyeong pulled out a fresh one and lit it. This was how she could smoke five packs a day, smoking only half a cigarette before throwing it away and lighting up a new one, and this without a break.

'If there were just one thing left in the world that you wanted, what would you do?'

Danyeong's mysterious tone of voice puzzled Hun.

'That which is on an unreachable peak must remain as a dream in the heart.'

'Can one be satisfied with just a dream?'

'Whether one can be satisfied or not isn't the problem; the problem is that there's nothing left but the dream.'

'If our dreams were enough, how easy life would be. The problem is that human nature makes us miserable when we cannot possess, touch, and caress the object of our desire.'

'But when we can't touch and caress that object, we can dream about it.' Changing his tone, Hun said, 'For instance, when the thing we want is love, but it's a one-sided love, dreaming brings us an incredible freedom. Let's say I was in love with you ...'

Being put at ease by Hun's joke, Danyeong finally opened up. 'I'm thinking about what the best course of action with Ilma would be.'

When he heard Ilma's name, he could finally able to discern the nature of the shadow clouding his heart.

'Dreams or sense, these things are of no use to me. Like when a tiger catches a rabbit, it has to catch it by the throat, claw it, and drink its blood until it's satisfied. Uninhibited desire is a natural thing.'

'Whether you could be satisfied or not I don't know; the question is whether you could become that kind of pretty tigress.'

'I have a request to make to you. Please help me meet Ilma one last time.'

'That's your request?'

'He says he won't meet me. I have no choice but to ask you for help.'

'Are you saying that if you meet him you want to bite and claw him? Are you asking me to deliver my friend to you like a helpless rabbit?'

'If you do, I'll grant any request you make of me. No matter what it is.'

'You want me to be Judas, but I can't be bought for thirty pieces of silver.'

'If you don't want silver, I'll give you something else. Anyway, life isn't that long, and I'd like to do the right thing. Wanting to meet Ilma one last time isn't an unreasonable desire.'

Watching her pour her heart out like this, Hun couldn't help but view Danyeong with pity. It was natural for Hun to feel sympathy for Danyeong as the loser in the contest with Ilma. If meeting Ilma was so important to Danyeong, even though he was Hun's friend, there wouldn't be any real harm in assenting to Danyeong's request. He did not think it was too much to ask of Ilma to give a few hours of his time in order to help a woman in need.

Hun agreed to Danyeong's entreaty and the two of them made their secret pact regarding Ilma then and there.

'Then I'll bring Ilma this evening.'

'I have confidence in you.'

'Why does it feel like we are plotting something? It's giving me the jitters. Fortunately, Ilma trusts me.'

After parting from Hun, Danyeong spent the rest of the day immersed in thoughts that caused her an almost uncontrollable excitement.

While Hun's careless use of the word 'plot' ate into her heart, it also caused a strong emotional response. In fact, unbeknownst to Hun, Danyeong was harbouring a plot of her own deep inside that she couldn't share with anyone. While trembling just at the thought of that plot, she coolly prepared herself for it.

This is the only way left to me, she thought.

It was an audacious plan. However, in a way it was a natural consequence of her decision to throw away everything.

There's nothing I wouldn't do for it ... she said to herself.

Danyeong had never been ashamed of the fact that she was a slave to her passions. She felt that it was her female nature to want to let her passion have free reign, blossoming as long as possible like the last flower of the season giving forth brilliant petals before disappearing.

She was not able to merely dream about the object of her love when it was right in front of her. She couldn't bear to not to have it, caress it, pluck at it – this aspect of Danyeong's nature would never change.

Arriving early at the small restaurant that she and Hun had agreed on, she had food brought to the room and gave the waiter the necessary instructions. As she sat looking at her watch and entertaining some doubts, Hun appeared. Sure enough, Ilma was with him. Danyeong arose in excitement and stood in front of the two.

Ilma looked surprised. Realizing what had happened, he looked with annoyance at Hun. 'What is this? You said we were coming here to talk about a novel or a script or something.'

'If I'm here you can't talk about your novel? Am I a thorn in your side?' Danyeong then softened her tone. 'I haven't seen you since you returned from Manchuria, so I thought I would treat you to dinner. Don't be upset. Even if you are thinking of your wife, you can sit down. Life is so short, you don't have to always be splitting hairs.'

'Do you know how hard it was to get him out? When he was single he was free as a bird, but now that he's married, he practically a prisoner.'

Hun's banter on the heels of Danyeong's comment had the effect of softening Ilma's face, and he had no choice but to sit down.

Turning from Hun's heckling, Ilma said to Danyeong, 'Nadia is a lot of woman to handle, especially now that we're newly-weds.'

Danyeong replied, 'If marriage means being stuck to each other twenty-four hours a day, it's no different than being in prison or being a slave.'

'Did you bring me here to abuse me like this?'

Danyeong's attempt to appease Ilma sounded more like making sport of him. 'I'm just jealous at seeing such a loving couple. Nadia knows me so there's no need to worry. If she asks what's going on, I'll explain it to all to her.'

'Are the two of you having fun? What am I doing here anyway?'

Seeing Ilma becoming angry and fearing he might leave, Danyeong attempted to soothe him. 'I received such nice treatment in Manchuria that I thought I would return the courtesy. And I want to hear about your trip as well.'

'Did you return without travelling in Manchuria?'

'Shall I tell you about how I was disgraced? Do you remember what happened at the cabaret and the hotel? While slandering other people you insist that your life is protected by special privilege.'

'Who slandered whom? You broke into my room, and now you say it was you who were slandered?'

'Just wait and see if I don't have my revenge. A savage that thinks he can disregard and step all over a woman's heart sooner or later will get what's coming to him.'

'Ohh, I'm scared. You're going have your revenge? Go ahead and try.'

'Don't be so cocksure of yourself. You never know what can happen.'

'I think I will be cocksure of myself. Let's see what this revenge is that you have planned.'

'Tomorrow morning your regret will be plain for everyone to see. They'll all see you crying like a baby.'

Of course, Danyeong was the only one who knew the meaning of her words. This was a secret buried deep in her heart.

Relaxing somewhat at what they took to be Danyeong's joking, the initially awkward atmosphere gradually changed to one of enjoyment.

'This drink tastes bitter.'

While accepting every glass of the unusually bitter drink that Danyeong offered him, Ilma's reticence gradually evaporated.

'Booze is a bitter thing, but a chivalrous man should surrender to the drink so that I can have my revenge.'

At Danyeong's cajoling, Ilma drank what he was offered.

And Hun was right behind him.

Who would have known that that very booze was the instrument of Danyeong's revenge? The unusually bitter drink contained a secret that night.

Both Ilma and Hun, who were normally pretty good drinkers, were dead drunk after only half the amount of alcohol it normally took to render them inebriated. It seemed as if it wasn't the alcohol itself that had caused this but something else. Suddenly the two collapsed in a deep, drunken sleep.

While being delighted at the result of her work, Danyeong was also somewhat frightened. Her voice, when she called the waiter and gave him separate instructions in how to deal with the two, trembled slightly.

*

The next morning, Ilma awoke in Danyeong's apartment.

He was greatly surprised when, awaking at dawn, he found himself in Danyeong's room. The shock of the happenings of the night before hit him like a bolt of lightning, causing him to shiver.

He was in Danyeong's bed under the same blanket with her. Pushing her away and jumping up, he saw that it was already light outside. Sunlight shone through the window. He became fully aware of the indelible stain etched onto his body and soul from the events of the night before. While feeling a sudden tension run through his enervated body and spirit, something sharp seemed to be piercing his spine.

'What the hell happened last night?'

Danyeong was awake as well. Her eyes were shut, but her senses were sharp as she squirmed lightly in the bed. She had woken earlier and, lost in thought and unable to sleep, had tossed back and forth.

Seeing that Ilma was up, she said, 'Are you awake?'

Sitting up as well and dropping her feet over the side of the bed, the realization of Ilma's body right next to hers caused a sudden surge of desire.

Leaning toward him, she tried to plant her hot lips on his neck.

'Ah! You she-devil!' he cried, and his shove almost sent Danyeong onto the floor.

'Don't be so prudish. You're not that innocent, you know.'

Standing in front of him, Danyeong's short chemise* caused him to feel a renewed sense of embarrassment, and he could not look directly at her. Realizing how he himself looked caused him to blush, and pulling his bedclothes around him, he jumped down from the bed.

'What did you do to me last night, you fiend?'

---

* The word used here was the transliterated English for chemise (슈미스).

He wanted to rush at Danyeong and give her a few knocks on the head, but, figuring that what was done was done, he quickly set about gathering up his underclothes and suit, which were strewn over the floor.

'You were the one who told me to go ahead and take revenge, and now you protest in a most unchivalrous manner. Do you think that will undo what has been done?'

'You call this revenge? This isn't revenge, it's wickedness, pure evil.'

'Anyway, if my anger is satisfied, it's revenge. It doesn't take a duel with swords or something like that.'

'If I were a policeman, you'd be in handcuffs right now. Knocking me out with doctored booze and then having your way with me, this is outrageous.'

'Go ahead and cuff me or whatever. Those are big words from a lamb that was sacrificed on my altar. You don't know how lucky you are. Be happy that my plan wasn't the same as Salome's and that your fate wasn't that of John the Baptist's. Do you think I wouldn't cut your head off?'

Shocked by the venom in her voice, Ilma, without replying, quickly dressed. He was well aware of the reckless, Salome-like nature of Danyeong's passion.

'Don't be so surprised. This might have been my plan, but what happened in bed was all your idea.'

At this unexpected comment, Ilma's hands suddenly began to shake and his face to burn.

'Wh–what? You make sport of a person and then ...'

'I said don't be so surprised. Between men and women, only the creator can tell who makes sport of whom. Did Adam tempt Eve, or did Eve tempt Adam? Since we can't confirm the myth, there's no way to know.'

'You deceive a person, and now you want to take it back?'

Before he knew it, Ilma's hand flashed out and struck Danyeong's cheek. Was she lying or telling the truth? If she was telling the truth ... The thought of that awful possibility made him shiver.

'There's no reason to get so upset. Ultimately, you're a man, and I found out exactly what men want through you. Instead of getting flustered, why don't we consider each other's feelings for a moment? Human nature and instinct are not such noble and divine things, and virtue is nothing more than an attitude, a posture. Your innocence as well is nothing more than a kind of posture. You have no right to act so grand while insulting others.'

With Danyeong's every word cutting him to the quick, Ilma was at a loss for a reply. What's more, he could not strike her again. His anger was no longer directed at Danyeong alone.

'How can you be expected to know what you do when you're drunk? You can't say anything about my behaviour after drugging me senseless.' His voice was small and weak as if his mouth were covered with something.

'I don't know if you were senseless or not, I'm saying that what happened was the result of your real nature. What makes me happy is the discovery that because of that nature all people are the same; there are no true saints or gentlemen; we are all the same with one nose and two eyes, ordinary husbands and wives. This was more important, more satisfying than discovering a new continent. I no longer fear anything, and I now no longer need to idolize you. That doesn't mean I despise you; in fact, I still love you. I just hate it when you put on airs.'

After dressing, Ilma stood ill at ease, lighting a cigarette he didn't really want, as every word Danyeong spoke sunk home.

'Are you saying we're both responsible? After committing the act, you don't want to be the only evil one so you're doing everything you can to rope me into some of the blame.'

'What are you talking about blame for? If some blame

comes to me, what do think will happen to you? Shall we announce it to the world and see who hides? That idea doesn't frighten me in the least. Talk about the pot calling the kettle black. While you are calling me a devil and the like, you're still acting the virtuous hero.'

Seeing no profit in confrontation, Ilma put out his cigarette and stood to leave. 'No matter how sweet one might be on the inside, a devil's a devil. And you're a she-devil. Do you think this feels any different to me than spending a night in a brothel?'

There was nothing he could have said that would have insulted Danyeong more. In an instant, her eyes flamed, and her lips turned blue.

'What? Like spending the night in a brothel? You bastard.'

The pack of cigarettes that Danyeong flung at Ilma hit him in the face.

'This isn't over yet. You just wait. See if you don't come to me on your hands and knees. With the secret I hold in my hands, I can smash your happy marriage to pieces. Don't make me any angrier.'

It wasn't an empty threat. In truth, there was no way of telling what Danyeong's vehemence would drive her to do. Ilma was taken aback and beads of sweat broke out on his forehead.

'Start thinking about what you're going to say to Nadia. "I suddenly had to go to the countryside on some business, and there was no way to send a telegram", or some such lie. Nadia's not going to fall for that.'

Without a word in reply, Ilma hung his head and left the room. He looked like a child who had just received a scolding. In reality, worried that he had stirred up a hornet's nest, he was as meek as a lamb.

Walking the morning street, Ilma couldn't get rid of the bitter taste in his mouth. He had made the comment to Danyeong about spending the night in a brothel, but, being somewhat familiar with brothels, he knew that his mood was very different than the ordinary, unexcited feeling one has after such an experience.

He was plagued by a complicated feeling that would not leave him. It was a mixture of fear and shame.

He felt like a child that had been caught stealing fruit from the pantry. He was scared and ashamed, but he also felt a kind of secret excitement.

He was afraid and ashamed of that excitement. That shame, of which he could tell no one, was an unpleasant thing. And that bitter taste in his mouth was not from the cigarettes. When he asked himself the question 'Who is more at fault?', his heart was heavy.

If Danyeong had trodden on his freedom, hadn't he done the same thing to her? It didn't matter who had tempted whom in the beginning, they had both committed the same act. Just as there was no reason for Danyeong to feel intimidated by Ilma, he had no right to berate and browbeat her. Recalling every word that Danyeong had spewed forth, Ilma could not raise his head in good conscience. He was a co-conspirator, an accomplice in the plot; he could not put all the blame on Danyeong.

Actually, she's rather pathetic.

So thinking, he felt a pang of pity for Danyeong at the thought that she would go so far to get what she wanted. He felt sympathy rather than dislike for her malicious intent. The passion of an imploring woman was, to a man, something to be appreciated like scenery. And scenery was always comforting.

However, this kind of sympathy only increased Ilma's agony. What good was it going to do to feel sympathy for her? Sympathy brought sympathy and misdeed bred misdeed. There was no way to erase a misdeed with sympathy. The agony he felt arising from his deed was not due to Danyeong as much as it was due to Nadia. Even if he could resolve his feelings regarding Nadia, he didn't know how to deal with the thing that had happened and that couldn't be taken back. A dark cloud appeared in front of his eyes, and his legs felt weak.

When he reached the hotel, the first thing he did was wash, and when he had calmed down, he went into the bedroom. Seeing Nadia jump up from the bed, he could find nothing to say.

Nadia hadn't slept a wink all night. Her eyes were red, and her face seemed to have become thin overnight. She, as well, could find no words.

'On my way out of the hotel, I suddenly had to go to the countryside on urgent business.'

The lie made him feel terrible. 'I want to build a house there next year, and the broker said that there was a good opportunity yesterday that I shouldn't miss so I had to leave suddenly.'

One lie led to another. Even while spewing them out, Ilma was surprised at his ability to do so. At the same time, he was keenly aware that it was Danyeong who had revealed the wisdom of lying.

'It was the countryside, and there was no way to send a telegram in the middle of the night. I knew you'd be worried, but I had no choice.'

There were times when it was necessary to lie. If not for lying, there would have been no other way to deal with the situation.

'Is the land more important than I am?'

'Don't be angry. It's land to build a house for the two of us.'

He moved to hug Nadia and, while she didn't resist, that didn't completely resolve the situation. Feeling anew how big the problem was that he had created, Ilma's body trembled.

Ilma wasn't the only one suffering. As the extent of what she had done gradually dawned on Danyeong, her heart grew heavier. At the time, it had been gratifying to give vent to her spleen in front of Ilma, but when she thought about it now, it wasn't pleasant at all, and she was filled with sad thoughts and a feeling of melancholy.

She had suddenly gotten what she wanted. It was the only way she could gain control over him. But what had she really gained from it? How much satisfaction had she really received from that shallow joy? She had only momentarily possessed his body but had let his soul slip through her fingers, and the satisfaction had been fleeting. Would it not have been better to gain his soul rather than his body? After possessing his body, the realization of the uselessness and insignificance of it left her with a feeling of sorrow.

Despite her preparedness to carry out her plan, the fact that she had upset the order and that one evil had begotten another tormented her heart. Her desire to get back at Ilma had been replaced with a feeling of shame. She didn't think she could face him again. It wasn't just Ilma; she felt a sense of shame regarding the whole world. She couldn't walk around with her head up.

Does the devil ever regret what he's done?

While ridiculing herself, she tried to pull herself together, but the more she reflected, the more tormented she felt.

She spent the entire day in her apartment besieged by all manner of thoughts, but no solution presented itself to her floundering heart. She had no strength to go out the next day.

She spent the whole day in her bedclothes, drinking tea, and listening to records. The guest who came to see her that evening was Hun.

'Did you catch malaria? Staying in your room all day ...'

The way she looked, she very well could have caught malaria, and hearing this caused her to suddenly cover her face with her hands. She was afraid her face might betray her. Realizing how awful she must look, she made an effort to hide her shame and act brave.

'It really feels like malaria. My face is burning.'

'You were supposed to cure yourself from this love malaria, instead you got it worse.'

The jesting Hun looked tired as well. It seemed like the spiked booze had done a job on him.

'Why didn't you stick to the target? Was there any need to drag me into it? Look at me. I'm like a rabbit that got pushed into the same trap.'

'Don't be angry. It wasn't such a great sacrifice.' Danyeong went to Hun with a sorry look. 'We made a deal and I will repay you for that sacrifice.'

'How are you going to repay me? Being tired isn't the problem – what are you going to do about my ruined stomach?'

'Don't you want me the same way I wanted Ilma? Just as you gave me Ilma, I'll give myself to you. Do to me whatever you like.'

As if intending to go through with the offer of her body, she practically threw herself at him.

'See, I'm like a lamb that's been thrown at your feet. Do what you like ...'

As she attempted to throw her arms around his neck and bury her face in his chest, he suddenly dodged, causing her to tumble to the ground.

'Have you fallen so far? Have you lost all pride? I don't want you this way. I want your heart.'

'If I give you my heart, what will you do with it?'

'I can't love a woman with no pride. I loved the haughty, arrogant Danyeong. Who would want this?'

That last statement cut her to the quick. Hun had just put into words exactly what she had felt from Ilma. There was no meaning to a love that didn't involve the heart.

11. GIFT OF THE MUSE

Like a gift brought by the season, nothing caused as much talk on the streets as the performance by the Harbin Symphony Orchestra. The newspapers were trumpeting the event, and colourful advertising posters fluttered above the streets. People gathered around the posters that stimulated their interest in the special autumn event.

All manner of people gathered in teahouses with the musical programme spread before them, offering their opinions on the selections.

'Ilma did a good job getting the symphony orchestra to come to Seoul.'

'Not only did Ilma do a good job, but this event will help to increase the level of cultivation of our citizens.'

'In any event, Seoul is the second most cultured city after Tokyo. That's why what Ilma accomplished is so important.'

'I have some objections regarding the programme. Why did they include so much Beethoven? If the goal is to mesmerize people, Beethoven's not the right composer.'

'You don't like Beethoven because you're a Mozart fan.'

'Has there ever been a greater musician then Mozart?

Mozart, Schubert, and Chopin are real musicians. Beethoven wasn't a musician, he was a lunatic.'

'That's your own personal opinion. Such a rash judgement will have Beethoven rolling over in his grave. Don't be so presumptuous before you even hear the performance.'

When criticizing others, one assumes that one's own level of refinement is the standard. No matter how lustrous a tradition something might have, when compared to one's own standards all manner of highbrow criticisms become possible. On the other hand, this is the kind of freedom that an individual can enjoy. At any rate, this talk itself showed the degree to which musical culture had progressed in Joseon and, therefore, was something to be welcomed.

While attendance at a performance might not be proof of cultural progress, the first evening's performance was an unprecedented success. Thousands of music lovers packed the hall; thereby, demonstrating Seoul's level of cultural interest to the visiting orchestra. This was the best possible way to thank the orchestra for its efforts, and the thunderous applause was immensely pleasing to the musicians.

After the incident with Ilma and the conflict with Hun, Danyeong, feeling ashamed, had remained in her apartment. The day she decided to venture out happened to be the day of the first performance.

Myeongdo had visited her several times and had wondered about the cause of her silence. On this day as well, he appeared with tickets for the concert. Danyeong felt ashamed in front of Myeongdo and hesitated to go with him, but in the end, she couldn't hold out against his insistence and agreed to accompany him.

The Danyeong that had boldly done as she pleased with Myeongdo before the events with Ilma was, today, meek and obedient.

The brilliant atmosphere inside the hall was dizzying to

Danyeong. She recognized many among the thousands of faces in the hall, and the feeling that they all knew her secret made it impossible for her to raise her head. Sitting next to Myeongdo in the line of all those gazes was unpleasant enough, but the eyes that recognized her and seemed to be studying her made it even more difficult to bear.

But then wasn't the point of showing up here to be seen? Naturally she had run into Ilma and had met Hun in a room on the second floor. What's more, Miryeo and Hyeju were in the audience also.

Due to his relation with the orchestra, Ilma was an important person that evening. He was seated right in front of the stage with Nadia, intently watching the performance.

The musicians on the stage, all dressed in black and bathed in light, presented an almost divine appearance. Adding to this impression was the inspired sound produced by the harmony of their instruments. The movements of the director's hands produced a spiritual voice that emanated from the instruments. The classical pieces of the masters were brought to life by their hands so that those sounds might once again move people's hearts.

The audience was silent, staring intently at the stage as the sonorous sounds of Beethoven's Fifth filled the hall. Was it that music conveys the deep emotions of the realities of life? The audience sat in silence, mesmerized by the suggestions of 'Fate'. The door to fate opens and closes and can't be controlled by people's desire; falling victim to that fearful will, all people can do is laugh or cry. The thousands in the audience, while listening to 'Fate', had a chance to reflect on their own fate and laugh or cry. Was there anyone listening that didn't either laugh or cry? The majority of people's fates were pinned to these two states.

As the quiet strains of the second movement died down, Danyeong was possessed by an odd feeling. Listening to the third and fourth movements, she felt a strange sense of fatigue and dizziness suddenly descend on her. Leaving Myeongdo in his chair, she got up and went out.

However, she wasn't the only one who wanted to cry over her fate, and she found herself in a crowd of people heading for the lobby. When she came out, who should she see but Miryeo and Hyeju. They as well, it seemed, had felt that sense of fatigue and come out to the lobby.

Danyeong, pulled by a feeling of empathy with them, walked in their direction. The outdoor rest area was quiet and almost deserted. Of course, Danyeong and Miryeo knew each other, but now, affected by the emotions of the concert hall, she couldn't help but feel closer to her. It appeared quite natural for her to take a seat next to them.

'Fate is a spiteful thing. It does whatever it pleases with your soul, like some frightful musician.'

At Danyeong's words, Miryeo turned to her with a look of familiarity. 'Has fate not been kind to you? It seems there are no bold or brave people when one's fate turns for the worse. You seem to me like one who could change your fate.'

'Do I look so brave? I think I'm the weakest person I know.'

Even while saying so, however, Danyeong didn't know herself whether she was strong or weak. Is it strength to throw oneself brazenly and brashly into any and every situation? If so, how can one explain the feelings of disappointment and anguish that follow? There was no way in which Danyeong could conceive of herself as a strong person.

'Without courage, what can one accomplish? Is it not strength to decide what you want and then try to make the world give it you?

Looking attentively at Miryeo, trying to decipher her meaning, Danyeong suddenly asked, 'Did you see Ilma sitting in front of the stage? Sitting there with Nadia, didn't he have a look that said, "I'm the happiest man in the world"?'

As Hyeju looked at Danyeong, wondering why she was

making such comments, Miryeo sat with anguish in her eyes, acting as if she hadn't heard.

'If fate ever had a favourite child, it's Ilma. He's the happiest and most steadfast I know. And if his happiness comes at the sacrifice of others, he's not concerned about that.'

'Why do you keep going on about Ilma?' Not being able to take any more, Miryeo glanced at Danyeong with a look of annoyance. It was a bitter look that seemed to ask, 'What kind of perversity is driving you?'

'It's a sad situation not to be able to hate or despise him.'

Whether this was Danyeong making an appeal to her own feelings regarding Ilma, or a guess regarding her heart, Miryeo had no way of knowing.

'Actually, I do hate him, but I don't wish him misfortune.'

Not being able to stomach any more of Danyeong's talk about Ilma, Hyeju rose to leave. 'What does Ilma have to do with tonight's concert that you keep bringing him up?'

The rebuke to Danyeong was a sign of sympathy for Miryeo; however, Miryeo, unlike Hyeju, did not stand up.

'I want to sit for a while longer,' she said, indicating that Hyeju should go first.

After Hyeju had taken a few steps, Miryeo turned to face Danyeong. It seemed that Danyeong had much she wanted to say, and there was a part of Miryeo that wanted to hear it.

Miryeo already knew that Danyeong was infatuated with Ilma and had followed him to Manchuria. It could be said that they both felt the same way about Ilma. The only real difference between them was that Danyeong was more proactive and bolder than Miryeo when it came to doing something about it. When two people contract the same disease, it is natural that they should commiserate with each other. On this particular day, unlike before, Miryeo did not find Danyeong irritating, but rather felt a closeness to her.

'Shall we have a cup of tea?'

Appearing to want to sit somewhere else, Danyeong arose,

her attention focused on the tearoom next to the rest area. Miryeo followed without a word.

Once they were sitting in their seats in the quiet tearoom with their tea in front of them, it felt as if they had come for this purpose alone and not to attend the concert. The concert had turned out to be a frivolous expense to these two who were the least involved in the performance of all who had come.

'Everyone acts differently when they are in love, but what does one have to do to be happy ...?'

Miryeo responded without hesitation to Danyeong's comment. 'Can one be content and secure if their love is one-sided? A more fundamental problem must be solved before one can be content.'

The fact that the object of both their desires was the same person was now an open secret. There was no need to mention his name.

'Lately I can't help but wonder if it is a sin to want what I can't have.'

'I feel differently,' Danyeong immediately countered and then boldly offered her opinion. 'If it is wrong to want something in your heart, how many sins would there be in this world? But the world isn't such a harsh place. Whether one secretly desires something or not is a matter of personal freedom, and if someone does allow himself or herself to do so, it's not wrong. I don't think you have done anything to blame yourself for.'

Thinking about Danyeong's words, Miryeo wondered, *Does that mean you have done something wrong? I wonder what is.*

'I'm different from you, my nature won't let me just dream about something. Once I make up my mind about something, I can't rest until I put it into action. I'm not a monk. I can't live on dreams alone.'

'How did you put your dream into action?' Miryeo said in reply to Danyeong's unusual comment.

'Don't be surprised, but I had my way with him. I put him under my thumb and toyed with him.'

'You what? You toyed with him?' As if struck with a bolt from the blue, Miryeo was dumbfounded with surprise.

'But in the end, it was all for nothing. I was wrong to think that I had won. It just appeared that way. It seems that sometimes dreams are better than the real thing. I doubt dreamers ever feel this kind of disillusionment.'

Miryeo was surprised once again at Danyeong's words.

Miryeo stared at Danyeong as if she couldn't believe what she was hearing, but Danyeong was unfazed.

'You must be wondering if I'm lying. This must all seem quite fantastic to you, but to me it's nothing out of the ordinary.'

Wondering if Danyeong hadn't lost her mind, Miryeo began to regard her as dangerous.

'What I really want to talk to you about is what is left after all of this. My sense of despair is actually greater now than it was before. It would have been much better to just go on as we had been, then I wouldn't be so miserable. No one but me knows the disappointment of knowing everything there is to know. You should be happy to just dream about it. Don't wish for more than that.'

'What you've just said is very frightening.' With a shudder, Miryeo turned her gaze to Danyeong. 'You're saying people can meddle in other's lives and do whatever they want. Do you think life is forgiving? How frightening. Why have you told me this? Secrets should be left buried. What's your intention in telling me? Are you trying to frighten me?'

'You hate me now, don't you? And you're afraid of me. You hate Ilma as well.'

Before Danyeong had finished speaking, Miryeo was shaking her head. 'Of course, I do. I can't stand any of you. It's all disgusting and filthy. There's not a decent human being among the lot of you.'

In fact, she already considered Danyeong nothing more than the outer skin of an animal. This feeling was not the result of jealousy; it came from her idea of purity. Ilma was no longer the object of her dreams, he was now just another run-of-the-mill guy. The sadness that resulted from the thought that he was just another vulgar man pierced her heart.

'So, it seems I've done a good thing. Just the fact that I've awakened a sense of contempt in you for Ilma is an important accomplishment. In helping you to forget Ilma, I've in effect saved you. Just think of it as me saving you from the same fate I suffered and as a woman in need of someone to share my pain with.'

Miryeo was heartsick. It was true that she was disappointed by Ilma, but did she have the right to hate him? Danyeong's unexpected words had filled her with anguish.

'You're a devil.'

'You should feel the same way about Ilma. It will make you feel better.'

Just at the moment that Miryeo could no longer stand to hear what was coming out of Danyeong's mouth, Myeongdo appeared in front of them. He had grown tired of waiting for Danyeong to return and had come to find her.

'What are you doing? The symphony isn't even over yet and you're out here. Was it such a boring performance?'

Knowing that Myeongdo would continue to carry on like that, Danyeong arose from her seat.

'Don't despise me. There will come a time when you will be thankful for what I've told you. I'll be going now.'

After Danyeong left with Myeongdo, Miryeo sat for a while as if in a trance. Who should she hate? There was nothing for her to do but blame the day's fate.

The first half of the performance ended, and there was an intermission. Some people had come out to the rest area and others remained in their seats.

Jongse, Hun, and Neungbo had all come out to the rest

area, and as they brushed past Miryeo, the three of them all recognized her at the same time.

'Isn't that Miryeo?'

'Her husband took off for Shanghai, and no one's heard a word from him since. The divorce proceedings are finished, and now she's a free woman. She has been liberated, but now Ilma's married. Nothing's gone right for her. How painful it must be for her to see Ilma with his new wife. There are probably many like her here who can't enjoy this performance. Life sure can be complicated.'

The second performance started with Tchaikovsky's 'Walnut Doll'. Every strain of the movement exuded the sentiments of the northern country.* Playing the music of the musician's fatherland elicited a strong response from the audience, and the second half of the performance started off very enjoyably.

Music, it can be said, is an invention. The chords and strains of a melody are very different from the sounds that permeate everyday life. No matter how beautiful and exquisite the sounds of nature may be, they can't match the sounds of music that come even from a lowly shack. Music is emotion squeezed into form and the invention of inspiration. The pleasant arrangement of a musical piece is something that can't be heard just anywhere, and it gives more joy than the sounds of nature. The audience inside the auditorium was entranced, soaked in the sounds of the music as if it were water that had been sprayed over them. It was as if Tchaikovsky's soul was alive in their hearts.

Absorbed in the music along with the other several thousand people in attendance, Ilma and Nadia were feeling the same emotions at that instant as the rest of the audience. The hearts of people hearing the same music are all bathed in the same light, just as those bathing in blue water are all dyed blue.

---

* Lee uses the word *bukguk* (북국) which was term used at the time to refer to Manchuria.

As the members of the orchestra were Nadia's fellow coun-
trymen, she was familiar with several of them. Having lived
in Harbin for years, they had come across each other in the
street or some other place. Hearing a performance in this
far-off land by people she was familiar with caused Nadia to
experience deep emotions different from those of the rest of
the audience.

In the orchestra was a man named Ivanov, who Nadia was
particularly close to. Fixing her gaze on him, Nadia spoke
incessantly into Ilma's ear in an effort to share her feelings
with him.

'What do you think? Isn't he doing well? I was worried that
there would be some mistakes.'

Ivanov sat, almost hidden behind his cello, drawing his
bow slowly back and forth. In fact, judging from Ivanov's
appearance, there was some cause for these concerns. He
looked weak and enervated.

'The cello is a slow instrument,' Nadia said, and Ilma made
the pleasant discovery that the calm tune of the cello harmonized well with Ivanov's composed character.

'I had no idea that the instrument Ivanov played was the
cello.'

'I didn't know he was going to come on this trip. There
are so many musicians in Harbin that it was hard for him to
make a living with music. That's why I'm so surprised to see
him here.'

This was the same Ivanov that Ilma had met with Nadia
at the cemetery in Harbin. He had no idea that there was
anything special about him. Ilma had noticed him not only
because of his odd appearance, wearing a thin summer suit in
the autumn, but also because he created a certain impression
in Ilma.

Ilma heard from Nadia what a hard time Ivanov had. That
instead of trying to make a living with music, he had gotten
hold of a used car to try and feed himself working as a taxi

driver, but not being able to do even that he suffered many hardships. Never in his wildest dreams had Ilma imagined he would see Ivanov here as a member of the orchestra. His surprise was even greater than Nadia's.

'I hope that the performance is a success and that this brings Ivanov some happiness. It would be nice if his life got on the right track and his hardships came to an end.'

'It will be a success. I'm sure the response will be positive.'

It was clear that Nadia was thinking of her home. She, more than anyone, was hoping for Ivanov's success.

When the performance ended, most of the audience crowded for the exits. Those who were left lounged around just inside the door, looking at the musicians.

In a room behind the stage, several employees of the *Hyundai Daily* newspaper who had sponsored the concert were milling around waiting to congratulate the musicians on their performance. The sound of applause still seemed to resonate in the empty auditorium. The back of the stage was covered with innumerable bouquets and wreaths of brilliant flowers that spilled over into the back room. The performance had been an unrivalled success. It was a joyous event for both the musicians and the citizens of Seoul.

In spite of their fatigue, the musicians were delighted by the praise of the sponsors and were more pleased than anyone with the results of the concert.

Ilma and Nadia, not sponsors or part of the orchestra, were in an odd position. That is, while receiving the thanks and congratulations of the sponsors and musicians, Ilma was embarrassed and felt his face flush at the praise heaped on him for making the event happen. For her part, Nadia smiled every time someone spoke to her and busily responded to the praise.

As the noisy proceedings came to an end and the people packed up their things and headed for the door, all those who had been loitering about gathered around the exit. That group included Hun and Neungbo and, off to one side, Danyeong and Myeongdo. Miryeo, however, was nowhere to be seen. After hearing those surprising words from Danyeong, she had sat for a bit trying to compose herself and, being unsuccessful, had left hurriedly for home. The spirited Danyeong had remained until the end.

Hun and Neungbo contemplated giving Ilma their opinion of the performance but were somewhat embarrassed to rush over to him in the unruly crush of people, and as they stood in one corner wondering what to do, the musicians one by one took their seats in the waiting cars. As Ilma and Nadia were staying in the same hotel, they got into the last car and left the crowd behind. The throng stood watching the long procession of cars leaving, but the image that remained most clearly in their minds was that of the couple Ilma and Nadia. The person in that crowd most affected by the image of the couple was Danyeong, who felt her heart throb at the sight.

'Do you want people to see me like this?'

This was her response to Myeongdo's proposal to take some air. Danyeong turned in the opposite direction and returned to her apartment. It was the first time she had come directly home so meekly.

Plopping down listlessly on the bed, Danyeong, in reproach to herself, muttered, 'I shouldn't have said anything to Miryeo.'

No matter how she thought of it, she couldn't avoid the conclusion that what she had done that night had been rash.

What have I accomplished? Was it just a boast on my part? Was I trying to change his life? Anyway, haven't I merely succeeded in making myself sick and tormenting Miryeo? I've acted senselessly, believing what I was doing to be important and have spoken carelessly. And now I can't stop my distress from growing ...

At the same time, Miryeo was lying in bed at this early hour but was too upset to sleep. After her husband had absconded to Shanghai, she had returned home, where she passed the lonely days with the housekeeper.

Danyeong is not wrong for telling me those things, and Ilma is not wrong either; it's my own feelings that I resent. What can I do to bring my feelings under control?

With the electric light shining in her face, she squirmed in her bed, unable to sleep.

After returning to the hotel, the group did not go immediately to their rooms but sat in a room on the first floor, chatting.

Nadia, who had grown day by day more accustomed to Seoul, moved naturally among the group as if she were a hostess. After being caught up in the group, Ilma wished they could now go up to their room, but Nadia had not sensed his wishes.

Even after he said, 'I'm tired, shall we go up to the room?' Nadia showed no sign of leaving.

Being the only woman in a group composed totally of men, Nadia's presence was not only resplendent but added to the enjoyment of gathering. For this reason, it was not easy for her to leave. Bringing a bit of joy to the group was a form of etiquette.

'I'll go up first.'

As he could not really pull her to her feet in front of these people, Ilma left the room and headed up to the second floor.

Not having the energy to even change his clothes, he flung himself on the bed fully dressed and lay there for a while. With closed eyes, he lay lost in thought, feeling an unidentifiable sense of emotional fatigue.

He couldn't say what the cause was of this confused feeling.

He lay like that for half an hour or so. There continued to be no sign of Nadia. When he opened his eyes, the room went black and he felt dizzy. He jumped up and, without thinking about what he was doing, headed out of the room and down the stairs.

There were only a few people left in the room. Most had

returned to their own rooms, and among the small groups that remained, Nadia and Ivanov were sitting, deep in conversation.

'Aren't you tired?'

As Ilma pulled up a chair and joined them, Ivanov smiled and said, 'We have a lot of catching up to do as we haven't seen each other in a long time. Harbin has turned cold, but it's still quite pleasant here. When we met in the cemetery, things were quite awkward; I had no idea that we would come to be connected like this.'

Ilma felt that Ivanov's attitude while delivering this long greeting to be more ingratiating than the situation called for.

'We were talking about our impressions of Joseon. Ivanov is very favourably impressed. He likes the fact that everything is so foreign and unique.'

Ilma nodded his head as he listened to Nadia explaining Ivanov's thoughts.

'That's fortunate. With all it took to get here, it wouldn't do to have a bad experience.'

'I like it very much. I'd like to live here if possible. I'm tired of Harbin. It can be such a cold-hearted place to people like us. I'd like to see what living in an unfamiliar place like this would be like.'

Ivanov's words were not just empty platitudes but seemed to be a sincere reflection of what he really felt.

'If you really like it here so much, I hope you can stay as long as you want.'

'Could I make a living playing the cello? If I could, I would certainly stay.'

'Well ...'

To ask any further questions would be an imposition on Ilma. While showing signs of fatigue, Nadia changed the direction of the conversation.

'Shall we say goodnight? It's getting late,' she said as she stood up.

As Ilma and Ivanov also stood, Ilma could not suppress a yawn.

While changing his clothes after coming up to the room, Ilma was troubled by a feeling of awkwardness between him and Nadia.

Seeing that Nadia was not as talkative as she normally was, she seemed to be feeling the same thing.

'Ivanov said he wants to live here. Did he mean it or was he just making small talk?'

What was behind this question?

If Ilma's discomfort was due to Ivanov, and if Nadia was aware of that fact, then this question was unnecessary and frivolous.

Nadia looked at her husband as if she couldn't understand what he was talking about.

'How do I know? If you think Ivanov a gentleman, then you'll take him at his word.' Her tone was not soft.

'Who said he wasn't a gentleman? But he's in a strange place where the circumstances are different, so I thought he was just making idle talk.'

'If those things are such a problem, then what am I doing here?'

Such a response might have been a mistake.

'Are you saying that your situations are the same? Why have you come here? Wasn't it for love? Wasn't it because you trust me and wanted to come with me? What does Ivanov want from this place? Did he also come because he loves someone?'

Ilma's voice was slightly agitated when asking this question, and Nadia remained silent. She did not know how to respond.

'If it's love, there's no reason to be afraid of a strange place, but if it's not, what would he come to Joseon for?'

At this point Nadia realized what Ilma was getting at. 'Is love the only thing people live for? Someone might go to a strange land to find work. Or freedom.'

'So, Ivanov is here for work and freedom?'

'Why are you asking me? Didn't you just hear that straight from him?'

'What sort of job does he think he can find here that would justify coming this far?'

Both of them fell silent for a while.

Nadia had stood up and was changing into her nightclothes.

'I know what you're implying. I sensed it earlier. That's why I've been feeling uncomfortable and depressed. It's depressing, and that's why I'm not going to take it.' She spoke in a dignified manner.

Hanging her clothes at the foot of the bed and tying the sash of her nightgown, Nadia said, 'You've misunderstood. All of your surmising about me is wrong. It's not even worth talking about, but you think there's something between Ivanov and me, and I'm telling you now that there's not.'

Hearing this directly from Nadia's lips set Ilma back on his heels. Overcome with a feeling of shame, his face burned.

Such words from Nadia, the first of their kind, certainly seemed to ring true. In fact, this made Ilma regret the excessiveness of his words.

'Who thinks that?'

'Well, if you didn't have such thoughts, then don't entertain them in the future.'

Ilma, with head hung, climbed into bed.

Was I really being needlessly suspicious of Nadia?

Ilma was still wrestling with himself.

Was he wrong in having suspicions about Nadia and Ivanov? Their conversation had seemed especially intimate, but is it right for a husband to have doubts about his wife based just on that? But then, isn't it natural that such thoughts should occur?

This might be a problem of the difference in culture and refinement.

This difference in feeling might be the result of the difference between East and West. When looked at from the perspective of the morality of individualism, his wife's attitude might be seen as natural and cultured. If that's the case, did his misunderstanding of her attitude mean that his attitude was unfair and uncultured? Compared to his constrained sense of morality, Nadia's seemed bright and clear, and he again felt ashamed. He was embarrassed to no end at having betrayed such selfish and primitive emotions.

What right did he have to be suspicious of Nadia? In fact, much stronger than his doubts regarding Nadia was his sense of shame regarding himself. A husband's selfishness – this sense of a husband's entitlement that people still held to – caused him to feel no end of shame. What right did he have, he who was with Nadia, to find fault with anyone else? Compared to his blunder, there was nothing in Nadia's attitude to rebuke. Could he keep the secret buried in his heart for the rest of his life? And even if he could, would he be comfortable with the fact that he was deceiving his wife?

On the other hand, how in the world could he ever tell her something like that? Was it possible that such a revelation would not result in a cataclysm of some kind? Lost in such contemplations, Ilma felt not only shame but fear as well. It was as if ruin was about to descend on him. The blame was his, and sin lurked in his body. It was preposterous to blame Nadia. It wasn't a matter of difference in the concept of morality. It was that he didn't have the qualifications to be her husband. What had started as a useless suspicion of his wife had resulted in anxiety and agony. Lying in bed, he could feel that this was going to be a long night.

'If you have something to say, just say it.' Nadia, who had been sitting lost in thought, just then got up and came to the bed.

'What would I have to say that I haven't already said?'

Ilma turned his head toward Nadia with an apologetic look, and she spoke to him. 'The thing about the heart is that one must have a clear conscience if one is going to have any peace.

We're going to be together for the rest of our lives, not just a day or two, and if there is the slightest prick of conscience, we won't be comfortable together.'

She spoke as if proffering a philosophy.

'What would be pricking my conscience? When two people live together, there are bound to be times like this,' Ilma said, forcing a smile.

Nadia's response was to smile back and throw herself into his arms. Smothering his face with her body in this way was her customary way of showing affection.

However, was this enough to solve all of their problems? Was the relationship between Ilma, Nadia, and Ivanov thus settled?

This unexpected happening had pushed Ilma into a state of confusion and served to change his thinking; however, the sudden appearance of a telegram at the performance the next night once again created a stir.

It was early evening, and the second movement of the first half of the performance had just started.

A lamp had been on for a while, illuminating a black signboard next to the stage, drawing the attention of the audience.

By the time Ilma noticed it, the sign had been circulating back and forth for quite some time.

Ilma was taken aback by the message on the signboard.

Mr Cheon Ilma, please come to the rest area. It's an emergency.

This was the message blinking on and off.

After reading the signboard twice, Ilma gave a start. It was for him. Looking around, there was no one else standing up to respond. There was no one else with the same name.

'What's happened that I would be summoned?' Ilma said to Nadia and stood up, wondering what to do.

At that moment, two people, crouching over, came quickly toward him. It was Jongse that came to a stop in front of him. He said in a shaky voice, 'A boy came from the hotel with a telegram for you. Hurry out to the rest area and read it. It's waiting for you.'

Wondering what the telegram was all about, he followed Jongse out to the lobby.

'I couldn't open it myself, so I came to get you.'

When they reached the lobby, the waiting boy stood up. 'It's urgent so I brought it with me.'

And with that he gave him the telegram.

Hurriedly tearing open the envelope, Ilma stood awhile, not able to make out what it was about. After reading it several times, it finally made sense to him.

Something has happened. Request you return immediately, Byeoksu.

It was from his friend Byeoksu in Harbin; the postage stamp confirmed it.

'What does he mean "something has happened"?' Jongse, who had read the telegram with Ilma, was wondering what was going on as well.

'How would I know?' Ilma answered, his curiosity deepening at the mystery. 'It seems something important has happened. At any rate, he said come as soon as possible so I'd better go.'

As he said this, he felt his heart flutter.

After standing blankly for a moment he came to his senses, and after sending the boy off, he went quickly to the lobby.

'Are you planning to go?'

'I'll take the last train. Even if I were to send a telegram to find out what's going on, it would take a day and it seems that things are urgent, so I can't just sit here.'

Returning to the auditorium, he informed Nadia as to what was happening. She was surprised and confused.

'Are you going to go, then?' she also asked.

'I'll go to the hotel first. Finish listening to the concert and then come.'

After convincing Nadia to sit back down, Ilma returned

to the hotel where he filled a small trunk with the things he would need.

He had a couple of hours before the train left. He was sitting absent-mindedly after packing when Nadia came in.

'I want to go with you.'

He was moved by his wife's proposal.

'I appreciate that, but it's going to be a quick trip so there's no need for you to go,' he reasoned.

To this Nadia responded, 'It will be tedious going alone. Harbin is my home and, even if it's a short trip, I don't mind.'

'There's no need to go that trouble. And there are the guests from the orchestra to take care of, so I want you to stay. I'll be back soon.'

'I can't believe you're leaving the one you love behind.'

Ilma was extremely thankful that his wife felt this way. But he had no choice but to explain the situation to her and check her impulse to accompany him. Noisily hugging and kissing him, Nadia reluctantly accepted the situation.

12. THE INCIDENT

Ilma announced his imminent departure to Harbin to his friends just before he left.

His every action had always been a source of interest to his friends.

In spite of her complaints about how tiring the performance was, Danyeong had come to the auditorium where she heard of Ilma's situation again this night.

Asking Jongse about Ilma's spiritless appearance, she learned what had happened. When she thought about Ilma going to Harbin again, she had a sudden longing to see the place again, and she felt her heart throb. The reason for this was that she was still not over Ilma.

Harbin was the place where her heart had been deeply wounded, and despite the fact that the wound hadn't healed, she still missed the place, especially when she thought Ilma would be there.

'What's happened that Ilma would go back to Harbin? Just thinking about that place makes me sick.' Myeongdo had still not gotten the taste of what had happened in Harbin out of his mouth.

'Remember the cabaret? The night we all cursed each other?' Danyeong chimed in. But inside she did not share Myeong-do's abhorrence of the place. 'What in the world would cause Ilma to return there? And so suddenly at that?'

While voicing her doubts on the subject, Danyeong was also feeling the temptation to travel.

The next day, Danyeong ran into Hyeju on the street and told her about Ilma. Hyeju was also interested in Ilma's doings, and when it came to talk about him, she paid special attention. This was, of course, because of her friendship with Miryeo.

After hearing the story, Hyeju rushed to tell it to Miryeo. Because Miryeo was without family and lonely, Hyeju visited her every other day or so. In this way, the news of Ilma came directly to her.

'Ilma suddenly left for Harbin last night.'

Trying to act normal while receiving this news, she asked, 'Why did he go?'

'He got a telegram from a close friend saying that something important had happened.'

'What could it be ...?'

'It seems that it was so urgent he didn't have time to say what it was about. We'll have to wait till he gets back to find out.'

'Did he go alone?'

'Nadia wanted to go with him, but he left her here and went by himself.'

'Is he going to be there a while?'

'We'll have to wait and see. He's coming back as soon as everything's settled.'

Miryeo was curious about a number of things. Afraid that her voice would betray her, she remained silent, but Hyeju gave her friend a knowing look as if she had read her mind and said, 'Ilma, who is usually surrounded by so many people, is going to be alone for a while. I think this is a one-of-a-kind opportunity.'

Miryeo looked as if she were trying to figure out a riddle.

'Ilma will be alone.' Muttering to herself, she suddenly realized what Hyeju was inferring. 'A one-of-a-kind opportunity.'

'The kind of opportunity that you shouldn't miss, one you should take advantage of.'

'Go after Ilma?'

'Go and figure things out once and for all.'

'What will that solve?'

'What are you waiting for? Grab this opportunity.'

Hyeju's insistence was almost like an order. Being taken by the idea, Miryeo was dizzy trying to decide what to do.

A few days later, a short letter arrived for Jongse from Ilma describing the situation. Jongse had been so curious as to what was going on that he had sent a telegram to Ilma and the lack of a response had only increased his agitation. The letter was both a welcome and a frightening sight. Since he was also involved in these events, he couldn't help but be excited, and in that state, he carried the letter around to all their friends.

Of course, a letter containing the same contents had come for Nadia as well. Therefore, there was no need for him to visit Nadia and let her know what was happening. In all of this, he was more excited than anyone else. The 'incident' turned out to be a personal matter of Han Byeoksu's, but it was so involved that he needed Ilma's help. Anyone reading the details of it could not help but be fascinated.

> This is the second time I've been in Harbin, but it has changed a lot: the weather is cold and the feeling is completely different. I am here in a very disorganized state of mind and am faced with an extremely delicate situation that doesn't seem like it can be resolved quickly. There is something about Harbin that I had not realized until now, and this new discovery has changed the way I perceive the place in a most interesting way.

I had known that in the breadth and depth of this place there were certain unknowable things lurking, but I didn't know how surprising they would be when they were revealed. Most people know about the evil flowering in the deep, dark recesses of this place, but not many are aware that with the evil and vice, there is also terror lurking there as well. I have become aware that Harbin is not only a city of nostalgia but one of terror also. It's a city that causes one to shiver. I have realized that it's not just a place of peace of mind and enjoyable days but one of danger and fright.

I'm telling you about my new impressions of the nature of this city, because I believe it will help you understand what has happened. Without an understanding of the complicated nature of the situation it will be difficult to comprehend events. I'm sorry to surprise you, but the incident is related to Han Byeoksu, more precisely, to his uncle Han Unsan. Simply put, Unsan has been taken by a gang. He's been gone for several days and while we get threatening notes every day, actual information is sketchy.

As you know, Han Unsan b

uilt up his fortune here out of nothing over a couple of decades. He now is a wealthy man whose holdings include the Daeryukdang Pharmacy. It was clear the reason he was taken was his wealthy status. The gang is large, and its members are mostly foreigners. As I said before, the fact that gangs like this exist here is unexpected and surprising, like something out of a movie, a scene that is being played out right in front of me.

We think he's being held either out in the border region or else right here in the city, and they are

demanding a three hundred thousand won ransom
for him. They want someone to bring the money
to a certain location in the border region. Noth-
ing like this has ever happened before, and so the
family is beside themselves. We are cooperating
with the police, but if we take too much time his
life could be in danger, so I think the best thing to
do is pay the ransom. Of course, there is danger
in that as well, so we are damned if we do and
damned if we don't. I'll send details as they develop
but understand that I am trying to help and
comfort Byeoksu, so news might not be so forthcom-
ing. Let everyone there know what's happening.

From Harbin,
Ilma

*

The Daeryukdang's shades had been lowered, and the days were being passed anxiously. The sadness of a house that had lost its master precluded any thoughts of doing business. Pass-ers-by were easily able to distinguish that building from those on either side of it by the cloud of darkness that enshrouded it. The entire family and all of the employees would all huddle listlessly in one room, hearts beating anxiously.

As far as family went, it was small. In the absence of Unsan, there was his wife, the children, and Byeoksu. Apart from them were the staff, who were like family and boarded in the building. In the wake of events, the household was desolate and dreary, and it was understandable under these circum-stances that Byeoksu would summon Ilma. It was difficult to cope with the affairs of the house and business by himself. The enervated household felt like a house of mourning.

The saddest of all was Unsan's wife, who had been through thick and thin with her husband over the years only to be suddenly faced with this calamity. The first day he was taken all she could do was cry, but as the days passed and the danger to him increased, her despair and despondency deepened. There was nothing that could be done to assuage the fear that the house had lost the pillar that held it up.

After returning from the police station to ask if there had been any news, it was an unbearable torture to spend the rest of the day in the silence of the house. On the day of the abduction, the police had come and set up camp at the house to keep a watch over it; from then on there was a rotating watch where officers would take turns guarding the house, which made it easy to ask for information. There was nothing they could do but depend on the police and wait for news of the investigation, but there was practically nothing that could be called news. The mental agony of waiting all day for any scrap of information was such that they were overcome with a strange tiredness.

In the evenings, Byeoksu would be unable to disguise the mental fatigue he was feeling, and it would manifest itself in a look of despair.

'There's nothing else to do but accept their demands; the only question now is what the best way to handle it is.'

The members of the household showed no surprise at this conclusion. The three hundred thousand won was not the problem. Byeoksu, who had not gone to work at the newspaper, had no problem putting together the amount required by the hastily reached decision. The police could easily inform the gang of the decision, but the remaining problems were what the safest way to convey the ransom money was and whether Unsan would be returned unharmed.

It was rare for gangs not to harm abductees. It was customary for them to kill their hostages for fear of their identities being revealed.

If it was their practice to kill their hostages, not believing that just blindfolding them would protect their hideout, then it was natural that fear for Unsan's life was the major concern.

'There's no way not to depend on the police to deliver the money. But I'm worried that their actions will somehow do more harm than good.'

Unsan's wife was also at a loss as to what the right thing to do was.

'They say that he's being held somewhere near the border, but this gang is no doubt hiding somewhere in the city. I'm worried that if we head for the borderlands like simpletons, something else will happen here.'

In this way, they spent another day helplessly without finding any solutions.

There was not much for Ilma to do but wait in the Daeryuk-dang with the rest of them and offer his friend Byeoksu emotional support. Although it wasn't as if sitting around would help solve the problem. In fact, sitting like that all day long left him exhausted and soon even frustrated.

There was no news of the situation that day, so Ilma took Byeoksu out to a local teahouse for a change of scenery.

After being shut up in the house for several days like a bat without seeing the sun, even the evening lamps seemed bright to him.

'I wish there was a way to figure out what's going on. No matter how I think about it, it doesn't seem like this is going to be settled easily or safely.'

Feeling rejuvenated in the fresh air, they could be free from these growing concerns even if only for a brief time.

'First, we'll do everything we can. After that we have no choice but to leave it to fate. Worrying won't solve anything.'

This response was not merely a platitude but represented Ilma's true feelings on the matter.

'It may have been a mistake to go to the police. Even so, there was no way to hide from what was happening. Gangs, by nature, are a nasty bunch, and you never know what they might do if they get angry.'

'I'm sorry to say this, but I feel like I'm watching an American gangster movie. I'm dying to see how this all turns out. It's like a movie is playing itself out in broad daylight here in Harbin.'

'Harbin is a huge city. Second in size to New York. There's no way to know what's lurking in its nooks and crannies. After this gang business, I can't help but think how dangerous this place is.'

Byeoksu had ruled over this city for dozens of years, but now, as if he had lost all his confidence, the fear showed in his eyes.

'Every time I think of what happened that night I tremble. Uncle left in the morning saying he had something to do, and he didn't return all day. I had the feeling he was going to the bank to make a deposit, so I set out for the bank and then looked for him at the hotel and at some of the other places he frequents but without any luck. When I got back, the ransom note was waiting. Three hundred thousand won is a shocking amount, but the idea that they had taken him and there was nothing we could do about it was maddening. From that day on, I couldn't shake the idea that this is a frightening city. The more I think about it, the more I feel how hard this place can be.'

'It's actually kind of funny. There's no way a couple of yahoos like us would ever be the targets of such a scheme. It's the millionaires that have no peace.'

Ilma's laughter was meant to lighten Byeoksu's mood. But, no matter what Ilma did, Byeoksu's mood was not to be lightened.

'I have several reasons for thinking it might have been a mistake to go to the police.' Byeoksu was plagued by a number of worries. 'As you well know, Uncle faced all kinds of hardship and danger in achieving what he has, and his methods have not always been legal. I'm worried that if we completely depend on the police, Uncle's history may come to light. In fact, it's even more dangerous because Uncle is still now engaged in such practices. I'm always pointing out the dangers and trying to advise him against such activities, and now I'm afraid that he's done something even worse than normal.'

'Your criticisms and concern for justice aren't going to do any good now. They can only complicate things and confuse you.'

Ilma couldn't help but criticize Byeoksu's 'conscience' while trying to instil some courage in him.

After several days of sitting around without being able to accomplish anything, Ilma wanted to liberate himself from this uselessness and have an evening to himself.

After parting with Byeoksu at the teahouse and returning to the hotel where he had dinner, Ilma had the feeling that he was free from any obligations, and he finally started to relax.

At that moment, an idea occurred to him as to how he could spend his leisure time.

I'll go see Emilia.

That was his plan. The thought cheered him up.

After arriving in Harbin, Ilma had spent his time going back and forth between the hotel and the Daeryukdang; he had not had a chance to venture beyond. In this wide city, without Nadia, the only person he knew besides Byeoksu was Emilia, Nadia's friend and his acquaintance. He wanted to convey Nadia's greetings and, considering that Emilia's health had not been good, see for himself how she was getting along.

When he arrived at the Sunggari Cabaret it was already night, and the dancers were gathered in a corner eating. He was excited, but he failed to find Emilia among them.

He asked a dancer that he knew and was told that she hadn't been well and so had not been in for several days.

'She's sick again?'

'It's always the same sickness. This time it's bad.' Her

comment showed a mixture of concern and fatigue with the situation.

'If she's sick again things have really gotten out of hand,' Ilma muttered to himself. There was nothing else to do but go and look in on her, so he asked if she still lived in the same place and then left the cabaret.

He was barely able to find the apartment that he had visited only one time. The darkness had deepened, and the apartment looked dismal in the gloom. However, the inside was even worse than the exterior. It was not only gloomy, but due to the change of the season, the room was cold and dreary. Lying on the freezing bed, Emilia looked worse than she had in the summer. Emilia stared at Ilma for a moment after he entered, and then, recognizing him, she jumped out of bed in surprise.

'Wha–what are you doing here? When did you come? Nadia ...?' she asked in a high-pitched voice.

'I went to the cabaret, where they told me you were sick, so I came here.'

He quickly informed her about Byeoksu's situation and told her that tonight was the first time he'd had any time of his own.

'I read about the gang in the paper. But why did you come alone? Nadia must be sad.'

'I'm only here for a little while, and the situation is complicated. Also, she has to take care of the orchestra members.'

'How's Nadia doing? Is she happy? I did receive one letter ...'

Emilia couldn't contain her curiosity about her friend, but from Ilma's point of view, she was the one that needed worrying about.

'What's this about you being sick so much?'

'It would be better if I just died. I don't know why my life is so tenacious.'

The feeling conveyed by Emilia's voice caused a lump to

form in Ilma's throat. The shabby appearance of the sick girl engraved itself on his mind and caused a feeling of pity to well up in him.

'You have to get yourself together and not lose your courage. You only have one life, and it's a precious thing.'

Oddly, the picture of Emilia's mother hanging on the wall seemed to be saying the same thing even more earnestly. The portrait was exactly where it had been the previous summer, hanging over Emilia's bed looking down on her misfortune.

While it was true that she was sick in body, she was also lying in bed shrouded in disappointment at the way her life had turned out.

Wanting to give her some courage, and perhaps a little enjoyment, he pulled her up from the bed and suggested a stroll.

The Emilia who had changed her clothes and freshened herself up looked like an entirely different person than the one who had been lying in the bed. Emilia had two enemies: sickness and poverty. If only she weren't poor, how much better her life would be. The evening's outing turned out to be very enjoyable for Emilia.

Leading the way, Emilia was the first one out the door. She seemed like the happiest person in the world at that moment. As Ilma was headed down the stairs a door opened, and the old landlord suddenly appeared. Looking down at the receding Emilia, he waved his hand at her and muttered, 'You're a slick one. You say you're sick, and here you are going out ...'

Ilma instantly understood what he was getting at. 'I'll take care of it, just tell me what you need.'

At Ilma's query, the old man counted on his fingers.

'She's three months late,' he remarked sarcastically. This was what Ilma had anticipated, and he was not surprised at the answer. He had intuited the situation the moment the old man had appeared.

'How much is three months' rent?'

After taking out his wallet, counting out, and then paying the amount the old man indicated, there was no need for further talk, and so Ilma disappeared in an instant through the door. Emilia was waiting a few steps ahead of him. She hurried to him and walked next to him, an apologetic look on her face.

'What were you doing?' she asked.

'I was delayed a moment.'

With this nonchalant answer they made their way out of the back street.

Dealing with the old man had only taken a moment. He was glad that his intuition had allowed him to quickly take care of the situation without Emilia being any the wiser. If events had occurred in front of Emilia she would, no doubt, have been embarrassed, and there is no way she would have accepted such kindness from him. Ilma thought it delightful and fortunate that he was able to successfully conclude the small affair without her knowledge.

Feeling good about what had happened, he was also pained when he thought of her situation. He had not known the extent of her poverty and misfortune. She had not even one person to look after and help her. All she had watching over her was the lonely picture of her mother. There was no more pitiable a girl anywhere, and the thought of her pathetic situation pierced his breast.

'Nadia's letter was full of interesting news about how much she enjoys it there, she seems very happy. I have always wanted her to enjoy as much happiness and contentment as possible. I know many people care about Nadia, and I am one of them. I met Nadia's aunt once in the street, and she asked about Nadia. I told her that Nadia is possibly now one of the happiest people in the world. She wrinkled her nose and went her way without another word. I don't know if she was scoffing or if it meant that her mind was at ease.'

A plaintive longing for her own such happiness could be heard in Emilia's words. As if Nadia's happiness were her own happiness, her voice became animated while she talked, but this excitement only brought her unhappiness into clearer relief.

To Ilma, it seemed that those people closest to him had always been the unhappiest. Perhaps this was because he himself had not been so happy. Tonight, Emilia was no longer someone with no real connection to him. He now thought of her as one of his own flesh and blood. For that reason, his heart contained both feelings of gladness and pain.

Wandering the teeming streets, Ilma and Emilia were not sure where to go; eventually they decided on the Sunggari Cabaret.

Emilia was worried about showing her face there as she had not been to work for so long, but, on the other hand, she also felt a duty to put in an appearance. Ilma decided to go there partly to relieve Emilia's concerns and partly because it was familiar ground.

Even though it was her place of work, due to her long absence she felt a bit strange, like a new customer. Perhaps this was because she was still physically weak. There was a vague awkwardness between her and the other dancers. Ilma, as if protecting the lonely girl, sat with her and didn't leave her side for a moment. She felt an obligation to Ilma and danced and drank with only him. Even though she was sitting with Ilma, it was her job to serve any customer that came by.

However, no customers approached her. This fact seemed to partly account for her depression. Her physical attractiveness had already faded. For that reason, and in spite of her failing health, she drank heavily and indiscriminately. With red face and drowsy-looking eyes, she would empty the glasses that she poured for herself. Watching this made Ilma ill at ease. What was supposed to be an enjoyable evening was gradually becoming depressing.

There's no escaping the sadness of being an empty husk.

The idea of the 'empty husk', which had occurred to Ilma

in the street on his last visit, once again came into his head. The sadness he had felt last time at the sight of the blind musician, the flower girl, and the beggars descended on him once again tonight while witnessing Emilia's situation. Emilia was the same kind of empty husk as the musician or the flower girl. Having fallen through the cracks of society, hers was a life without a ray of hope. Blood ties had nothing to do with being an empty husk. The unity of blood ties could not save empty husks. Only by overcoming blood ties and skin colour, only through empty husks caring for each other and coming together could they find salvation. This was the reason that Ilma, on this night, felt a strong closeness to Emilia as well as pity and compassion for her.

Considering Emilia's appearance, Ilma felt himself becoming increasingly sad and depressed. He was besieged by thoughts like, *Will there ever be a world without empty husks? When will it come?*

'Do you know what I'm thinking?' Emilia spoke as if her sadness were several times deeper than Ilma's. 'I was wishing that it wasn't alcohol in this glass but poison. I'd down it in one gulp.'

This bold statement startled Ilma.

'You've had too much to drink,' he said and took Emilia outside the dance hall.

In the long hallway attached to hall were a number of sofas.

Sitting Emilia down in the one furthest from the hall, Ilma said, 'Emilia, you must listen to me tonight. I have a request to make.'

With a sober look, Emilia sat up straight.

'There's one thing that you need right now, and that's your health. For the sake of your health I want you to accept the request I'm about to make. It's not that I'm better than you, it's just that I can't stand to see you like this.'

Emilia, intuiting what Ilma was talking about, said, 'Are

you proposing to save me? I'm already too far gone. What good would momentary salvation do?'

'I want you to rest and recuperate for six months or a year. I can take care of that for you.'

'Thank you. And I know that would be a good thing for me, but what right do I have to accept such kindness from you? If it's because of my friendship with Nadia ...'

The thing that was making Emilia hesitate was a sense of morality concerning Nadia. Just as Ilma was trying to find the right way to tell her not to worry about that, someone appeared unexpectedly in front of them. It was Byeoksu.

'What are you doing here?' Ilma was surprised, knowing that there was no way Byeoksu had the leisure to be hanging about in the cabaret.

'I came to find you.' Byeoksu's answer was even more surprising.

'To find me?'

'You should have told me earlier that you were coming here, I looked for you all over the place.'

'What's happened?'

'After leaving you I went back to the pharmacy when someone suddenly showed up there. They said they had come from Seoul just to find you. Can you think of anyone who might come here to find you? It's a woman.'

'A woman?'

'Not Danyeong.'

'If it's not Danyeong, who else would come here to find me? This is unbelievable.'

Muttering to himself, Ilma was confused by this unexpected news. No matter how much he shook his head and racked his brain, he couldn't come up with the single name of a woman that might come here to find him.

'It's unfortunate that I've never met her before, she's a real beauty. Danyeong can't compare to her. If one were to pick the most beautiful of all the women you know, it would be this one.'

'The most beautiful woman I know? Do you think I know that many women?'

'Whether you know a lot or not, she's the finest. There was nothing else to do but direct her to the hotel you're staying at. If you meet her, tell me about it. She must have a reason for coming all this way, so don't create an incident.'

'What do you mean? If there's an incident it'll be because you caused it,' Ilma retorted, but he had been bowled over by this news and was still trying to figure out the riddle of the woman's identity.

'I've given you the message I came to give so I'm going to go back to the pharmacy. You might as well stop goofing off here and go to the hotel. If I'd have known where you were, I'd have brought her here with me.'

After Byeoksu gave his admonishment and left, Ilma sat lost in thought, momentarily forgetting that Emilia was sitting next to him.

'What's happened that has caused all this excitement?'

Emilia's voice brought Ilma back to his senses.

'Ah, we were talking about rescuing you and getting you some rest and recuperation. And you were saying that because of the matter of appearances with Nadia that you were going to decline the offer ...'

Returning to his earlier self, he determined that as he had started the evening with Emilia he would finish it with her, and that he would finish the conversation he had started about helping and would insist on giving her material assistance no matter how much she refused. What did it matter right now to him if a beautiful woman, or any woman had come looking for him? As he muttered this to himself, he went back to his earlier thoughts about 'empty husks' and concentrated once again on Emilia.

However, the next morning at the hotel, Ilma faced another surprise.

Ilma had returned to his room after waking up late and breakfasting, when the bellboy brought an unexpected visitor to his room.

Ilma was so surprised that he was speechless. He was not only speechless, his heart nearly stopped.

'Are you surprised?'

The visitor greeted him first, and he was barely able to stammer, 'It's you ...'

'I came by last night, but you weren't here, so I came again this morning. I asked about you at the Daeryukdang, and they told me you were here.'

The female visitor that had so surprised Byeoksu that he had run to the cabaret to inform Ilma was none other than Miryeo. Seeing Miryeo standing right in front of him, Ilma, who the night before had not been interested enough to come back to hotel to see who had come, could not contain his surprise.

'Even if I had stayed up all night thinking about who it could be that had come here to see me, I never would have guessed it was you.'

It was impossible to discern whether Ilma's tone during this frank confession was one of pleasure or of annoyance. Even if he was not pleased to see her, he wasn't annoyed either. In fact, the look on his face was closer to fear. Miryeo did not miss the look, and there was no reason for her not to know its meaning.

'You must have been very surprised at my presumptuous behaviour, but I had no choice. I heard from Hyeju that you had come here so I just took a risk and followed you. I hope this isn't too intrusive.'

'It's not intrusive. You are free to go wherever you want.'

Miryeo didn't miss the strain of sadness in the cold, off-hand tone of Ilma's matter-of-fact answer. She knew there were other words that she wanted to hear.

'I don't want you to feel like you have any responsibility to me, no matter what; my coming here was the free choice of a free woman. I have no husband or family to tie me down. There's no reason to be annoyed or think too much of this.'

Miryeo explained what had transpired in her life of late. She told Ilma about the rupture of her marriage with Manhae and the legal proceedings that had led to her new, free life. She seemed to be trying to put Ilma's mind at ease.

'No matter what your reasons for coming here, it was a mistake of you to come to Harbin when it's in the midst of a transformation. It's in between autumn and winter; the streets are bleak, and there's nothing right now worth seeing here.'

Following this allusion to their situation, which was delivered somewhat sarcastically, Ilma began to express his unvarnished feelings.

'It's too late. Events have already taken their course. You've gone through some drastic changes in your family and personal life, but that has all been the result of a kind of chance and not because you made any particular effort to realize a goal. Even if things turned out the way you wanted them to, it's too late; things have already been decided.'

'I know. I'm aware of all that. And because I know, I am at a loss as to what to do.'

'If by chance, even though it doesn't mean anything, Nadia knew that I was in a hotel room with you right now, what would she think and how would she feel? What's more, I'm in love with my wife and don't want anything to change ...'

It felt like she was being scolded. Miryeo's face burned, and she hurt to the marrow of her bones. What made her even sadder was that she had no right to get angry or cry. She had no choice but to soften her voice even more.

'I have no intention of causing you any further trouble. I had one reason for coming here. How can I possibly change everything that's happened? I don't have the ability nor am I that brazen. I came to ask you one thing, to hear one thing directly from your own lips. I don't know if I have paid too high a price coming all this way to hear that one thing from you, but I came because I would never get this chance in Seoul, and I believe that here you'll be honest with me.'

Listening to Miryeo's composed words, Ilma found some courage. 'What's the one thing you want to hear?'

'I need a lot of courage to tell you.'

No matter how difficult Ilma's position was, Miryeo was his guest. And, among the people who could have visited him, she was actually a welcome one.

While putting on a chilly front, he couldn't lie to himself. He had his guard up and a frown on his face, but how could he so easily forget the feelings that he had had for Miryeo? As his surprise slowly subsided, his manner toward Miryeo began to soften. This softening was furthered by her dignified demeanour.

While taking an early meal in the hotel restaurant, he treated her like the special guest she had once been to him. This was due, no doubt, to the relief he felt at the knowledge that all Miryeo wanted was to hear something from him.

'What is it that you want to hear?'

It was not that he was trying to pressure her, but his curiosity had been aroused.

'It's not easy to say if you press me like that. It would be a lot easier if it just came out naturally. Otherwise, I won't be able to collect myself, and I won't be able to say the right thing.'

Miryeo seemed to be stiffening up. She was even having trouble eating her meal. 'Can you please spend the day with me?'

'I have to check in on Byeoksu. I have some things to do.'

'Just for today, I won't ask any more of you.'

'Byeoksu is worried that instead of helping him with his problem, I'm going to create one of my own.'

Of course, this was Ilma's own take on the situation, but it was the only thing he could think of to say.

'Couldn't you just spend half a day taking me around the quietest part of the city?'

'The quietest part of the city?'

'That kind of place will give me courage. The courage I need to say what I want to say.'

'Is what you have to say so serious?'

'I want to hear your sincere answer.'

Where is the quietest place in this city?

For the life of him he couldn't think of a quiet place other than the outskirts of the city. And the quietest place that came to mind was the cemetery. It was more secluded than a crowded park or the riverside. The cemetery would be the best place to hear what was deep in a woman's heart.

There was no other way but to give his day to Miryeo, and so without dropping in to the Daeryukdang, they left the hotel and got in a car for the cemetery.

A sudden thought occurred to him, and he stopped by a flower shop where he bought a bouquet of flowers. He intended to lay them at Nadia's mother's grave. The car flew down the road.

The cemetery looked entirely different than it had in the summer. Owing to the somewhat overcast day, the place was deserted and chilly. All that remained of the thick foliage of the woods were bare tree branches, which could all be taken in with one glance.

The wall of the shrine, which could be seen through the barren trees, looked bleak, and the leaves that had carpeted the path had lost all trace of colour, giving the entire grounds a feeling of desolateness. The trunks of the silver poplars looked starkly white, and the bare branches of the elms looked like the scribbling of a pencil against the sky. Even the benches, devoid of people, looked cold and dreary.

Miryeo, who was seeing such a sight for the first time, at first felt her desolateness increase and doubted whether this was the right place to speak her heart.

Ilma found the grave of Nadia's mother, placed the flowers before it, and then made his way back along the long path to where Miryeo was waiting.

'It can't get any quieter than this place. Now, what is it that you want to say to me?'

'How could I possibly presume to upset your happy family life? Because I have no desire to do so, I was able to come to you like this. If not, how could I show my face? I wish for your happiness as much as anyone.'

It was difficult for Ilma to listen to Miryeo airing her personal feelings like this, especially here. This was the place he had walked together with Nadia. Nadia's mother's grave lay just yonder, and it felt as if the grave was gazing sadly on the two of them. This thought caused Ilma to feel a tightness in his chest.

'If you really wish me to be happy, you won't do anything to hurt me, you'll just let me be.'

'I know. You don't know how hard I have tried to control and conquer my heart. I've just barely managed to calm my battered feelings and am now trying to find my own way forward. Even if I were to have inappropriate desires, as you've already said, it's too late. There is one thing I want you to know, though. Settling this one thing may be the key to bringing me permanent peace.'

Miryeo paused, took a deep breath, and continued.

'It has to do with the past. Seven or eight years ago, when I was still innocent in mind and body, fate or vanity, I don't know which, made me lose my footing, and I've been walking this path of unhappiness ever since. In the midst of my unhappiness, the only thing I have to enjoy is the memory of that time. Those memories play themselves over and over in my mind, and it is possible that I will live inside those memories in the future as well. When I'm lost in those memories, I wonder about how you felt at that time. The depth of your feelings, I mean. That's what I want to know.'

'I was very angry back then. I was so angry and miserable that I wanted to just burn everything down. The fact that all that anger has completely disappeared is a miracle.'

'What do you mean you were angry and miserable?' Becoming excited, as if she were being given a long sought-after clue, Miryeo hung on Ilma's every word. 'If the situation was so unbearable, does that mean that you ...'

'...'

'Were you in love with me?'

The word fell from her lips like an anvil. There was a strange look of courage in her face. This was the thing she had wondered about and desired to know. She had come thousands of *li* for that one word.

'Did you love me?' The tone in her voice was close to pleading. More even than courage, there was a gleam of something like passion flashing in her eyes.

'It was unbearable because I was in love with you.'

When Ilma finally forced the words out, Miryeo practically jumped.

'Love! Oh! That's exactly the word I wanted to hear. No matter how things are now, you loved me once! I came all this way to hear that. Today I heard a word I haven't heard for oh so long now. I couldn't be happier.'

Like a young girl, she danced around, spreading her arms and grabbing aimlessly at the tree branches. Watching this sight, Ilma was surprised anew, not knowing whether he had done the right thing or not in letting those words loose.

Going further down the path, the elms and birches became thicker and their branches entwined overhead to cover the sky. The layers of leaves were soft underfoot and with the cold air, trees, and sky, it was as if they had entered a deep mountain valley. There wasn't a trace of any other living soul, and not even the sound of a bird broke the silence. In this isolation, it was if they had entered another world.

The quiet and chilly forest seemed to gradually affect their bodies' temperature. The thing coursing through their bosoms was not passionate love but self-possession and tranquillity. Ilma's thoughts of the past and Miryeo's emotions were not inflaming their passions but, rather, cooling them, bringing composure. Was this because the day had turned so cold?

However, Miryeo was oblivious to the beauty of the season. Neither the cold nor even the season's first snow could intrude on the thoughts that filled her heart as she took up the conversation again.

'I have a competitor.'

Ilma was surprised by this sudden revelation.

'A competitor?'

'Someone competing for you. Do you know whom I'm talking about? It's Danyeong.'

'Danyeong?'

'I know everything. Danyeong told me what happened. I didn't ask her to, she just suddenly let the secret out.'

'Secret? What secret?'

'The secret of what happened that night in Danyeong's apartment.'

It was perhaps a bit cruel of Miryeo to go so far with her explanation. Hearing these last words, Ilma's face turned blue and his lips trembled.

The surprise and shame left him unable to speak.

'I was shocked and disgusted when I heard about it and couldn't suppress my repulsion. However, when I realized that everything was the result of Danyeong's rashness, my anger subsided. It already seems like somebody else's story from long ago. I'm not concerned about it any more.'

'...'

'What's more, I discovered something interesting today. I know who won the contest between Danyeong and me. The reason I'm so happy right now is that I know I won. When Danyeong told me her secret, I swore to myself that I had to find out how you felt.'

'…'

'Just knowing what I now know means that I've won. You didn't love Danyeong, you loved me. I'm not envious of what happened in her apartment. That love, even though it is a love from the past, can make me happy for the rest of my life.'

Watching Miryeo's emotion and passion, Ilma's shame gradually changed to fear. Sitting next to him like a burning coal, he realized that she was dangerous, and he began to be afraid of her.

'I want to thank you. The one thing I really want to say to you is thank you. I want you to know how wonderful the word "love" is to woman.'

'Don't work yourself up too much in this cold weather.'

Thinking her excessive excitement strange, Ilma had actually begun to worry about her health. The steady snowfall had already filled the crevices between the fallen leaves with white.

After returning to the hotel, Miryeo seemed to transform into a different person, cool and composed. The excitement and emotion of the snow-filled wood had been replaced by reticence and a calm demeanour.

She was travelling without any luggage to speak of and only planning to stay a day or so, and so she had left her trunk for the time being in Ilma's room.

To Ilma the day had been a waste. The shock he had received during the first half-day he had spent with Miryeo had so completely occupied his mind that for the remainder of the day he could think of nothing else. The things that Miryeo had said and her expression and attitude would not leave his mind. In this state, there was no way he could visit Emilia again or be of any use to Byeoksu. He had no choice but to spend the rest of the day with Miryeo.

Snow had continued to fall and soon the streets were white. The people walking in them seemed delighted to see the snow as they went about their business. Ilma felt chilled by the cold and ordered coffee as he sat looking out of the window of the hospitality room, which faced the street. As the cof-fee warmed his throat, his body slowly warmed as well while he looked down at the street below. Watching the men and women come and go on the paved road, Miryeo took in the warm steam coming up out of her cup, and her body began to warm also, but at the same time, there was something sad about the smell of coffee on a snowy day. The loquacious Miryeo from the cemetery was gone and, in her place, was a sad and lonely-looking woman. The steam from her coffee had warmed her face, wafting into her nostrils, causing her to winkle her nose, and formed beads of dew on her eyelids.

After hearing from Ilma the words she had come to hear and expressing her thanks, she had accomplished her objec-tive, and there was nothing left to do. Could the delight she had felt in the forest continue? Could the word love that she had heard solve all of her problems and bring her satisfaction? Sadness never really ends, and that meant that life would be forever sad.

'There's nothing left to do but leave. There's nothing left to say, and nothing left to hear. My purpose here is finished. I'll leave tonight.'

These words were not motivated by a sense of satisfaction, but by sadness. They were like a final moan of resignation.

'Well, I won't delay you further. Just remember, there's nothing to do but think that the past is the past and the pres-ent is the present. Is there any way that the satisfaction of the present can last forever? You should know that forgetting those things that do you no good is necessary in life. What other choice do you have?'

There was no reason for Ilma to delay her departure, nor did he have any further words to offer. What they both needed more than anything else was to part from each other as quickly as possible.

'Change your clothes and come down. Let's eat together.'

Sending Miryeo up to the room, he ordered the bellboy to

prepare dinner and then waited for more than an hour. More time passed, and the other guests had all begun their dinner, but Miryeo had not appeared. Waiting fifteen more minutes, Ilma had no choice but to go up and knock on the door of the room.

Without waiting for an answer, he entered the room where he found Miryeo lying on the bed crying. She wasn't crying softly but was racked with huge sobs. He was at a loss as to what to say or do.

'You said to forget, but how can I? Why do the past and the present have to be so hard? And what about the future?'

'You need a special courage. You need a greater courage than that which you showed me at the cemetery. That courage will allow you to forget and figure out the right thing to do.'

Had his words gotten through to her?

13. SONG OF SORROW

The days when one could go out for a walk lightly dressed were already past.

Returning from her half hour stroll, Danyeong's lips were blue, and her arms and legs were shaking. The red hawthorn berries she had picked and brought back looked shrivelled in the cold morning air.

The mountain stream even sounded cold, and the leaves of the trees, which had already been through several morning frosts, had lost their colour and were shrivelled up, thereby announcing the end of the season. Of course, the greens were gone, but even the reds and yellows of autumn had faded into the colourlessness of winter. All looked cold and dismal, and everything under the sky was desolate.

She had been at the mountain hot springs for about five days and could feel the change of the season. She realized that her body was reacting to the cold. Then again, hadn't she taken the train* north a day's ride to this valley in search of

---

* In the original text it says she takes the Kyeongui line, which was the railway between Seoul and Shinuiju that opened in 1906.

solitude? She had come here for a few days with the intention of relaxing. Coming here in the off-season when there
were practically no other guests, Danyeong thought again of
her objective. Coming to this quiet place and walking in the
woods morning and evening had brought peace to her heart
and had helped her rid herself of worldly desire. However, the
morning air was so cold on her flesh that her lips froze, and
her arms and legs shook. There was a sadness in the inevitabil-
ity of these sensations.

Returning to the hotel, she went down to the bath. Immersing herself in the hot water thawed her frozen body and resuscitated her spirit. As her blood warmed in the hot steam, she
felt the joy of being alive soar in her bosom. The morning
sun coming in through the tall window bathed the otherwise white, steamy bathhouse with a red tinge. The interior
of the bathhouse was entirely covered in white tile with the
exception of the bottom of the tub, which was tiled blue, and
the sunlight hitting the clear water made it look like the sea.
Splashing around in that little sea like a mermaid, the quiet
mornings in the deserted bathhouse were the most enjoyable
time of the day for Danyeong.

Coming out of the water and sitting against the tub, her
red skin looked beautiful against the white tile like a piece
of fruit just coming into ripeness. Bending this way and that,
and running her hands over her well-baked body, Danyeong
thought how beautiful it was. The lines, the elasticity, the hue;
was there anything in the world as beautiful as the human
body? Thinking of how the years up until now had etched
themselves in every nook of her body, she studied herself,
openly realizing her beauty anew and feeling the happiness of
being alive. For that moment at least, happiness was all that
she was aware of, the unpleasant memories of the recent past
having disappeared from her mind. She was momentarily distracted from her secret 'objective' by the pleasure of her warm
blood and the beauty of her body. But could human and

worldly desire be shaken off so easily? While in the baths, she experienced powerful desires. Before she could finish her bath, and while she was still lost in thoughts of the body, someone called her from outside and a maid appeared in the door.

'You have a visitor. Someone has come from Seoul to see you.'

'To see me?'

Even as she answered, she guessed who the visitor might be. Of course, she wasn't pleased by the thought.

Returning from the bathhouse, just as she had anticipated she found Myeongdo sitting in her room like he owned it.

'What are you doing here?'

Her tone was a mixture of lamentation and reproach.

Sitting calmly, Myeongdo, who had entered her room without permission, presented a tenacious appearance to Danyeong. The feeling of happiness she had experienced that morning in the bathhouse evaporated.

'Is this how you greet a guest that's come this far to see you?'

Smiling easily, Myeongdo pushed his trunk into a corner of the room. This, his normal demeanour and temperament, was completely different in nature from that of Danyeong.

'Why have you gone to the bother of finding out where I'd gone and following me all the way out here?'

'Can you only complain? Where's the concern for what I went through? It was easy to find you. I just started with the closest hot springs resorts and worked my way here. It's already been a few days since I left Seoul. I had no idea you'd be hiding in a place like this. I can't tell you the pains I took trying to find you.'

'Who told you to take any pains?'

Without any change in her expression, Danyeong went and sat in front of the dressing table.

Myeongdo also could see the unblemished face reflected in the mirror. A woman who has just come from the bathhouse is particularly beautiful. That morning, Myeongdo couldn't take his eyes off the sight of Danyeong wearing only a bath-robe. Was this only because it had been a while since he had seen her?

'You suddenly disappeared, and people at the movie com-pany were wondering where you went, so I sent them to search the city for you, but you were nowhere to be found. I asked at your apartment, and their guess led me here after a lot of searching. Of course, I was lonely, but I was also worried that something had happened, so I didn't have a minute of peace.'

'Am I supposed to thank you? How can you be so ignorant of my feelings?'

There was nothing new about her speech or attitude. Things resumed between the two right where they had left off. Per-haps this combination of vitality and stubbornness was the reason that their relationship lasted so long. Myeongdo, for his part, while dull, pursued his affection for Danyeong per-sistently and passionately, while on Danyeong's side, she was spirited and hard to handle, constantly blocking his advances. Seen superficially, they seemed very comfortable and close to each other, but there was a line that was carefully guarded.

'I'll get right to the point. You have to come back with me right away, tonight if possible.'

'What right do you have to tell me where and when I must go somewhere? Why don't you just leave me be?'

She had put on foundation and rouge and was applying lipstick.

Was it a woman's nature to want to put on make-up? Danyeong went through her normal routine in that isolated mountain valley as if she was getting ready to go out.

'What right indeed? You wouldn't say such things if you knew how much trouble you were causing other people. We are ready to start filming and you disappear.'

When it came to talk of business, Myeongdo was the one who was responsible, so he did not easily yield.

'Hun has already written the script, and the casting has all been done; this is no time for you to be loafing. You can't only think of yourself. We can't afford for the season to completely turn.'

'Are you giving me orders? I have my own plans. What promises did I give you that made you create such a fuss?'

What had begun as Myeongdo's intention to woo Danyeong had unavoidably become awkward appeals on behalf of his business. His fretfulness was part desire and part concern for his company.

'Even if you offered me the world it's too late. What do you think I want that would make me obey you?'

'There's no need for more talk. Think about it while I bathe. And just remember that I can get angry too.' Myeongdo dropped his clothes right there and looked for a towel on his way to the shower.

*

It was true that Myeongdo was experiencing difficulties in filming due to Danyeong's disappearance, but as he was unable to overcome her obstinacy, he gave up on his objective of retrieving her.

After doing absolutely nothing for half the day, by evening Myeongdo still showed no intention of leaving and, instead, looked as comfortable as if he were here on vacation.

'Okay, so you're saying that no matter what you won't go back. Shall we see who can hold out longer? I won't be leaving either.'

In fact, even as he said these words this was exactly what he had hoped would happen.

Of course, there was no reason for Danyeong not to know what was in Myeongdo's mind. In fact, she had perceived, even more clearly than Myeongdo, the reason for making this trip that lurked in his heart. This time, Myeongdo was even more impatient than ever to realize his intentions with Danyeong. This impatience arose from the fact that he had been harbouring these intentions for such a long time. He had sacrificed all manner of things for that one goal. Put another way, he felt he had already more than paid the price for what he wanted. And Danyeong had guessed that in Myeongdo's heart he felt this was the time to demand she give him what he wanted.

While walking in the wood behind the inn, Danyeong thought about her situation with Myeongdo. In spite of the fact that there were no leaves left on the trees, the denseness of the forest gave it a cosy feeling. There were so many fallen leaves underfoot that it seemed as if one were walking on a yellow cushion. It seemed a shame to tread on that cushion with shoes on, so Danyeong took her shoes off. She lay down in the leaves. Lying on her back, the sky looked like a thread tangled in the tree branches. Above that, a tuft of cloud floated leisurely in the sky, but Danyeong's heart, far from being at leisure, felt like those tangled branches.

What's the right thing to do? Should I give Myeongdo what he wants, or not?

She lay there for several hours, such thoughts running topsy-turvy through her mind.

Finally, she got up and resumed her walk through the woods. Taking out her frustrations by shaking a tree, the remaining leaves fell like yellow snowflakes.

Returning to the inn without having been able to reach a decision, she found Myeongdo sitting in the room with the lights off, drinking. He had been drinking alone like that for half the day.

When Danyeong came in, the maid who had been pouring his drinks got up, assuming her services were no longer required, and left the room. His eyes dulled by the drink, Myeongdo stared at Danyeong as if to ask if she had been doing some soul searching. Danyeong plopped down, feeling exhausted.

'What have you been doing in the forest all day? Is it right to leave me in this room? No matter what, you only live once – why are you wasting your time doing all that thinking? Sometimes the waters of life are muddy and sometimes they're clear. There's no use being so stubborn. Here, have a drink.'

'...'

'Ah, to be drunk. I feel like fighting. No one can get the better of me today. Today, I'm unbeatable.'

Fearing that he was getting ready to do something rash, Danyeong was suddenly frightened by Myeongdo's rough chest thumping, something she had never seen before.

'So, even if I offer, you won't have a drink with me?'

This roaring Myeongdo was a completely different person than the one she had known up until now. This was not the helpless Myeongdo, prostrating himself and entreating her favour. This was an unyielding Myeongdo, bent on asserting his will. Where did he get this courage? Just as the stone Buddha is sometimes roused to anger, if someone is pushed far enough they can become enraged. That is what had happened to Myeongdo. He had finally had enough of having his entreaties ignored, and this had led to anger. There is no soul braver than an angry one. This was a Myeongdo that she had never seen before, a savage Myeongdo.

'How strong can a woman be? Today we'll find out once and for all. Until now you've walked all over me. But I won't be stepped on any more. Today we're going to see who's stronger.'

'What's the cause of all this bluster? Are you going on like this just because I said I didn't want a drink?'

'Why won't you drink? Why won't you take a drink from me? Do you have blisters on your lips? Am I not a human being?'

With foam-flecked lips, he was practically growling.

'Did you follow me here without being asked just to upset me? Is that also a man's prerogative? I have my life and you have yours, how in the world can you force someone to do something they don't want to do? Go ahead, do your worst.'

Danyeong retorted in her fashion, but she was not as spirited as she had been earlier. Her dispiritedness, of course, was not the result of a new fear of Myeongdo but came from the conflict she was having with herself. The problem was not how her relationship with Myeongdo was ultimately going to play out but was the much more fundamental issue of her fate. She had neither the energy nor the inclination to put up with Myeongdo's drunken behaviour.

'Is Ilma the only man in the world? Is there some law that says that Ilma is the only one under heaven worth loving? What is it about him that's so attractive? A pretty, white face, tall and slim, familiar with music, involved in culture activities or some such thing, is that what it takes to gain a woman's affection? Are these the rules of love? If you don't possess these traits, does that mean you'll never have the love of a woman? Does that mean that a black fool like me is doomed to be lonely my whole life? Who made these damn rules? What's the point of such unfairness? Why don't I smash those rules? That's what I'll do. This fool is going to get his piece of love, too.'

As Myeongdo muttered disjointedly, part in protest and part in appeal, his eyes gradually took on a fevered look.

'We're all children of the creator – when did he say that some of us could not be loved? Even the ugly duckling has the right to be loved. But love doesn't happen so easily. If it was easy, would you be going on like you are, and would I be in such agony? Do you think love is an easy thing?'

'If you're talking about loving one with your heart or some such thing, I have no use for such love. I will take what I want by force. Whether I'm despised for it or not, if I take what I want, that's the end of it.'

As he was talking, Myeongdo suddenly caught Danyeong by the arm. His strength was such that he was able to easily pick her up, but, in fact, she wasn't resisting and seemed to have already resigned herself to this.

'Do you think you'll be satisfied if you take what you want? I've already tried that. The fact that it didn't bring me satisfaction is why I'm suffering now.'

'I don't give a damn about ethics. Desire is all I feel and all I care about is satisfying it.'

Danyeong had harboured the thought for some time now that there would come a time when she would have to compensate Myeongdo for all the sacrifices he had made for her. Now that thought was growing toward a decision.

This was an exceedingly bold thought. It was true that this decision had arisen from the fact that she was in a state of self-abandonment. She had two reasons in mind: one was the thought that she owed Myeongdo something for his kindnesses; and the second was related to her final intention, quickening death by self-effacement and abusing her body. She already thought of her body as a soulless machine. So what difference did it make if, with that machine, she satisfied a man's lust or disillusioned him, thereby creating another person like her, disappointed with life? Bestowing this favour in the final hours of her life was a way to settle accounts for the chequered way she had lived. Wanting to change Myeongdo's appearance from what it had heretofore been, even if just for a moment, she imagined that she saw the gentleness of a lamb in the vulgarly inflamed face and tried to find beauty in that ugliness.

When dinnertime arrived, Myeongdo was still drinking, and Danyeong was preoccupied with her thoughts. She needed to make her final preparations and firm up her determination. In one corner of her heart she was calculating her remaining time and counting the final drops of life left to her. Realizing that Myeongdo's coarse attitude and loud grumbling had disappeared, she surreptitiously glanced at him, wondering when he had calmed down, only to find that he was weeping with his head bowed. He was leaning against the table with one hand covering his face and crying. When he lifted his face, his cheeks were lined with tears. On his face was an expression gentler than a lamb's. All tears are pure things, except maybe the accidental ones that come from a yawn. Tears only come from pure feelings. Without knowing why these tears were flowing, Danyeong was touched by them. It was somewhat embarrassing to see a big, strong man cry, but she thought that this was the most beautiful Myeongdo had ever looked to her. In those tears, Danyeong found the one thing of beauty she had been looking for. It was the one thing that her body had requested. Those tears washed away her loathing and made it possible for her to give him her body.

'Would you like to use my mirror? You look like a toad crying like that,' she joked.

'There can't be many men in the world as pathetic as me. I don't know if it's because I'm pathetic, or I'm too nice, but I couldn't go through with it.'

This genuine appeal served to finalize Danyeong's resolve.

'Then is it my turn to be brave? Hey, pathetic man, buck up.'

As if putting herself entirely in his hands, she stroked his face.

*

Danyeong's plan was a success. Things had proceeded in the way she had prepared herself for. Her heart was suddenly taken with a feeling completely different from the one she had felt before the act had happened and now, all that awaited her worn-out body was the doorway to oblivion. Before he could again shed the tears that had momentarily veiled his vulgarity, he was once again his ugly, lust-filled self and just looking at him caused a shudder. Danyeong, her body ruthlessly defiled, felt herself a fool now filled with a shabby sense of disillusionment, and she shivered at the thought of what had happened. There was nothing left for her in this world. She had gone as far as she could go. The last step, carrying out her final resolution in the midst of this enormous outrage and degradation, was going to be easy. Her plan had succeeded.

Laughter had changed to tears. Lying on the bed, wiping away her tears, she tried to gather her wits. The satiated beast next to her was asleep. It was the final, quiet moment.

If I have to die because of this, does that mean that I'm old-fashioned? Even so, that classic practice is the best solution. Will fate allow me to meet Ilma in another life?

Calmly she took out what she had been keeping on her person, dissolved it in a glass of water and swallowed it in one gulp.

It must have been some special kind of intuition that woke Myeongdo from his tired, drunken sleep. The moans coming from Danyeong, who was lying next to him, were not loud enough to have woken him. Awaking from an empty dream and hearing a strange moaning sound, he was surprised by what he saw. Next to Danyeong, who was writhing in pain, he found the empty medicine packet and, realizing what had happened, jumped out of bed.

Myeongdo shook her, but she was deep under the influence of the drug and, while writhing in pain and foaming at the mouth, she did not open her eyes. As if the mind was removed to a place far from the agony of the body, her mind did not respond to what her body was trying to tell it. Realizing the urgency of the situation, Myeongdo, gripped with fear, burst through the door and into the hallway.

'Somebody help!'

His cries brought the maids, who were still up, rushing out of their room.

It was late, and due to the isolation of the inn, there were not many guests staying there. It was as quiet as a tomb until Myeongdo's voice resounded thunderingly in the silence of the yellow lamp-lit hallway.

Several maids came running and crowded into the room, but surprise was all they could muster; no one had any idea what to do. It is not just anyone that can save a person's life, and when that is beyond one's ability, the only response is surprise.

Neither the maids nor Myeongdo knew what to do, and it was suggested that they wake the owner. However, in that secluded mountain valley, their combined wisdom was not going to be enough to save Danyeong. Emergencies are so rare that most people are not ordinarily equipped to deal with them. For that matter, Danyeong was rare as well, a modern woman in love with an old-fashioned sensibility.

Fortunately, there was a car in the yard of the inn. This car, which was used to ferry guests back and forth from the station to the resort, was normally parked at the station; however, that night the driver had decided to spend the night at the resort. The owner woke the driver and Myeongdo urged him to drive them into town at top speed.

The town was the nearest place with a hospital and a doctor. There was nothing else to do but summon the doctor. It was the middle of the night in a country backwater; Danyeong couldn't have chosen a more unfavourable place. But then again, for her intentions it was the perfect place.

Due to the urgent nature of the situation, the driver raced down the mountain road without a complaint. The road to town was not only narrow, but the rugged scenery for which the area was famous also made it winding and dangerously steep. The car sped down the mountain with the weeds of the road dimly illuminated in the headlights.

'What's going on? Why did she take poison?'

In response to the driver's question, Myeongdo replied, 'Who knows?'

While giving this offhanded answer, Myeongdo's insides were a jumble.

'Someone might look like they don't have a care in the world, but inside they may have their own torments. How could someone that young take poison?'

'...'

In the silence, Myeongdo was focusing on one thing.

Was this all my fault? Was it me that drove her to make that final decision to take her own life? She had seemed despondent. In that state, did she use me as the final stepping stone on her way to death?

He was racked with pangs of conscience, and his heart felt like it was being squeezed by a great sense of guilt.

He was a greedy man. But why had he not been able to leave one woman's virtue intact?

Is a woman's heart really such a beautiful thing that she would choose to demonstrate her virtue with her own death? Ilma must be the happiest man in the world.

It was not only his body that was chilled by the cold air, but his heart as well.

It was a thirty *li* drive one way, making it sixty there and back, and dawn was already approaching when they reached the town.

The doctor of this small town was a bit slow and thick, and he practically had to be coaxed out of bed to come with them.

Myeongdo's trust in the doctor put his mind somewhat at ease, but still, the cock had already crowed by the time they got back to the hot springs.

In the room, a maid was dozing, and Danyeong was still moaning.

Myeongdo, in his urgency, was as anxious as a child, but the doctor, whether he was calm or just unconcerned, rendered all the aid he was capable of giving in an unhurried manner. He gave her an injection and fed her some medicine. In her unconscious state, she couldn't swallow the medicine, and it ran down her chin. There was nothing else to do but wait for the medicine to take effect. After doing all that could be done, they all sat waiting for a change in her colour.

'Is there a chance that she'll recover?' Myeongdo, in his trepidation, was barely able to ask this question.

'Well ...'

'She has to recover.'

'Fortunately, she didn't take that much which is cause for hope.'

The doctor had picked up and was examining the medicine packet that lay next to Danyeong.

It had contained only a few capsules of white powder. According to the doctor, while this was enough to accomplish her objective, there was a greater chance that it would not. It seemed that Danyeong had, out of fear, not taken the full dosage. This one fact gave Myeongdo hope, but then the doctor added, 'However, she seems to have a very weak constitution and so will have a harder than normal time recovering.'

Myeongdo knew better than anyone that of late Danyeong's health had been unusually fragile. Due to the worries that had not given her a moment's peace, her otherwise good constitution had suddenly crumbled, surprising Myeongdo. And now this tragedy on top of that was almost too much for him to bear.

'Doctor, you've got to save her, do everything you can.'

He wanted to put his hands together and pray.

However, the doctor had already done all that he could, and the only further help he could render was to sit and provide some companionship to Myeongdo.

But being a busy man, he could not tarry longer and so the car took him back to town.

Somehow the dawn finally broke.

Myeongdo, who had not slept a wink, met the morning with wide-open eyes. He was not tired, however, and had not left his spot at the head of Danyeong's bed. He thought this the only way he could show his devotion to her. He was willing to put his own body through anything if he could save her, so this was the least he could do. There was nothing in his power he would not do for her, but for now this was the extent of his options.

With the morning, he planned to summon by a telegram a close doctor friend of his. He would be able to arrive by evening. There was nothing he was not prepared to do. He realized anew that Danyeong was the most important person in the world to him.

Gradually awakening to the depth and sincerity of the love he felt for her, he stared blankly at her face with an aching heart.

How her face had changed. It was no longer the healthy face of yesterday but was white and gaunt. It was full of pain and sadness. She could not be more pitiable.

Whether it's Danyeong or me, why can't things turn out the way people want them to? Why do people have to be so sad?

His eyes began to fill and when he shut them tight, a large tear fell onto his lap. Rubbing his eyes with the backs of his thick hands, Myeongdo looked just like a child.

14. THE WAY OF THE COUPLE

There were not many households as quiet as Professor An Sangdal's. It was just him and his wife, Hyeju. There were times when Hyeju felt an emptiness at the lack of a child; on the other hand, her body was still unmarked by childbirth, and the quietness of the house gave her the comfortable feeling that they were still newly-weds. Just the two of them staring at each other like two birds in a nest occasionally became tedious and boring, but that was perhaps the price two satisfied people must pay for not being troubled by the cares of the world.

An Sangdal was not that busy at school and was fairly untroubled on weekdays; however, Sunday was always anticipated, as it was the day the two of them spent together. The couple, as a rule, looked for ways to break up the monotony of life by coming up with new plans and by discovering new things; however, when it came to fascinating new plans, there were none. They were forced to rely on the same things as others to bring some interest to life: the usual entertainments or a degree of extravagance.

As they tended to sleep later with the cold weather, by the

time they had finished breakfast and were sitting in the main room, the sun was high in the sky.

Mozart's chamber music filled the quiet room with splendour and a touch of sadness, but as it was the same music they always listened to. When the piece ended, the room felt even quieter.

Hyeju had brought in her knitting and was working on it in her chair. Her husband had been making noises about skiing that winter, and so she was knitting something warm to protect him from the cold. The knitting coiled about her feet and looked soft in the sunlight coming in through the window. The more his heart was warmed by that cosy picture of the season, the more Sangdal felt a kind of loneliness.

'This is no way to live; we should at least raise a kitten or something.'

'You're the one who is always absorbed in a thesis or a paper or the like. Why are you acting so bored on Sunday of all days?'

Actually, Hyeju felt the same as her husband, and her sharp comment was a sign of her annoyance with the monotony.

'Since you mentioned boredom, I'm so bored I can barely stand it. I'm cooped up at home all day doing nothing, just watching the time pass. Sometimes it feels like I'm in hell.'

'Outside the wall are flowers, inside are books. The house is small, but there are the shadows of the trees in the spacious yard, a steady income and a loving wife. The satisfied wife, envious of no one. She enjoys being a prisoner of the house, singing together with the birds in the yard. The small house, steady income, loving spouse, healthy body and contented heart; have you ever seen anyone that has it as good as I do? Have you already forgotten reading that poem? Are you saying that time changes the things that poem celebrates?'

'What flowers and shadows are you talking about? Does the poem about flowers remain after the flowers have withered? Look at the yard.' In the midst of her retort, Hyeju seemed to have been abruptly struck with a new thought. 'Wait a minute. Who is the one that has forgotten that poem? Me? Or you?'

'I don't know. Did I forget it? Anyway, why can't I forget a poem that you've forgotten?'

'What? Is that a man's prerogative? Is it a man's special right to neglect his family and insist only on his needs?'

Was it that Hyeju thought that a man should worship his wife and feel that his home was paradise? From the husband's perspective, such ideas on the wife's part were unacceptable.

'We are both in the same boat so there's nothing to get excited about. Let's go see a movie.'

It being Sunday, this was a very easy thing to do.

Eating at the same restaurant and going to the movies was their normal Sunday routine, and this day their route did not vary; however, even though there was nothing especially stimulating about the experience on this particular day, returning from their outing they had once again been able to enjoy that special Sunday mood.

In her mind, Hyeju was still going over the debate as to who was more to blame for the ennui of married life, and it still bothered her, yet she had enough discretion to understand the etiquette of following her husband's lead on their outing.

Sangdal rose from his chair and, with his wife, came out to the lobby with a pleased look on his face. The musical they had been watching had just finished. Being exhausted with academic life, he had enjoyed the popular music of the film much more than he would have the heaviness of a dramatic film. All he wanted was to be liberated for a while from mental fatigue and act like a fool swaying and singing along with the music.

'It a good thing the movie wasn't *Southern Carrier*; that's no movie for a married woman to see.'

He said this nonchalantly with a laugh, but he was clearly

intending to call to mind what had happened to Miryeo, and Hyeju turned on him with a serious look.

'What about *Southern Carrier*? Why don't you spare me the useless criticism? There are already enough movie critics in the world.'

'Think about it. If more and more women imitate what happens in that movie, what will happen to the family? Do you think ten out ten people would approve of what Miryeo did?'

'So what if they don't? What good does it do to stay in a loveless marriage? You can't find a fingernail worth of fault with what she did. And why are you getting involved in other people's business?'

'Why do you get so excited at the mention of Miryeo's name? Were you two so close?'

'It's not because we're close that I'm speaking in her defence, it's because, as a woman, I understand her position. Are you saying that men can do whatever they want, and women should just follow them?'

'In the end, all wives, in fact everyone, has a bit of *Southern Carrier* in them. It's a scary thing. *Southern Carrier* was all about Nora. It's a dangerous thing.'

'What about men? Do you have any idea what kind of man Miryeo's husband was?'

The debate continued as they sat down on a sofa in the lobby.

'Well, even if Miryeo's was a special case, if the majority of couples can't trust each other like that, how in the world can a person ever have peace of mind?'

As a family man, Sangdal was a proponent of reliability and propriety. He did not like the idea of reform and believed in preserving harmony through compromise.

It was not that Hyeju disagreed with such an opinion, the problem was that it was only welcome when it was applied to the wife but not so much when it was centred on the husband.

'Ultimately, when the husband respects the wife, all problems are solved.'

'There is a more fundamental aspect to this problem. One should not enter into a loveless marriage. If there is love, even if ennui settles in, this can be safely worked out through compromise; married life requires effort. When there is only ennui and stubbornness, things can't help but break down.'

'You are stating the obvious.'

With Hyeju's agreement, they had both arrived at the same conclusion, and it became unclear what they had been arguing about in the first place. Perhaps this is just what it means to be a couple.

*

Ilma was freezing the entire time he was in Harbin, and when he returned to Seoul he found it to be just as cold. Winter was the same in both places, and in Seoul the light and temperature were now the same as Harbin. On his way north, he had packed winter clothes and a winter coat, and on his return, he was glad that he had.

His happiness with his winter clothes extended also to seeing his wife again and returning to his own life. He felt a fatigue he had never before experienced from this short trip, which gave him a new desire to see his wife and enjoy the atmosphere she created. He felt a kind of impatience thinking that this was the only place for him.

It seemed as if a great deal had happened on his short journey, and he couldn't hide his complicated emotions. He now wondered why he had ever left. He had left to help his friend with the unforeseen incident and had become involved in one of his own. His heart was furrowed, and gloomy shadows had formed in those furrows.

The kidnapping of Unsan, the Daeryukdang owner, was close to a resolution, but Ilma had returned without seeing his release. The gang that had kidnapped him was large and well connected and was not easily intimidated. It was decided that negotiating was the best solution, and the ransom money had been paid. Now the only thing that could be done was to wait for him to be released. When considering that the gang had a sense of chivalry and morality, it was deemed that they would keep their word. It was now just a question of how they would return him. Waiting for Unsan's return, his family and friends were, of course, curious about how it would be effected. Since negotiations had progressed to this stage, Byeoksu, who felt much relieved, suggested that Ilma return, which is what he decided to do.

Of course, Miryeo had left Harbin before Ilma. She was concerned that her emotions would become even more overheated, and so she left the hotel that night right after dinner with Ilma. For several days after Miryeo's departure, Ilma's tangled emotions had kept him on edge. Remaining cool and dignified in front of Miryeo to the last had required great effort on his part. This was the result of a secret war within his body in which he had to bring under control the passion rising within him. He knew how fierce and dangerous the fire raging in him was. With his feelings at the time, it was a very dangerous situation. The truth of how he had practically broken out in a sweat in trying to calm his emotions was a secret hidden in his heart that only he knew. In addition to his love for Nadia, the other things that had helped him pull back on the reins of passion were the knowledge that when order is upset by passion it means the destruction of social life and the common-sense notion that immorality does humanity no favours.

The reason he stayed a week longer after Miryeo had left was that he needed the time to organize his thoughts about what had happened and to calm himself. Sickness can arise in the space where two people face each other. If Ilma had not met Miryeo in this way, such anguish would not have visited itself on him. Their reunion created emotions in him and revived intimate thoughts that now vexed him.

The thought that suddenly came to him as he fought to bring his feelings under control was of Nadia and their life together. When he returned excitedly to Seoul and was met by his wife, who was overjoyed to see him, he discovered a new emotion. Thinking that his wife and his overcoat were the two best gifts he could have received, his feelings regained their composure.

Even though there had been a good reason for it, the newly wed couple's separation had been even harder on Nadia than on Ilma, and she couldn't help but think of it as an unpleasant occurrence. At the time, as she'd had the symphony orchestra to take care of and Ilma had to leave to help his friend, she'd naturally thought that he should go; however, after her duties were fulfilled and she had time to herself to think, she was taken by an unbearable loneliness, and thoughts of her husband suddenly filled her breast.

Meeting her husband with such feelings, she was happier to see him than she had ever been, and the excited emotions of being a newly-wed returned to her.

She was even more excited than Ilma, and her woman's sensibility could be seen in the tears in her eyes. She was like a lonely animal that had been living in a cave. Hugging, licking, and biting like an animal might be the most natural form of expression for people as well. Nadia's enthusiastic reception was a sincere and natural outpouring of her feelings.

'You don't know how much I regretted that you had gone. I thought about how unnatural it was that I stayed behind by myself, and what a mistake it was. It was like a nightmare.'

As Nadia excitedly compared then with now and described the changes in her mental state, she placed all of the blame on herself.

'After I was done taking care of the symphony orchestra, I wondered why I was so wound up about something that wasn't really so important ... I thought that I should have gone with you ...'

Ilma felt sorry for the fact that she been even more devoted to the task of taking care of the orchestra than was needed.

'What do you mean not important? It was my responsibility, and while I was gone who else could have taken care of them as well as you? That kind of devotion is not often recognized. How can you dismiss it so easily? We were both doing what we had to do.'

'It's already been quite a few days since the symphony orchestra left for Tokyo. How lonely I was for nearly a week. After they left, that was the end of it. I was exhausted, and I couldn't figure out what I had been so excited about. I thought how much better it would have been if I had gone on that trip with you.'

'Harbin was too cold to be any fun. And besides, I had my own headaches while I was there. While we were both caught up in dealing with symphony orchestras and friends' problems, we missed out on our own life. Now that things have settled down, from now on, it will just be the two of us.'

Even though Ilma had changed the subject, Nadia stuck stubbornly to the topic of the symphony orchestra.

'The members felt extremely grateful to you. Especially Ivanov, he insisted that I give you his special thanks.'

Why had she brought up Ivanov? Was she worried that he still harboured doubts about him? He was touched by her attitude and saw nothing in her innocent expression to give him cause for new doubts.

If the relative innocence of the couple were measured, Ilma could not even lift his head in front of his wife. While what had happened on this trip had been unexpected, if Nadia learned that he had met Miryeo, she would certainly be surprised and suspicious. He was thinking that, for the peace of their marriage, he had best not mention anything about that business. The possibilities for misunderstandings between couples were endless, and the keys to a good relationship were trust and an open mind. Somewhere along the way, Ilma had developed this philosophy. The last few months, although a short span of time, had been very complicated.

'Anyway, it's all in the past now. There's nothing to worry about now. The only thing that's important now is our love.'

*

Danyeong was lying in the small room of a hospital on top of a hill. The walls were white, the bed was white, and Danyeong's face was white. Even with its unusually pale complexion, her face was more beautiful than it had ever been. When a woman with a good complexion like Danyeong looked frail and weak, she seemed unusually beautiful.

Since her admittance several days ago, her condition had been gradually improving, and she was now waiting for a full recovery. When she thought about what had transpired, she found it fantastic that she was lying in this hospital bed. She wondered how it was that she was lying here when she was supposed to be dead.

She did not know whether to be thankful for the competence of that country doctor or to resent him, but his treatment in the mournful room of that inn had snatched her back from the jaws of death. She had spent a day moaning in a delirium, but by the time the doctor had arrived from Seoul that evening, she had returned to the side of the living and regained consciousness. As if it were his own life, Myeongdo was overjoyed that she was no longer in danger.

Seeing him, Danyeong's mood turned sour and, regretting that she had been resuscitated, she cursed the stubbornness of life, but the die had already been cast. She did not have the courage to make another attempt. She had lain in a room in the hot springs inn until she been well enough to move, and then she was brought to the hospital in Seoul. How shall we describe her state? Like a sword that had been drawn only to be returned unused to its scabbard, she felt herself to be useless, cowardly, and foolish; and she felt ashamed. She was filled with a sense of self-loathing. Even if she could be stoic about what had happened, saying it was fate or destiny or the like, when she thought how it must look to those around her, her face burned. Wondering how she could put together the pieces of her broken life, she felt unhappiness in the bottom of her heart. The future was going to be an extension of the life she had been living; could she hope for a miracle to change it? There was no way that her failed decision could bring any value or pride to her remaining life. Thinking that she would have to spend the rest of her life with this festering wound made her teeth chatter and thinking of her cursed life made her toss uncomfortably in the hospital bed.

The more she saw of Myeongdo, the more she was reminded of that unpleasant memory and she decided, for the time being, not to allow him in her room. The fact that the man who had been meekly and conscientiously waiting on her would not be around caused her to feel both sad and relieved.

Why can't I love that kind, simple man? Shall I try to drive him away? Would I be comfortable spending the rest of my life with him?

The more she thought of Myeongdo's devotion the sadder it made her to think that this too was a kind of fate.

She had many visitors, such as Jongse and Hun, but, for some reason, she was most pleased to see Miryeo. She brought flowers, put them a vase and spoke words of consolation and encouragement, and Danyeong felt closer to her than anyone else. Was it because women truly have a special way of communicating with each other? Anyway, had she not already completely revealed herself to Miryeo? In fact, there was no one else she could share the anguish of her heart with.

'Danyeong, you've always been braver than me. That was true in Manchuria, and after you returned as well. And this time too, this was a brave thing to do.'

'This is what I get for trying to be brave. I become a pathetic clown.'

'Since I seem to be following you in everything you do, perhaps I will turn out the same way.' She had already told Danyeong that she had followed Ilma to Harbin. 'I thought I would win if I went there and heard from him that he had loved me, but I was wrong to think that there could be a winner in all this. And how could I beat such a brave woman?'

Like a couple of soldiers who had lost the war they were fighting, the two unburdened themselves to each other, holding nothing back, and in the process, became best friends.

*

Secretly, Hun had been interested in Danyeong, but when she had rashly thrown herself at him, he had refused her with a rebuke. But, seeing how wretched she was, Hun was no longer able to remain cold to her and, taking pity, came and sat with her often.

From Danyeong's perspective, Hun was of a different calibre than Myeongdo. If there was another man in the world that she could love after Ilma, there's no doubt she would have chosen Hun. Due to her fixation on Ilma, she had been oblivious of the existence of Hun right beside her. When she had offered him her body to arrange the meeting with Ilma, she had not felt the same aversion as with Myeongdo. It was a proposal that had been possible after receiving the consent of her heart. After missing her chance with Ilma and, now, having given up on him, the man she felt closest to was Hun. She was happy to see him for different reasons than she was to see Miryeo.

However, these were Danyeong's thoughts; Hun had different ideas. There had been a time when he had been tormented by a secret desire for Danyeong, but in his mind, that time had passed. Danyeong had fallen as far as she could fall. With her damaged body and soul, there was no way that he could look at her with the same fresh thoughts and want the same things from her as before. While he could have pity on

her and feel sympathy for her, this was different than thinking of her as someone he could love. He was not thinking of
her as a love interest but as a friend in need of pity.

Whether it was because Danyeong knew his mind or not,
while she was happy that he came so often to see her, she
was also embarrassed by it. Not only was it hard to face him,
but she was also ashamed of the fact that she felt she did not
deserve his kindness.

'Your life would have seemed much more glamorous if you
had succeeded. But you took the pie out of the oven before it
was done and now look at you.'

He had always been able to make these kinds of jokes with
her, and she knew that his jests carried no ill will. This knowledge made her even more embarrassed as she realized how she
must look.

'Who knew things would turn out like this? I thought my
plan would succeed. But now I don't have the courage to try it
again, and so I have no choice but to be laughed at by life. If I
get tired of living in the days ahead, well, I'll cross that bridge
when I come to it ...'

'As we say, life is hard, and living and dying don't always go
as we want them to. Anyway, whether it's your bravery or your
harshness, you're a frightening woman.'

'Don't go too far. If I get mad, there's no telling what could
happen ...' Danyeong covered her face with a hand towel and
turned away.

'What, and add to Ilma's good fortune? Is there anyone in
the world happier than him? Are there not women who will
give him their hearts, and women who will give him their
lives? It's hard enough to win the wholehearted love of one
woman, and Ilma has two or three clamouring for his love.
He must be happier than King Solomon. If you're going to
be born a man, you might as well be born a man like him. Is
he such a catch or is it that women have such poor taste? No
matter how you see it, it's quite a spectacle. Could things be

more unfair? Cupid must have lost his mind to give one man all the luck in love.'

Hun's diatribe caused Danyeong to turn back to him again. 'Are men so jealous of each other? How unbecoming.'

'Of course, we are. If I have to despise a friend for the sake of the men of the world, so be it. So after all this, do you still want to see Ilma? Shall I bring him around?'

'...'

'That's what I'll do alright. I'll drag the lucky boy down here to your bed where you can look at him until you're sick of his face.'

*

Hearing about the suicide attempt from Hun, Ilma was naturally surprised. More surprising than the pluck required of such an extreme act was the fact that she had done it because of him.

He thought about Danyeong's personality. Considering her strong disposition and passion, he knew she was capable of carrying out such a thing. What was unexpected was that, in light of her somewhat chaotic lifestyle, she could be so clear and single-minded in pursuing that one objective. He knew that the reason she had acted so brashly was that she was in love with him, but he had not anticipated that her feelings had been so powerful and pure. He could not but be surprised at the terribleness and immensity of the decision to choose death in the absence of love, but he could not believe that he deserved to be the object of that lofty expression of her heart. His surprise slowly turned to a heavy feeling of responsibility and he began to feel overwhelmed by it all. However, the fortunate fact that Danyeong's life had been snatched from the jaws of death served to alleviate his sense of responsibility somewhat. He thought how miserable and guilt-ridden he would have been had Danyeong not survived.

'You should know what a charmed life you live; you hold someone else's precious life in your hands.'

Sitting face to face with Ilma, Hun could not stop himself from saying this. He thought that Ilma deserved to hear such unpleasant words repeated over and over.

'I might seem charmed to you. But I don't think I'm fortunate at all, in fact, I'm not sure that I'm not unfortunate.'

'That's being greedy. Fortune is fortune, and misfortune is misfortune. Seeing happiness as misfortune is the nonsense of someone with a full belly.'

'Are you making a fuss because you can't have Danyeong, who you think is the giver of all this happiness?'

'So, you're happy because I can't have her? You can't be happy if a woman is with another man? Why don't you visit her? Don't you think that kind of devotion deserves some response from you? If all men were so cold, what in the world would women have to believe in?'

'When did you suddenly begin to worship women?'

'I want to let the world know that not all men are like you. I'm completely on Danyeong's side this time. I don't understand your cold attitude.'

This degree of goodwill from Hun toward Danyeong was natural considering how he had felt about her. He thought that by fulfilling her hidden wish that Ilma be brought to her once again, he could give her a small degree of consolation.

Feeling somewhat awkward, Ilma bought a bouquet of flowers and went to Danyeong's hospital room.

Danyeong's colour did not change as she lay in her bed, a calm, unblinking expression on her face. She was alone, and it was a good thing she was. If there had been someone else in the room, what would they have heard come out of her mouth in that sharp voice of hers? The scolding of one lover by another? Some sort of appeal?

'I thought I would see you in hell, but we meet again in this world.' She spoke in a tone one only uses with a loved one.

'What do you mean hell? Why wouldn't we meet in heaven?' Picking up on Danyeong's coquettishness, Ilma replied with a joke of his own.

'Is there any way a woman with as many sins as me could get into heaven? Hell is more appropriate for me and that would be just my luck.'

'In any event, we meet again here and not in heaven or hell. If you had not come back, I never would have heard the end of it.'

Danyeong shot him a fierce glance, but it was a woman's instinctual coquettishness.

'Did you think what you were doing was wise when you made that foolish decision? Or did you do it knowing it was stupid?'

Thinking Ilma's question foolish, Danyeong shot back a retort. 'What do wisdom or foolishness have to do with it? Do you only do things you think are wise? Can't you do something even while knowing it's foolish?'

While she was rejecting Ilma's utilitarianism, he had his own ideas on the subject.

'So, you think passion is the best thing to base decisions on. If we all followed the dictates of our passions, what kind of place would the world be? Don't you know there's nothing as individualistic as passion? And where did your passion lead you? You couldn't control it, and it made you do that stupid thing.'

'That's why I intend to quietly let my passion burn all alone.'

'And what did that burning passion lead to?'

'My original intention was obviously not this failure. Failing was the result of fate; whether one fails or succeeds, there's always a reason.'

'The outcome is that you were unable to contain your passion, and now you're lying broken in this bed. But tell me why, what's the reason?'

'Did you come here to harass me? I don't think there's a

crueller person in the whole world than you. You wish I would've died, and now you're afraid that I'll recover to come back and annoy you again.'

Clearly, she was exaggerating for his benefit. With a smile, Ilma softened his voice.

'Aren't you supposed to be one of these new women? At the same time, you have the heart of an old-fashioned woman. Is what I'm saying so foolish? Why would you want to throw away your precious life for someone as worthless as me? What century was it that Chunhyang pledged to Lee Doryeong that she would keep her virtue for him?* What use is such a thing in this topsy-turvy, cold-hearted modern world? You're trying to live in a dream and not face reality as it is. Your emotions are moved by the whims of others. Do you think people will regard that as admirable? Do you think they'll erect a monument to your virtue?'**

Ilma had intended his words as a criticism of himself, but Danyeong heard them as directed at her alone.

'Whether I'm Chunhyang or not, why are you ridiculing me? What I did was my business which hasn't affected you in the least, so don't concern yourself with it.'

'Right now, all I see in front of me is an actress, an actress on a stage. This room and bed are stage props, and you're a pitiful actress standing on the stage. It's not a tragedy but a comedy.'

Here as well, Ilma had himself in mind while speaking, but it seemed he had taken it too far. Danyeong sat bolt upright in anger, her face instantly turning red.

---

*   This is another reference to the 'Tale of Chunhyang' that was first mentioned in the beginning of the novel. Chunhyang vows to save herself for Lee Doryeong, who must go to Seoul and take the civil service exam. His return is delayed and Chunhyang's virtue is severely tested.

**   The word for monument used in the text was *yeolnyeobi* (열녀비) which was a monument erected for women of exemplary virtue in the Joseon dynasty. Virtue here meant remaining chaste after one's husband leaves or dies.

'What? An actress? An actress in a comedy? So, you're saying what I did was all an act? Say it again. I dare you to say it again!'

She buried her face in the crook of her arm, her body shaking in rage. Ilma could see by her violent reaction that his words had been extreme, but he was at a loss as to what to do. There were tears forming in Danyeong's eyes. They were dangling from her lashes, and her lips were screwed into a frown, making her look just like an upset child.

'You're right. I'm an actress. That's all I've ever been. I'm just a no-good actress that acts a lie to fool my audience.'

As her voice rose, she pointed at the door.

'Leave. Leave now. Why would such a haughty soul as you come to the room of a lowly actress? I want you to leave.'

Never having imagined that things would go so wrong, Ilma was frightened by Danyeong's anger. He regretted upsetting her in her current condition.

'Don't misunderstand. I'm telling you these things for your own benefit. I'm not looking down on you. If I were, why would I visit you like this? I'm saying these things because I was so surprised and shocked by what happened, don't read anything else into it.'

'You are acting like this because you've always thought of me as a kind of actress, and this is the result of that.'

'Why would I look down on an actress? This happened because of your stubbornness, I've never doubted your character. I am so embarrassed at myself that I can hardly stand it; what right do I have to find fault with you?'

'In any case, what I've done is nothing more than acting. That's why I'm being treated like this. So enough of your ridicule and your cajoling, leave my room right now. What have I done to deserve this? I couldn't throw my life away, and I can't escape this agony either.'

While speaking, Danyeong felt indescribably lonely. This was the result of the fact that she had done this to forget Ilma, and just when she thought she had done so, here he was in front of her speaking to her. She was unbearably lonely and frustrated. Her intention had been to forever free herself from this frustration, but looking at her failure, she saw it was all her own fault. She immediately began to plan again how to free herself from the anguish he caused her. There was no choice but to put a great deal of distance between herself and Ilma. Distance brings longing, while closeness, even though enjoyable, brings only frustration and the desire to be far apart again. These contradictory feelings were the perverse result of a stubborn, ill-natured temperament.

In spite of her agony, she wasn't sure if showing Ilma the door was what she truly wanted to do or not.

'I said leave right now. And promise never to show yourself again.'

Stretching her arm toward the door, she pushed herself to the foot of the bed, contorting her body and looking as if she were about to tumble out. Her gyrations were too much. Her face burned red, and her hair became dishevelled.

'Why are you getting so excited?'

Thanks to Ilma rushing over and grabbing her, he prevented her from falling from the bed. But she continued to shake, and her eyes rolled. She did not try to break Ilma's grip, rather, she sat up straight and calmly looked at the wall fixedly. She wished she could just evaporate. The anger of a moment ago had disappeared, and now, supported by Ilma's arms, she suddenly became docile. Her desire for him, body and soul, had been real love, and she had been starving to receive such love for most of her life. This was what she wanted, but fate had not granted it to her. Being consoled like this by Ilma was perhaps life's last gift to her, and she was filled with joy, feeling as if she were in dream.

'You have a long life yet to live. Just remember that life can change when you're tempted to have foolish thoughts. Isn't the most important thing to calmly consider how your fate can change?'

'Don't be giving advice like you know what you're talking about. No matter what course my life takes, this is where we part. I'll deal with things as they come.'

Danyeong had regained her wits and gently pushed Ilma away.

Was Ilma a genius? Or was this the nature of all men? He had been able to treat the various women he had known according to each of their situations, and his calm and peaceful expression masked a broad and diverse inner world.

Standing in front of his wife with the same face that he had worn in front of Danyeong was not in the least awkward for Ilma. Of course, he was not sure whether to tell Nadia of his visit to Danyeong. If doing so would damage their happiness, then silence should be seen as the proper expedient. What's more, he did not see this as an affront to his wife. As his last visit to Danyeong had closed the final chapter of their relationship, he did not think it should be a *casus belli* between himself and Nadia. It was true that Danyeong's heart-rending look in the hospital room was disorienting; he had never been in love with her, and it was the matter of only a moment's work to put it behind him. He decided that, from this point on, all negative elements would be rejected, and he would recover the pure spirit of his relationship with Nadia.

That Ilma felt no sense of shame toward Nadia was because even though events on the surface had been chaotic, there had been no changes in his innermost feelings for her. Those feelings had been the same from start to finish. His sentiments for Miryeo as well had been consigned to the distant past as soon as he had met Nadia. In the end, his love for Nadia was stronger than all other things and, for that reason, he felt he had no cause to be ashamed.

It wasn't that he was not sceptical of the morals associated with marriage. To what extent was a perfect relationship possible? Even if one said a couple was like water merging with water, would there be no murkiness or impurities in that union? When it came to the man, how many women other than his wife would he meet in his life? And what direction would their emotions take when that happened? Only the creator and the devil were able to assay how pure or how murky those emotions might be. In the case of the devil, there was no need for him to carefully measure said emotions; rather, all he does is bring forth confusion and anxiety. It is enough to contemplate and desire a perfect relationship, there is no need to analyse it.

Did I not meet Danyeong and Miryeo without the knowledge of my wife? And our relationship faced a crisis. However, it's not right to measure the strength of our relationship based on that fact. I love Nadia. Can there be a more complete merging than that? I have nothing to be ashamed of.

What was needed was not an analysis of feelings, it was maintaining the focus on one's partner with the goals of the relationship in mind, that and effort. Originally, marriage is the beginning of a new life that requires that the old one be reorganized. It meant the reorganization of one's dreams. Chasing the various dreams we have in our short lives is a difficult and tiring business. Marriage means choosing one among many of our dreams and settling down to live within its limits, abandoning the rest. Whether one chooses the best dream or is handed the worst, or whether one's marriage is ideal or not are all decided by the good or bad luck of chance; however, whichever way it turns out, eventually the fatigue sets in. What is important is the effort to overcome this and to not have any illusions.

While ruminating on the morals of marriage, Ilma did not feel in the slightest that there was anything lacking in his relationship with Nadia.

Ilma and Nadia were enjoying some pleasant time, just the two of them, in their room. It was not Ilma's habit to feel tedium, in fact, this evening he was particularly looking forward to their time together.

The temperature had dropped suddenly the night before, and the chilliness had Nadia bundled up in the room.

Even going down for tea being a nuisance, the two were lazing in the room while the bellboy made repeated deliveries.

While they had this leisure time, Nadia took the opportunity to continue her study of the Joseon language that she had begun some time earlier. Ilma was a patient teacher. While he was impressed with her devotion, the study of language is a never-ending task. At times Nadia's progress seemed to be rapid, at other times it seemed slow. She whiled away the time learning the final consonants, remembering vocabulary, and returning to the first chapter of her textbook, repeating, '*Ga-gya, geo-gyeo, gu-gyu ... Ah-ya, eo-yeo, woo-yoo ...** *Ya, yoo.* The fact that one letter represents a sound is really similar to Russian.'

Watching the joy with which Nadia expressed her delight at this fascinating discovery, Ilma could not help but be delighted also and was filled with an inexpressible sense of satisfaction.

He did not feel it to be peculiar when he spoke a foreign language, but when foreigners did so, it seemed exceedingly strange to him. He did not give it a second thought when Nadia spoke her native language, but, with her blonde hair and blue eyes, hearing her awkwardly pronouncing the Joseon language was wondrous. Not only was it admirable that she wanted to learn the language of the one she loved, but the cuteness of her awkward pronunciation drew a smile from Ilma and filled him with a sense of satisfaction. Respecting and wanting to learn the customs of a loved one is an attempt to adapt oneself to that person and is, perhaps, the greatest act of devotion that love inspires.

'Foreigners say that the Joseon language is difficult to learn; what do you think? Most quit in the middle ...'

Ilma assumed the attitude of a benevolent teacher and gave

* Nadia is practicing the vowels of the Korean alphabet.

her a smile, to which Nadia replied confidently, 'Wait and see. I'll have it figured out in a few months. The harder something is to learn, the more value in learning it.'

Trusting in his wife's ability and enthusiasm, Ilma's confidence that she could do what she said increased.

'Just see if I'm not able to talk with Miryeo before too long. I want to be able to get to know her and be able to enjoy myself with her in the Joseon language.'

It was an honest statement. There was no need for Ilma to be concerned at the mention of Miryeo's name. She was the first woman that Nadia had met in Joseon, and she had been taken by Nadia's beauty. It was Nadia's wish to become friends with her.

When evening fell, they felt the room suddenly grow warm, and, upon inspection, found the heat coming from the steam heater by the wall. It was the season's first test. With the smell of metal heating up, the room began to warm.

Nadia left the desk and, carrying her textbook, went to the heater, where she beamed like a child, pressing her stomach against it.

'There's nothing I love more than the first cold spell. Doesn't it suddenly feel like spring in the room?'

She suddenly put her book down and took on a worried tone.

'We have to find a house. Winter is coming, and we can't stay in the hotel.'

Ilma as well was worried about the same thing and had been looking at several locations. 'I'm planning on building something on the outskirts of town in the spring. We just need something for the winter. I'm waiting to hear on several inquiries I've made.'

15. DESIGNING A LIFE

The human being is a tenacious creature that can be reborn several times in one lifetime. It is inevitable that he or she will experience misfortune; it is equally inevitable that that misfortune will pass. Something like a monkey hanging on the rope of fateful and eternal time, the human will struggle with life, enduring its vicissitudes. It is unavoidable that one's history will change with every bounce of the rope. While vexatious, this can also be welcome, for the change that comes may be liberation from a stifling impasse.

Whatever pains Miryeo might still be concealing in her heart, there was no doubt that the return of her peaceful expression and calm demeanour was the result of one such change. Hyeju was relieved to discover this change in her friend's face.

'It seems like there are two Miryeos inside you. The Miryeo of today that is talking and planning is completely different from the Miryeo of yesterday.'

'What else is to be done? As long as we breathe we have to stay busy taking care of our affairs; and when one stays busy, one naturally forgets what has passed.'

f this orchestra performance has made people
usic. Now is a good opportunity.'
r it was sufficiently publicized or not, this is
l in right now. I want to see what it's like to
ie culture business. In several ways it brings
me hope.'

The topic of conversation was planning the Nokseong
Music Academy. This had been in the works for quite a while
now, and while the catalyst that had stimulated Miryeo's
renewed determination to develop the academy was her unexpected reconciliation with Ilma, she had always had a better
than average understanding of music and art and had been a
sponsor of the symphony orchestra as well. This declaration of
her intentions regarding the academy was not only the result
of what had happened with Jongse but was also an expression
of new hope. This change in her frame of mind was the cause
of her renewed enthusiasm for promoting the planning of the
academy. In fact, the will to plan and administer this enterprise had injected her with fresh hope and courage.

Hyeju's strong feelings of friendship were an important
source of support for Miryeo, who sought her counsel because
it was always helpful and also because she enjoyed their chats.

'Just thinking about the young, beautiful Miryeo sitting
in the director's office makes me happy. The beautiful young
director will be enough to make the academy the talk of the
town. What with the stagnant state of culture nowadays, this
will be just the breath of fresh air our society needs.'

Hyeju was already enjoying the thought of the academy.

'What's a more important and a more difficult task than
me being director will be your role as dean. I believe you'll
make a better dean than anyone else.'

'What need is there for a dean? A director and instructors
are all you need, except, of course, for a beautician. You can't
have your women musicians running around looking a mess.
You want the atmosphere of the school to be luxurious and

high-class, and you want the students to be beautiful and polished. You need to create a unique atmosphere without a trace of old-fashionedness. Art should never be sullied by the mundane world.'

'Those are great ideas. I want you to make an administrative plan for me.'

'Candidates should be chosen more for their appearance than for their grades. If possible, you should admit and train beautiful women, and this should be the Nokseong Music Academy's first policy. In spite of talk about fairness in educational opportunity, when it comes to art, certain privileges are assumed in selecting students. In creating the best artist, appearance must be considered as well as talent. When it comes to painting or literature, the artist can hide in his studio and then present his finished creation to his audience. But with music, the artist must appear on the stage, and the combined appeal of their appearance and their art is what moves the audience, and this gives more weight to the performance and more joy to life. It's likely that my emphasis on appearance will be misconstrued, but if people understand my real intentions, I think most will agree with me.'

Hyeju's idealism completely captivated Miryeo. She enthusiastically approved of her friend's ideas.

'That's right. I agree. It might seem aristocratic and high-handed, but it's a good, original idea. Originally, certain races are better at producing musical art than others. No one can argue with the fact that the conditions of such races are unique, and so isn't it proper that those selected as artists should contribute more to human life? My original intention was not to create an academic organization but to build a beautiful garden. I want to build a schoolhouse on top of a hill and plant grass around it. There will be roses, and it will be thick with trees so that it looks like a garden right out of a dream. A beautiful house filled with beautiful people, it will be like heaven on earth. It'll be even more ideal with a beautician there to take care of our beauties morning to evening. I'll see that this happens and make the best academy in the country.'

Miryeo was completely carried away by her daydreaming.

'We shouldn't stop with beautiful students. We'll hire only beautiful women as instructors, and it'll be an oasis of beauty. There won't be any place for me in all that beauty. There won't be anything for me to do, and I wouldn't fit in.'

Miryeo was taken aback at Hyeju's display of modesty.

'What are you talking about? If you're not beautiful, I don't know what beauty is. Stop talking nonsense and promise me that you'll help.'

'Well, the beautiful director certainly is good at teasing people.'

The two had a hearty laugh at this.

'We'll have a department for voice, instrumental music, and composition. In addition, we'll have a choir, chamber music and a symphony orchestra. After the students finish their three-year course, they won't leave the academy but will remain and sit in the chamber chorus or symphony orchestra. In other words, the academy will be organized around education and practical experience so that members trained this way will be able to work in society while living together like a family.'

'It'll be like a small utopia. The meeting of life with art, just what we've longed for.'

The two were enjoying their fantasy immeasurably.

That day the steam heater had been turned on in the quiet theatre, helping them forget the cold outside. Talking about her plan with her friend in her warm room helped melt away the loneliness that Miryeo had been feeling in the big empty house.

A short time later, Miryeo brought in a sketchpad and pencil and started to draw up plans for the academy. The hand holding the pencil was practiced, and she was full of hope and courage. She looked like a skilled technician who had recently come out of a period of sadness. Hyeju was surprised at the sophistication of the drawing, which took shape as if Miryeo had been deliberating on it for some time. In an instant a building, yard, and flower garden appeared in their appointed places. The interior of the building was laid out as the sanctuary that Miryeo had been planning was reproduced on the sketchpad.

'When did you become such an accomplished architect?'

'Since it's my academy, I should design it to my liking, don't you think? Do you know how long I've been planning this?'

The act of designing a structure being a creative process, these words were a subtle expression of the pride and joy she felt at her own creativity.

'The flower garden, rear yard, and lounge will be large; this will be more of a place for rest and recreation.'

Miryeo explained the different aspects of the design that Hyeju pointed to on the sketch.

'Yes, it should be a place for rest and relaxation. What I want to do is combine study and leisure so that every day is one of enjoyment, excitement, and emotion. Call it turning life into art. A lifestyle where art and life are harmonized so that they can't be separated, isn't this the ideal of human life? I'm going to design the Nokseong Academy to meet that ideal, that's why it won't only be comprised of classrooms but will have everything needed.'

Pointing here and there on the sketch with her pencil, Miryeo continued, 'We need a lounge and a hall. There must be a restaurant. Here will be the library, and here the practice room ...'

She lifted her head and put the pencil to her cheek.

'We'll have ten pianos in the practice room. The students can practice any time they want. In the dusk of the evening, or the light of an early moon, the music wafting out into the garden, blending with the chirping of crickets, will create a beautiful mood for the academy.'

'It will be the perfect academy.'

'And I'll put soft sofas in the lounge so that people can relax any time they want, and we'll serve delicious food in the restaurant, and the hall will be large enough that we can have concerts and stage plays, music, and works of art, and there will be literary publications in the library so that people can read them at their leisure.'

'That should do it for the main building.'

'On the porch of the main building there will be roses that climb an arched entryway. The front yard will be covered with grass, and there will be flower beds here and there.'

'Of course, we'll import the grass from England.'

'One of the characteristics of the academy will be the grounds, which will be entirely covered with green grass without a patch of earth showing through. And we'll cover the pathway to the porch with white gravel. On the green background of the grass will be spelled "Nokseong Music Academy" with flowers.'

'And will you plant trees in the rear garden?'

'That's right. We'll plant trees close together so that we'll have deep shade in the rear and side gardens. There will be poplars, elms, maple, and interspersed between them, evergreens like juniper.'

Tired of sitting, Miryeo took Hyeju and left the hospitality room, heading for her own room.

The *ondol** heating was on, and its warmth was different from that of cultures that sit above the floor in chairs. Sitting on the warm floor, the two continued to indulge in their fantasy.

---

* *Ondol* is the system of heating used in Korea whereby warm air is circulated under the floor in flues.

'And that's not the end of it. I have an even bigger plan.'

Miryeo delighted in surprising Hyeju with new ideas.

'Why don't you just bring a corner of paradise and put it there?'

'I'm going to build an annex next to the main building with a gymnasium and a greenhouse. In the gymnasium the women, wearing only underwear, will run and jump, play with balls, and enjoy themselves. The exercise will help them grow straight and tall like bamboo, and they will plant flowers and tropical plants in the greenhouse where they can stroll in the warm sunshine.'

'What else are you going to surprise me with?'

'There will be something amazing in the shade of the trees in the rear garden.'

'Are you going to plant the tree of knowledge that Adam and Eve stood under?'

'What do you mean Adam? This is a world for Eves only and I'm building it for them.'

'What other surprises do you have for me?'

'How about a pool? I'll dig a pool. It'll be framed with marble and fresh water will constantly flow into it and run over the sides. In the summer, the water will be blue in the shade of the trees, and in the autumn, red and yellow leaves will flutter down and float gently on the surface, which will ripple in the wind ...'

'And the Eves will swim naked in the water?'

'They'll swim and play tag and have water fights and cavort. The water will refresh them and help them recover when they are tired from their studies. That won't be the end of their enjoyment; the beautiful landscape will be a source of healthy pleasure.'

'Okay. Stop. I can't take any more.'

Hyeju was exhausted from just listening, but Miryeo volunteered more.

'Actually, all this is related to leisure, so I plan to establish a department of leisure and let it operate according to its own needs. Related to that, I have something important to discuss with you.'

Looking Hyeju straight in the eye, she said, 'I'm thinking of using Danyeong. What's your opinion?'

'Danyeong?'

This was absolutely unexpected. She opened her eyes wide in surprise and stared at Miryeo.

'I'm thinking of hiring her as head of the department of leisure. Of course, you'll be the dean. That means the three of us would administer the academy. With the three of us working together, there's nothing we won't be able to do.'

'Hiring Danyeong isn't the problem. Are you completely over the unpleasantness that occurred between the two of you? If so, and you think that you can start fresh with her, then I have no objections.'

'I've been alright with Danyeong for some time now. What happened between us is all in the past. We've both suffered failures and are trying to start fresh and giving Danyeong a chance for redemption is the duty of one woman to another. What's important is that I have always liked Danyeong and will have no problem being her friend. The question is whether or not she will accept my offer.'

'Why would Danyeong refuse such a generous offer? The best thing she can do for herself is get out of that sleazy film industry world. If you can get her to agree then both of your problems will be solved.'

Even though these were still only ideas, talking like this filled them both with endless pleasure.

*

Danyeong, who had been moved from the hospital to her apartment, was now fully recovered and ready to leave her sickbed behind. She had been up for several days and would suddenly rise from her chair, pace her room, and then go down the hall to peer into every nook and cranny of the apartment. It was as if she was feeling an unfamiliar new energy. She touched her toes and stretched. Doing light calisthenics, she tested her body's vitality like a technician checking the performance of his favourite machine.

Why did I do it? Was I caught in a nightmare?

She had not really regretted her past mistake, but now, thinking about it again, she did not want to repeat it. With a newfound appreciation for her body, which had been brought back from the brink of death, she came to think of her past action as something that had happened in a dream.

Her face was thinner than it had been before the incident, which ended up making it appear lovelier, and looking at the upper half of her body in the mirror, she was taken by the mysteriousness of it. It was unblemished and white like something grown in a greenhouse. Her earlobes, nose, and fingers were smooth and pliable as beeswax. She couldn't stop looking at her body, wondering when it had become so beautiful.

The chrysanthemums she had put by the window continued to bloom, oblivious to the cold, filling the room with their fragrance and filling her with a new joy and vitality. She experienced inexpressible admiration at the sight of those flowers and their ability to overcome the adversity of the season. While staring at the chrysanthemums, she suddenly recalled the sight of Miryeo, who had come to see her, and recalled what she had said:

'Let's work together. Let's show people that women are not weak.'

Miryeo's sincere intentions and kind words had convinced Danyeong to accept her offer. While they could have continued their animosity toward each other, Danyeong was impressed with the magnanimity of the warm affection being shown her by a member of her own sex. In addition, an enterprise related to the development of culture was very intriguing to her.

Not only would she be able to forget her past dream of love by immersing herself in this new work, but she felt she could even come to disregard it completely. She was thankful for Miryeo's offer and pledged to work together with her.

'What the people need is not a path to destruction, but one to revival, to resurrection. We must always be brave.'

These words spoken to her by Miryeo remained engraved in her heart.

On this evening, there was to be a dinner for the organizers of the Nokseong Music Academy. Danyeong, to show her commitment to the project, had promised to attend. She had been at her dressing table since early in the afternoon, busily preparing herself. Her make-up, an indispensable part of a woman's everyday life, was the announcement of her return to life, her first new step, and her first order of business. Her clean complexion became milky white with cream and powder.

The day before, Miryeo had appeared wrapped in a thick black overcoat. It had been a good look for her and had served as an impetus to Danyeong. That thick overcoat had been an indication of a strong will to live. Danyeong pulled her overcoat and muffler from her wardrobe. She would take her first new steps wearing them.

She also could not forget the black shoes that Miryeo had worn. The faintly shining black shoes had seemed to be fuelling a ravenous desire for life. She was immensely pleased at the thought of wearing her own black shoes and seeing the blue sky and white clouds reflected in their shiny surface.

*

Hyeju was talking to her husband, An Sangdal.

'We're still not in agreement on when to open, but there are things that will be difficult for women to do, so I want you to be involved as well.'

'So, *Southern Carrier* has changed to the Nokseong Music

Academy, eh? I generally think it's a good idea, but you said that men weren't permitted inside.'

'Well, it is just for women, but there will be times when we will need a lackey.'

'So you do need men after all. I guess women can never really be independent.'

'What? Don't be so full of yourself. If you're not interested, just forget it.'

'Did I say I wasn't interested? I was just wondering out loud about how things will turn out.'

However, as things did turn out, An Sangdal spared no efforts in helping with the preparations. As his wife, in good conscience, could not ignore her other responsibilities, he filled in in her place where needed.

Originally, the idea for the academy had been related to the sponsorship of the symphony orchestra, and as the *Hyundai Daily* newspaper had been the sponsor of the orchestra, it was the paper that had first thought of the academy. In order to follow up on the idea, the newspaper organized a sponsorship committee. While listening to the sponsors, Miryeo appealed for a smooth launch of the academy project. Directly involved in the sponsorship committee were the president of the *Hyundai Daily* and Jongse. An Sangdal, as well, lent his name to the project and used his influence for the sake of his wife.

Attending the dinner that evening were the editor and Jongse from the paper, An Sangdal, and, from the academy's side, Miryeo, Hyeju and Danyeong.

The six practically filled the room in the restaurant, but the relatively small number did not diminish the significance of the meeting. The group, gathered there in that well-prepared room to celebrate the creation of the music academy, looked dignified and elegant. The refined and splendid appearance of the three women lit up the room, creating a bright and cheery ambience.

In all of that brightness, Danyeong looked as splendid

as anyone. Her past was all behind her. If her surroundings shone on her, she naturally reflected that brilliance. Not only was the entire party free of any prejudices regarding her past, but they all accepted her, and this in turn helped her to free herself completely from that past and shine in their midst. Having washed the stains of her past from her soul, she looked somehow sublime sitting elegantly in front of her new and bright future. That night, she looked as she never had before, and her appearance brought repeated glances. In a word, a new person had been born, a new personality created. She was no longer her former self.

Sitting with Danyeong on one side and her good friend Hyeju on the other, facing these three socially prominent men, Miryeo could not have been happier. It was not only the way they all looked that night that made her feel as proud as a peacock. It was that her heart was filled with an even greater brilliance than that given off by her appearance.

I'm embarking on a new career. I can now go out in public again.

The more she thought, the more she was filled with strong emotions. Life is long and wonderful. She could not have imagined a few months ago that such a wonderful new life could be possible. Her emotions caused her heart to swell and her eyes to fill with tears.

'What is really amazing about the creation of the Nokseong Music Academy is not only the fact that there has never been such a cultural facility in this country before but also the wholly original nature of a project of this scale. We have all felt the need for such a facility and have been eagerly awaiting its appearance. And now, our wish is about to be realized. It is not only us here who will appreciate the meaning of this; there are many other people in this country who will be delighted by the news.'

After the congratulatory remarks were concluded and Miryeo and the others had given short speeches, the dinner began, and conversation turned to friendly chitchat. The chief editor's conversation was basically an extension of the congratulatory comments, and it seemed that was all people wanted to talk about.

An Sangdal picked up the conversation where the editor had left off. He too had nothing but praise for the project.

'What will surprise people more than anything is that this facility is run by women and is for women. This is a first, and I'm anxious to see the kind of attention it's going to get. The task is to bring everything to a successful conclusion by continuing to hold people's interest and giving them a good impression.'

'This is even more important seeing as this is a project related to music. Are there a people anywhere in the world that are more ignorant of music than we are? When we consider that the more cultured a society is the greater the role music plays in everyday life, this academy becomes even more important. If we work continuously to promote and popularize music, sooner or later we'll see development in our culture.'

Jongse continued with his oft-heard theory about the necessity of music.

'No matter how much human society might change, the love of music will never change. Literature and painting are important arts, but they can't match music for directly moving the human heart. Whether you're sad, or angry, if you listen to music it always lightens your mood. Music can truly bring harmony to people. If the emotions of people absorbed in music could be harnessed and used, all those politicians and great thinkers of antiquity would be able to build the ideal state of love that hasn't been possible up until now. The inspiration one receives from music is more enjoyable and effective than the hundreds of theories produced by philosophers. Because it has strength, music provides a kind of sustenance or perhaps something more. In fact, if you were to ask me what the best thing in the world is, I would say music. It's better than food, clothing, love, or ambition; it's better than anything I can think of. If one has music, then all can be forgotten in an instant. You might think I'm crazy, but I'll never change the way I think about music.'

Jongse's unexpected passion drew smiles and applause from the rest of the group.

'What's more, as you heard earlier, the plans and aspirations of the sponsors are unique and admirable, and we give them our full endorsement. Furthermore, as we believe that this enterprise will contribute significantly to society, we will do all we can to support it.'

As if waiting for her turn, Miryeo took the opportunity to express her thanks.

'Thank you. I believe that with your support we will achieve an excellent result. Even though we three are short on experience, we will work as hard as we can for this project.'

After speaking, she glanced at Hyeju and Danyeong, who sat looking dignified.

'The president should have been here but was unable to make it due to another engagement, so I came in his stead. Tonight's toast is a special one.' While making small talk, the editor made several toasts.

The other engagement that the president could not avoid was actually a small gathering in honour of Ilma and his wife in the same restaurant. It was overdue, but tonight was the night that the president had decided to host a wedding reception for Ilma. It was also in thanks for Ilma's role in making the symphony orchestra's performances such a huge success. The president was personally hosting the couple that night as a gesture of appreciation. This was the reason that he had sent the chief editor in his stead to the music academy dinner.

Both dinners occurring in the same restaurant on the same night was not an accident. The president had planned it that way. Holding both dinners in the same restaurant was a matter of convenience; it was economical for the president to entertain in one room and send the editor to do the same in the other. There was nothing more to it. As this was an un-co-incidental coincidence, nothing would disturb the course of what went on in the two rooms, and for that reason there is nothing further to add to this part of the story. In other words, it was a simple 'coincidence', and these kinds of 'coincidences' sometimes happen. Yet, when Miryeo heard of that coincidence, she was vaguely stirred.

'Ilma is here in another room, what a pleasant surprise. There are two wonderful celebrations taking place here tonight.'

She spoke in a composed manner, but her heart was anything but composed. She had lost the calmness that had been with her all evening, and her heart was in a flutter.

Danyeong was feeling the same thing as well, and Hyeju immediately perceived what was happening.

'In that room a reception, in this one a congratulatory dinner, both happy events.'

'It would have been better if we had joined the two together; there was no need to hold them separately.' Hyeju, with a mischievous grin on her face, poked Miryeo in the ribs.

Before she could go on, Jongse joined in. 'I see no reason we couldn't have done that.'

Miryeo's face turned even redder.

'The two gatherings are different, there's no need to combine the two. We are celebrating an enterprise for and by women, there's no reason to add more men to the mix. We are thankful for what our sponsors have done for us tonight, but men are strictly forbidden in the music academy.'

'Oh ho. So, men are forbidden. That's impressive.'

Jongse chimed in with a smile on his face.

'In any event, I pray that both parties are blessed with happy, bright futures,' Jongse said and momentarily left the room. He was going to Ilma's room. Going back and forth between the two rooms, he had two roles to play this evening.

Before he could enter the room, he ran into Ilma at the corner of the hallway.

Hearing from Jongse about Miryeo, Ilma's face flushed.

'I had no idea. I mean, I heard talk about the music academy, but I didn't know a sponsorship committee had already been formed. That's good news.'

'Danyeong, Hyeju, and Miryeo looked very dignified talking about their plans for the academy. Once a person makes a plan, they grow into the task in terms of dignity and presence. After seeing Miryeo tonight, there's no reason to think she can't be a good director.'

'There's nothing that women can't accomplish these days. And Danyeong is a completely different woman.'

'Um hm.'

As he and Jongse opened the door of the room, Ilma was deep in thought.

In the room sat the president, the director, and the chief of the entertainment bureau with the couple sitting in the middle. More than anything else, the cheerful mood of the room was created by the happy couple. More precisely, it was the result of Nadia's pleasant attitude. This was what the aged president had hoped for, and a harmonious mood pervaded the room.

The happy atmosphere was in contrast to the dignified and solemn mood of Miryeo's room. The dignified poses of the three women were a good thing in that they helped lend a sense of certainty to the new plans for the enterprise. They had gathered to celebrate the academy project and toast its success, and the women had created just the right mood. And in Ilma's room, the atmosphere of harmony and warmth was perfect for the occasion. Now it was up to Ilma and Nadia to live a happy, peaceful life together. The times of turbulence and excitement were in the past. Miryeo's life was now designed around gratitude and Ilma's around joy, and the atmospheres of the two gatherings reflected those two emotions.

When Jongse entered the room, Nadia was sitting awk-wardly on the floor with her legs stretched out in front of her, looking with wonder at the table of food.

'What do think of Joseon food? Do you still find it strange?'

'Strange? Not at all.'

Jongse saw that she was much more practiced with the chopsticks she held in her hand than she had been before.

'Do you like the *ondol*?' Jongse asked.

'There's nothing better than the warmth of the *ondol*. It's better than our Russian stoves, steam heat, or furnaces. I'm in the process of convincing Ilma to put an *ondol* room in the house we intend to build this spring,' she said while smiling at her husband.

In fact, this was not the first time that Nadia had expe-rienced *ondol* and Joseon food. Her exposure to them had gradually turned her into a fan of both. That night as well, she could be said to be an admirer of Joseon culture. She sam-pled everything on the table. She enjoyed the sweet steamed rice, the honey-ginger cakes, rice nectar, and honeyed fruit. While it is true that what is palatable to one might not be so to another, Nadia was unusually fond of Joseon food.

'This cinnamon-flavoured persimmon punch tastes like coffee,' she said, comparing the tastes of the two.

'And this sweet rice tastes like sweetly prepared stew,' she added, but her evaluations of the food seemed unnecessary as she was already once again engrossed in her meal.

The sight of Nadia sitting in front of the low table eating Joseon food suddenly seemed very natural to Jongse, and the awkward impression she had once given had disappeared without a trace. This brought up an important point: whether one's hair is black or red, whether one speaks the same lan-guage or not, all sit at the banquet of life as equals, and there is nothing remotely unnatural about this. Differences in life-style are not fundamental obstacles to harmony. Whether one eats bread or rice is an inconsequential difference. When love is strong enough, the assimilation of the human race is as simple as can be.

The gathering was not a noisy drinking affair, as official events ended after about an hour, and the room became somewhat quiet, but the director and the chief kept the mood alive with witty conversation.

After Jongse had returned to the other room, Ilma as well thought it time to wrap things up and went out for a last breath of fresh air.

It was still early evening in the restaurant.* In the hallway, the sounds of revelry could be heard coming from the various rooms.

Something was on Ilma's mind, but for the life of him he could not put his finger on what it was. Something in his subconscious had a grip on his thoughts but would not reveal itself. Being lost this way in thought, he took a wrong turn in the hallway after coming out of the bathroom and, as he was passing by the open door of an unoccupied room, was surprised by the sight of someone sitting inside.

Who is that? Who's in there?

He was momentarily befuddled and could not make out who it was. He thought this could not possibly be due to the couple of drinks he had had.

Standing stone still like a totem pole, his senses suddenly cleared, and he recognized who was sitting in the room.

Why, it's Miryeo.

This all took no longer than an instant, and as he shook his head to clear it, he was suddenly taken with a feeling of shame. What had caused him to momentarily lose his wits? Had it been thoughts of Miryeo submerged in his subconscious that he had not been able to identify? Had he become befuddled because the thing that was submerged in his mind had been

---

* Actually they are in a *yojeong* (요정) which is a high-class Korean restaurant used for entertaining and sometimes employing *kisaeng*.

suddenly come into focus? Feeling uneasy, he could not suppress a sense of embarrassment.

'Why are you in here by yourself when your party is in there?' Ilma asked, standing just inside the door. Miryeo gave him a penetrating look and then bowed her head.

'I came here to catch my breath. It's getting noisy in there,' she replied.

A sudden feeling that this would be the last time he would see her came over him, and impulsively throwing prudence to the wind, he shut the door and sat down in front of her. He felt he had to say something at their last parting.

'I heard from Jongse about the establishment of the Nokseong Music Academy. I hope that all goes well and that you're successful.'

It seemed that Miryeo had felt the same thing as Ilma. She looked boldly into his face, and there were countless things in her bright eyes that could never be said.

'It's I that should congratulate you first. I wish you all the happiness in the world in your married life.'

Whether she was sincere or not was not clear, but Ilma couldn't help but wonder if there was a touch of sarcasm in those words.

'We may both be living in the same city of Seoul, but for some reason I have the feeling that we won't meet again.'

'It's better if we don't. What's to be gained from seeing each other?'

'Even if we don't meet, I will feel better knowing that you are in Seoul.'

This last comment seemed sincere, without any hidden motives.

'Even though they say life is short, it's not. And who knows what will happen in the future?'

'I sincerely wish you peace and success. Goodbye.'

Being careful not to let her voice tremble, Miryeo, telling herself not to cry, bit her lip and got a firm grip on her emotions.

*

Thanks to the help of the people at the newspaper. Ilma was easily able to find a place to live.

It was a small house on the hill facing the British Consulate, and Nadia loved it at first sight. Ilma as well thought it fortunate the way things had turned out and was no less delighted than Nadia on the day they went to look it over. It was a brick house that had been occupied by foreign missionaries and had a large yard. The yard was so big that it made the house look small. The hill the house was on overlooked the entire neighbourhood. On the lawn, now withered yellow, stood thickets of rose bramble interspersed here and there with maple trees, giving the place the feel of a garden in the midst of the city. Vines grew on the old bricks of the wall, and among their withered tendrils wild grapes hung in abundance. It was easy to imagine how beautiful this house would be in the summer, but even now in winter with only the vines, it was a pleasant sight. Thinking that this would be their home, if only for a short time, brought the couple a sense of satisfaction. They would be here until they built their own house the following spring. A half-year is a long time when each day is filled with joy. This place would be even more memorable because it was their first house.

Half the city was visible from the window of the first room in from the porch. The dense houses and bustle of the city seemed so close one could reach out and touch them. What was more, the view at night with the twinkling lights was so clear and beautiful that it increased the happiness the new house gave them.

On the day they looked at the house, they had coal brought in and made a fire in the fireplace. They also had a bed delivered and moved their things out of the hotel. There were so many things to arrange in the new house that they planned to take their time putting on the finishing touches. In the way of belongings, there were merely two trunks from the hotel, some household items that Ilma had left at Neungbo's, books and bookshelves, a wardrobe, and the like.

As this was a new house, they had to buy all the household items they would need. This was not an easy task. While enjoyable, it was also tiring. It was a laborious job that required patience, meticulous planning, close attention to detail, and clever bargaining. It was not just chairs and wardrobes that were needed; a length of twine and a nail were also essential items. Worrying about twine and needles and nails and hammers got so confusing that in the end, Ilma did not know if he was coming or going.

'Managing everyday life is not such an easy thing to do.'

'Of course not. This goes all the way back to the beginning of history; how could it be easy? Among all the things one can design, designing a new house is one of the most important. It's both aggravating and enjoyable.'

Every morning when Nadia woke up, she faced the day with a fresh spirit and new courage. As she arranged the numerous chairs, tables, bookcases, wardrobes, and the bed – mostly unwieldy things – each in their place, the house began to take shape. However, what were most important to Nadia were the kitchen and its utensils. At what point she had become such a devoted housewife was unclear, but she selected every teacup according to her own taste and gave her full attention to the selection of each plate and dish.

After the kitchen had been fully arranged, and while she was first testing her skills there, she also began making curtains for the many windows. According to Nadia, curtains were the most important factor determining the impression a house would give. She felt they were an expression of taste and refinement. Gathering scraps of material, she sat in front of her sewing machine, whistling along to its rhythm while creating her own unique designs.

Due to their efforts, after a few days the place had become a cosy nest for its new inhabitants. Colour was a precious commodity in this season, and, seen from the drab yard, the exterior of the house seemed bulky, but it being winter, the inside was kept cosy and warm. The curtains that Nadia had made, when seen from outside, were a brilliant touch that decorated the entire house. They looked luxurious and seemed to hint at the plenitude inside those dull brick walls. The smoke that rose all day long from the square chimney looked like steam rising from a cup of tea.

With her apron on over her winter clothes, the young mistress of the house gave the appearance of a typical housewife. While being a sweet wife, she was also an earnest homemaker. There was talk of hiring a maid, and they were looking for one, but until she came, Nadia would play the role of homemaker. Even after a maid was employed, she intended to maintain her special rights as mistress of the house.

'Aren't we missing something?'

'Really? What else do we need?'

'Oh, right. Music! We don't have any music.'

They had been too busy for the past few days to think of music. The fact that these two, who could not live a day without music, had forgotten about it was a testament to how absorbed in work they had been.

Nadia was greatly pleased by the piano that was placed in the drawing room.

Every day, she would take off her apron and sit in front of it. She would invariably clean herself up, change her clothes and her frame of mind, and sit down to enjoy herself. She was drinking life to the lees without missing a drop. The more enjoyable life is, the healthier one's spirit is, and one's spirit must be healthy for life to be enjoyable.

When she would play the waltz which sang of the Danube river, Ilma would stand next to her and watch her fingers dance on the keys while his mind wandered back to Harbin. Memories of Harbin were always intertwined with this waltz.

It was the night of the waltz that his and Nadia's hearts had found each other.

The nostalgia for the Danube was, for Nadia, nostalgia for the Songhwa river in Harbin, and her fingers tripping over the keys seemed to be an expression of this.

On clear days, the piano strains flowing from the house seemed even more distinct and gave the house on the hill its life and character. The house now had a different character than it had when its previous owners had occupied it and a different one than it would receive from its future residents.

The sky was particularly blue, and the couple was standing by the window in a state of total bliss. What more could they need?

'Endless blue sky ...'

Both happiness and unhappiness were endless. Staring at the endless blue sky that seemed like endless life, Nadia now felt that her entire body had been dyed azure by that sky of blue.

'What do you think will fall from that sky?'

'I don't know. But it seems something will fall.'

Nadia looked at Ilma. 'Shut your eyes and you'll find out.'

'Here.'

He shut his eyes, but there was more.

'Open your mouth.'

'Ah.'

What fell on Ilma's open mouth and face, which was turned to the sky, was the soft touch of skin and a warm body. That which fell from the blue sky was Nadia's body and her love.

Could there be anything better than this gift from the blue sky? Ilma's body once experienced anew the happiness his wife could give him as he surrendered himself into her hands.

16. A DIGRESSION

The next day a new tenant moved into the room of the Cheongun apartment that Ilma had recently vacated. It was Eunpa. Neungbo had brought someone even closer to him than his old friend Ilma to live there.

While outwardly the two had often traded abuse, somewhere along the way their relationship had become much closer. Their friends had all been surprised when the two, who were always fighting like cats and dogs, suddenly ended up living together. Was this the result of some hidden attractiveness that Eunpa possessed? Was the external animosity actually an expression of love?

Neungbo had not started his business yet, but was financially stable enough to support two people. It had been Eunpa's hope to quit her lowly job at the Sillagwon and live with Neungbo, and now that hope had been realized. She was not concerned about the annoyance of conventions regarding marriage but was happy to live under one roof with him as long as they got along; she did not bother herself with the burden of additional worries. As for Neungbo, he thought this arrangement much better than living alone, as did Eunpa.

All that Eunpa brought with her were two trunks. Even though they were living together, it was Eunpa who was joining Neungbo. The trunks looked small in the large, empty room.

'Wouldn't it be better if I put them in your room?'

Eunpa, looking small in the middle of the large room, was unhappy about how barren it was.

'That doesn't make sense. We both have our own ways, and we need to be able to go to our own rooms when things get complicated,' Neungbo replied.

'This still feels like Ilma's room.'

'He has left to be with Nadia and taken all of his things, there isn't a trace of him left here.'

In the end, Eunpa occupied this room, but, in reality, it was also something of Neungbo's room as well. Eunpa had her two trunks, but she used all of Neungbo's household items: his bookcases, his chairs, his wardrobe. They both ended up using this room as their bedroom. The two rooms were actually like one, just as their two bodies were like one. Only a thin wall separated the two rooms, and with the addition of this new occupant, the house took on a new personality and customs. Eunpa was daily much happier and freer than she had ever been at the Sillagwon, and it was as if she had re-discovered paradise. She no longer was an object of contempt, but now had self-esteem. Living now like a devoted housewife, taking care of these two rooms was a source of delight, and she could not help but continue to look back at her old self and wonder at this second chance at life. After Neungbo would leave for his office, Eunpa's duties consisted of cleaning and straightening up the two rooms. She would tie a towel around her head and whistle while swinging her broom, taking to her duties like a mother hen.

She was concerned about pleasing Neungbo and would show the greatest care when polishing the microscope that he valued so highly. Of course, she enjoyed all this.

Seeing the way her face lit up when he returned home, this was possibly the most enjoyable moment of her day. The sight of Eunpa jumping up from her chair made Neungbo smile, and he wondered by what appellation he should address her. Eunpa was wondering the same thing when she suddenly said, 'Let's go out for dinner.'

They both decided it was most comfortable to dispense with any appellations.*

Hun came to visit Neungbo with a large box of matches as a housewarming gift. He was surprised at how neat and tidy the place was.

'It seems living together has got living alone beat hands down. The place feels totally different.'

'How is it different?' Even as he asked this, Neungbo knew the answer.

'Was there ever a bohemian like you? You were dirty, lazy, messy, a real low life. But look at you now. Not only is this place clean, but you're clean too. You have a crease in the pants of your suit, you wear clean underwear every day, and your shoes are shined. This is a completely different you. Women are like a groom that takes a dirty man and cleans him up.'

'Groom is a little extreme, don't you think?' Eunpa, who had been brewing tea over a kerosene stove, was not happy with the comparison.

'There's nothing extreme about it. Think how great a responsibility it is to care for a horse.'

'Then I'm nothing more than a horse.' It was Neungbo's turn to be unhappy.

'So, neither a horse nor a groom are good enough for the

---

* Here the text is referring to the Korean custom of referring to someone by other than their name. In professional life it is always a title. Here it could be whether Neungbo is going to refer to Eunpa as *yobo* or 'honey'.

two of you. Eh? You don't want to be either a groom or a horse? You're both being greedy. If the right groom came along, I'd gladly be a horse.'

The three had a good laugh at Hun's analogy that had initially ruffled feathers but ended up being a pretty good joke. Eunpa put the boiled tea on the table and poured a bit of whiskey into each cup.

For Hun, this was a different kind of tea. The fragrance of the whiskey in the hot tea seemed to seep warmly into his entire body. This was the tastiest cup of tea he had ever had.

'Is this the taste of home? This warm, fragrant taste?'

'Actually, there are many benefits beside this to living together.'

Neungbo explained his thoughts on this one by one to Hun, who agreed with everything he heard.

'This tea is great, and I'm a lot cleaner. In addition to that, I have calmed down a lot, daily life is more convenient, and I don't spend as much money since I'm not out drinking every night.'

'Hmm. That last one makes the most sense. That's a benefit I never would have thought of.'

'It turns out that what I'd been dreaming about was right next to me. The loftier and farther away one's dream is, the more impossible it is. The dream right in front of your nose and the one a thousand miles away are the same if you can catch them. If you can realize one dream, no matter which one it is, the next thing to do is find a way to find peace within that dream.'

'I'm sorry I couldn't be the thousand-mile-away dream.'

Despite being slightly miffed, Eunpa was not unhappy with Neungbo's attitude. They had been this way with each other from the beginning, and it was, perhaps, the reason they were together.

'You may have found peace in your dream, but we have lost the enjoyment of drinking at the Sillagwon. Without Eunpa, the place seems empty, and now we can't joke around with her like we used to.'

'Then don't let Danyeong get away. Don't you fiddle around too.'

Even if Hun had not heard this from Neungbo, he had lately been unable to ignore Danyeong. She had made a clean break with Myeongdo, had started over with a new outlook; she seemed like a person reborn. He felt the surge of a new desire.

On this day, Hun had decided to go and visit Danyeong. Seeing the way Neungbo and Eunpa acted together only increased his desire to do so.

*

Ilma learned about what had been going on in Manchuria through a letter from Emilia that had come for Nadia.

Ilma was happy to learn the latest of the Daeryukdang, about which he had been wondering. He expected a detailed letter from Byeoksu, but in the meantime, he was able to hear from his wife what Emilia had to say about it.

As expected, the family had paid the three hundred thousand won to the gang, and Unsan had been released unharmed. As rumoured, he had been held in the remote region by the border. It was fortunate that he was released without incident and without having been hurt or mistreated. It was unclear through which route Unsan had been released, but Ilma expected that Unsan would be able sit his large body somewhere comfortable and relax, and that Byeoksu, Unsan's wife, and the rest of the family, whose anxiety had come to an end, would finally get a good night's sleep. This had become a hot topic of conversation on the street, and now that the fear and anxiety were a thing of the past, there was a mood of excited reassurance. The gang member's identities had not been discovered, and they were hiding in anonymity as they always had. The fact that Emilia had passed on this much information made it easy to guess how much attention this story had received on the streets of Harbin.

When he thought about how hard this terrible, once-in-a-lifetime experience must have been on Han Unsan, who had made his way with nothing but his will in that lonely foreign land, Ilma was left with a strong impression as if this was not merely an incident that had happened to someone else. While it was shocking and dispiriting, it also provided a valuable lesson that could alter the way he made decisions. This might be incentive for Byeoksu, who had not been happy with the way his uncle did business, to help Unsan clean up his affairs so that he might play a part in the development of Manchuria. It was as if he had seen how fortune and misfortune could be intertwined, and this gave rise to all manner of complicated thoughts.

'The fact that they couldn't uncover the gang, and that they are still lurking somewhere, means that Harbin continues to be a dangerous city. How can one travel there with any sense of comfort?'

'What do we have to fear from a gang? Things happen when you draw too much attention to yourself. Ordinary citizens have nothing to worry about. Rising above the crowd is not always a recipe for happiness.'

'Well, hopefully there'll come a day when the dark underbelly of society will disappear.'

'In any event, all's well that ends well. I couldn't have hoped for a better conclusion. Now you don't have to go back to Harbin and leave me here,' Nadia said with a laugh. This joke was a better way to tell Ilma how worried she had been last time he left than coming right out and saying so. 'One thing worries me more than that gang.'

With a slight change in his tone of voice, Ilma asked what that one thing was.

'Emilia. I worry about her health; she must be having a

terrible time in the cold. Even though she doesn't come right out and say it in her letter, it's obvious.'

Ilma knew that Nadia was probably closer to Emilia than she was to her aunt.

'I have a request.' She said this hesitantly.

'What is it? There's nothing you can't ask me.'

'I'd like to bring Emilia here for a while. So she doesn't have such a hard time with the winter.'

To Ilma, this was not a difficult request. He thought that he should have volunteered the idea himself.

'If Emilia agrees, what objections would I have? Will she want to come?'

'You'll do it? Oh, thank you. I'll send her a reply right away. She'll be overjoyed. I'll tell her to leave immediately.'

*

Jongse went to visit Neungbo, and he took Ilma along with him.

'I should have visited your house first, but I haven't gone yet because I can't decide what to get you for a housewarming present. I can't very well bring you a box of matches.'

This was Jongse's excuse for still not having come to see Ilma's new home.

'What do you mean, housewarming present? Just bring yourself.'

'It wouldn't be a problem if only one person was setting up house, but all my friends are setting up new homes, and it's a tricky question as to who to go visit first. At any rate, making a new home with someone seems to be the road to happiness.'

'I'm sorry I made you worry about something so trivial. I didn't realize setting up house would cause this kind of problem.'

'Anyway, I thought I'd go see Neungbo today.'

'I was thinking the same thing.'

The two were sitting at the window of a teahouse facing the street, while outside the window the sidewalk was a jumble of people coming and going. It was a typical busy winter street.

'I'm not complaining about you having a new home and all, it's just that with you in your warm little sanctuary, what do you expect the rest of us to do? When Hun and I leave you guys and go home, all we have waiting for us is a cold room.'

There was a tone of regret and loneliness in Jongse's voice.

'When I put it like that, it sounds like I'm jealous. But what I really mean is that you are doing the right thing.'

Looking outside, they could see that it had begun to snow. The large flakes came down to land on the pedestrians' shoulders and brush against their legs. Judging by the fact that the street was already white, it seemed this was going to be a heavy snowfall.

'Why don't you enjoy single life a little while longer? Such large dreams shouldn't be thrown away so easily.'

'No matter how large my dream might be, is there any way the results can be better than what you got? All dreams are the same if they can be realized.'

'Don't get distracted. Keep your mind on what you're trying to do. A big pumpkin is not going to come rolling along.'

'Well, even if it's small, the pumpkin that has already rolled up to you is better than the big pumpkin that might come rolling along,' Jongse said as he stared out of the window at the falling snow. 'This winter I'm going to relieve some stress by going skiing. There's nothing better than sports to clear your mind.'

'Skiing? Good idea. I want to go along. I haven't been able to ski for a couple of years, and I'm looking forward to it.'

'Are you saying you're going to bring you wife to the ski hill?'

'If that bothers you I'll go alone.'

'An Sangdal said he's going to start this winter, and he's

already bought boots and gloves, and he's chomping at the bit. It looks like our ski circle will get bigger this year.'

'We'll form a team and head for Sambang every weekend.'*

'If An Sangdal goes, do you think Hyeju's going to stay behind? The ski trips are going to become couple outings as well.'

'Does that mean that the entire staff of the Nokseong Music Academy is going to be mobilized?' As he was asking this, Ilma suddenly changed directions. 'By the way, do you meet Miryeo often these days?'

Ilma's question sounded natural, but Jongse immediately perceived that he was fishing, and so he merely stared at him in reply.

Ilma seemed to be trying to sound out Jongse's relationship with Miryeo, which made Jongse feel somewhat awkward; however, the problem was that he himself was not sure of his own mind on the subject.

'I haven't seen her since that night. But even if I had, Miryeo's not the kind of woman to easily give her heart to someone,' he answered, and then searched his feelings, wondering if he was actually contemplating trying to win her heart if it were winnable. He felt a sudden shiver. Everything that was happening lately was so incredible and frightening.

'I have no idea how easy her heart is to win.'

'Who knows what the future holds? The only way we can know what's waiting around the corner is to turn it. The only thing that can determine what's going to happen to us in life is life itself. Life ... We have no choice but to live and see what happens.'

After rambling thus to himself for a moment, Jongse came back to the here and now.

'What am I talking about? What does Miryeo have to do

---

* The first ski hill in Korea was developed by the Japanese at Sambang in 1929.

with me? Forget Miryeo, I haven't told you yet about Cheong-mae. I just got a letter from her in Shanghai. Here, read it and see what Shanghai is like.'

He pulled a wrinkled letter from his pocket and gave it to Ilma.

'A letter from Cheongmae? I haven't heard that name for a long time.'

'There's no way to know whether she's suffering or enjoying herself on her flight for love, but if I were in a strange land, I know I would think of home. I'm happy to get a letter from her.'

'Is it a love letter? I feel funny reading someone else's mail.'

Looking uncomfortable, Ilma unfolded the letter. Considering the woman who'd written it, it was well written in a very literate style.

> *It's already been several months since I left, and the seasons have changed. I've been so busy I haven't had the wherewithal to write and ask about home until now. My home, far across the sea, is now like a small lamplight faintly flickering in my heart. For the first time in quite a while I've had time to think and, taking my pen in hand, I feel a surge of emotion.*
>
> *The last few months it's as if I've been in a trance. My actions were so sudden and rash that I've had to ask myself if this is all really happening or if I've been taken with wild illusions. At the time, I thought that was my only option and was the best solution, and even now, I don't regret it. Having done it, I realize the enormity of the deed and am even surprised at myself. I am vexed, and my heart is heavy at the thought that you will misunderstand and wish to reproach me. However, what's done is done and there's no*

*use wishing it were otherwise. What's happened
is a kind of fate. I can't help but think this is
karma. I'm terribly sorry to go on about myself
like this. Please forgive me. I am in the process
of trying to develop some resoluteness of heart.*

*There is no use in going over what hap-
pened again and again. I must follow the path
I've chosen. I have resolved to be strong.*

The letter went on. It was thick and seemed as long as the
Great Wall of China. Even skipping over some parts, reading
it was a tedious task.

*… Shanghai. I'd heard about how big it was, but
seeing it for myself, I couldn't help but be surprised
at its size. It seems an endless stretch of land.*

*I slept on the trip over, and then we sailed up a
river so large I couldn't see the bank until, finally, I
disembarked on this huge slice of land. This place
doesn't seem like a city inhabited by people but
the very centre of some barbaric region. It was as
if I had come to test myself in this enormous place.
Well, that was what I had come to do, but arriving
here, I found that I was no more than a grain of
sand in the sea. No doubt there are people here
who have come to either test themselves or to hide,
but I just couldn't believe how many there were.*

*The place literally seethed like an anthill with
so many people that if thousands or tens of thousands suddenly disappeared, it wouldn't make a
dent. And I was like an ant in that hill that could
be squashed, and no one would know the difference.*

*Even though I've been here for a few months, I
have hardly left my apartment and so have no*

idea of my way around. As we couldn't stay in a hotel forever, we got a two-room apartment with the intention of a long-term stay. When I sometimes go out and walk the streets, I suddenly feel just how unfamiliar this place is.

The sense of refinement, social conditions, and even popular sentiments are completely different from those back home. Since everything is different, there are times when I feel freedom from worry, but there are also times when I am suddenly annoyed and frustrated. Recently, I passed by the foreign resident's neighbourhood and headed to the river where, while staring at the bridge, I couldn't suppress a feeling of concern about home. Is the sky clear or overcast? It was then that I felt a sense of anxiety as to whether I would ever be able to return to my homeland, and I wondered if I hadn't done a foolish thing.

... I can only imagine the extent of the rumours flying around about me. People naturally like to vilify others; it's much more enjoyable than praising them. I'm sure that my actions have been judged and that my name is being trampled on. Joseon becomes an even more difficult place for me and seems to be even farther away. Such thoughts are extremely frustrating.

I am with Manhae constantly. I love him and can't help but do so. I did what I did because I love him and, because of that, will come to love him even more. If I didn't love him, what would be left for me? And the fact that he loves me draws me to him even more.

Since it seems I'll be here for a long time and I can't continue to remain idle, I'm planning to try my hand at something, but nothing's for certain.

Who knows, I may even be successful here. When I left, I brought everything I had with me, and that should be enough to do something with. Anyway, as I've resolved to make a go of it here, it seems I'll be away from my home for quite some time. I'm sorry to only talk of myself this way, but please don't misjudge or criticize me. And please forget about me. I ask you that for your sake. In the meantime, please try to stop rumours from spreading. I'll try to write again. As this was my first letter, please forgive me for writing only of myself. Please take care.

Yours,
Cheongmae

After finishing the long letter, Ilma was left with a deep impression. Even though he had never been close with Cheongmae and had only read the letter at his friend's insistence, her honest confession had affected him.

'They say women are weak, but in reality, that's not true. Somewhere along the way, Cheongmae turned out to be quite strong.'

Ilma and Jongse were in agreement on this point.

'If she was weak, she couldn't have left in the first place. Even if it was for love, look at the place she ended up in. She's an amazing and dauntless woman.'

'She was able, it seems, to accept her situation in spite of missing home, and has resolved to make the best of it.'

'Well, when someone faces such a situation, they have to become strong, there's no other choice. When you come to a stream, there's nothing you can do but jump it. It seems true that the conditions make the person.'

'At any rate, I'm glad I read the letter. It's been a long time since I've been this impressed by such dignity in a woman.'

Ilma really did seem to be impressed.

'Whether what she did was right or wrong isn't the most important thing. And even if someone were to say what she did was wrong, then what in this world is right? When we consider that she did what she did for love, that judgement will change.'

On this point as well, Jongse was in agreement.

'Talk on the streets is critical of Cheongmae. But isn't that how it usually goes? When something like this happens, people blame the woman and say that she seduced the man. That's extremely unfair. If the truth were told, it's actually almost always the man that instigates things. What can the woman do if the man isn't willing?'

'Manhae decided to run to Shanghai when his business went under, and Cheongmae got caught up in it, so the source of the problem is obvious.'

'No matter what her actions, and no matter what our relationship may have been, I have nothing critical to say about her. In fact, as she asks me in the letter, I want to stick up for her and set the record straight. And I'm going to write her back and tell her to forget about coming back, that she should stay in Shanghai and succeed in her business.'

'Are you able to forget a past love so easily? That takes a lot of courage – to stick up for Cheongmae and not hate Manhae.'

Jongse just stared silently for a moment and then replied, 'Think about it. If Cheongmae came back now, what would happen to Miryeo's plans and the Nokseong Music Academy? Of course, Manhae and Miryeo are divorced, but who knows what kind of complications could arise? Even if I can't completely forget Cheongmae, for the sake of the academy I have no choice but to give her such advice.'

'I understand what you mean.'

It turns out that Jongse was somewhat conflicted. As Ilma listened carefully to every word his friend spoke, he was able to see into his feelings.

'Ultimately, this is all because of Miryeo.'

'Why do you say that? This is all because I'm worried about the music academy.'

'Isn't the music academy just another name for Miryeo?'

Ilma said this with a smile on his face and started to get up from his seat to stop Jongse from further prattling on. The topic was beginning to make him feel uncomfortable.

'We were supposed to be going to see someone's place, instead we've sat here gabbing.'

As they left the teahouse, the couple he saw walking in the snowy street ahead of them aroused Ilma's curiosity.

'Do you see that? There's a surprising sight. This is the first time I've seen such a modern couple walking in the street like that.'

'They're even more than modern; using the new popular phrase, they're chic. That's quite a sight. It's enough to make your eyes pop out of your head.'

The woman was wearing a black overcoat with a scarlet muffler that hung down her front. She presented an elegant and beautiful sight. Pieces of shiny glass sparkled on the heels of her black shoes. The man was dressed equally elegantly.

'Wait a minute.' Jongse looked again as if not believing his eyes. 'Isn't that Danyeong?'

His surprise caused Ilma to start.

'It's Danyeong alright. She's changed, I didn't know it was her at first. And look. Isn't that Hun she's with?'

'Isn't that something? They're dressed so chicly we hardly recognized them.'

In his astonishment, Jongse couldn't take his eyes off the couple. 'Look at the two of them strolling together. Since when did they become an item? Let's go surprise them, whaddya say?'

'Okay.'

With Ilma's agreement, they set out after the two, but before they had gone very far, Ilma changed his mind about harassing them.

'Let's leave them alone today. We'll give it to them next time we see them. It would be a shame to rock the love birds' nest today.'

Jongse did not like the idea of giving up on their fun, but he had no choice but to agree, and the two ducked into an alley so as not to be seen.

Hun and Danyeong continued on, completely oblivious to the fact that they had been discovered by their friends. Whether they were aware or not of the stares their extravagant appearance was drawing seemed not to matter as the two calmly sauntered along the street.

'This would make a good novel. It wouldn't have to be embellished at all; one could just write what really happened. Sooner or later I'm going to do it.'

Danyeong immediately agreed with this idea. 'You should write a novel about what has happened, with yourself in it as well.'

'Well, since I'd be in it, it will be an even better novel. After all, it's a novelist's duty to depict himself truthfully.'

'That's why I don't like novelists. Everything they see and experience they want to write a story about. It must be in their nature.'

'What else is there to do but write? Whether it's your story or someone else's, it all becomes material. As an artist yourself you should know that.'

It was Danyeong's habit to be obstinate, but in the end, she had no choice but to agree with Hun. 'Well, if you're going to write a novel, write a good one, don't write a piece of garbage.'

'That's like a model posing for a painter asking him to paint her face beautifully. That's not very artist-like.'

As Hun laughed, Danyeong jabbed him fiercely in the side and gave him a sidelong glare. 'Let's see which is more successful, my music or your novel.'

Danyeong had already begun taking music lessons. It was true that she was beginning her studies late, but it was part of her responsibilities as an administrator of the music academy. She was now on her way with Hun to see her piano teacher. This was the way the day had been planned.

'Wait a minute, I'm competing with someone who has been studying writing for ten years, and I'm just starting now; I take it all back.'

In her relationship with Hun, Danyeong felt slightly inferior. But as this did not cause her any concern, there was no reason for anyone else to concern themselves with it.*

---

* This is a rather abrupt ending and one gets the feeling that Lee brought the story to a close somewhat prematurely, as sometimes happened with serialized novels.

A NOTE ON THE ILLUSTRATION

Lee Kyutae is a Seoul-based artist who creates distinctive illustrations that are often observational. His signature style has appeared on numerous Korean book covers, and Honford Star is proud to have commissioned Lee Kyutae to create the cover illustration for *Endless Blue Sky*. In this evocative image, Ilma can be seen walking arm in arm with the *hanbok*-wearing Nadia past *choga*, traditional Korean houses made of straw, wood, and soil.

honfordstar.com